Trinity

The Koldun Code

Sophie Masson

First published by Momentum in 2014
This edition published in 2014 by Momentum
Pan Macmillan Australia Pty Ltd
1 Market Street, Sydney 2000

A CIP record for this book is available at the National Library of Australia

Trinity: The Koldun Code (Book 1)

EPUB format: 9781760082017
Mobi format: 9781760082024
Print on Demand format: 9781760082031

Cover design by XOU Creative
Edited by Deonie Fiford
Proofread by Thomasin Litchfield

Macmillan Digital Australia: www.macmillandigital.com.au

To report a typographical error, please visit momentumbooks.com.au/contact/

Visit www.momentumbooks.com.au to read more about all our books and to buy books
online. You will also find features, author interviews and news of any author events.

Born in Indonesia of French parents, and brought up in Australia and France, Sophie Masson is the award-winning author of more than 60 novels for readers of all ages, published in Australia and many other countries. Her adult novels include the popular historical fantasy trilogy, *Forest of Dreams* (Random House Australia). Sophie has always had a great interest in Russian myth and history, an interest reflected in several of her books for younger readers.

*For him who does not believe in signs,
there is no way to live in the world.*
                    (Russian proverb)

A Note to the Reader on Russian Names

Russians have three names – their given or forename, their patronymic (which is formed from the person's father's first name) and their surname, or family name. When addressing people formally, you use the first name, followed by a patronymic name. In the countryside, sometimes only a patronymic might be used. Sometimes you'll see initials used in written material (for example, V.I. Lenin, V.V. Putin) but Russians never use the Western-style form with an initial in the middle, such as Vladimir V. Putin.

Endings of both patronymics and surnames are different depending on whether the named individual is male or female. Patronymics end in "evich" or "ovich" (meaning "son of") for a male, and "ovna" or "evna" (meaning "daughter of") for a female. Surnames of Slavic origin always end in "a", for a woman, so, for instance, you would know if a doctor is a man or a woman. Surnames of non-Slavic origin, however, such as Kersh and Blok do not follow this rule.

Pet names and diminutives of given names are also frequently used for friends and family. So for instance "Nikolai" becomes "Kolya"; Alexey "Alyosha", "Lyosha", "Lyoshka"; Mikhail "Misha" or "Mishka"; Yelena "Lena" or "Lenochka" and so on. There are often many pet names or diminutives for the one name, but I have kept to one or two to avoid confusion.

Western titles like "Mr" and "Mrs" aren't used in modern Russia, though "Dr" and "Professor" certainly are. In the

Soviet past, Tovarish (Comrade) was used, but not now; and in pre-Soviet Russia, "Gospodin/Gospozsha" (literally, "lord" and "lady" rather like the French "monsieur" or "madame") were commonly used. But all these have now fallen into disuse. To denote respect or formality, people call others by their first name and patronymic, though this can also be used between family on occasion too, usually only when addressing older members of the family.

Chapter 1

The Volga River, the longest in Europe, winds majestically through a million square kilometers of the Great Russian Plain on her way to the Caspian Sea: past forest and farmland, marshland and meadow, factories and power plants, shipyards and timber yards, and through countless villages, towns and cities. The lifeblood of her people throughout history, the center of myth and legend, even today the river known as "Mother Volga" ferries more than half of Russia's water traffic, everything from creaking old barges to vast timber carriers, smart speedboats to aluminum dinghies, little sailboats to luxurious cruisers, and the big tourist ships that ply up and down the waterways from May to October, when the water's ice-free.

For the tourists, whether Russian or foreign, it's a welcome chance to experience the enchantment of Russia the old way, by water. But for the settlements along the routes, the arrival of the tourist ships spells another kind of magic: a true end to winter as hibernating shops and markets suddenly wake up, teachers transform into guides, wooden toys march out of workshops, musicians brave monstrous mosquitoes and sudden spring showers to perform *al fresco*.

On a beautiful sunny afternoon in late May, the spring bustle was in full swing when the latest ship docked at the quay below the Volga town of Uglich. There was already one ship moored there, another on its way, and the usual small crowd of musicians, touts, and local guides waiting for the alighting throng. Most of the passengers wouldn't be here more than a couple of hours, for them Uglich was only one short stop on a long cruise.

A small fraction of the tourists might break their journey here for a day or two, and head to the town's few hotels. But the two women who stepped off the ship, wheeling suitcases behind them, were not bound for a hotel.

One was in her mid-forties or so, small and chic in pencil skirt and close-fitting shirt, short dark hair cut sleek as a helmet. The other was young, slightly taller than the other woman, dressed in jeans and a lace top, and her dark red hair was in a single thick plait that hung to her shoulder-blades. It was odd, thought Sergey Olegovich Filippov as he picked his way through the milling crowd toward them. From behind, you'd suppose the two women couldn't possibly be related. But from the front, you'd see the same anxious expression appear in the same kind of large, long-lashed brown eyes, and you'd have to guess again.

Not that Sergey had to. He knew they were the closest of relations – a mother and child. A Mrs. Clement and her 22-year-old daughter.

They hadn't seen him yet. Of course, they'd expected Professor Bayeva herself to meet them. She'd meant to, but "I've been called away unexpectedly, Sergey," she'd said, "would you mind picking up my friends? I'll be back by nightfall."

Sergey didn't mind. Not only did the professor pay well but he always appreciated a chance to practice his English. And besides, he thought, smiling to himself as he picked his way down to them, having two such pretty ladies in my car is no hardship at all.

"Excuse me, ladies," he enunciated carefully, in English, as he drew close to them. They turned to look at him. "You come with me, please." He gestured toward the road.

"No. Please go away and leave us alone," snapped the older woman, in fairly good Russian, her dark eyes imperious. "We are not buying anything."

Sergey was not put off. Persisting in English, he said, "Madam, I am not selling. I am driver. For you."

In the same language, she said, "We didn't ask for a driver. A friend is picking us up."

"Yes. That is Professor Bayeva."

"Professor Bayeva Simmons, you mean."

"She is Professor Bayeva here," Sergey said gently. He looked into the woman's lustrous dark eyes – he'd always loved dark eyes most of all – and went on, "And she is sorry – ah, Mrs. Clement –" he pronounced the name and title carefully " – but she must go on urgent business today. So she ask me. I drive taxi. Often she take it. You see?"

"I do see," said Mrs. Clement, a smile softly lighting up her face. "Well, Mr. – "

"Filippov," he said, promptly, returning her smile. "Sergey Olegovich Filippov, at your service."

"Well, then, Mr. Filippov, where's your car?"

"Close. I take bags for you please," said Sergey, cheerfully, reaching for the handles of the two big suitcases. There was a little exchange then between mother and daughter which he didn't understand because they'd spoken not in English, but in French. Professor Bayeva had told him that Mrs. Clement was originally French, but now lived in England, and had once been married to an American. But though he could not understand the words, the meaning was clear enough. The girl wasn't keen on him taking her bag. It didn't offend him – he had a much-loved niece about the same age, and she could be just as snippy about anyone touching her things, as though they contained State secrets. Shooting an understanding glance at them, he took Mrs. Clement's bag, studiously leaving the girl to handle hers, said, "Come with me, please," and led the way toward his vehicle, an old but well-kept blue Lada.

All the slow way to Professor Bayeva's house, as he guided the car carefully around the potholes in the road, Sergey kept up a gentle patter of conversation.

"Professor Bayeva told me Mrs. Clement was famous journalist," he said, glancing into the rear-vision mirror.

"Oh not that famous," Mrs. Clement said with a smile. "I just write travel articles for magazines."

"And you plan to write on Uglich?" he went on.

"And other towns nearby, I'm writing a series about the Golden Ring. I've written about Moscow and St Petersburg in the past, but never come here."

"Oh, here much better than big cities! Here you find real Russia. Real heart. And real soul."

"Well, that's certainly what I'm looking for," said Mrs. Clement.

Encouraged by her reaction, Sergey launched into full flow. "Uglich, most beloved of all, because of Saint Dimitri you understand. You have seen his church from river? Is beautiful, *da*?"

"Oh yes," agreed Mrs. Clement. "Enchanting."

"In Russia we say churches, they are alive," Sergey observed. "And Saint Dimitri on Blood, it is most alive, because this little Prince Dimitri, he is innocent child killed by wicked men right there. It still mystery who do this terrible thing though many people suspect." His voice dropped. "But not only mystery here. You see this street here? Up there is Makarov *dacha*. Country house, that is. Belong to Ivan Mikhailovich Makarov. You hear of him perhaps?"

"No," said Mrs Clement. "But do tell us."

"Ivan Mikhailovich rich man. Very, very rich." Sergey rolled his r's with relish. "His company named Troitsa – I do not know in English ..."

"Trinity," said Mrs. Clement.

"Trinity. Yes. This very special company, it" – he struggled with the words – "like – like police, with mysteries, only private, yes?"

"Ah. Private investigators."

He nodded vigorously. "*Da*. Troitsa – Trinity – have three leaders. Makarov, Galkin, Barsukov." He paused dramatically. "And now all dead. Strangely."

"Murdered, you mean?"

He shrugged. "No one know for sure. Police say accident. Because all drown."

The girl spoke for the first time. In the rear-vision mirror, Sergey saw her face had paled. "Here? In the Volga?"

"Oh, no, no," he said, hastily. "Thanks be to God not here." He shot a glance at her. "Miss, you must not worry." A pause, then he went on, "These men, they die different times. And different places. Galkin in Finland. Barsukov in France. Makarov in Australia. No one see what happen. No one know. And some people call this Rusalka curse." He saw his passengers' puzzled expressions, and explained, "Rusalka, she is spirit from water. She look like beautiful girl, but she drown men."

"What?" said Mrs. Clement. "Are they saying it's a girl who –"

"*Nyet. Nyet*," Sergey said firmly. "No one know *who*. Is big, big mystery like murder of Prince Dimitri. And now company belong to only son of Ivan Mikhailovich Makarov. Alexey Ivanovich. He is rich young man now. But not interested in Trinity." He had turned into a quiet little cul-de-sac road, sprinkled with wooden houses behind birch trees and grassy verges. "They say he sell company. Some say he needs sell, or Rusalka curse get him too."

"Maybe we'd better talk about something more cheerful now," said Mrs. Clement, with a wary glance at her daughter.

"*Nichevo.* No problem," said Sergey, turning into a little lane and pulling up outside a house right down the end of it, just before the shaky asphalt petered out at the entrance to a little wood. It was a traditional timber *izba*, or cottage, two-story, with walls of silvery weathered boards, the golden light of late afternoon picking out the delicate tracery of carvings around the windows. "Here is house of Professor Bayeva."

"Oh, it's lovely," exclaimed Mrs. Clement.

Sergey went to open the car door, ushering them out. As the girl stepped out, he said, a little anxiously, "Please excuse if I frighten you, Miss."

The girl looked at him. Beautiful eyes, but too serious for one so young, he thought. At her age, she should be full of joyful sparkle, like his niece Masha. She said, softly, "It's okay, Mr. Filippov. I'm just a bit tired, that's all."

"It's Helen's first time in Russia," explained her mother protectively.

Sergey nodded. "Ah. And you have come from Moscow, of course. Much too big, noisy, tiring city. I myself go there only once. And this enough. I want to run away. But here is different. You find peace, Miss, I think."

*

The taxi driver turned his back to them as he opened the front door of the house, and didn't see the look that passed over Helen's face. He was quite right, she *had* been freaked out by Moscow. But unlike Sergey, she came from a big city, so it wasn't that. And it wasn't that the Russian capital was ugly or frightening, either, quite the opposite. Partly, it was because the physical contrast to home was so great, and so sudden. They'd left a mild gray London spring morning and emerged into a Moscow afternoon so bright blue that it seemed painted on with a lavish brush. Everything had culture-shocked her, from the sublime to the ordinary: the candy-striped domes of St Basil's cathedral flaunted against the intense sky, Red Square vast as a rolling stone plain, wide streets strung with garlands of lights, weird little railway kiosks like tiny general stores, impassive people whose faces she didn't know how to read. And most of all, the barbed-wire look of Cyrillic script fencing her off from any real understanding of what was going on.

But it wasn't just culture shock; she knew that.

Chapter 2

Inside, Irina's cottage was like a wooden nest, with its timber floors and ceilings not silvery-weathered like outside, but glowing a soft gold. The simply but attractively furnished large downstairs room, which served as a combination of kitchen, dining-room and living-room, clustered around a white-washed traditional brick stove. But cozily traditional though it might look, the *izba* didn't lack for modern comforts either: a gleaming new stove, fridge, and microwave oven, and a modern, compact bathroom.

Up a set of narrow stairs were three smallish but comfortable bedrooms, each furnished with a wooden bed covered with an embroidered spread, a chest of drawers, a small rug, a spindly chair, and a bedside cabinet. Each of the bedrooms had a window looking out over a pretty view: from Helen's mother's there were the silver-scaled onion domes and white-washed walls of a little church; from Irina's, the back garden with its mauve and white lilac bushes and the renovated study that had once been a bath-house. And from her room, Helen looked out over the quiet lane at the front of the house: asphalt edges crumbling into the flower-threaded long spring grass, a tall silver birch like a giant candle, and the faded-blue walls of the house across the road.

Just then, a magpie flew down from the top of the birch and landed on the window-sill. Cocking its head, it surveyed Helen briefly. As it flew off again, she caught a flash of silver on one of its legs. A tag, she thought. It's some kind of …

"I can understand why Irina likes it here," said her mother, in French, behind her. Helen jumped.

"What? Who? Oh, Irina, you mean."

Her mother looked at her a little oddly. "Who else would I mean? It's lovely, isn't it?"

"Oh yes. It is."

"She spends most of the year here now, from what I gather," said Therese. "Still overwinters in LA though. Well! It's going to be good to see her. Haven't caught up with her for ages." Helen knew the two women had first met twenty years ago at a summer school in LA, where Irina was tutoring a class in comparative myth.

Helen said, "And I don't think I've seen her since I was, oh at least fifteen."

"That's about right. I did see her briefly a few years ago in Paris but on my own. She seemed just the same as ever, nose to the grindstone. That new book of hers on the folk-lore around bears, she's been at it for, oh, I think at least seven or eight years. I'm sure she rewrites chapters twenty times over. That level of perfection would just bore me. Which is why I'm a freelance journalist and she's a respected academic, I suppose."

Helen flinched as her mother's innocent remark triggered an unwelcome scenario in her mind. Mom talking about her work. Irina raving about hers. And then the professor would turn to Helen and say, "Well, honey, last time I heard, your mom told me you were working as a researcher and writer at that funky little film production company – what's it called again? Changeling? Said you were doing real well. So I want to hear all about it, and about that good-looking boyfriend of yours too, Simon, isn't it?" And she'd sit there with a brightly expectant expression, waiting to hear all about the success her friend's daughter was sure to be making of her life. And Helen would sit there with nothing to say and Irina would see the truth in her eyes and know that in just about every-thing that counts Helen got it so wrong, and she'd look away, embarrassed, or worse still take pity on her.

Hurriedly, she brushed the thought away. "Shall we go for that walk you were talking about before?"

Her mother smiled. "If you're not too tired, then, yes, let's go!"

Under a milky blue sky, they set off, through a riot of greenery and bright washes of spring flowers, past a couple of shabbily pretty churches, and lots of lovely wooden houses. Some were of silvery-weathered timber, like Irina's, some newer, the fresh timber glowing like gold, while others were painted in greens, pinks, blues, yellows and browns, with carved scrollwork like gingerbread lace set around the windows. Some had flowers in the windows, scalloped curtains, scrubbed paintwork and tidy vegetable gardens; others were less well-kept, lapped by long grass with higgledy-piggledy piles of firewood toppling at the side, yet still charming. Even the odd ugly spot, such as a dilapidated block of apartments squatting toad-like amid the green, could not detract from the magical look of the place. And somehow it seemed familiar to Helen, though she couldn't work out why at first. And then it came to her.

"Remember that book Irina once sent me for my birth-day?" she said to her mother. "*The Tale of Prince Ivan, the Firebird, and Gray Wolf?*"

"Yes," said her mother. "How could I forget? You were only six, and I remember thinking that it was obvious Irina didn't have kids as it was a strange story to pick for a child that age. I thought it might give you nightmares."

"I *was* scared, but I still loved it," said Helen. "I loved everything about it, the story, the characters. But most of all I loved those pictures."

"Yes, you did," said Therese cheerfully. "You practically wore them out, poring over them for hours. I remember you saying once that if you stared long enough, it would work like a spell and you'd fall right into those pictures."

"I was a weird little kid," said Helen.

"No. Just very imaginative." Therese linked an arm with her daughter's. "And here you are, *chérie*, fallen right into your book. How does that feel?"

"Nice," said Helen. She smiled. "Very nice, actually." She hadn't thought of the book in years; it had vanished somewhere in one of their moves, long ago. And yet now, in this place, she remembered the exact breathless feeling she'd had, as a young child, turning the pages of *The Tale of Prince Ivan*. "I think I'm going to like it here, Mam," she said softly, using the half-French, half-English term for her mother that she'd called her from childhood.

"Oh, I'm so glad," her mother said. "So very glad. You were so subdued in Moscow that I feared I'd pushed you too hard. That I was selfish, dragging you so far away."

"No, Mam. Don't think that. I wanted to come."

She had, very much. Not because she wanted particularly to see Russia, but because she was desperate to get away. Far away as possible from the old life, the old surroundings. Far away from the memories of *that day*. So what if it was not facing things, if it was running away from "confronting your issues", as Simon had said? He'd always managed to make her feel like it was her fault, and never his.

She jerked her attention back to her mother with an effort. "I'm sorry, what did you just say?"

Therese Clement pointed down the street they had just come to. "There's that place Sergey was telling us about earlier. Looks like Fort Knox with all those high gates, doesn't it? Makes you wonder what they're hiding."

At that moment, a big black Mercedes nosed out of the high metal gates, heading down the road toward them with sinister grace and power that made Helen instantly think of a gangster's cortège in a movie. Her mother stopped to watch, shamelessly curious, but Helen hurriedly walked on, pretending to be interested in someone's garden. But as the car turned the corner, it came to a halt not far from her. She caught a glimpse of figures in the front: a chauffeur in a peaked cap and another man, younger, dark-haired. And in the rear passenger side, a face, framed for a moment in the window that had just opened: a hard young man's face under slickly combed dark blond hair, eyes hidden behind sunglasses, broad shoulders in a smart jacket. She looked at him; he looked at her. He had the advantage of her, for she couldn't see the expression in his eyes behind the dark glasses. For an instant, she thought he was about to speak, and she held her breath. But he didn't. He turned away, the window whispered shut, and the car glided on.

"Well, how about that," said her mother, behind her. "Checking out the outsiders for future reference. I suppose they think they own this road. Can't escape New Russia even in fairytale country."

"What do you mean?" said Helen, watching the car as it disappeared up the road. Her palms were prickling from the unexpected encounter.

"Pure Moscow swagger, swollen with loads of dodgy money and enough arrogance to sink the *Titanic*. Well, so that was the famous Trinity heir." She looked at her watch. "Anyway, darling, Irina's going to be home any time now. Shall we head back?"

*

It was a shock to Helen, how much Irina had changed. She hadn't seen her mother's friend for years, and Irina was at least ten years older than Therese, but she looked every year of it now. She'd never been a large person but now she was actually thin, the sharply expressive lines of her face almost gaunt. Her pixie haircut had gone quite gray, she had taken up smoking, and the jacket of her tailored suit was smudged with ash. But what hadn't changed was her personality; the blue eyes behind the horn-rimmed glasses were as bright as ever, and her manner as direct and friendly as Helen remembered it.

Over a simple but delicious dinner of smoked fish, omelet and salad, they talked about what had happened since they'd last seen each other. At least, Therese and Irina talked. For Helen soon realized the scenario she had feared wasn't about to come true. Her mother must already have briefed Irina on her situation, because there were no questions about boyfriends or careers, just chit-chat about the trip, and how Helen was liking Russia so far, and so on. There was only one awkward moment, when Therese went to the bathroom and Irina said, "Sorry I missed you when you were in the States last year, honey."

It had been a holiday with Simon. The last. Trying to sound offhand, Helen said, "That's okay. You were busy with that conference in Alaska. I understand."

"That was the first time you'd been back in ages, right?"

"Yes."

Irina shot her a look. "Didn't try to see your dad, I suppose?"

Helen shook her head. Her father, Sam Byrd, an American special forces officer, had been divorced from Therese since Helen was five. After the divorce, she saw him hardly at all, because her mother took her back to Europe. She spent a few holidays with him on and off over the years, but never felt comfortable with him. It wasn't just that he was a moody, taciturn man, and she was used to her lively, bright, communicative mother. It was also that she didn't know how to draw him out; his silence only made her silent too. She endured the visits more than enjoyed them. She didn't know what he felt. He never told her. They never had a real relationship, at least not the sort she had with her mother.

Not that it hurt her. Long ago, she'd learned to deal with it. Except that she had recently seen the fear in her mother's eyes, when Helen was drifting for weeks in the gray world of unhappiness after *that day*. She had known what lay unspoken between them. The fear that Helen was turning into her father. *You can't help over-reacting to things, because you have a genetic predisposition to depression.* That's what Simon had said. Simon was good at turning banalities into unexpected weapons.

Irina was looking quizzically at her. Helen mumbled, "Sorry, didn't catch that." Her mother had come back and she and Irina had been talking, but lost in her thoughts, Helen hadn't heard a thing.

"I was just telling your mother that I have to go chasing off to St Petersburg for a few days to follow up a lead. I'm sorry, I know I'm a terrible hostess, but –"

"Don't worry. We don't mind at all," Helen's mother cut in. "Do we, Helen?" Helen shook her head. "We've got plenty to do around here, exploring," Therese went on. "And when we need to go further afield, there's Sergey and his taxi."

"He's a good guy, you can trust him. Even if he does talk your ears off."

"We got a taste of that yesterday," said Therese, smiling. "He told us all about the big news, about that Trinity case."

14

"Oh yes. The talk of the town it was for a while. Died down a bit recently as nothing much more has happened."

"We saw the Trinity heir today, actually. Looked a bit dodgy, didn't he, Helen?"

Helen shrugged. "We didn't even speak to him."

"And if I were you, honey, I'd keep it that way," said Irina.

"Why?"

"He just sounds like the kind of guy best kept away from," said Irina firmly.

Helen opened her mouth to argue but Therese said, "Never mind, it's not important. Irina, you haven't told us about your book, how's it going?"

Irina was instantly distracted. "Fantastic, though I haven't finished it by a long shot yet. It's much less academic than my other books, and my publisher's got high hopes for it to reach a wider market."

"Ah, a bestseller then!"

Irina smiled. "Let's wait and see, huh? Anyway, it sure seems like it's a book that was meant to be. You know how I was in Yaroslavl today? My mom's family was originally from the Yaroslavl area and that's where I heard the story that sparked it all off, years and years ago when I first visited Russia ..." She looked at them with a twinkle in her eye. "But maybe I'm boring you."

"Not at all," Therese protested. "We want to hear all about it, don't we, Helen?"

She nodded, smiling. "Sure we do."

"Okay. So this is how it goes: a thousand years ago, Yaroslavl was a wild place known as *Medvezhy Ugol*, or Bears' Corner, which was inhabited by a fierce tribe of river raiders who worshipped a bear-god. In the eleventh century Yaroslav the Wise, a Christian prince of Rostov, and one of the sons of the first king of Russia, Vladimir of Kiev, turned up to convert them and also to bring them under the control of his people. He was captured by the locals and a huge bear was set on him. They thought he'd die for sure. But the story goes that he wrestled the bear to the ground and killed it with his club. After that, they all fell at his feet and did what he wanted. Even now, the arms of the city feature a bear with a club over his shoulder. "

"That's a bit of a black joke, isn't it?" observed Therese Clement.

"You could say that. A paradox, too. Very Russian, actually. And that's what started me thinking about the Russian attitude to bears – on the one hand it's one of their most powerful national symbols. In myth the bear is seen both as brother and god, demon and helper; in fairytale and folklore he is Misha, friend and enemy: sometimes so close to humans as to adopt them, sometimes an implacable foe. But on the other hand, to this day the phrase *bears' corner* means not only an actual forest area where bears roam, but also shorthand for a primitive sort of place. And then of course there are all the stories of real-life encounters, not only past but present, because there's still a lot of bears in Russia."

Helen said, a little uneasily, "Are there any around here?" She remembered her father, in one of his few loquacious moments, telling her of a terrifying encounter he'd had with a grizzly while hiking in Yellowstone National Park with a friend, when they were teenagers. The friend had been badly mauled before Sam had managed to scare the bear off. It was the kind of story you never forgot, especially because it was one of the few stories Helen remembered her father ever telling her.

Irina smiled. "I don't think so. Certainly not in the little wood just past my house, honey. You can safely go for a walk there without any chance of coming nose to nose with any big bad wild animal. But there are bigger forests outside the town and it's possible there are both wolves and bears, though they tend to keep to the deepest parts of the forest well away from people. But further north in Karelia there are big, dense forests, and lots of bears. I saw one myself there a few years ago. Very close, actually, about as close as here to the other side of the room."

Helen breathed, "What did you do?"

"Nothing. I just stopped and kept very still. The bear knew I was there, but he didn't care. Looked at me for a moment then just turned and ambled away." She paused. "It's funny, but I wasn't frightened at all. And yet I knew what he could have done to me if he chose. It was just – I can't describe it. It was like seeing the spirit of the forest, the soul of this land. Absolutely unforgettable."

Chapter 3

Helen woke the next morning to bright sunshine flooding the room. For a moment, confused by the unfamiliar surroundings and the ghostly outline of the silver birch through the thin curtains, she felt disoriented. Then she remembered. She was in Russia. In Uglich, at Irina's place. And she'd had the best sleep she'd had in a very long time. Utterly dreamless, and perfectly restful. And the jumpiness of the day before had completely gone.

Going downstairs after a shower, she found Irina and her mother deep in conversation over breakfast. A cheerful smell of warm bread and coffee filled the room. They both looked up and smiled when she came in.

"Slept well?" said Irina.

"Fabulous."

"Great. Now, honey, sit down. Here's some coffee. Bread. Butter. And my own home-made forest berry jam."

Helen raised an eyebrow as she helped herself to the food. "Hey, Irina, I never pictured you as the jam-making sort!"

"Yeah, well, I wasn't, before. But here it's different. Making jam. Growing vegetables. Gathering mushrooms and berries. Everyone does it here. I love walking too. There's a lovely little stream in the wood right near here where I go to think, it's my favorite place."

Therese shook her head. "Sounds like you've become a real country girl!"

"I used to think I was one hundred percent urban, but I guess I was wrong. Never too old to learn, are you? And this country, it's opened me up to new experiences. More than that – if you'll excuse the psychobabble – it's like I've found myself here. And I didn't expect that at all. You see, I didn't exactly have positive ideas about Russia when I was young. Mom's family defected when she was a baby, and they just wanted to forget about the place and become American. And me, well, I didn't really care. It was only when Mom died a few years ago that I decided I should at least come and visit, have a look. The rest, as they say, is history."

"How do you get on with the locals?" asked Helen, thinking she hadn't heard Irina mention any Russian friends.

"*Normailno*, as they say here. Fine. But we don't live in each other's pockets and that's good, I'm not keen on social stuff, I've always been perfectly happy in my own company. And I'm very busy anyway. Besides, I don't kid myself that I can ever hope to be a real Russian, despite Mom's background and the fact I speak the language pretty fluently. I'm an American born and bred, plus Dad was sixth-generation American and I never try to deny that."

"But you don't use your full name, do you?" said Therese. "Sergey said you preferred to use Bayeva here."

"That's right. Simmons is on my visa but I don't use it. Just makes it easier. Bayeva is a familiar sound. And it is Mom's family name after all. In fact, usually I introduce myself as Irina Petrovna Bayeva. Because Dad's name was Peter. I'm Peter's daughter – so, my patronymic would be Petrovna. People feel they've got a bit of a handle on me then, even if I'm still that eccentric foreign lady who writes about bears."

Soon after, Sergey came to pick up Irina, and she left them with all kinds of last-minute instructions. "Help yourself to whatever you want," she said, as she finally got into the taxi. She looked up at Helen with a cheeky smile. "But whatever you do, don't get on the wrong side of *domovoi*."

"Dom *who*? Is he a neighbor?"

Irina laughed. "Closer than that, hon. Much closer. He came with the house. Have a look at the books on my shelf, and you'll find out. See you."

And she was off, a grinning Sergey tooting the horn in jaunty farewell. He was clearly in on the joke too.

"Tell you what," said Therese, as they went back in, "I was a bit worried about Irina at first, she's so thin I thought she must be ill and hadn't told us ... and all that mystical stuff about finding herself here, that just isn't like the old Irina. She always used to scoff at that kind of thing. But now I can see it's just that she's fallen madly in love. With a place, not a person, that's all. And all her passionately obsessive nature has gone into it, as per usual."

"Plus remember back in L.A.," Helen said, "she never went for walks and she used to eat a lot of junk food. It's like she's gone on a health kick here. That's probably why she's lost all that weight."

"Yes, and going back to smoking, which isn't so good. But I guess here where people smoke like chimneys, it must bring the craving back. Anyway, I'm glad that she seems happy in her own funny way. Pity though she hasn't met some nice man to ..." She broke off, looking shamefaced. "Okay, forget I said that. Engaging mouth before brain. Sorry."

"It's okay, Mam," said Helen gently, knowing her mother was worried that the mere mention of a relationship might set her off brooding again. "I can cope. Really. And I know what you mean. Irina's a bit intense sometimes. Lived on her own too long."

"Yes," said her mother, looking relieved. "That is what I meant." She kissed her daughter on the cheek. "Anyway, *chérie*, listen, I've really got to write up some of my Moscow notes this afternoon, so if you don't mind being left on your own for a bit ..."

"Course I don't," said Helen affectionately. "I've got big plans of my own. Like – how about a cake for dessert tonight?"

Her mother beamed. "Great idea. Look forward to it." And she left her daughter to it and went upstairs to work.

It was only recently that Helen had felt like cooking again. Humming to herself, she mixed up ingredients for a berry fruit cake. It was a lovely process, every ordered step of the way, each gesture a little ritual, and while she was doing it, she didn't think of anything other than the sheer sensual pleasure of it.

There. The cake was made, and in the oven. It would take forty minutes or so to bake. Time to do something else. Her gaze fell on the bookshelves.

There was a bit of fiction, but most of the books on Irina's shelves were non-fiction volumes about myth and folklore. Much of it was dry and academic but Helen found an illustrated book on Russian folklore that was written in a lively and interesting way, and she soon became absorbed in it.

Back at Changeling, they'd once produced a special documentary on the mythological allusions behind Harry Potter. She'd done some of the basic research for it. She'd loved it – she'd always been into fairytales as a child and it had been like plunging back into that heady enchanted world. Now the same kind of fascination returned as she happened almost at once on the answer to Irina's parting riddle.

For *domovoi* wasn't a person but a thing. A house-spirit. Something like a house-elf in *Harry Potter,* only *domovoi* were most certainly not meek and cringing, and you couldn't enslave them or even expect them to work for you. In fact, unlike the industrious tailor elves of Western folk tale, *domovoi* were damn lazy. It was *you* who worked for them. You who had to leave bits of food for them near the stove or in the cellar, where they usually lived. You who had to be polite and ask after their health. Your visitors who had to duck their heads in greeting to the *domovoi* when they entered your house, or he'd give them a nasty crack on the head. If you didn't do these things, he'd take his revenge. Send things flying around the place. Trip you up. Upend pots and pans. Spoil sauces. Send plagues of mice and insects to eat your stores. So you had to be very careful. And if you moved house you had to ask your *domovoi* to come with you or you'd get bad luck. Sometimes they didn't feel like moving and then if the next person brought along their own *domovoi*, there'd be a real brawl between them. But the important thing was to ask. Nicely.

She read on, about other sorts of spirits, many much less homely than the *domovoi*: the *bannik*, who lived in the steambath-house, and might suffocate or burn you if you bathed without his permission or after midnight; the *leshii*, who lived in the forest, ranged from dwarfish to gigantic, and could set bears and wolves onto you; the *vodyanoi*, who manifested in the form of a hideous old man and whose main purpose in non-life was to drown people and animals and who you had to placate with gifts ranging from vodka to dead chickens. And the unhappy, dangerous *Rusalki*. She remembered Sergey mentioning them. But a *Rusalka* was considered a bit differently to other dangerous spirits, because as well as fearing her, people pitied her, as she once had been a human being. *Rusalki* were most active around a time called "Rusalka week", the week just before the religious feast-day of the Trinity, or Pentecost, as it was known in the West.

Trinity – the Rusalka curse. Yesterday, Sergey's story had spooked her. Today, with the image of the Trinity heir flashing through her mind, she tingled with curiosity. She wished she'd asked Sergey questions. But she couldn't wait till the next time he turned up. She'd have to google it on her smartphone, right now.

*

Most of the stuff on the Internet about the so-called "Rusalka Curse" was in Russian. But there were also a few articles in English, with the most useful being from an Australian newspaper which had reported on Ivan Makarov's death, two months previously, in March.

MYSTERIOUS DEATH SPARKS SPECULATION
TRINITY FOUNDER DIES IN GOLD COAST CANAL

The mysterious drowning death of wealthy expatriate Russian businessman Ivan Makarov, 47, in a canal near his Gold Coast home, has stunned the Russian community in Queensland. Makarov, whose body was found in the early hours of yesterday morning by a local dog walker, is believed to have died sometime during the previous night.

No signs of violence were found, apart from a bump on the head, which investigation indicates is probably accidental, due to Makarov slipping and striking his head on the bank, possibly after a sudden heart attack. The last person to see Makarov alive, a waitress in a local restaurant the businessman frequented, said he'd left the establishment around 10 pm, saying he was walking home as it was a fine night.

A founder and director of the secretive Moscow-based investigative company, Trinity, Makarov had been living in

Australia for the last eleven years, but retained property in Russia, and flew several times a year to Moscow for board meetings. Police have confirmed that he was due to fly to Moscow again next week.

Mr. Makarov is the last of the company's three founding directors to die in unusual circumstances. Semyon Galkin, 47, and Sergey Barsukov, 48, who were co-founders of Trinity with Makarov twenty years ago, also drowned. Galkin died in a remote Finnish lake while on a hunting trip two Junes ago, while last year in May, Barsukov was found floating in the pool of a luxury hotel in Nice, France, where he was holidaying.

In each case, autopsies showed that the men were probably unconscious when they hit the water, but in none was there a sign of violence, and toxicology reports were negative. It is believed that Galkin had a history of heart problems which could have contributed to his losing consciousness and drowning, but there was no such indication in Barsukov's case. Despite the heart attack report, Makarov had also been given a clean bill of health by his doctor a few months before.

No witnesses to the men's deaths have come forward, and in each case they are believed to have been alone at the time.

Makarov's only surviving child, his 24-year-old son Alexey, a music graduate, who was interstate when his father died, has inherited all Trinity shares and assets outright.

Under the article were readers' comments. Helen skimmed a few.

sjholmes11: Probably a Russian Mafia job. Rumor has it they've been after Trinity for some time. Apparently the Makarov kid is not interested in running it and it's likely to be sold off.

Truthteller: More likely somebody in the secret services got rid of those guys. Probably been *sitting on some dangerous secrets. Easy to disappear in Russia if you offend powerful people.*

Georg75: Read in Russia Today *that some people say there's something weirder than that going on, they're calling it "The Rusalka Curse" after the mermaid who lures guys to their death.*

Frappyman: People believe in that shit, no wonder Russia's screwed man.

Helen clicked out of the comments and looked at the photo illustrating the article. It showed the three dead Trinity partners at some function. Of all of them, Barsukov looked the most classically dangerous, like a character out of some underworld film – big, tall, with a bald bullet head and unsmiling black eyes, massive shoulders under a smart suit. Galkin was small and wiry as a jockey, with a thin face and restless eyes. But Ivan Makarov looked ordinary, like someone you might pass in the street and hardly notice – gray eyes, dark brown hair, average height. Helen thought of the face she'd glimpsed in the Mercedes. Ivan Makarov's son, Trinity heir. Alexey. He didn't look much like his father. Perhaps he took after his mother. But she wasn't mentioned. Was she dead, or just absent? And the article had also said he was the "only surviving child", which implied there must have been others, once. So the young man had ended up alone, far from home, living behind high walls, his father dead in suspicious circumstances, minders around him, shadowy enemies lurking in the wings, and a question mark over his future. And yet he's only a little older than me, thought Helen. She shivered, remembering the young man she'd fleetingly glimpsed in the car. How lonely it must be for him, despite the extravagant trappings of wealth.

Chapter 4

The next day dawned clear and blue and at breakfast Therese announced an intention to go and visit the cathedral of Saint Dimitri. "Would you like to come?" she asked Helen.

"Would you mind awfully if I didn't? We did see a lot of churches in Moscow."

Her mother laughed. "Sure, no problem. You take it easy. I'll be back around lunchtime."

"And I'll have some lunch ready when you get back," said Helen, brightly.

"*Formidable!* I certainly think I'll stay in this hotel again." Her mother blew a kiss to her and set off.

Left alone, Helen wandered for a while in the garden, picking flowers for the table, watching bees buzzing around the blossoms, peeking in at the window of Irina's study – a pleasant room with tall filing cabinets and a big desk with everything in its place, not at all like Mom's untidy desk back home. That made her think of what Irina had said, about the "magical stream" in the wood. She'd go exploring, see if she could find it. Her grandfather in France had a farm by the edge of a similar small wood and she loved it there. And Irina had said there were no bears there.

Walking down the track, she breathed in the pine-scented air, delightedly taking everything in: the sun shining through leaves making green-gold coins on the path, the silver gleam of birch trunks, a bright flurry of fragile flowers, and whispery clouds of butterflies. A few mosquitoes, too, but nowhere near as bad as by the river. She startled a hare sitting bolt upright in the middle of the path. He took off like the wind, lolloping off through the trees. A little further on, a squirrel bounded up a tree at her approach. There were birds, too – a cuckoo calling coolly from the depths of the woods, pigeons cooing, little birds twittering.

And then, coming around a bend, she saw something on the track ahead. It was a magpie, injured by the looks of it, flapping, uttering little cries. "Oh you poor thing," whispered Helen, approaching it carefully, so it wouldn't get scared. Closer up, she could see a silver tag around one of its legs. "My God," she breathed, "it's you ..."

She bent down. Reached out a hand, and ...

The roar of a powerful engine burst behind her. She only just had time to fling herself sideways before the big red motorbike went racing past in a stinging cloud of dust and pebbles.

"Effing pillock!" she screamed at the black-clad, black-helmeted rider's back. She dashed to where the magpie had been, fearing the worst. But not only was there no pitiful mash of blood and bone and feathers, there was *nothing*. The magpie had vanished. It must have flown away. She couldn't believe it. She was sure it had been injured. Stunned, at least. It couldn't just have ...

She jerked her head up. Down the track, the biker had turned his machine around and was heading straight for her! Half-blinded by panic, she plunged into the undergrowth, not seeing the fallen sapling till it was too late. She went sprawling, coming down painfully on her right ankle. "Fuck it!" she yelled in pain, trying to scramble up.

Too late. The biker had already jumped off his machine and came towards her, minus the black helmet that had made him look so alien and menacing.

"Oh hell, I'm so sorry." He must have heard her cursing, for he spoke in perfect English, with an unusual accent highlighting a deep voice. He bent down to her, his leathers creaking. "Are you okay?"

She'd only caught a glimpse of him yesterday. Up close he was *gorgeous*. High cheekbones, straight nose, tough jaw: hard, masculine lines, but softened and brightened by an extraordinary pair of blue-green eyes, framed in short dark lashes under that thatch of thick blond hair. She'd seen faces like his in paintings in the Tretyakov art gallery in Moscow: great knights and princely warriors from Russian history and legend, an impression reinforced by the black leathers he wore. But the painted faces did not have a fraction of the stunning vitality, the warmth of his. Trying desperately to recover her scattered wits, she said, tartly, "Hardly. My ankle hurts. I think it could be sprained or even broken."

"Oh God. I'm so sorry." He hesitated. "Can I – can I check your ankle, see what's wrong?"

"Are you a doctor or something?" she said, truculently. Then she relented. "Okay. For all the good it'll do." She winced involuntarily as he pushed back her sock, exposing the ankle. It was throbbing now, really hurting.

His touch was light, gentle, but it made her tremble. And then it happened. She felt a jolt as his fingers touched her skin. He glanced quickly at her. There was an extraordinary expression in his eyes, surprise mixed with joy, and it made her heart race. His fingers held still on the ankle for a moment more, and a flood of warmth rushed through her. Then he took his hand away, and with a shock she realized that her ankle had stopped throbbing and that the pain had gone. She looked at him, but before she could speak, he said, rapidly, "It was only twisted, thanks be to God. Can I help you up?"

Part of her longed to ask what exactly had happened when he had touched her ankle. But another part of her didn't want to know. Something very weird was going on. She couldn't believe it. Correction, she *had* to believe it. She just didn't know what to make of it. And it wasn't just her ankle, though that was strange enough. It was the startling power of her own reaction to him.

Her mind was flapping around like the injured magpie. That hadn't been injured after all, but only ... She shivered. "Thanks," she muttered, "but I can get up by myself."

But her ankle was still weak, as she soon found out, and so he helped her anyway. He said, "I don't think you should walk on that yet. Can I give you a lift somewhere?"

"On that machine?"

He laughed. "I'm afraid so. But I promise to be careful this time."

They looked at each other, and in that moment something came into Helen's mind, an image so startlingly vivid and sharp that it was as if it was something right before her, and yet as otherworldly as a dream.

There was a crossroads. Two paths. One on the right. One on the left. A tingle rippled coldly over her, a tremor part excitement, part fear. For she had no idea where the vision had come from: but she knew it was important. And she knew *exactly* what it meant.

Take the right-hand path: the safe path. Say *no thanks, it's okay, I'm fine, I'll make my own way back*, and it would be business as usual. Take the left-hand path: the dangerous one. Say *yes*, get on the back of his motorbike, and then – God only knew.

She took a deep breath. And plunged into the left-hand path. "I'll hold you to that," she said.

A smile lit up his face. "Fair enough." He held out a hand. "I'm Alexey, by the way. Alexey Makarov."

"Hello. I'm Helen. Helen Clement." She returned the shake, but withdrew her hand quickly.

"I saw you yesterday," he said.

"Yes – yes – we had just arrived from Moscow, we'd gone for a little walk, we're here on holiday, my mother's a travel writer." She knew she was speaking too much but was unable to stop. "We're staying with Professor Irina Bayeva, in a house just near here. Maybe you know her."

He shook his head. "I think I've heard the name, but I haven't met her. I haven't lived here very long. And I'm not always here. Have to go to Moscow quite often. So I'm not really up with the locals." He gave her a wry sidelong glance. "But, as I expect you already know, the locals are well up on me."

She looked away. "Er – yes."

"You're English, right?" he said, smiling a little at her discomfiture.

"No. That is, not technically speaking," she said, hastily. "My mother's French, my dad's American. I live in London. Have done since I was about nine. And you – your accent ..."

"Russian with an Aussie veneer, I guess," he said, "which is why it probably sounds weird. Lived in Australia from the age of twelve till now, see. Well, we're quite a mixture, then, aren't we, you and I?" he added, lightly.

Helen swallowed, and trying to match his light tone, said, "I guess so. But then lots of people are now."

"You're right," he said, with a little smile that Helen knew had nothing to do with what she'd said and everything to do with what he'd seen in her eyes when he'd said "you and I".

She said, sharply because she was feeling so nervous, "Well, now we've been properly introduced and all, how about that lift?"

The smile didn't leave his face. "Sure thing, Helen." Picking up the bike, he sat astride. He handed her the helmet. "Here, put this on."

"But you …"

He brushed that aside. "I don't need it. Okay, you comfy?"

"Sure."

"You can put your arms round my waist if it helps," he said. "I won't bite, I promise."

She stammered, "It's okay, I can hang onto the sides here, it's fine."

"No worries," he said, calmly. "Whatever you want."

Chapter 5

As soon as they drew up outside Irina's cottage, Helen hastily dismounted. Taking off the helmet, she handed it to Alexey. "Would you – would you – er – like to come in for a drink or something? I think there's beer in the fridge."

"A beer would be fantastic," he said, smiling, and followed her in. She was so aware of his nearness she was sure he could sense it, but he seemed perfectly at ease.

"Lovely place," he said, looking around the room, as she pulled two beers out of the fridge. "Feels like a real home."

"Yes," said Helen, "it does." It was a singularly uninspiring answer, she knew that, but she couldn't help it. Away from the woods, and the troubling atmosphere of their meeting, she should have felt more normal. But she didn't. Far from it. She took a swig of beer. "Irina's been coming here for years now."

"But this is your first time. It must seem strange to you."

"In a way. But I thought it would feel stranger than it does, actually. I mean being in Russia. You hear all this stuff about it, don't you?" She saw his expression. "I'm sorry, I don't mean to be rude ..."

He smiled. "It's okay. I know what you mean. Truth is, nothing is simple here. And yet everything is."

She was struck by his words. For wasn't that precisely what had happened today? Something so magically simple it made her heart sing. Yet so complicated her head spun at the thought of it.

"Helen," he went on, "may I ask you something?"

She swallowed. "Sure."

"What were you doing when I – when I tried my best to skittle you?"

"What I was doing?" she repeated. "Oh, you mean – the magpie. On the path. I thought it was hurt. But it flew away. It must have."

"I suppose so," he said, gravely.

"Didn't you see it?"

He shook his head. "It all happened so fast."

"It did," said Helen. Their eyes met. Hastily, she added, "I saw it yesterday too. When we arrived. I knew it was the same magpie," she explained, seeing his raised eyebrow, "because of the tag. Around its leg, that is. Funny coincidence, right?"

"Maybe. But you know what Albert Einstein once said about coincidence?"

She shook her head.

"Coincidence is God's way of remaining anonymous," he said.

She glanced at him. "I'm not sure that I ..." she began, uncomfortably, but he laughed, and drained the last of his beer. "It's okay. Just a cool saying. Right?"

"Right," she agreed, a little uncertainly.

He got up. "Look, Helen, I'm sorry, but I've got to be going. My godfather's arriving at mine any time now and we've got to talk business. Really wish I could stay a while longer, but I can't."

"Oh. Sure. Of course," she said, scrambling up in her turn and following him to the door. There, he stopped and said, "And look, I'm so sorry about before, about sending you flying, I mean." His eyes were on her face. "Hope you won't hold it against me too much."

She choked out, "Oh no. No. Really. It's ... fine."

He smiled. "Good. Because I'd really like to continue this conversation. Very soon. If you don't mind."

"No. Yes. I mean, I'd – I'd like that too."

"Awesome. Look, I'll be tied up for a few hours now. But can I call you later?"

Her throat was dry. "Sure." She gave him her number.

"See you again soon, then, I hope," he said, as he walked to his bike.

"Yes," she murmured. "See you."

His face lit up with an impish smile. "And keep an eye out for that enigmatic bird. I think it brought us good luck." And before she could answer, he roared off up the street, waving a hand in farewell.

When the motorbike had turned the corner and disappeared, she went slowly back into the house. The clock was reading 11.45. Her mother would be back soon. She'd promised to make lunch, and she hadn't even half an inkling what. There was no time now to make anything hot. A big salad, maybe, with bits and pieces from the garden and the cupboards. Mechanically, she began gathering ingredients together: green leaves of various sorts, preserved beetroot, onions, gherkins and olives. She boiled some eggs and a couple of potatoes, made a dressing of mayonnaise and mustard and a splash of vinegar, set the table and cut some bread. But all the time, she couldn't stop thinking of him. He stirred her in a way that scared her and thrilled her. And now the muted colors of her world had suddenly acquired a golden tinge, warm and unfamiliar as the patina of this room.

Her mother came back clutching a plastic bag full of bits and pieces she'd bought at the riverside craft market, and full of chatter about her morning, to which Helen listened with only half an ear. Therese soon noticed her abstraction, and said, "And what did you do, darling, apart from prepare this scrumptious lunch?"

"Went for a walk in the wood."

"Oh. Good. Was it nice there?"

"Yes. Lots of flowers and so on." She hesitated. But there was no point in hiding it. "Oh, and guess what? I met Alexey Makarov."

Therese looked puzzled. "Who's that?"

"You know – the guy from Trinity."

Therese stared. "You mean that young man we saw in the Mercedes the other day? Was he on his own?"

Helen nodded. "When I was in the woods, walking – he came tearing through on his motorbike. I was startled and fell over. I thought I'd twisted my ankle so he – he gave me a lift back."

Therese gave her a sharp glance, but all she said was, "I see. And how's your ankle now?"

"It's absolutely fine. Not even bruised. I just fell heavily, that's all." A pause. "I invited him in for a beer."

Therese raised an eyebrow. "Okay. I see."

"He's nice, Mam. Much nicer than I expected." *Nice*, she thought, her skin tingling. Such a dull ordinary word for a man who was anything but that.

"I see," repeated Therese. Her calm tone was belied by the anxiety in her eyes. "So. Are you going to see him again?"

"I don't know. Maybe. Probably."

"Do you think that's wise, darling? I mean, what Irina said …"

"It's just gossip. She doesn't know him."

"Neither do you," said her mother.

"I can't keep hiding from people, from life," Helen flashed out. "Or is that what you think I should do?"

"Of course not! Sweetheart, all I'm saying is please be careful. People like that – I mean," she hurried on, seeing her daughter's expression, "from that kind of background, used to lots of money, used to having whatever they want – they see life differently to other people. And you – you have been through such a hard time. I just don't want you to get hurt again."

"I know, Mam." Helen laid a hand on her mother's arm. "Don't worry. It'll be okay. And anyway, I may not end up seeing him again."

Her mother's expression said she thought that was highly unlikely. But she nodded, and to Helen's relief turned the conversation to the subject of the market she'd been to that morning.

"It was really interesting. Amazing display of all sorts of crafts. Bought up quite a storm as you can see." She gestured at the collection of little lacquered boxes, nesting dolls, painted wooden objects and embroidered cloths laid out on the table.

"They're so gorgeous," Helen said, picking up one of the boxes, painted with a winter scene.

"Yes. It was hard to choose. There were so many nice things there."

"Are they still open this afternoon? I might go take a look." She'd rather be out of the house if Alexey did call. Holding a conversation with her mother hovering anxiously would be too awkward, and she was jumpy enough as it was.

"I think they're open all day. Do you need me to come too? To translate, I mean?"

"No! I mean, no thanks, Mam," she added, hastily. "I should have a go at doing things myself. If I can't find the right words, I'll mime or something." She hesitated, then added, "And, Mam, I know I've been – out of it – but I'm much better now. Really I am. And since being here – well, I feel even better. Do you see?"

"I do," said Therese, with a little smile. "That sparkle in your eyes is back. And I'm so glad. I don't mean to be a worry wart, sweetheart, I just ..."

"I know, Mam," said Helen, kissing her mother on the cheek. "I know."

*

The craft market consisted of two long rows of covered stalls in the big town park, close by the river-boat quay. When Helen arrived, it was thronged with tourists from two cruise ships that had just docked. They were picking over the items in the stalls, closely but not obtrusively watched by the sellers. Judging from what she could hear, one lot seemed to be mainly Russian, the other mainly American, with a good sprinkling of other nationalities – French, British, Canadians, Japanese, Antipodeans. Helen soon gave up any thought of buying souvenirs and instead sat on a bench to people-watch. She hadn't done that for quite a while.

It was so funny, she thought, how when they were in a group, people behaved as if they were following some national script written by Stereotype Central. Russians were impassive, made quick decisions and didn't go in for chit-chat. Americans marched up confidently, showered cheerful greetings on the sellers, picked things up and turned them over, then asked complicated questions the sellers couldn't understand with their limited English. Canadians were humbler, but more impulsive. The French cast disdainful eyes over the displays, as if to say it was all far beneath their notice; then walked away with a big haul, discreetly bought when you weren't looking. The British hummed and hahed and looked like they were thinking of buying up the entire stall but rarely bought more than one thing. Australians tried to bargain, not very successfully. The Japanese never bargained but paid first price.

She was so absorbed that the tug on her sleeve startled her. She turned. Someone else had come to sit on the bench. An old lady, frail, birdlike, with cloudy blue eyes and a flowery scarf over thick silver hair. She was carrying bunches of lily of the valley. And a clear plastic bag half-full of small painted wooden figures.

"Good day – I mean, *dobree dyeyn*," said Helen, awkwardly.

The old woman nodded, acknowledging the greeting. She reached into the plastic bag and handed Helen a tiny wooden figure of a girl in traditional dress. Simply but strikingly carved and painted, it sat snugly in the palm of Helen's hand, and she loved it at once. She looked at the old woman, rummaging in her mind for the right word. "Er – *krasivee*," she finally remembered. Beautiful.

The old lady beamed, showing a row of rather crooked teeth. Lifting a thin hand to Helen's hair, she touched it very lightly. "*Krasnee*," she said. Red.

Helen remembered reading somewhere that the two words used to be identical, and that "red" was synonymous with "beautiful", so that Red Square's name long predated Communism, and the "red corner" was where you kept the family icons. She knew the old lady was paying her a compliment, and she smiled. "*Spasiba*." Thank you.

The old lady nodded in a pleased sort of way.

Helen pulled out her wallet, and started to take out some notes. "*Skolko?*" How much?

The old woman's glance flickered over her face, and Helen had the sudden unnerving feeling that the pale, cloudy, half-blind eyes actually saw right into her. *Deep* into her. The old lady growled, "*Nyet, nyet,*" and pushed the notes away.

Helen said, helplessly, "You mean – it's not enough? Or it's not for sale?"

"*Nyet*," she repeated, loudly and sharply, "*Nyet*," so that several people turned around to look what the commotion was. Helen colored. "I'm sorry, I don't understand ... do you want it back?" She held out the figure. The old woman made an explosive sound, turned her back on Helen and went marching off through the crowd without a backward glance.

A nearby stall-keeper, a young woman with a friendly face under an ash-blonde perm, had seen the little scene. Helen caught her eye. "*Izvenityeh* – excuse me – do you speak any English?"

"*Choo-Choot*. Little bit," explained the young woman, thumb and forefinger showing how much.

"That lady – who is she?"

"That Olga Sergeyevna Feshina. She is widow. She have one daughter in Yaroslavl." She jerked her head at Helen's hair. "Child of daughter, she has hair same you."

"She seemed like a nice lady." She held up the figurine. "And a good artist."

The young woman shot her a look. She did not respond directly to what Helen had said, but instead observed, casually, "People say she is *zhanarka*." She saw Helen's puzzled expression and added, "This means, woman who knows."

"I'm sorry, I don't understand."

"She knows," the woman said, patiently. "She know to heal. Also, she might see who you marry. If you get money. And more."

Helen stared. "You're not saying, she's some kind of *witch*?"

The other woman's face closed up, more at Helen's tone than anything. She said, indifferently, "I tell only what people say," and turned away to serve a customer. Helen was dismissed, and knew it, and muttering, "Thanks," she walked away with as much dignity as she could muster, the little carving still in her hand. As she left the market and turned down the river path that led to Saint Dimitri, she couldn't help feeling uneasy. Of course she didn't believe in witches, not any more at least, not since childhood. But the memory of Mrs. Feshina's expression as she looked into her eyes was still vivid. What if the figurine she'd given her was some kind of voodoo thing? What if she was being jinxed? She half-wanted to throw it away in the bushes. But that was too stupid. It was lovely, and there was no way it could possibly do her any harm. To think otherwise – well, that way lay madness. She pushed the figurine into her bag. Maybe she'd ask Alexey about it. If he called ... but maybe he'd have thought better of it by now. For what had happened in the woods – it was something out of time. Like a dream. Something marvelous, but that you couldn't fit into ordinary life.

She was by the river now, not far from Saint Dimitri's. Up close like this, it was even more enchanting, with its five sky-blue onion domes studded with golden stars, its deep red walls and towers elaborately iced with white pilasters, cornices and carvings. She might as well go in and have a look, she thought, if only to get away from her restless thoughts and from the equally restless clouds of big fat mosquitoes under the trees, dive-bombing her mercilessly. There was a tour party waiting to go in, so she joined it.

The cathedral had looked quite big from the outside, but just as with St Basil's in Moscow, that was deceptive, for the space inside was much smaller. Warm and close, it was very different to what she was used to in the great cathedrals of Western Europe, with their soaring spaces and light falling through stained-glass windows. Here it felt much less spacious, much more dim, yet color glowed everywhere, from the frescoed walls and the iconostasis, or wall of icons, with its rows of saints, angels, prophets, apostles and Jesus and Mary, Mother of God. Their sad, steady eyes followed Helen around; their very stillness seemed living, breathing.

There were no statues. No pews, because congregations never sat in services, but stood or knelt. No altar to be seen either – that was behind the iconostasis, in the middle of which was the golden door through which only the priest may enter. For in front of the iconostasis, the guide told them, was this world. Behind it, the other world.

Now the guide said, "As you know, this is the very spot where little Prince Dimitri, last son of Tsar Ivan Grozny, you say Ivan the Terrible, was murdered. He was only nine years old when this happened." She took them to a series of wall paintings in the nave, which told the whole story somewhat in the manner of a comic strip. There he was, playing by the Volga with his friends. And there was someone creeping up on him. And there the poor kid was, lying on the ground, with a blade in his throat and blood spurting from his wounds.

"Nobody can say exactly who did this," said the guide. "Many say it was his uncle Boris Godunov. He was regent after Ivan died. He send investigators, they say Dimitri stab himself in epileptic fit. But nobody believe this. People in Uglich then, they are sure Godunov order this murder, and they rise up. But maybe is someone else. Nobody knows. What is certain is Boris become tsar after Dimitri's death. But Boris Godunov was not long tsar. After his death, many, many problems. We call this Time of Troubles."

A wag in the party said, "How do you Russians tell that time of trouble apart from all the other ones you've had?"

The guide serenely ignored this. "Polish kings, they say Dimitri not really dead, they say he hiding in their country, they bring false prince and try to put him on throne of Russia. There is much, much trouble and war. But all the time, real Saint Dimitri here, in this place, and Russian peoples know this. His body stay sweet and uncorrupted, and that is why he is saint." She led the way back to the main part of the church, and pointed at the big bell that hung there on a stand. "This bell rang signal for rebellion that started in Uglich after Dimitri died. So Boris Godunov, he order that clapper of bell be cut out, like man's tongue, and bell is exiled to Siberia."

There was a gasp, half-amazed, half-amused, from the audience. The guide smiled. "Yes, this really happen. Bell only come back hundreds of years later. It has new clapper now." She gently lifted the clapper, letting it softly hit the side of the bell. Once. Twice. Three times.

The bell's voice was softer than Helen had expected, given its size. Deep, but soft and sad, the sound reaching right into your bones as it reverberated in the hushed church. Helen suddenly thought of what Sergey had said: *In Russia, we say churches are alive.* She understood what he meant now. Oh, I hope you were happy here, poor little Dimitri, she thought. I hope that before you died and became a saint that there were lots of ordinary happy days, sunlight on the river, birds singing in the trees, games to play, trees to climb, honey cakes to eat, not too many mosquitoes, and no bad dreams. I hope you never knew what was coming.

As she walked out of the church, her phone rang. It was Alexey. On the phone, his voice was even deeper.

"Hi, Helen. How's it going?"

She tried to keep her voice level. "Fine." Walking away from the church to a quiet spot by the river, she went on, "I've just been to visit Saint Dimitri's."

"And what did you think of it?"

"Beautiful. But sad. Poor little boy. I guess he got to be a saint but somehow I think he'd have preferred to grow up."

"I'd say you were right. You know, when I was a kid, I used to think that one of the pictures of Saint Dimitri looked like my brother Misha. Same sulky look." There was a smile in his voice. "Misha hated it. Used to chase me around yelling he was going to turn *me* into a saint if I didn't shut up."

"Does he still hate it now?" Helen asked, smiling into the phone.

There was a short silence, then Alexey said, "Misha's … he's dead. A few years ago."

What a fool she was, what a fool. How could she not have noticed that he'd spoken in the past tense? How could she not have remembered that the newspaper article she'd read had mentioned he was the only surviving child? "I'm so sorry, Alexey," she whispered. "I'm so sorry."

"Don't be. You weren't to know and it was me who mentioned him. Anyway it does me good to speak about him. He wasn't the easiest of brothers, but he *was* my brother. Poor old Mish." He sighed. "Sorry to be a downer. You probably wish I hadn't called now."

"No." She clutched the phone closer to her ear as a couple of people walked by. "Not at all. Really. I – um – did your meeting go well? With your godfather?"

"Sure. He's a great guy, even if he does worry a bit too much. And he's been awesome in getting me up to speed on things with Trinity. Steep learning curve, that's for sure. Listen – what are you doing right now? Are you on your way home?"

"No. I'm sitting by the river, just near the church."

"Good. I'm not far away. Mind if I drop by?"

"If you like," said Helen, her pulse racing.

He laughed. "I do like. See you very soon, then." And he clicked off.

He was as good as his word. Just over five minutes had passed when she heard him calling her name and, turning, saw him walking across the grass towards her.

"Hi," she greeted him, trying to sound casual, as if she hadn't spent the last few minutes with her stomach full of butterflies.

"Hi there. Good to see you. It's been a while," he said, and grinned, so that she knew he was only kidding.

"I was beginning to wonder when we'd catch up next," she answered, matching his light tone. They looked at each other and laughed.

"Want to walk a bit?" he said. "I've just spent hours over some very tiresome formalities and I really need to stretch my legs a bit before I have to go through yet another lot of papers. That okay with you?"

"Sure." She wouldn't have been able to sit still, anyway. Not with him sitting next to her. At least now the flush in her cheeks might be put down to exertion. "I like walking." On an impulse, she added, "How did you do that?"

He blinked. "What?

"My ankle – the other day – it was so sore." She gave him a sidelong glance. "And then – you touched it. And it wasn't sore any longer. Please don't tell me it was my imagination. I know it wasn't."

There was a small silence. Then he said, "I don't know how it works."

"What do you mean, you don't know?"

"Just that." For the first time since she'd met him, he sounded shy, reticent, even a little nervous, and she didn't press him. Instead, she fished in her handbag and, bringing out Mrs. Feshina's figurine, handed it to him, recounting the story of how she'd got it, finishing with, "So what do you think?"

He'd accepted the change of subject with obvious relief. Turning the little figure over in his hands, he said, "You mean, should you be worried about this doll?"

She nodded.

"I don't think so," he said, gently, and handed the carving back to her. "If she's a *zhanarka* – well, they are the good sort of witch. Her giving you this – it's a good sign."

She faltered, "You mean – you think it's actually *true*, what that woman said?"

He shrugged. "Could be." He handed the figurine back to her, and smiled. "Don't look so worried, Helen. Witch or not, I'm sure the old lady hasn't called down a curse on you or anything."

She blushed. "Of course I didn't think that. It's just so – so –"

"So out there?" he suggested. She nodded.

"You'll get used to that," he said. "Magic is so popular here that the government actually regulates witchcraft."

She stared at him. "What? Like in *Harry Potter*?"

He smiled. "Kind of. They know they can't ban magic, so they just try to keep tabs on it, and forbid witches and wizards and *ekstrasens* – those are psychics – from claiming their services can cure terminal illnesses, that kind of thing. Doesn't stop them from getting tons of clients, from all walks of life, who come for potions, and curses and fortune-telling and whatever. And let's not forget those that can help you stave off energy vampires."

"You're kidding me! What on earth are those? *Twilight* types on speed?"

He laughed. "Sort of. Except more like they're on downers. Energy vampires suck all the energy out of you. They're the kinds of people who bring you down all the time, who make you feel that life's a drag, who take away your joy of life, who turn the world into a gray fog."

Helen gave an involuntary shiver, thinking of Simon. Alexey saw it and said, quietly, "Makes sense, doesn't it, in a strange sort of way? We all know people like that. It's just that some of us prefer to think it's a kind of spell. Because you can break a spell, if you have the right formula. Gives you hope. Do you see?"

"I do," said Helen, very much struck by his words.

"Helen, can I ask you something?"

"Of course."

45

"What brought you here? I mean, I know you came on holiday with your mother. But if you don't mind me saying so, it's kind of unusual to see a girl your age traveling with her mother."

She swallowed. "I – I happen to like traveling with my mother." Defiantly, she added, "Is that so strange?"

"No. It's unusual, that's all. You're lucky. My mother …" He paused, and she saw his eyes darken. "I never got to know that about her and me. She died of cancer when I was twelve, but I still miss her so much."

Her throat swelled. Impulsively, she reached out a hand to him. "Oh, Alexey. I'm so sorry."

"Thank you," he said, and clasped her hand. Though his touch was brief, Helen's breath caught in her throat, for the flood of warmth she'd felt when he'd touched her ankle had surged through her again. Only sweeter and more piercing this time. And from the expression in his eyes, she knew he felt it too.

There was a small silence, then he released her hand and went on, "It's the one thing I really understood about my father. The fact he loved my mother. I think she was the only person he ever truly loved."

His eyes were shiny. His emotions were so close to the surface, she thought, and she was helplessly drawn to that in him. Still a little shaky, she whispered, "Oh, it must be so hard for you."

"It has been. But I think it just got easier." Their eyes met.

And then, it was as if some barrier had broken between them, and as they walked by the river and back through the park, the talk blossomed between them as easily as if they had known each other for a long time, and yet it was sparkling, piquant with discovery; intimate and unfamiliar, all at once. For though there was so much that was different between them, there was so much too that rang common bells: uneasy family circumstances, shunting between different countries, different cultures, the feeling of being set apart, somewhat solitary but needing company too, and concentrating on school work to escape the confusion. But whereas Helen's interests at school had always tended to words, Alexey was drawn to music. His interest led him to the conservatorium and training as a classical singer; hers to Changeling. But he didn't dwell on the music school. "I want to know about *you*," he said. "Tell me about Changeling and what you do there."

"Nothing now," she said, softly. "It was an internship and I was so excited to get it because it's really sought-after. You see, Changeling's one of the coolest small production houses in the UK, they do great quirky documentaries. And they made it pretty clear that if I did well, they'd offer me a job. I really thought I was doing well. I worked really hard, and I even came up with a couple of story ideas which I pitched. Well, my internship expired – and they said they had to let me go. When I asked why, they told me I didn't quite fit in, that I didn't have what they called a 'proper team spirit'. I knew then what it was really about. Those story ideas I'd pitched. I hadn't gone to my immediate boss first, I didn't play office politics, I just had no idea. I thought – I thought that none of that mattered. I thought Changeling was – different. Creative. Cool. So uncorporate." She grimaced. "I learned the hard way they weren't. That they'd pinned me down as a troublemaker. I was an idiot. I should have kept my head down."

"No," said Alexey, his eyes flashing. "What they did was not only unjust but stupid. A company's only as good as the people who work for it. And if they treat staff like that – well, in the end they'll get what they deserve. You'll see."

"That's sweet of you, Alexey, but that isn't how it works," she said, wearily. She thought of that last hour at Changeling, of stumbling blindly out of the office and into the Tube, heading home desperate for comfort, and walking in on Simon and Annie…

She couldn't tell him that part. Not yet. Maybe one day. If they got to "one day". Right now, it felt like a violation. Telling him about Changeling was a relief, but it wasn't the worst of it, not the coup de grâce that had sent her reeling out into the street.

Chapter 6

Not long after, Alexey had to leave. But not before he had made a date with Helen for the next day. "No snatched moments, this time," he'd said. "Let me take you to lunch. Agreed?"

"Agreed," she echoed, and as she made her way back to Irina's, she was so happy she felt as though she were floating. Her mother had said she should take care, because "people like that" saw life differently. "But that's what I want," said Helen to the bright sky. "To see life differently. And no more energy vampires!" And she laughed.

The rest of the afternoon and evening passed quietly, but cheerfully. Helen's mother clearly saw that her daughter was in a buoyant mood, but she didn't ask any questions, and when Helen told her she was going out to lunch with Alexey the next day, she only nodded and said, "That sounds nice. I suppose being a local he must know the good places around here." Helen knew her mother was making an effort for her sake, and it touched her instead of irritating her as it might once have done. She showed her Mrs. Feshina's figurine, and told her what the stall-keeper had said, and her mother shook her head and said, "That reminds me of old Madame Latour in the village in France when I was a child, everyone knew she was a *sorcière*. Even the mayor of the village went to her in secret once, and he was supposed to be a Communist and not believe in God let alone magic. She really had a gift, you know. She knew people. Could see inside you. Or that's what it felt like."

"That's what Mrs. Feshina was like too," Helen exclaimed, and then the rest of the evening passed happily swapping stories of the unexplained over dinner, and then watching a DVD of *Dersu Uzala* that Irina had on her shelves. The touching story of the old Siberian hunter Dersu Uzala and his friendship with the young Russian surveyor Arseniev, and the grandeur of the Siberian landscape, were enthralling, so that when Helen went to bed, her head was full of snowy vistas and huge dark forests, and hard-faced, soft-eyed men for whom life was never a gray fog.

*

Dreaming, Helen was back in the wood. The same wood as where she'd met Alexey, but it felt very different. The trees pressed in much closer, the shadows grew across the track. Unseen eyes were in every tree, and there were whispers, rustles of footfalls all around. She could hear her own heart beating. Could feel the sweat growing cold on her skin. She wanted to turn back, but couldn't. Could only go forward, deeper into the heart of the woods.

There was someone right behind her. Something. She turned her head to look and saw a bear. A huge beast the size of a grizzly. It was a short distance away, loping down the track toward her. Small, intelligent eyes, mouth open on a soundless roar. She began to run, but the bear kept coming, calm, purposeful, while the breath tore in her chest and through her throat. She ran and ran, and the bear still kept coming, and soon, soon, it would catch her up ...

Helen woke. Her heart was pounding. Her skin felt cold. For a moment, the dream's menace still lingered in her, like a warning, a threat. She looked at the time. It was well past ten o'clock! She hadn't slept so long for ages, and yet she didn't feel very rested because of the dream. And then she remembered. Alexey was picking her up at midday. And that immediately chased away thought of everything else.

Whoa, girl, she told herself. Slow down. Yes. You're going on a date with a gorgeous guy who you clearly click with. But he's a stranger, from a dangerous world so different to yours that it might as well be on another planet. After that business with Simon, surely she'd learned her lesson. And then it struck her. That dismissive phrase, the one an indifferent stranger might have used: *The business with Simon*. No grief, no shame, not even anger. That was suddenly all in the past. Finished. Done with. All that mattered was here. Now. Seeing *him* again.

She showered, and dressed, changing clothes several times before finally deciding on a simple dark blue cotton dress sprinkled with daisies. It was short, and her legs felt strangely bare, so she pulled on a pair of cable-knit tights, and ballerina pumps, and a pale blue cotton cardigan. She twisted her hair up, and put on some lip gloss and mascara and some daisy earrings. She looked at herself in the mirror. Well, hello, little Miss Clement, she thought, Bo-Peep with your sheep, butter wouldn't melt. Not classy or elegant. Not sexy. Not dangerous at all.

When her mother saw her, she raised an eyebrow. "You sure you're wearing the right sort of clothes for this?"

"For what?" Helen flashed out.

Her mother looked surprised and a little hurt. "I just mean – Russians dress up, you know."

"We're not going to a posh restaurant, Mam. I mean, this is a provincial town in the middle of nowhere, not Moscow or Paris!"

"You never know," said her mother, mysteriously, and Helen shrugged, trying to look calm and collected when in fact she felt anything but.

*

A short time later, he arrived. Helen was in the back garden when the Mercedes pulled up outside the house, and by the time she went back in, Alexey was standing in the kitchen, talking to her mother who was arranging some flowers in a vase. Dressed in a white shirt, a fine blue linen jacket and trousers, he looked not only elegant but unbelievably sexy.

Her mother said, "There you are. Aren't these lovely?"

They were creamy-white roses, very fragrant, Helen could smell them from across the room. "Lovely," she echoed, stammering a little. "Thank – thank you."

"I hoped you'd like them." The words were ordinary, but his sea-change eyes were expressive, and she swallowed. She said, a little clumsily, "Right – are you ready, then?"

"If you are," he replied, holding her gaze, and she saw the alarm dawning in her mother's face. She said, hastily, "Okay, Mam, see you later," and went out with Alexey.

There were two people in the front seat of the car – the chauffeur and a young man with crew-cut blond hair. Alexey saw her glance and said, "Sorry about that, it's more to keep Kolya happy than anything. He doesn't like it when I ditch security like I've done recently." He held the gate open for her. "Anyway, don't worry, Slava and Yuri are not going to be breathing down our necks at the restaurant, they'll wait outside."

He introduced her to the two men. Helen murmured greetings, not meeting the bodyguard Slava's eye as he jumped out and opened the rear door for them. What would he and the chauffeur think of their boss taking some unknown foreign girl out to lunch? She was prickly with nerves, but

Alexey seemed perfectly relaxed, chatting about the weather, the news, the houses they passed, while she sat uncomfortably aware of the silent presence of the men in front. Yet even more acutely aware of Alexey's nearness, though he didn't try to touch her.

Soon they were purring in through the impressive gateway of the hotel, a grand pillared building in the style of the Bolshoi Theatre in Moscow, standing in landscaped grounds right on the banks of the Volga, with a sweeping view over the huge river. Taken by surprise, Helen said, "Hey, that's not bad. Someone's old mansion, was it?"

"No, actually. It's pretty much brand-new. They just wanted it to look like it came from the time of the tsars. Done it pretty well, too."

Inside was just as grand, all turned balustrades, crystal chandeliers, crimson and cream walls on which hung oil paintings of imperial court scenes, and a magnificent central marble staircase leading up to the first floor. This was nothing like what Helen had expected.

She blurted out, without thinking, "Alexey, this is going to cost you a fortune."

"Don't worry about that," he said, grinning. "My fortune's big enough to take care of itself."

"I didn't mean that," she said, blushing scarlet, because of the appallingly stupid thing she'd said, and because she was afraid he'd think she was a gold-digger, and also because she was disconcerted that he should be so open about his money. People didn't do that. Not in the circles she'd been in, at least. Simon's circle, that's to say. Most of them had money – or at least their families did – and it was expected they – and you – pretended it didn't matter. When actually, of course, it did.

She saw the laughter in Alexey's eyes and knew he understood what she was thinking. "Sorry, Helen," he said, as they sat down and ordered cocktails. "Couldn't resist teasing you. You looked so sweetly serious and practical. Kolya would approve. He's always at me not to be extravagant. To be careful."

She was blushing even more now, not only because of the funny little compliment, but because of the warmth in his eyes. She said, primly, "Well, one does have to be careful, doesn't one?"

He laughed. "Oh, does *one*?" His expression changed and he added, seriously, "Trouble is, Helen, when does one live, then, eh?"

Their eyes met. She said, very quietly, "I don't know."

The cocktails arrived. Alexey said, "Shall we make a toast, Helen?"

She nodded.

"To life," he said, and she echoed, "to life," and drank.

"One toast is never enough," he said. "You need at least three. The best things come in threes." He looked at her with an impish smile. "You choose the next one."

She returned his smile. "Okay, then. To magic."

"I'll second that," he said, laughing. "To magic!" And they clinked glasses and drank.

"And now?"

"One more. What's it to be, Helen?"

"To joy," she cried and he looked at her with the strangest look on his face, so that for an instant she thought that somehow she had offended him. Then he whispered, "My God, that was *exactly* what I was thinking," and she knew now that the expression in his eyes was awe. She felt awed herself, thrilled beyond words by what was happening to her, to them. As they drank the toast, she thought, I can't describe it. Only feel it filling up my whole body, my mind, my heart, my whole being, infusing the world with a sparkling sweetness much more intoxicating than the Crimean champagne cocktail I'm drinking.

The timeless moment was ended by the waiter bringing their shared entrée, red caviar and lobster salad with tiny, perfect buckwheat blinis and a tangy mayonnaise on the side. It was delicious and for a short while all they talked about was things to do with food. Alexey turned out to have quite a fondness for cooking shows, while Helen disliked them on principle, but loved food blogs and was even thinking of starting her own. At least, she'd decided on the spur of the moment she would, and then Alexey jokingly suggested some silly titles for it. The main course arrived – pike-perch fillet with fennel for him, and duck breast in lemon sauce for her – and by then they were both so easy and mellow with each other that it felt perfectly natural for Helen to say, "Yesterday, you said you thought that a company is only as good as the people who work for it. That sounds like you've really thought about it. But I thought you weren't interested in running your father's company?"

Too late she realized that her words revealed she'd been reading up about him. He noticed all right, but he didn't seem to mind. He said, "It's true I wasn't, at first. When I came back to Russia, it was just to bury Dad next to my mother, as he'd wanted. I fully intended to get rid of Trinity. I never had anything to do with it before – my father kept me well away from it – but the little I knew about how it operated didn't make me feel well-disposed to it. I certainly didn't want to be lumbered with it, anyway. Plus, I thought I was too young to think of taking anything like that on. And then everything changed."

"Why? If you don't mind telling me."

He smiled. "I'd love to! It's just I'm afraid of boring you with my pet subject."

"Try me," she said, smiling back. "I'll tell you if I feel like yawning."

He laughed. "Deal! Really, it was all down to Kolya. You see, as well as being my godfather, he's also Trinity's general manager and he's been running the company since Dad died. And Kolya pretty much ambushed me. He said I must understand that as my father's heir, I had responsibilities. That I had to realize that many people, including him, had given years of their life to the company and it wasn't fair to simply wipe out its existence without facing them in person. They deserved at least that."

"Oh! And what did you say to that?"

"Well, I was stung, of course. I told him okay, get all the staff together for a meeting. I was all set to tell them that I appreciated they'd worked hard, but that it was over. And then I met them. These were *good* people, Helen. Hard-working, intelligent, dedicated. And so I had to face it. The age thing – that was a total cop-out. Dad and his mates had started Trinity when they were not much older than me. And I did have to take responsibility, no matter what I decided. You see, if I closed down the company, the staff would be out of work and good work isn't necessarily easy to come by here. But if I sold it on, it was likely the new owners would be dodgy. I'd already had offers for it from a couple of people who looked legit but who Kolya told me were a front for gangsters."

Helen's eyes widened. "Wow. That would have freaked me out."

"I didn't like it, I can tell you. I didn't want the staff to be at the mercy of people like that. And so I couldn't tell them I was abandoning them. I just said that I needed time to think about our options, but that as far as I was concerned, they could get on with their work, with Kolya as acting director. I still thought I might pull out, even then. But I wanted to do it from an informed viewpoint."

Her pulse raced. Imagine being in that position at his age, having to decide such things! It was awe-inspiring, extraordinary. Terrifying. She asked, eagerly, "So what did you do then?"

"I went on a crash course about Trinity. Talked to Kolya and the rest of the staff at length. Waded through hundreds of files to check out what Trinity had been up to over the years. Basically, it's a private investigation firm, specializing in business cases, such as breaches of company security or industrial espionage, and a few hand-picked personal cases. For instance one guy, this wealthy banker, wanted his daughter's boyfriend investigated. Also, Trinity does some work for government departments, and in recent years consultancy for foreign companies setting up branches here. The company's methods weren't always what you'd call absolutely ethical – but it wasn't what I had feared." Again he paused, and now Helen said, "You don't have to go on, Alexey. It's okay. I understand."

"No. I want to tell you." His eyes were fixed on hers. "From that first moment in the woods, I knew that there was a deep connection between us. And that I can trust you, absolutely. As I hope you know you can trust me."

She nodded, shakily, not trusting herself to speak.

"But if you'd rather not know," he went on, "if it scares you – I quite understand. We can talk about something else."

"No!" she said, so explosively that he looked a little startled for a moment. "I mean – I want to hear. I'm glad – honoured. Please – go on. What was it that you feared?"

His expression changed, became grim. "I thought, you see, that Trinity might have been a front. That it was actually a criminal organization carrying out hits and major fraud for selected clients." She stared at him, stunned. "You really thought that your father might be that kind of—"

"I know it sounds extreme, but my father – he was an extreme sort of guy. Secretive, remote, ruthless. And his family background ..." He paused. "Well, let's just say ruthlessness ran in the family. His father was in the KGB. Not the external service either, but the internal one, the really terrifying bastards. Worked out of the Lubyanka. And *his* father before him."

Helen's eyes widened. Even though the Soviet regime had fallen before she was born, she'd heard stories, watched movies about the KGB. The dreaded secret police of Soviet days and its Moscow headquarters had a fearsome reputation.

"You see why I thought it was possible," Alexey said quietly. "Quite a few of those KGB guys switched to dodgy business after the fall of the Soviet Union. I knew Dad had clients who'd diversified like that." His mouth twisted wryly. "Dad might have turned his back on a career in the security services but he thought like them, in some ways. And I knew nothing really about what he'd been up to with Trinity. Anyway, there was nothing like that to be seen in any of the records. Not at least in the stuff that was *officially* recorded. But then Kolya told me that occasionally the three directors took on a case themselves. Nobody else at Trinity knew what went on. There was no paper trail. No computer records. It was totally secret."

Helen spoke softly, "Do you have any idea what those cases were?"

"No. Not a clue. Still don't. Not sure I want to know, actually. What really matters was that the staff hadn't been involved. So I decided I would keep Trinity going. But how? Did I want to be directly involved, or leave things in Kolya's capable hands while I continued my studies? To be honest, I think that's what Kolya expected. He thought I was all set on a career in music."

"And weren't you?"

"In those weeks at Trinity I'd changed. And I'd realized something important. That *this* was what I wanted, now." His eyes were shining. "Running Trinity was not what I'd ever imagined myself doing before, but that was what really excited me, the sheer unexpectedness of it! It's such an adventure, such a challenge, I feel like I'm ten times more alive than I was at the conservatorium, much as I love music. And being back in Russia – it's been such a big thing for me! Oh, don't get me wrong, I really like Australia. It was my home for twelve years. I had friends there, a life. But back here, I realized that this was where I truly *belonged*." He looked at Helen. "Have you ever read Gogol? The writer Nikolai Gogol I mean?"

"No, I haven't."

"Well, in one of his stories he compares the Russian character to a ride in a troika, you know, one of those three-horse sleighs. You just race along, not afraid of getting hurt, of consequences, just going for it, no matter what might happen. Well, that was me. I jumped on board that troika and went for it. Just keeping on Trinity wasn't enough. I decided to change it. No more dark secrets. No more being snoops for corrupt bullies. Trinity would be transformed."

So just like that, she thought, he'd changed his entire life. Thrown himself into something whose path he couldn't even predict. It was startling, brave, mad, inspirational, magnificent! Her voice trembling a little, she said, "How, Alexey?"

"In my country ordinary people have always been left out of the picture. And I hope we might use Trinity's skills to help them when they're in trouble."

"That's beautiful," said Helen, deeply moved by the simplicity and modesty of what he'd said. "So right. So *real*."

His smile was very sweet. "You understand. I'm so glad."

"So what's happened? How many new cases have you taken on? Or can't you talk about them?"

He smiled at the tumble of questions. "Well, I would if I could, Helen – but I can't. Not because it's secret but because we haven't taken on anything new yet. It's very early days. Not everything's settled, legally. But it shouldn't be long before it's all done and we can make a fresh start."

Helen blurted out, "Oh, Alexey, aren't you just a little bit – nervous about it?"

"Of course." His expression darkened. "Sometimes I'm freaking terrified of what I've started. I wake up in the middle of the night and my heart's pounding and I'm thinking, what in God's name am I doing? How on earth do I think I can make a go of this? And then ..."

"Yeah, what then?" she breathed.

"Then I just roll over and go back to sleep," he said, lightly.

She frowned, not sure whether he was being serious or not. "As easy as that?"

"Not easy at all," he replied. "Just the only way it can be, Helen. Do you understand what I'm saying?"

"Yes," she whispered, and her throat felt dry. "I think I do."

Chapter 7

Maxim Antonovich Serebrov was troubled. And when he was troubled, he turned from a gentle giant into a growling bear of a man. At least, that's what Marina used to say. In the days when she could be bothered to say anything even halfway agreeable about him, anyway.

Maxim knew that in this mood, he didn't help himself. He knew that, coupled with his impressive physical bulk, a bad mood made him intimidating to the general public, and challenging to his superiors. The first wasn't a problem – he always managed to surmount the fury and treated even insolent *urkas*, street thugs, with as much impassive calm as he could muster. The second had always been more of a problem because Maxim, a natural rebel who'd grown up in a tough Moscow suburb, had always had an issue with authority.

He knew that his kind usually hated the *militsiya*, the police. And were much more likely to join the ranks of the *urkas* than the *mients*, the cops. But he'd been different. Emerging from a scarifying experience as a young army recruit in the First Chechen War of the mid-1990s, he'd gone to university and studied languages. With his experience and background, he could have joined the intelligence services afterwards, but he stunned everybody – his family, who hated the police instinctively, and Marina's intellectual family, who thought that only thick-headed country clods with no education or ambition would even think of such a thing – by joining the police force.

Truth was, Maxim had dreamed of change. Of a world where ordinary people could live in peace and respect, and not be treated as cannon fodder or brain-washed sheep or prey to be exploited. In the intelligence services, it was the State you protected from its enemies. In the police, you protected ordinary people from predators. That was what he wanted to do. Oh, he knew the force was a very long way from perfect. It had a bad reputation in Soviet days. But he'd thought that now things had changed, it would be reformed.

He'd soon realized he was kidding himself. Not only were the time-servers and bully boys of the past still in the force, but with the lawless chaos that reigned in the country at that time, the police, now not merely under-resourced as in the Soviet past but starved of even their meagre pay packets, had morphed into a gangsters' protection society and vicious extortion racket. Many officers had left the force for much more lucrative positions in private security. Others supplemented their pathetic pay with bribes. Worse still, some police became involved in violent crime, from armed robbery to rape and murder. Psychopaths, thugs and alcoholics held sway, and guidebooks for foreign travelers warned that the *militsiya* were much more dangerous than gangsters. And, of course, criminal investigation fell into the absolute doldrums.

Marina begged him to leave the force and join one of the private agencies or at least to retrain for work in the procurator's office. But he refused. He had no illusions anymore but he was determined. He wasn't going to be beaten, he told Marina. In our country, people too often allow themselves to be beaten down by bastards. Or join them.

But he wasn't going to do either. For a while Marina had seemed to accept it, especially after he was given his one and only promotion, from lieutenant to senior lieutenant, by some miracle of oversight. But there he'd stagnated.

And then one day he was approached by an ex-colleague, who was now a frontman for one of the city's most powerful crime gangs. Maxim was offered a good salary and conditions if he came to work for them as a consultant investigator – for apparently his intelligence and initiative had been noted. Maxim had sent him packing – but it had been the end for him and Marina. She'd collapsed in tears of fury, accusing him of being a selfish good-for-nothing who was deliberately trying to destroy their lives, and walked out. She didn't return.

Things had become better in recent years – not between him and Marina, that was over long ago – but in the country itself, and in the force. But Maxim knew it would need more than codes of conduct, the doubling of police pay packets, Ministry of the Interior video clips about helpful police action, and the renaming of the force from the Soviet term "militia" back to the more civilian sound of "police" to change ingrained public perceptions. It would take years. Generations, maybe. And there was nothing Maxim could do to hurry that along. He was just a miniscule cog in the huge wheel of history. But he *could* do something about his instinctive attitude to his superiors when they thwarted him. He should be more cunning. More patient. Sometimes, it worked and he actually managed to keep a guard on his tongue. This time, though ...

"You're off the Rusalka case," Korolev had said when Maxim entered his superior's office that day.

Maxim stared at him, trying not to show how stunned he was. "May I ask why, Fyodor Mikhailovich?"

"The procurator's pissed off that there's not been a resolution to this case. It's all going far too slow for his liking."

Maxim stiffened. "I've tried my hardest," he growled, "but there aren't enough resources, we have to do everything on the cheap, and I get stonewalled all the time by people who'd much rather make us think those Trinity deaths were accidents. What the hell does the procurator expect?"

Korolev shrugged. "He expects us to wrap this up, and double quick, Serebrov. It doesn't look good for it to drag on. Besides, nothing you've uncovered yet points the finger at any suspect."

"I just need more time." It wasn't in Maxim's nature to beg, but he forced himself to add, "Please."

Korolev shook his head. "Sorry. Can't be done. The procurator's already decided the case is going to the Organized Crime Unit."

"What?" Maxim was livid. "Those OC gorillas will make a hash of it as usual. Might as well bury the case completely."

"That's enough!" Korolev snapped. "Your own report raised the possibility Trinity had links to organized crime, so it's bizarre you should question what's being done." He glared at Maxim. "You have obviously lost all sense of proportion, Serebrov. You've got too close to the damned case." His mouth twisted. "Do you think you'll make a name for yourself at last, if you solve it? Or is there something else you're not telling me?"

At that, Maxim's control snapped. He couldn't hold back the angry swear words that burst scalding from his lips and hung blue in the air, giving Korolev exactly the excuse he had been waiting for.

"Go home, Maxim," he said. "You're obviously over-tired and stressed, and under the circumstances you can't do your job properly."

"I'm sorry, Fyodor Mikhailovich," said Maxim, apologizing with ill grace.

"Go. You're on two weeks unpaid leave, as of now. You're lucky I think so highly of you, Senior Lieutenant Serebrov, or you'd be in serious trouble."

Maxim knew there was no point in protesting. It was true that Korolev was within his rights to discipline him much more severely. It was also true that despite the fact they did not click at all – Korolev being not only a desk man but a dab hand at internal politics, neither of which was Maxim's forte – his superior had not hindered him before. The procurator and who knows who else must really be breathing down his neck, Maxim thought, and there was nothing he could do. So he shrugged, said, "Very well," and left the office, cursing himself for an impulsive fool.

Now, back in his tiny apartment, re-reading the copies of the notes he'd made on the Rusalka case (he always secretly made copies and kept them at home, not trusting in office security), he felt more troubled than ever. Yes, it was true he'd reluctantly conceded in his report that, given the available evidence, the deaths of Galkin, Barsukov and Makarov looked like accidents. "Looked like" and "available evidence" were the operative words.

Maxim liked to use his eyes and ears as well as his brain when on a case but because the men had died abroad, it hadn't been possible for him to personally visit the scene of the crime and talk to people locally. The exception had been the first death, Galkin's, because that had been in neighboring Finland, and the anorexic travel budget of the department had stretched enough to grant Maxim a cheap flight to Helsinki. Not that it had done much good; there had been no direct witnesses to the death, and though Maxim visited the scene, he gained nothing of any significance. And that failure, that waste of good police money, as Korolev had tetchily called it, had ensured that when Barsukov had died in Nice, Maxim had to make do with reports sent over by the French police, and frustrating, garbled phone conversations in bad English. And, of course, there was absolutely no question of his going all the way to Australia, especially as Makarov's death completely put paid to the theory he'd been leaning toward – that the surviving Trinity director had a strong motive for eliminating his partners, so as to gain complete control of the company.

Over the course of the investigation, Maxim had several times visited the Trinity office, housed on the first floor of an office block not far from the Duma, the Russian parliament building, and interviewed all the staff. After Galkin's death, he'd interviewed Barsukov – both he and Galkin had been Russia-based; Barsukov in Moscow, Galkin in St Petersburg. After Barsukov's death, he'd even interviewed Makarov, who had flown over himself to "help the police with their inquiries", as he put it. And he *had* been helpful. Suspiciously so, in fact. He had answered all Maxim's questions with apparent openness, had explained what business his company did with apparent honesty, and had instructed all his staff, from manager Nikolai Volkovsky to receptionist Alla Chernina, to give Maxim full co-operation.

The policeman had soon realized that while some of the companies and individuals on Trinity's published list of clients were reasonably respectable, others were on the shady side, though not straight-out criminal. In any case that wasn't his concern. He was investigating suspicious deaths, not companies operating on the windy side of the law. He interviewed the clients, who all – including the shady ones! – praised Trinity as being thorough and discreet. Though Maxim wasn't altogether convinced by these clients' complete sincerity, he didn't find any reason to really doubt them, or to suspect their motives. But what he did begin to suspect was that the work that Trinity did in plain view was only the tip of the iceberg, and that there was more to the company than was obviously apparent.

But it was one thing to suspect, another to prove it, and though he'd tried to surprise Ivan Makarov into admitting it, he'd failed. Yet he'd been sure he'd been on to something when one very early morning, he called round unexpectedly on Makarov in his swish Moscow apartment, and snapped, "I want to see the real files. The hidden ones that your friends were killed for," and Makarov's eyes had widened in shock. Only for the merest flash of an instant; and in the next moment, the man shrugged and said, in an amused tone, "You've seen all our files. You know all our secrets, Senior Lieutenant. I hope you won't use them against us."

Oh, he'd tried. Gone through all the computers. All the filing cabinets. Through the apartments of all three men. And he'd found nothing. He ran up against a brick wall of frustration. And copped a complaint from Makarov into the bargain. He'd alleged "police harassment".

Maxim had been hauled over the coals. Makarov might have deserted his country to live on the other side of the world, Korolev bawled, but he was still an important man, with influential friends in Russia. Maxim had no such leverage. In fact he'd pissed people off so much he could be transferred to the boondocks if he was keen on stubbornly persisting with his investigation. "Concentrate on the men's deaths, man," Korolev warned him, "not on mythical secret files!"

Maxim had to swallow both his pride and his hunch. And a little while later, when Makarov, back in Australia, had also drowned, the detective had had to swallow his prime suspect theory as well. Now he had no suspect. And he was no nearer the truth of any possible motive. All he had was a bad feeling about the case being taken off him. And one single, solitary clue that his hunch about the hidden files had perhaps not been so stupid and far-fetched after all.

It had started with one of the witness statements compiled by the Australian police after Makarov's death. Makarov's housekeeper had said that the day before her employer died, he'd been "edgy" and, later that evening, she heard what she thought was the shredder going in his home office. But she hadn't actually seen her boss, and no shredded documents had been found at the house, so it was concluded that either she'd been mistaken, or that Makarov had disposed of whatever it was. And though Makarov's computer and cell phone had been seized, and combed for clues, there was nothing. According to the Australians, that is. Maxim asked for and received copies of the files and painstakingly went over them. There was so much stuff, most of which he'd seen already, that he nearly missed it.

It was just a tiny mention, buried deep in the welter of deleted emails from Makarov's hard drive. The email in question was several months old, and was from Sergey Barsukov, a couple of weeks before his death. It was short and to the point:

Possible Koldun leak. S.

Trinity cases were usually filed under nicknames – "Millennium", "Mercury", "Volga" or other such things. "Koldun", "wizard" or "sorcerer" in Russian, fitted that pattern. But not only was there no file labelled "Koldun", it was completely invisible anywhere else apart from that one mention in the deleted email. Maxim checked and rechecked. Nothing. But he had an instinct that it was important, that it was part of Trinity's secret side, and that it was linked to whatever it was Makarov had destroyed the night before his death.

But try as he might, Maxim could not get a single idea of who or what Koldun might have been. When he spoke to Trinity's staff they were clearly as baffled as he was. Whatever or whoever "Koldun" might be code for, nobody seemed to know. And once Korolev had found out what he was doing, he hit the roof; told him the "Koldun" trail was a wild-goose chase. With heavy irony, he asked what was next in this absurd quest. Would Maxim perhaps go on to theorize that this "Koldun" was none other than Dima Koldun, the Belarusian pop singer, who would turn out to be some kind of criminal mastermind? "Finish your report," Korolev had said. "Present it to me. And we'll see where we go from there." The scene in his office this morning had been the result.

Maxim chewed on his lip. Now the case had been taken from him, the gorillas in Organized Crime would either royally stuff it up – the most likely scenario – or take the glory for cracking it, if it could be cracked. He wasn't going to let that happen. He had one tiny lead, and he was going to follow it, no matter what Korolev or anyone else said. He was his own man for two weeks of forced holiday. He was going to use it to the full.

There was one person he hadn't spoken to yet. Makarov's son and heir, Alexey Ivanovich. His secretive father had probably not told him anything about Koldun, but he'd lived with the man. Without knowing it, he might have heard something. Observed something. Something that might not mean much to him, but that might help Maxim.

He knew the young man was back in Russia, living in Uglich. He could easily have found out Alexey's number and spoken to him on the phone, but Maxim much preferred to speak to people face to face, you got a lot more from them that way. And his old car wasn't brilliant, so it might take him most of the day to travel the 200 kilometers or so to Uglich, but he thought the car would make it.

Once the idea had taken root, he knew it was the right one. Unfolding a map of the region, he began to plot his journey.

Chapter 8

"Russia's one of the most cynical countries in the world," Alexey was saying over cakes and coffee. He and Helen had been talking for hours. "I think that's what makes real reform difficult. We're always looking for the hidden agenda, the secret motive, the truth behind the honeyed words. And our concept of good and evil – well it's not quite like that in the West."

"How so?"

"It's not that we think those things don't exist – more like we feel they can shade into each other, and that there can be no permanent victory over evil. Not in the human world at least. All that black and white stuff, are you with us or against us – people just don't go for that. Maybe it's because that black and white stuff was all they heard in Communist times, maybe it goes further back because our religion places a different emphasis on those things to the Western churches." He sighed. "And yet, you know, despite the cynicism, we're such idealists! There's no one quite like Russians for getting bowled over by grand ideas."

At high school, Helen had thought a lot about what one of her friends had called "the big things", but mostly she was too choked by the "bigness" to express out loud what she felt. So she wrote about it, reams of poetry, most of it pretty bad, but deeply felt, as she thrilled with the sadness, the grandeur, the strangeness of life and of people. Later, when she'd got into Simon's worldly circle, she'd learned to restrain those feelings, unless, of course, she was being ironic. But now, she was free to do as she liked. Think as she liked. And she tingled all over with excitement.

"Oh, but Alexey – doesn't it make it really hard, trying to make your own path among all that confusion? Trying to do the right thing ..."

"Yes, it is," he said. "But it also makes you look at things with more humility. And that's no bad thing."

"It sure isn't." She knew just what he meant. Humility wasn't something that was fashionable in the world she'd lived in. "Alexey – you said that Russians are cynical. And yet they also seem to believe in stuff like – like witchcraft, for instance. It doesn't make sense."

"Doesn't it?" he said. "Some things just are, that's all, even things you don't understand, that aren't clear. Being cynical doesn't mean you reject mystery. It means you stop trying to put labels on it, to tidy it away neatly." He looked at her. "You accept that some things are meant to be, even if you can't explain them. But we're not always ready. Like that first time I saw you, in the street. I wanted to speak to you – so much – but lost my nerve."

She smiled. "Okay, sure. Like I believe that. You, losing your nerve!"

He said, softly, "It's true. I was struck dumb at the sight of you. You are so beautiful, Helen."

Helen's heart was racing so fast she thought it must jump out of her chest. Her face felt so hot she was sure her cheeks were flaming. Her eyes met Alexey's.

But before either of them could say anything, the spell was broken by Slava. Excusing himself for interrupting, he handed a cell phone to Alexey, who turned to Helen. "I'm really sorry," he said, "but I'm going to have to take this. Back in a second." And he took the phone from Slava's hand and walked off.

Left alone with Slava, Helen felt uncomfortable. She said, lamely, "Would you like to sit down or something?"

His face stayed as impassive as ever, yet she had the impression she'd said the wrong thing. All he said, in heavily accented English, was, "Is okay, Miss."

Helen smiled nervously, wishing he would go away instead of standing by Alexey's chair as though he were a dog waiting for his master. She fiddled with her napkin, with her cell phone, with the cold dregs of her coffee cup. It seemed like ages but was only a few seconds before Alexey returned to the table. He handed the phone to Slava, and spoke to him briefly, in Russian. The bodyguard nodded and left. Alexey turned to Helen. "That was Kolya. Something's come up."

"Is anything wrong?"

"No, but I have to go home. Got to make some calls." He ran a hand through his blond hair, a little nervously. "Actually, I was hoping you might come back to my place too. If that's okay."

She looked at him, her heart pounding. "Sure. If – if you're sure I'd not be in the way."

He laughed. "You might just be a bit bored, that's all. Never in the way. And I know Kolya would really like to meet you too, after all I said about you."

"Oh." She imagined a brusque bear of a man, who would regard her, a stray foreigner who'd caught his rich godson's eye, with great suspicion. She'd felt uneasy under Slava's scrutiny. How much more uncomfortable would she feel being given the once-over by a hard-bitten businessman? But she couldn't back out now. Not that she wanted to.

As they emerged out of the restaurant onto the steps of the hotel, Alexey stopped and said, "Helen, I should have said this before – but I wasn't brave enough. But now – I have to."

"Yes?" she murmured, feeling a twist of fear.

"I don't want to make things hard for you – so if there is someone back in London who you – well, if there is anything that –" Uncharacteristically, he seemed to be having difficulty choosing his words, but Helen understood.

"There's no one. Not anymore. My ex-boyfriend – he – he didn't think fidelity was for him and so I ..." Her throat thickened. Her eyes filled with tears, and she couldn't finish what she had been about to say.

"Oh, Helen," was all he said, but he gently took her hand, and she clung to it, the comfort in his touch and in the tender expression in his eyes so deep that she could have wept for the sweet relief of it. But she did not cry. "I believe in fidelity," he said, very simply. "I believe in it with every breath in my body." Their eyes met, and she knew for certain that he was not only telling the absolute truth, but that he was making her a promise that he would never break.

Chapter 9

As they drew up outside the tall iron gates of the Makarov *dacha,* Slava got out. He pressed a buzzer, the gates opened, and the car swept down a long graveled driveway lined with trees toward a big house that had not been visible at all from the road.

At first sight, it looked rather like an overgrown version of one of the traditional local houses. Much bigger, of course, and with extra embellishments – there was lots of wooden lace around the windows, plus pillars, and a flight of painted stone steps leading up to the massive front door, which itself was decorated with pillars and extra lace. Three storys high, the house, whose neat walls were painted a creamy yellow, also boasted a large balcony on the top floor. Ivy grew thickly up one side of the house, there was a riot of flowers in the small garden in front of it, a small glasshouse to one side, with a path leading to what looked like more garden, and on the other a large garage. As the car pulled up outside the house, a dark-haired young man emerged from behind the garage, holding a pair of leashed Dobermans. It was the dark-haired man she'd glimpsed that first day with Alexey and Yuri in the car. In a small voice, Helen said, "You've got some big dogs."

"They're not mine. They belong to Oleg over there. He's a mate of Slava's." The bodyguard had not got back into the car but had walked in and was now standing chatting with the other man. Alexey saw her expression. "Don't worry. The dogs are tied up most of the time. Bloody nuisance if you ask me. Eat their heads off and scare people for no good reason. Wait a moment." He touched her gently on the shoulder, and got out of the car. She watched him walk over to where Slava and Oleg were standing, saw them glance at the car, at her, at Yuri still sitting silently in the driver's seat. Moments later, the other two men walked off with the dogs, and Alexey returned. He opened the door for her, led her up the steps to the front door, and ushered her inside.

"So, then, what do you think of our *dacha*?" he said, smiling at her.

Some "country cottage" this was! Not at all like Irina's modest wooden house. She looked around her, at the large hall, with its sweeping but plain white iron staircase going up to the next floor, the two large abstract paintings on the walls, and the severe white tile floor. She searched for the right words to describe it, but could only come up with, "It's really different inside to what you'd expect from the outside."

"Isn't it just? Outside's a bit full on, but it's really local. As if your standard *izba* has taken a deep breath and swelled up like a self-important bullfrog."

Helen laughed. "That's so true."

"But inside, it's like every place Dad ever lived in. He was into modern. Gleaming surfaces. Clean lines. He hated old, cozy and traditional. He only bought this house because it was going cheap. The original builder went bankrupt, you see. It was just a shell – Dad had all the interiors done up. He just never got round to doing anything about the outside."

At that moment, a man came down the hall toward them, hands extended, smiling. In his mid to late forties, he was of medium height and slim build, with light brown hair receding a little at the sides, and deep-set dark eyes in a creased face. Dressed plainly in a white shirt, gray jumper and trousers of the same color, he could not have been called handsome, but he had a pleasant, kind face.

Alexey said, "Helen, may I present Nikolai Pavlovich Volkovsky, my godfather, the manager of Trinity. Kolya, I'd like you to meet Helen Clement."

If in appearance Alexey's godfather had been quite unlike the grim picture in Helen's imagination, his manner was even more so. "I am most pleased to meet you, Miss Clement," he said, cheerfully, as they shook hands. His English was excellent, the Russian accent discernible but not all that strong.

"And I you," she responded, a little shyly. "Please call me Helen, Mr. Volkovsky."

"A very pretty name indeed. Yelena in our language. But if I am to call you this, then let there be none of this Mr. Volkovsky either. Please call me Nikolai."

"Thank you. I will."

"I look forward very much to speaking further with you, Helen, but just now Lyosha and I have to make a conference call to Moscow. Would you mind waiting in the living-room till we finish? We will have Katya bring you coffee, or something stronger if you desire?"

"Oh no. Coffee will be fine."

"Very well, then, I will arrange for it and set up the call. See you in the study in a few minutes, Lyosha." He turned on his heel and disappeared down the corridor.

As they entered the living-room, Helen said, "Alexey, if you –"

She never finished her sentence, for he'd kicked the door shut behind them and taken her in his arms. And just like that, they were kissing, again and again, desperately, as if they couldn't stop, his fingers entwined in her hair, her arms around his neck. The delicious warm masculine scent of him made her dizzy, her limbs were melting, senses reeling – the taste of him on her lips mingled salt and heat, the sea-change eyes had the pull of a tide in which she would happily have drowned. As they emerged breathless from the kiss, he said her name, softly, and she felt a sharp stab of mixed delight and foreboding and cried, "Oh, Alexey, oh Alexey – can we risk this ... oh, we're from such different worlds, you and I."

"We have a saying in Russia," he responded, smiling down at her. "He who never takes risks never gets to taste champagne."

She laughed a little shakily. "Typical! I suppose you swig champagne in that troika of yours while you go hell for leather down the road scattering passers-by as you go!"

"You've got it in one," he said, exultantly. "It's all about joy and passion and commitment, about seizing every moment and living it to the full because you never know what's coming next." His eyes gleamed. "Do you see, Helen? Do you see?"

"I do," she whispered, "oh, I do." She held him tight as they kissed again and her heart swelled almost unbearably with desire and a huge golden heat as powerful as anger. It was what her mother would have called *la rage de vivre*, the passion for life. Even before Simon had cast his pall, before he'd made her retreat before life, the world had not beat with as furious a pulse as it did now. She gave herself up to it. She was not in control, but so what? The everyday had cracked wide open, revealing the molten core of life itself: joy, passion, commitment – and the unexpected!

She pushed him gently away and said, "You'd better get to that conference call of yours, or your godfather won't be happy with me," and he grinned and said, "And we can't have that, can we?" As he spoke there came a tentative knock on the door, and a young woman came in; a thin, short girl with brown hair whose tips were inexpertly dyed in what Helen privately thought of as the "vanilla-and-chocolate ice-cream look", layers of blonde and black. She wore an apron over jeans and a flowery top, and carried a tray on which reposed a miniature version of the tea-urn Russians called *samovar*, a couple of lovely tea-glasses, and a plate of exquisite little pink and white iced gingerbread biscuits.

"*Spasiba*. Thank you, Katya," said Alexey, and smiled at her. Helen felt a twist of ridiculous jealousy. "Katya's our chef," he went on in English. "She had the morning off though and I didn't think it was fair to expect her to cook lunch."

"Oh, right." She held out a hand to Katya. "Hello," she said. "Pleased to meet you."

Katya shook Helen's hand. "I am pleased to meet you," she echoed shyly, in hesitant English, and then left the room.

Alexey turned the tap of the samovar and poured out some tea into the glasses. He handed one to Helen, and drained the other one in one gulp.

"She seems pretty young to be a chef," said Helen.

"She is. But she's awesome." He gave her a wry glance. "Oleg's her boyfriend, by the way."

She colored a little. "Oh. Right."

He smiled. "Helen, are you going to be okay? I'll be quick as I can. And if you get bored, there's some magazines in that shelf over there – some of them are in English, a bit old, but …"

"Don't worry about me, I'll be fine," Helen said, and impulsively reached up to kiss him on the cheek.

He laughed. "Yes, better keep it cool right now or I won't know what the hell I'm saying to those officials, will I?" he said, teasingly, and, squeezing her hand, he was gone.

Left alone, Helen sat drinking her coffee, nibbling on the delicious little biscuits, and looking around her at the room she hadn't really noticed till now. It was all chilly muted colors: clinically white walls, two large pale gray leather sofas, a smoked glass coffee table with steel edges, a TV and entertainment unit hidden behind black glass, a simple gray shelf housing some black leather files with magazines stacked neatly in them, and a large gray-and-green abstract painting on one wall. All very modern and chic but impersonal, like a set-up in a magazine. No family photos or clutter or books. And only one incongruous touch, on a small table in a corner: an icon depicting three angels sitting around a table. Helen remembered seeing a similar one in Moscow, and remembered too her mother reading out a comment from her guidebook: *"In the Russian Orthodox religion, the Holy Trinity of Father, Son and Holy Spirit is very important. And it is always depicted as three angels, because of the great medieval artist Andrei Rublev's famous icon. One of Russia's most beloved religious images, it is reproduced again and again, and many homes have a copy of it."*

This was a very good copy, Helen thought, looking more closely. It wasn't simply a foil picture glued onto a wooden backing, as was the case in most of the reproductions she'd seen for sale in churches and souvenir shops. This one had been painted, and very delicately too. And it looked old. Antique, even. She wondered if Alexey's father had called his company after it, or if he'd bought it because he had a company of that name.

She went to the shelf and started looking through the magazines. There were a few old publications in English – *Time, The Economist*, and a thick glossy publication called *Company Life*, a magazine aimed at foreign companies looking to do business in Russia. She was flipping idly through *Company Life* when she happened on something that made her pause. It was an ad for Trinity, made to look like a typewritten page extracted from a private investigator's files.

In the colorful world of Russian business, Trinity is a quiet ghost. You won't see splashy stories about it in the press or on

TV. Its directors don't believe in throwing champagne parties or riding in stretch limousines with blonde bombshells or being seen at grand openings with the élite of Russia. And yet ask around. Listen. On the lips of everyone who matters will come one word, one whisper: Trinity.

With family backgrounds in the security services, the three young army mates who started the firm in the difficult early 1990s vowed that discretion, attention to detail and efficiency must be their watchwords at all times. But they also vowed to never forget the imaginative leap without which those other qualities are hollow forms. It is an understanding that has taken the firm from humble beginnings at a rickety kitchen table in a cramped communal apartment to large offices in Moscow and St Petersburg; agencies in Helsinki, Copenhagen, Vilnius and Riga; and an enviable network of international links. We can't sway you with details of Trinity's highly qualified staff and excellent contacts in business and government. We can't tell you about Trinity's impressive list of successes and we can't reel off the names of their most famous clients.. All we can tell you is this: there are private investigation companies. And then there's Trinity.

The only illustration was a blurry photograph of three men seen from the back. And under that, a phone number. And that was all.

Cheesy or what, Helen thought, smiling, just as the door opened and Nikolai Volkovsky came in. "Lyosha's just wrapping up one or two things with the lawyer. He asked me to come and keep you company," he said, moving to sit by her. "Ah, I see you've found the famous blurb." He glanced at the magazine on her lap. "Ivan Mikhailovich – Alexey's father – was furious about it at first. He said it trotted out every Western cliché about Russia, and that it would make Trinity a laughing-stock."

"Didn't he know it was going in?"

"No. It was Semyon Danilovich's idea. One of the other partners, Mr. Galkin. He didn't write it of course." He grinned. "A rather pretty young English lady at *Company Life* did that. Semyon Danilovich was partial to pretty young ladies. Curvy brunettes or foreign girls were his preference. She was both."

Helen smiled. "What happened? Did it work – the ad, I mean?"

"Seems like the brunette knew what she was doing when it came to Westerners and stereotypes. We got quite a bit of foreign business over it. And Ivan Mikhailovich stopped grumbling." He sighed. "It's ancient history now. We are on a new path, as I'm sure Lyosha has told you."

She gave him a swift glance. Was there some reproof for Alexey in his tone? But he seemed quite relaxed. "Yes, he did."

"It's not easy to change direction, Helen."

"I can imagine that. How long have you been working for Trinity, Mr. – er, Nikolai?"

"Oh, almost since it started," he said. "They were very hard years, the early '90s, and many people fell by the wayside. But Ivan Makarov was well ahead of the game, he wasn't the son of a KGB major for nothing. He understood instinctively about the value of information, and in not only finding people with the right skills, but developing their skills and their confidence. For instance, I started as a humble fact-checker and ended where you see me now. "

She gave him another quick glance. He was so much more open than she'd imagined. Much more willing to share than she'd feared. He must be taking his cues from Alexey, she thought. They were obviously very close.

"I think that's great," she said, hurriedly, seeing his questioning expression.

"Yes. It is. I don't know what Lyosha's told you, exactly, but though Ivan Mikhailovich and the others had their faults, they also had many good qualities. And one of them was respect for us, the staff. We were all, from manager down to the cleaners, treated well; not like buddies, that is not our way, but with respect. Some of us, who were to deal with foreign clients, were also paid to undergo extra training, like intensive language courses."

Which was why, she thought, he could speak English so well. "Alexey said he and his father weren't close."

"That's so. But he is more like his father than he might care to admit. Though don't tell him I said so," he added, cheerfully. "I used to think poor Misha – his late brother Mikhail, that is – did he tell you about him?"

"Only a little."

"Then I will let him tell you the whole story himself in his own time. But suffice it to say that because Misha looked more like his father than Alexey does, people tended to assume he was more like him in character too. Not so. Poor Misha was a troubled soul. Weak. Easily influenced. But Alexey's strong, Helen. And his determination – his conviction – is so much like his father's. But no, they were not close. It is a real shame."

He looked at her, earnestly, as if expecting a response. She wasn't sure what to say. She felt a little awkward about talking about Alexey's family when he wasn't there. But she also didn't want to offend his godfather.

"Yes," she said, "it must have been very difficult."

"Yes. Trouble was, Ivan closed himself off to everyone after poor Svetlana died. And that impinged on everything. I understand why he felt he had to leave Russia – but it was a pity, for us, for Trinity. We kept expanding, we even opened small offices in Helsinki and Copenhagen, he came often on visits, and Galkin and Barsukov were still around, but it just wasn't the same. Even when Ivan Mikhailovich was here, it wasn't like the old days. Our relationship had changed. Business was booming, never better, but it felt empty, somehow."

Was that the shine of tears in his eyes? Touched yet embarrassed by his obvious emotion, and wishing Alexey would come back, Helen murmured, "Oh. That's sad."

"Yes. But it was more than that. I had the uneasy feeling that there were secrets being kept from me and the other Trinity staff. But what could I do? I wasn't about to endanger my job on the ghost of an uneasy feeling. So I said nothing." He paused. "Sometimes I lie awake at night thinking – if I had been braver, if I had spoken out, would things have been different? But I will never know the answer to that question."

The expression in his eyes was both sad and fierce. On an impulse, Helen said, "Do you think Alexey's father and his partners were –"

"Murdered?" he finished her sentence. "One accident, yes, two even – maybe. But three? It stretches credulity, even if the police seem slow to agree. Yes, I'm sure they were murdered. I don't know *how*, but I have a fair suspicion as to *who*."

She stared at him. He said, "Let me rephrase that. I do not know the identity of the actual individuals. Just that I can guess the *milieu* they are likely to come from."

"Gangsters, you mean?"

He smiled. "They call themselves businessmen, these days. The days of guns blazing in Moscow streets and tattooed *vory* strutting around are long gone. Everything looks smooth and ordered now. The wolf is still there, but he wears a sheep's pelt." He paused. "Did Lyosha tell you about the offers he got for the company?"

She nodded.

"We have suspicion as to who might be behind them, but no proof. On my advice, rather than just refuse them out of hand, he stalled them. Told them he was still weighing up his options. It bought us time. But they'd know by now what he's decided."

Her breath fluttered in her throat. "Does that mean that … he could be in danger from them, if they're – if they're angry about it?"

"It's certainly possible."

She felt a cold hand grip her heart. "Has anything – have they done anything to …"

"There's been a couple of incidents. Nothing very serious. Yet."

Helen faltered, "What sort of incidents?"

"Some anonymous phone calls. And an attempted break-in at our Petersburg office. But they didn't get in." He looked at her. "As I said, it's minor, at the moment. Lyosha says there is nothing to worry about. He is brave, Helen. He will not back down. And I'm glad of that. Trinity must go on. But that doesn't stop me from being concerned about his safety."

"The police …"

"Will not do anything unless something happens," he said. "You know how it is. So we deal with things ourselves. Lyosha lives here because we can protect him more easily than in the city. Strangers are more easily spotted, you understand."

She shivered. "Yes. I do."

"But Lyosha's quite headstrong, and it can be the devil's own job keeping up with him." He smiled at her. "As I'm sure you'll find out."

She was saved from answering by the reappearance of Alexey, looking harassed. Flinging himself down in an armchair, he said, "Bloody bureaucrats! Tie you up in knots over the simplest thing, and so slow about everything."

"They are annoying, I grant you, but we're almost there." He smiled, his obvious affection for his godson lightening his creased face. "You're doing so well, Lyosha. But that patience of yours still needs a little work."

"True enough," said Alexey, laughing.

Chapter 10

Alexey drove Helen home a little later that afternoon. He stayed for a drink, and when he'd gone home, Therese said, in a resigned sort of voice, "Well, I suppose I won't see much of you for the rest of the holiday," and Helen laughed and said, "I'm sorry, Mam, do you mind?"

Therese shook her head. "It's great to see you looking so happy, even though it scares me a little too, for what do we really know about him?"

Helen kissed her mother and said, "Everything that matters and nothing that doesn't. You mustn't worry, Mam, you mustn't worry about me anymore because everything's going to be all right now." And just like that she found she was able to finally talk with her mother about what had happened that day back in London.

It wasn't that her mother didn't know the basic outline. She knew that punch-drunk from her ignominious departure from Changeling, Helen had come home to the apartment she shared with Simon and walked in on him in bed with Annie, who of all Simon's circle, was the closest thing to a friend Helen had. The shock of it was so great that at first she couldn't move. Then she stumbled away down the stairs, but before she reached the front door, Simon came after her. "Listen, Helen, it's just sex," he'd said, "she doesn't mean what you mean to me." When she'd whispered, "Was that the first time?" he'd shrugged, and she knew it wasn't. She said, "Do you love her?" And he'd said, impatiently, "Of course not, it's nothing, I tell you, it's no big deal. What the fuck's the matter with you, you turning all suburban on me or something?"

As he spoke, she felt as though her feet were slipping out from under her, as though the very earth itself had tilted and turned traitor. She looked at Simon and saw a stranger, she looked at herself and saw a stranger. She had no words or feelings or thoughts for what was happening to her. She had no idea how she pushed past Simon, got out of the house and onto the bus that brought her shaking and speechless to her mother's door.

Yes, her mother had known most of that. Not what Simon had said, though. And not how it had felt. Helen hadn't been able to express it. Not out loud. Until now.

Her mother clearly knew what an important moment this was. When Helen finished, she put an arm around her daughter and said, gently, "You know, when I went to collect your things that week, Simon followed me around the apartment telling me that you'd 'overreacted' because of losing your job but that you knew your relationship was on the rocks anyway. He acted all concerned and smarmy, said he hoped you would be all right but that it was better if he didn't see you again. I didn't believe a word of his excuses but I was so relieved that he'd no longer be in your life that I didn't question him at all. Which suited that slimy little creep just fine."

"You never liked him, did you Mam?" Helen said, affectionately.

"No. He was much too pleased with himself. It set my teeth on edge. And I hated the way he was always correcting you. Putting you down. Lecturing you, as if you weren't good enough, when you were worth twenty of him. And he was trying to turn you into someone you weren't. Cutting you off from your old friends, trying to drive a wedge between us too, forcing you to be one of his shallow set."

"It wasn't just his fault," said Helen. "I didn't have to do as he said. Thing is, I *wanted* to make myself into someone else because I was scared to be me. I was scared I'd never fit in if I didn't. And so you see when he – when he said those things to me, it was as though a veil had been ripped from reality, as though I had been stripped bare. I knew then I'd been wrong about just about everything. About the job, about him, about myself. But I had no idea who I was, any longer. I had got lost, and I didn't know how to find my way back."

"Oh, darling," said her mother, softly, and there was the shine of tears in her eyes. "I – it hurt so, to see you suffering. I've felt so damned helpless at times, so useless." She bit her lip. "And once or twice – I've even been afraid that – I'd lose you, like I'd lost your father."

Helen hugged her mother, tightly. Her mother had never admitted it out loud, and that was an important moment, too. "I know," she said, gently. "And you did understand, Mam. In the best way possible. You were there for me. And that's what helped me get over it. And now – it feels like it's *really* over." She paused. Took a deep breath. "You like Alexey, don't you?"

"Oh yes. Who could help liking him? He seems like such a genuine person. And so vital and intelligent, not to speak of drop-dead handsome. It's easy to see why you're attracted ..." She hesitated. "But ..."

"Please don't *but*, Mam. It's making me happy – *he's* making me happy."

"I can see that," said her mother softly. "And I'm glad." She paused. "And – I'm glad you could talk about it with me. I really am."

Helen smiled. "I know." They hugged. Then Helen said, cheerfully, "But I never asked you about your day. Did you get much work done?"

"Quite a bit. Then Sergey turned up about three – I'd asked him to drop in to discuss plans for tomorrow, we're going to Rostov you know – anyway he ended up staying a good hour or more, we had quite a chat."

"Did he tell you any more gossip?"

"Actually, no. We talked about his family, his sister, his niece – he's proud of her, she's studying at Moscow University. And we talked about books. Quite a lot about books. It was very interesting, actually."

Helen smiled. "Uh, uh."

"Don't be silly, darling. It was just a chat. By the way," her mother added, hastily, ignoring Helen's raised eyebrow, "Irina called. Said she'd be stuck in St Petersburg for a few more days. She was concerned we'd be put out. I assured her we were getting on just fine on our own. Told her you'd even gone out to lunch with the local celebrity."

"What did she say?" said Helen, successfully distracted.

"Nothing much. Just sighed and asked if you knew it was a small town, and gossip would be running wild by now."

Helen laughed. "Let them wag their tongues off if it makes them happy."

*

That night, she found it hard to sleep. She lay in bed tossing and turning, remembering every detail of the day. She was in such a whirl of feelings: astonished, afraid, content yet frantic with longing to see him again. She wished she was with him right now, in his arms, kissing him, over and over, or talking *dushi-dusha*, as he'd called it, soul to soul, laughing, just being together.

Every part of her was coming to life again, every dormant nerve and feeling sending out tendrils like green shoots in the spring. He is my spring made flesh, she thought, laughing at herself for not being in the least embarrassed anymore by something that only a few short weeks ago she would have labelled, by sheer force of learned habit, "extreme". How shallow, how stupid that felt now! She felt free for the first time in her life, free to choose the life she really wanted, and the rush of it buzzed wildly in her veins.

It was ages before she managed to doze off. And then she was woken from a jerky, disconnected dream with the sensation that something was wrong. Someone was in the room with her. So strong was the impression that her heart was pounding with fear when she opened her eyes onto bright moonlight and an empty room. The sensation must have been in her dream. But the shock of it had woken her properly. She looked at her phone. The time read 1.30 am. She got up, padded to the kitchen, got a glass of water, went back to her room and stood at the window, looking out into the silent lane and the silver birch shining with an otherworldly glow in the light of the moon. She gave a little shiver. The scene outside suddenly felt like a still moment in a movie, just before something bad happens. She glanced up into the branches of the tree, half-expecting to see the magpie perched there. But there was nothing.

It was then she saw the car, coming slowly down the road. It was one of those boxy old Russian cars, like Sergey's taxi. Only it wasn't his. This car wasn't blue, it was white.

It was probably someone who lived in the lane, returning home late from a party or shift work. But even as the reassuring thoughts flashed through her mind, she felt the hairs prickle at the back of her neck.

The car came quietly to a stop, right outside Irina's house. The door opened and a figure got out. It was a man wearing dark trousers and a bomber jacket. He was as burly as Slava and Oleg, but taller even than Alexey, a giant figure of a man with short dark hair. She only caught a brief glimpse of his face: tough, coarse features, with a bushy moustache under a crooked nose, though she couldn't tell the color of his eyes, or anything much else. She'd never seen him before, but he made her skin creep. Maybe it was because, despite his bulk, he moved with a light-footed grace that suddenly made her think of a forest predator. Not a wolf. A bear. She remembered what Volkovsky had said about the dark forces arrayed against Alexey. What if this man was part of them? What if he was here because he'd seen her with Alexey and …

Now he was locking the car door and heading toward the woods. Soon, he had plunged down the track and disappeared from sight. Helen's breath returned. She got a grip on herself. She'd been in a strange state after that dream, and had turned a perfectly ordinary incident into some kind of menacing scenario. She shrugged, went back to bed, and when she woke again, it was to a cloudy morning and the smell of toast wafting up the stairs. When she glanced out of the window, she saw the white car had gone.

Not long after breakfast, Alexey turned up, on foot this time, with the stolid Slava in tow, a few paces behind. Sergey had just arrived too and was having a cup of tea in the kitchen with her mother before they set off for Rostov. It was amusing to see Sergey's reaction to Alexey's arrival. It wasn't that he looked surprised, exactly. Clearly, Helen thought, just as Irina had said, the gossip grapevine was humming, and he, like everyone else in Uglich probably, knew that the Trinity heir and the young foreigner had hit it off. The feelings that flitted over Sergey's expressive face as Alexey extended a hand for him to shake were a conflicted mixture of social unease and natural curiosity. But when he caught sight of Slava, his face became expressionless, shut down. It was quite striking.

She said as much to Alexey, on the way to his house, the bodyguard still plodding behind. "He has that effect on a lot of people," Alexey said. "I guess that's the point."

"I can't say I feel comfortable around him either," she whispered.

He laughed and took her hand. "Don't worry, we'll give him the slip later on, okay? Like I did the other day when I went out on my bike. Can't do it while Kolya's around though or I'll get a lecture about security precautions."

"Alexey, he told me about those people who made offers to buy Trinity, and how they're likely to be angry that you."

Alexey shrugged. "That's their lookout."

"But Nikolai told me about what happened. The calls. The break-in."

He sighed. "He shouldn't have told you. It was nothing. Only an attempted break-in. And they didn't get anywhere."

"But do you have any idea who's behind it?"

"There's this guy in Petersburg called Boris Repin – Kolya suspects he's behind one of the takeover offers. This Repin's got quite a reputation."

"He's a gangster?"

"In the papers they call him a businessman. But there's no proof it's him. Could be anyone, really." He saw her expression and said, "Relax, Helen. The way I see it, whoever it is that's playing funny buggers is hardly going to try and kill me. What good would that do them? Trinity still wouldn't belong to them."

He took it so lightly, but she couldn't. The unease crept into her as she said, "But they could put pressure on you. Try to frighten you into ..."

"I'm not frightened," said Alexey, simply, and looking at him, she knew he was speaking the truth. "Besides, unless you count the stupid calls – and they were put through to Kolya, not me – no one's made a move against me, personally. To get

Kolya off my back, I've accepted Slava and Oleg and the dogs, at least temporarily. But I'm damned if I'm going to spend my life looking over my shoulder. Okay?"

His tone was almost fierce, and Helen winced. "Okay. Sorry."

He was instantly contrite. "I didn't mean to bark at you. It's just I'm used to hearing it from Kolya. Sometimes I think he forgets I'm not the little boy he used to bounce on his knee." He squeezed her hand. "Don't worry, Helen. I'm not such a pushover – did I tell you I used to do judo, back in Oz?"

"No," she said, smiling. "You didn't."

"Well, it so happens I'm a black belt, Miss Clement, so what do you think of that?" He looked at her with a teasing expression in his eyes.

"I think I'd better be extra careful around you, Mr. Makarov," she said, demurely, looking up at him under her eyelashes.

Their eyes met. He laughed, huskily. "If you keep looking at me like that," he said, quietly, "I can't answer for what I'll do."

She breathed, "Can't we lose Slava right now? Can't we run away somewhere totally private?"

"I'm working on it," he said, and his grip on her hand was so tight it almost hurt.

*

But when they arrived at the house, Nikolai Volkovsky was there to greet them, and in no mood to let them sneak away. "How very nice to see you again, Helen," he said, firmly ushering them in. "I hope you don't mind, but I'm going to have to claim Lyosha again for a little while." Turning to a crestfallen Alexey, he spoke to him briefly in Russian.

"Sorry, Helen," Alexey said. "A guy called Lebedev – who we hope might have some information for us – has turned up unexpectedly. I've really got to have a word with him. I'll try not to be long."

"I can wait," she said, with a little sidelong smile. Their eyes spoke to each other.

"Have you had breakfast, Helen?" Volkovsky said, discreetly. "Katya can bring you some if not."

She dragged her glance away from Alexey's. "Thank you, Nikolai," she said, formally. "I'm fine. I'll find something to do. Go for a walk in the garden or something. If you don't mind."

"Of course not," said Volkovsky. "Make yourself at home."

"See you very soon," said Alexey, flashing her a rueful smile, and the two men walked off, leaving Helen alone.

She felt restless so she headed out of the front door again, down a path to the back of the house and a big sweep of garden that was like a cross between a small park and an overgrown orchard, with fruit trees in blossom mixed in with birch, aspen, linden and other trees she didn't know, long grass growing in among them, and clumps of flowers dotted here and there. She found a tree to sit under, the air was bright and fresh, the sun had come out properly now, and she was dreaming of Alexey, when all at once the peaceful air was shattered by the furious barking of dogs and the Dobermans bounded into the garden. She scrambled to her feet and kept dead still, totally silent, pressed against the tree trunk, knowing instinctively she must not move, must not try to run.

The dogs circled her, not barking now but growling deeply in their throats, their gleaming eyes fixed on her. Quite what would have happened if Oleg hadn't appeared just then she did not know. He whistled to the dogs, and yelled something.

The dogs ran to him, and he clipped leashes to them and tied them up. But Helen still couldn't move. She felt sick, her palms were prickly, her knees shaking.

Oleg hurried to Helen, babbling away in Russian. Though she didn't understand the words, she knew from his stricken expression that he was frantically apologizing. Maybe he thinks he'll get the sack if Alexey finds out, she thought, so she forced herself to smile and say, "It's okay, I'm okay."

He gestured, miming that he'd escort her back to the house. She nodded and followed him, avoiding looking at the tied-up dogs. No harm done, she was cool about it now. She wouldn't say anything to anyone, she didn't want Oleg to get into trouble. She'd just make damn sure next time that the dogs were tied up.

Back inside, Oleg said something whose meaning she half-caught, something about Katya and coffee. She nodded, and seeing he still looked anxious, said, "It's okay," and put a finger to her lips. His expression cleared. He said, "*Spasiba, spasiba bolshoi,*" thank you, thank you very much, and then he insisted on taking her to the living-room and fussed around settling her on the sofa. Finally he left her in peace and she sat back and took a deep breath.

She'd coped. She'd managed. Even if Oleg hadn't come at that moment, it would have been okay, as long as she'd kept her nerve. Take another deep breath. You did it, girl.

The door opened, and Katya came in, carrying a tray with coffee and also a shot glass filled with pale golden liquid. She said, nervously, "Honey pepper vodka – good medicine, yes?"

Helen couldn't help laughing. Taking the glass, she downed it in one gulp. As the sweet, piquant warmth of it rushed down her throat, she said, "Thanks. It's very good."

Katya beamed. She poured out some coffee. "Oleg very sorry for you."

"I know," said Helen. She felt a little light-headed now, but pleasantly so. "Tell him not to worry. I won't tell anyone. Not even Alexey."

Katya nodded. She said, solemnly, "Thank you. It not happen again." And she flashed the other girl a grateful glance and went out.

Had she been right to promise not to tell Alexey? Well, it was done now, and she couldn't take it back, so she might as well stop thinking about it. Sipping on the hot, strong coffee, she got up and opened one of the drawers of the entertainment unit, expecting to see CDs or DVDs. Instead, there was a large photo album of the lavish old-fashioned kind, with a shiny black cover, the photos held in with corners on thick paper sheets, and translucent dividers between each sheet. She took it back to the sofa to have a look.

The first photo showed a severe-looking elderly woman, holding a smiling, curly-haired little girl in her lap. Underneath something was written in Cyrillic script, so Helen couldn't read it. But the date read 1970. Perhaps this was Alexey's mother and her grandmother.

She turned the page. This time, the photo was of a sturdy boy of about ten or eleven, standing almost at attention next to what must be his parents. The mother was looking directly at the camera, but the father's face was turned away, as if he'd seen something. But there was something about this man's profile that made her catch her breath. He looked so like Alexey. Or Alexey looked like him. Or was that just a trick of the way the light fell on his half-turned face? The child definitely wasn't Alexey, couldn't be Alexey, because of the date: 1973. But still, the boy's features were vaguely familiar, and in a moment she realized why as she turned the page and came on the next photo, of a young man with a defiant chin and a steady gaze, smoking a cigarette, and posing against the background of Red Square. She'd seen exactly that gaze in a newspaper photo. This was Ivan Makarov. Alexey's father. She flipped back to the childhood photo. Yes, no question about it. The boy and the young man were one and the same.

"So, you found the family photos," Alexey said behind her, and she jumped. "Sorry. Didn't mean to startle you." He sat next to her.

"I hope you don't mind that I ..."

"Of course not." He put an arm around her and kissed her very softly on the ear. "I'm glad you've been looking." She leaned into him, loving his closeness. "How have you been?" he added, smiling. "Not too bored, I hope?"

The image of the dogs flashed into her mind. She said, quickly, "Oh no. I'm fine. Your meeting – how did it go?"

"Waste of time, actually. This guy Lebedev claimed to have important information about that break-in. Turned out he knew nothing. Thought he'd get us to pay him for a bullshit story. Anyway, we sent him packing pretty damn quick once we realized. But then I got a call from the Moscow office. Nothing sinister – just a bureaucratic snarl-up. Took a bit of time to sort out. Sorry."

"That's okay."

Looking down at the photo, he changed the subject abruptly. "I suppose you've noticed I look like him. My grandfather, I mean. KGB Major Mikhail Petrovich Makarov."

She glanced at him. "Mmm," she said, cautiously, knowing by the tone in his voice that the resemblance didn't exactly please him.

"Wait a minute." Getting up, he opened one of the drawers and took out a small black case with metal clasps. Inside was a pistol, with engraved Cyrillic script on the grip. "This was my grandfather's service pistol – they engraved it for him when he retired. See, it says," and he translated, "*To M.P.M, a true patriot, for services to the USSR.*"

"What was he like, I mean, as a grandfather?"

"Can't say. Never met him. He died of a stroke before I was born."

"What about your dad, what did he feel about his father?"

"Oh Dad didn't talk about his relationship with his father. But I knew from what Mama said that he'd been scared of his dad, as a kid. But admired him, too, from a distance. But they were not what you'd call close." His mouth twisted wryly. "Seems like that too runs in the family. Anyway, he kept this pistol preciously enough."

"Oh," said Helen, doubtfully eyeing the weapon. Her French grandfather had a hunting rifle, which had in turn been owned by his father, and which he was very proud of. But the service pistol was different to a gun you took out to shoot ducks and rabbits for the pot; it smelled of a darker and more disturbing history.

Alexey saw her expression. He closed the pistol case and put it away. "Remember I told you Dad wasn't much of a one for following tradition?" he said. "It was quite a big thing for him to turn his back on the family profession and go into business instead of joining the service. I doubt his father was too happy about that, though by the time Dad was old enough to get a job, the regime was imploding and even the KGB wasn't much of a sure-bet career. But his background sure didn't hurt when he started Trinity. Gave him useful connections. And to the people who mattered, it made him trustworthy. The KGB was feared by many people of course, but to many others it was a badge of honor. And that worked in Dad's favor. Especially when his business partners Galkin and Barsukov also both came from KGB families, though they didn't meet till they were adults."

Helen said, "What did your mother think about all that?"

"She kept out of it. She had nothing to do with the business. Her world was family, it was what mattered to her – Dad, and my brother and me, and her parents. The other side of the family – well, she said Dad's father made her nervous, that he was the coldest man she'd ever met. Very polite, formal even. But with dead eyes. She never knew what he was thinking. And knowing what he did for a living didn't exactly help. But Dad's mother was a nice woman, even if pretty meek, and the scary father-in-law died only a year or so after she and Dad were married, so he wasn't around to cast a shadow on things for long. Her parents had been against her marrying Dad at first – not only because of the KGB connection, but because they were religious, and he was pretty much an atheist – but they came round to quite liking him." He paused. "Dad could be – could be charming. When he felt like it. And he truly loved my mother, and her parents saw that, so it made a bond between them."

"Are they still around – your other grandparents, I mean?"

"No. They died a while back. But they were nice, from what I remember of them. And they doted on Mama." He leafed through the album. "But here she is, aged about sixteen. My mother, I mean. Svetlana Gavrilovna Makarova, *née* Egorova."

The picture showed a small, sweet-faced teenaged girl with a cloud of teased fair hair, laughingly posing arm-in-arm with two other girls in front of the statue of the Bronze Horseman in St Petersburg. "She came from Peters originally," Alexey explained, "she only moved to Moscow in her university years." Another showed her in a pinafore dress at a summer barbecue party on a riverbank, among a crowd of other young people. "Dad's university mates," Alexey said. Another photo in winter, bundled up in fur hat and coat, posing in front of St Basil's, peeking between her fingers. "She's so pretty," said Helen. "And she looks like she'd be fun."

"Oh yes, she so was!" His eyes were very bright. "It sounds corny, but she was like a light – lit up everywhere she went, everyone she met, and you felt warm just being near her." He turned another page. "Here are my parents on their wedding day." A stiff portrait, professional this time, the bride in a drop-waisted dress and bouffant hairdo, and her groom, a beaming young man with a bad haircut, wearing a large-lapelled suit. Alexey said, lightly, "Check out the daggy fashions."

"*Daggy?*"

"I keep forgetting you don't speak Australian. Means old-fashioned. Uncool."

"Oh, right. Well, my mother says the '80s is the decade style fled howling from," she said, instinctively matching his light tone. "But she still looks beautiful anyway," she added, more seriously. "And they look happy."

"They do," he said, and smiled. He might look like the scary grandfather, Helen thought, but he had a sweet smile exactly like his mother's.

He flipped through more pages. "There's their Moscow apartment – one of those communal ones, totally cramped – oh, and a Black Sea holiday they took before we were born. Wait, here we are. Baby photos. That's Misha. Their first child. My older brother, Mikhail. He was a funny little thing, wasn't he?"

"He looks very serious," said Helen, looking at the unsmiling little boy with gray eyes under a straight fringe of dark hair.

"Scowling as usual," said Alexey. "That's why I thought that Dimitri icon looked like him. And that's me," he added, pointing out the photo opposite, of a laughing baby with a white-blond quiff sitting up in his pram.

"Oh, you were so *cute!*" said Helen.

"Not like now, eh," he said, and she colored and said, "You know I didn't mean that, you're just fishing shamelessly for compliments you don't even need, Alexey Makarov," and he said, laughing, "Shameless is right, you've got me in one, Helen Clement." And he kissed her, long and lingeringly.

"Check this out," he said, a little later, taking up the album again. "Here's Misha and me in our hideous boarding-school uniforms, in Australia. Not so cute there, are we?"

"You sure don't look happy."

"We weren't. We both hated it, but I put up with it." His face darkened. "Mish couldn't. Wouldn't. He was in revolt against everything. Dad, well, he'd never been close to us – but he got totally remote after Mama died. It really got to Misha. He wanted Dad to notice him and he only did that when my brother played up, and then he'd roar at him. Meanwhile I just tried to keep out of the way."

She said, gently, "It sounds very difficult."

"Yeah. It was. The worst of it was that – Misha and me – we were brothers, but we didn't understand each other, even though we were only just over a year apart in age. Maybe that was the trouble. He didn't cope well when I was born, Mama told me once, he was jealous and they had to watch he didn't try and poke my eyes out! And then, as we grew up, we just were interested in such different things, he thought I was soft, and I was freaked out by that temper of his, which only got worse. He was just so – so angry about everything."

"I used to wish I had a brother or sister," said Helen. "I thought it would be so good to have someone to share things with. And who'd look out for you."

He said, very sadly, "Well, it wasn't like that, for us. We were like a family out of Dostoyevsky, constantly at odds with each other, and constantly missing the point about each other." He paused. "Anyway, after school Mish started a law degree, but dropped out before the year was out. So Dad got him a job with a mate of his called Anatoly Tretyakov. He was an expatriate Russian like us, and he had a boat business in Surfer's Paradise. Anyway it might've worked out if Mish hadn't got matey with Tretyakov's son Dima, Dimmer I used to call him, bloody idiot he was, though his dad thought the sun shone out of his backside. So did poor Mish, he never was a good judge of character. To cut a long story short this creep got my brother into boosting cars, Anatoly found out but Dimmer made out it was Misha who was the bad influence so he was sacked. He had a massive fight with Dad, walked out and never came back. Wouldn't answer emails, ditched his old cell phone number and deleted his Facebook account. And that was it, for years. Until – until the day when my father got a call from the Mexican police. Misha had been killed in a car accident near Hermosillo, in the north. They were pretty cagey about it and it was only when we went over there that we realized why. The accident was hardly an accident. His car – it had been blown up, with him in it."

"Oh my God!" She was white to the lips.

"They told us Mish had been in the States, working in some crap job, when Dimmer turned up and persuaded my brother he had a good thing going in Mexico. Small-scale dealing in marijuana," he said, "not big-time, but it got them on the wrong side of some very dangerous people who have that trade all sewn up. So then Dimmer dreamed up some bird-brained scheme to sort it out, and sent my brother to a meeting." He clenched his fists. "The only reason we knew was because Dima wrote to the police, confessing what had happened. He said he was sorry. Sorry! As if that made a difference. You know, there was nothing left of Misha for us to bury but a handful of ash, and the few things he'd left behind in the flophouse he lived in. And that cowardly bastard Dima disappeared. And no, I'm sure he didn't get whacked," he went on, "because he always managed to get out of things. Right now he's probably conning some other loyal sucker into doing his dirty work for him." His voice carried such a freight of bitterness that Helen felt the weight of it settle heavy on her own heart. There was nothing to say. And he didn't want her to. He just wanted her to listen, to the very end. She knew that as clearly as if he'd told her. She took his hand and held it, tight, as he went on speaking.

"Dad said he never wanted to hear Misha's name spoken again, that as far as he was concerned his eldest son had never existed. The weird thing was," he continued on, bleakly, "that he said that, and I hated him for it, but do you know what? When he died and I saw his will – Helen, he *hadn't changed it*. He'd left it just as it was before poor Misha's death. Everything was still left to me *and* him – just as if – as if in a part of himself my father couldn't bear what had happened. Couldn't bear the loss of his son. That's when I understood that – well, that I would *never* understand my father." He paused, and went on, quietly, "So, there you have it. That's us. Mad, bad, and dangerous to know. You still want to be around me?"

"Of course I do!" she said, hugging him fiercely, tears in her eyes.

He cried, "Oh Helen – the thing that wakes me up at night sometimes is – I just wish I had … Mishka was hurting real bad, and I didn't understand. I had my music, my books, my dreams. He had so little. He was my brother. I should have helped him. I should have tried harder."

"You can't help a person if they won't let you in," she said. "They have to want it. If they won't let you in – then there's nothing you can do." And haltingly at first, then with her voice growing surer, she began to tell him about her father. About all of it. Not only the difficult visits, her father's silences, her growing distance from him, but how it had all ended, too. How, six years before, Sam Byrd had come back from a mission in Afghanistan, resigned from the service, and vanished. Eventually, they found out what had happened. Narrowly escaping a roadside ambush that had killed several of the Afghan soldiers he'd been training, he'd returned home and been diagnosed with severe post-traumatic stress.

He'd been offered help but refused it. Instead he'd taken off, holing up in an isolated cabin deep in the woods of Montana, shunning all contact with the outside world. No phone, no Internet, not even a postbox. Helen had sent a letter anyway, care of the little post office nearby. He'd written a curt note back, saying he thanked her for her concern, but that he was trying to deal with things in his own way. He'd added a PS: *You are better off without me.* And that was it. There'd been not another word or call from him in the years since, though she knew he was still living in his remote cabin.

Alexey listened in silence, and when she finished, he hugged her and said, "Oh, Helen." That was all he said; but the expression in his eyes showed her that he understood.

Chapter 11

Maxim had arrived in Uglich the day before, much later than he'd hoped. It had been a particularly slow and frustrating trip, cursed by more than the usual number of delays. He was held up first by the usual traffic snarls in Moscow and then, on the open road, he endured ages in the tailback of a lumbering old truck which his almost equally ancient vehicle was too gutless to overtake, and achieved the hat-trick of a flat tire as well. When at last he drove into the town, it was dark, he was furious, ravenous and dog-tired, and not inclined to be civil to the nervous young hotel receptionist who told him the kitchen had already closed and the cook gone home for the day.

A pile of hastily cut ham sandwiches and a couple of glasses of beer later, he was feeling more benign, and not a little ashamed of himself. He went down again to excuse himself to the girl, but was told by the impassive night watchman that she had gone off duty but would be back in the morning. Cursing his bad temper, Maxim went back upstairs and, after a shower, fell into bed and into a heavy sleep from which he woke a mere couple of hours later, jumpy and tense.

He tried to go back to sleep but couldn't, so instead he got up and went for a drive. It was very late and the town was utterly quiet as he drove aimlessly around, ending up at last in a quiet little street which backed onto some woods. The look of it brought back poignant memories of staying as a child at his grandmother's in just such a little provincial town as this, and, sharply, an image of a night-time walk he'd gone on, once, when everyone was asleep. It had felt brilliant, like the whole world belonged to him. So on impulse, he parked the car, and set off into the woods. He didn't walk long or go far, but it had done the trick and cleared his head, so that by the time he got back into his car and drove back to the hotel, he was feeling much calmer. This time, his sleep was a good deal better and he woke late, refreshed, and determined to make amends to that poor girl in reception.

It was already ten o'clock, so he did not even try to get any breakfast at the hotel. On his way out to find some in town, he called in at the reception desk, where he awkwardly apologized to the girl, who stammered that it was all quite all right. Maxim hadn't told her that he was a policeman, but it was clear from her manner that she'd guessed. He asked her gently for a map of the town, and when she hastily handed him one, he asked if she happened to know on which street the Makarov house was. He knew already, but wanted to see her reaction to the mention of Makarov.

Her face lit up at once with curiosity. She pointed out the street on the map. He said, "Have you been to the house—" He looked for a non-existent nametag, "what is your name?"

The girl's eyes widened. "Norova. Anastasia Kirillovna Norova. Oh no, I've never been there."

Well, Anastasia Kirillovna, perhaps you've met the young man ..." He pretended to hesitate. "What's his name –"

"Alexey Ivanovich Makarov," said the girl, promptly. "No. I haven't. Never spoken to him, that is. But I've seen him about. And my friend – he works at one of the other hotels

– he saw him yesterday, in the hotel restaurant, having lunch with a girl. Not a local person," she added. "A foreigner."

"I see. What's your friend's name, and the hotel's?" Not that it was important, but she looked as if she thought it was. She told him, and he made a show of writing it down. Then he said, "What do people say about him, hereabouts?"

She looked at him, suddenly cautious again. "I – I don't know."

"People must have an opinion," he said. "It's the biggest story to hit your town in years."

She hesitated. "Well, I've heard that – that he does not seem much grieved by his father's death."

"I see. Tell me, were people surprised when he moved here?"

"Why yes, especially as he'd never come before. Not when his father was alive, I mean."

"Why do you think he came here?"

"Me? I – I don't know."

He sighed. "Very well. Have you heard what *other* people think about it?"

"Some say he is hiding."

"From who?"

She shrugged, but didn't answer.

He said, quietly, "Gangsters, you mean?"

She looked at him. "Perhaps. Or perhaps – something else."

"What?" And then, suddenly, he understood the expression in her eyes. "You mean the curse." He sighed.

The girl was blushing but determined. "I read it in one of the Moscow papers – an *ekstrasens* – said it must be a curse made by a powerful sorcerer. She said the police would never be able to solve it on their own."

"Oh, that one," said Maxim, knowing the psychic the girl was referring to. "She came to see us. But it was no good.

She knew nothing." He'd forgotten about that, it had been after the Barsukov death, and before Makarov's. The psychic had come to see him and had gone on about sinister forces and bad karma; she'd placed her hands on the photographs of the Trinity founders and claimed that the sinister forces were particularly concentrated around Ivan Makarov. It was at a time when Maxim was leaning toward the theory that Makarov had engineered his partners' deaths, so he asked her what she meant. But when she told him that there was a sorcerer at work, he lost his temper, accusing her of wasting his time, and threw her out. She'd sold her story to a trashy newspaper, which the receptionist must have read. Now he looked at the expectant face of the young girl, and said, "I'm afraid she was just a charlatan, thought she could make some easy money. That's all."

Her face fell. "Oh. But …" She broke off.

"But what?" said Maxim, sharply.

"It doesn't matter."

"Let me be the judge of that," he said, sternly.

"There's an old lady my mother knows – she's a wise woman, sees things – and she said she had seen it in a dream."

Maxim suddenly felt like *Alice in the Land of Miracles*, a book he'd read in his youth. "Seen what?"

She looked at him, wide-eyed. "That it was true. About the sorcerer."

Maxim wasn't surprised to hear this talk of sorcerers. He knew that before the 1917 Bolshevik Revolution, every village had its resident witch or wizard. Under the Soviets, such traditional practices were banned and persecuted, like religion. But the Soviets were still fascinated by things like telepathy and remote sensing, investigating them as mind-control tools. Maxim remembered going to a lecture at school on paranormal phenomena and how they might be used to the advantage of the State. And now the Soviets had gone, traditional magic had come surging back, alongside continued scientific exploration of the paranormal.

Like most Russians, Maxim didn't dismiss the reality of the supernatural and the occult. He didn't think it was irrational to believe in such things. Life itself was irrational, after all. But experience had taught him that all too often people claiming to have supernatural powers were just unscrupulous crooks looking for easy marks, and he usually reacted poorly to such claims.

But he didn't want to take out his feelings on poor Norova again. Instead he said, "I see. Thank you for being so helpful, Anastasia Kirillovna."

For the first time, she gave him a smile, a faint, timid little smile, but a smile nevertheless. "I am glad to be of help," she said, simply. "And if perhaps you'd like to speak to the lady in question – her name is Feshina, Olga Sergeyevna Feshina, she lives in –"

"Thank you," said Maxim, hastily. "I will see about that later. In the meantime, I am going out. Please be so kind as to inform the kitchen that I will be requiring both lunch and dinner today."

"Oh yes, of course, sir," she said, with a bright, darting look at him, and he knew that while he might have wasted time listening to excitable guff about sorcery, at least he had repaired last night's mistake. And that could well stand him in good stead in a small provincial backwater like this, where gossip ran like wildfire, and an unfortunate reputation as a contemptuous city cop might well close doors and lips that might otherwise have opened.

*

He was sitting over a very good brew of thick dark tea and fresh rolls and cheese, leafing through the crashingly boring local newspaper (which did not have a single mention of the Makarov mystery) when it suddenly struck him – *Koldun*, of course, meant "sorcerer". He hadn't thought twice about the name, before, just accepting it to be a code-name but after the conversation with young Norova this morning, and remembering that *ekstrasens* and her prattle about sorcerers, the name seemed more meaningful. But could it be more than mere coincidence? Could it be there was a connection between a file named "sorcerer" and an *actual* sorcerer? Could the Trinity partners have been employing a sorcerer in secret?

The thought was stunning, but also made a strange kind of sense, and a prickle of excitement ran up his spine – after all, Trinity had used just about every other covert means at their disposal: surveillance and computer hacks, bugs and black-mail. Why *not* magic?

Maxim had once arrested a man who had made a pretty good living practicing a kind of hypnosis which had been described by his victims as "real sorcery". Using a honeyed voice, a stream of gibberish and a penetrating stare, he had spellbound them into handing over their wallets. Sometimes, under the same spell, a victim would take him back to their apartment and hand over all their remaining valuables. It was a clever trick; for he couldn't be accused of either mugging or burglary. He had only been small-time, and he had been caught when one victim, less frightened and ashamed than the others, had gone to the police. But it had worked well, in its limited way.

What if the Trinity partners had found someone with much less limited skills? Someone *really* gifted in the black arts of sorcerous persuasion and mind-control, perhaps even a person who combined traditional magic with the more scientific paranormal, and who might give them the ultimate advantage in their information-gathering. He'd never met anyone like that himself, but he remembered hearing from an veteran cop about a woman he'd once questioned in the backblocks of Voronezh over a moonshine-distilling racket. She had a reputation locally not just for racketeering but for foretelling deaths. The old cop had told Maxim how he'd never forgotten the look in her eyes when she'd turned to his colleague and hissed, "September twenty-fourth."

"And on that very date," the old cop told Maxim, "my poor friend was felled by a massive stroke. He was only forty-two. Coincidence, you might say; but some things, you just can't explain. She was a real old villain, that one. But she had something. Something real."

And Maxim remembered, too, that lecture on the paranormal at school, and how it mentioned that people with psychic gifts had been employed by intelligence services to track down American spies, amongst other things. Those cases were real enough, even if they might have been overblown for propaganda purposes. So – what if the Trinity men had found someone like that? Someone whose identity had been kept top-secret, which is why he'd found not a trace of them – apart from that one cryptic reference in Barsukov's email.

In a society as superstitious as ours, he thought, even a person with fake psychic powers can make a tidy living. But if a person had *real* powers, then that person could be very use-ful to a company such as Trinity. And dangerous, too. Maybe very dangerous. But useful. Worth trying out, anyway. He – and the word *Koldun* indicated a he, not a she – was so important his identity was not shared with anyone other than the inner circle – or rather, the triangle – of the three founders.

And if that was the case, then the leak referred to in Barsukov's email might well have been fatal. To Barsukov and Makarov. More than ever now, Maxim was convinced that the answer lay in the files Makarov had destroyed the night before his death. They might not exist anymore, but the only person who might know – who had been described as someone who was not "much grieved for his father" – was still very much alive, and it was time to visit him.

*

The gates of the Makarov house were closed and everything looked quiet when Maxim pressed the buzzer. A sharp voice said, "This is private property. No salesmen or canvassers."

"I am neither," said Maxim, calmly. "My name is Senior Lieutenant Maxim Antonovich Serebrov, of the Criminal Investigation Department, Moscow. And I am here to speak to Alexey Ivanovich Makarov."

There was a small silence. "He's not expecting you."

"No, that's right. But I am here to speak to him nonetheless. Tell him it's urgent."

Shortly, a burly young man appeared, shoulders big in a sharp suit, fair hair harvested to a wheat-field stubble. He asked for and was shown Maxim's police card, opened the gates for him, and once Maxim had parked the car, the man ushered him into the house, saying, "Wait here," leaving Maxim standing in the hall. Like a servant, he thought, with an inward smile. He knew the type well. They served the true masters of the universe, the rich, so why should they be impressed by a mere policeman?

He could hear voices coming from down the hall. Whoever it was wasn't speaking Russian, but English. A language he knew, having studied it at university. He moved closer to try and catch what was being said, but before he could do so, the tough returned. He wasn't alone. With him was a familiar figure. Trinity's manager Nikolai Volkovsky.

"Senior Lieutenant Serebrov! What a surprise! Please excuse us for keeping you waiting."

His wasn't the voice Maxim had heard. And he decided to keep his knowledge of English quiet for the time being. Aloud, he said, smoothly, "Something's come up. Something I need to check with Alexey Ivanovich, regarding his father."

"I see," said Volkovsky. "It must be important, to bring you all the way from Moscow."

"Yes," said Maxim, ignoring the implied question, and following Volkovsky as he led the way down the hall and opened the door to the living-room.

The first thing Maxim noticed was the almost dead quality of the room, with its chilly paleness and impersonal surfaces. It made the bright spots of color – the icon of the Trinity, and the two young people sitting on the sofa – all the more striking. Not that they wouldn't have been striking in any circumstance – the slim young woman with her rich dark red hair and big brown eyes, wearing a little yellow dress that could only have suited someone of her coloring and shape; and the young man, tall and broad-shouldered in an open-necked blue shirt and black jeans, and the strong, hard, handsome face of a legendary hero, a *bogatyr*, under a thatch of thick blond hair.

"Senior Lieutenant." The young man advanced toward Maxim, extending a hand. "I'm Alexey Makarov. And this is my friend Yelena – Helen Clement."

This must be the foreign girlfriend Anastasia Kirillovna had mentioned, Maxim thought. He was a little surprised to see the disconcerted expression on her face, surely more disconcerted than the situation merited. But he showed no trace of curiosity as she stammered some kind of broken-Russian answer to his formal greeting.

The young man hadn't noticed his girlfriend's reaction. He said, in Russian, "You have come a long way, Senior Lieutenant. So whatever you have to say must be important. Won't you sit down?"

"Thank you," said Maxim, doing just that. There was a photograph in the Ivan Makarov file, a copy of an ID photo of the KGB major, his father. It was uncanny how much this young man looked like him – how those striking looks had jumped a generation to land on the grandson Mikhail Petrovich Makarov had never met. In the grandfather's case, good looks had gone with a merciless heart, an unswerving devotion to the Party, and an intuitive intelligence so sharp it was feared even by his colleagues. How many lives he'd destroyed Maxim didn't know, but his formidable reputation remained decades after his death. Who knew, Maxim thought, perhaps the major had handed more than looks down to his grandson. He'd certainly given a ruthless legacy to his own son, even if Ivan Makarov hadn't followed the same path.

Alexey said, "Is there new information perhaps, Senior Lieutenant?"

"It could be," said Maxim. He glanced at Volkovsky, who said, smoothly, "Of course you'd like to speak to my godson in private, Senior Lieutenant." And motioning to the girl, he left the room with her.

Turning back to Alexey, Maxim said, "I've come to ask you personally if you have any idea what was in those files your father destroyed before his death."

Alexey shook his head. "You must know I don't. I told the inquest so."

Maxim cut in. "Perhaps it just slipped your mind. Or perhaps you might have remembered since then."

Alexey stared. "No!"

Maxim's voice was hard as he said, "Please think carefully before you answer my next question. What is Koldun?"

Alexey said, stiffly, "Is this some kind of joke?"

"Not at all. Did your father ever speak to you about a project, a person, or a file called Koldun?"

"My father never spoke to me about his business," said Alexey, tightly.

"Are you quite sure?"

"Of course I'm sure."

"Did you dislike your father?"

"No. Yes. What business is it of yours?"

"Very much my business. I am investigating your father's death. I discovered a passing reference to a certain Koldun – and I learned that your father destroyed files just before he died. I wonder if perhaps, living in the same house, you might know what –"

"I don't," cut in Alexey, sharply. "As you must know, I was nowhere near home that week. Not that any trace of the shredded files was found. You must know that."

"You seem very informed on everything in the case, Alexey Ivanovich."

"For God's sake!" exploded Alexey. "Of course I am! I might have disliked my father – even hated him, on occasion – but he was still my *father!* I *want* to know what happened to him! And now you accuse me of, of having a hand in his death. It makes me feel sick." His color was high, his eyes flashing.

Maxim said, with a faint smile, "I am not accusing you of anything. I simply want to get to the truth."

"So do I," said Alexey, softly. "So do I."

"Then search your memory. If you have not heard of Koldun itself – perhaps you might have heard of something connected, whose significance you did not realize. Had your father recently shown any sign of interest in the occult? Had he for instance mentioned visits to psychics? Started consulting astrological columns in the newspaper, even? Did you come across anything that might indicate he was taking an interest in such things?" He was fishing in the dark, he knew that, but it had a completely unexpected result.

Alexey stared at him. Then he said, slowly, "I thought maybe he'd been trying to – to contact my dead mother or brother."

It was Maxim's turn to stare. "*What?*"

"The business card I found, when I was sorting through his books – none of which were occult, incidentally. Dad's reading taste was for business biographies and Russian history. I found the card in a book about the siege of Leningrad." He paused. "It was the business card of a psychic, specializing in contacting the dead, according to the card."

"Why didn't you say anything to the police at the time?"

"In God's name, why would I think it could have any possible connection? I thought – well actually, it touched me, rather."

"Didn't you find it surprising?"

"Absolutely. Dad had never shown much interest in psychic things. That is, we never discussed it. Not ever."

"And what about you, Alexey Ivanovich? What do you think of such things?"

"Me?" Something flickered in the young man's eyes. "I suppose I'm with Hamlet."

Maxim quoted, softly, "*There are more things in heaven and earth than are dreamt of in your philosophy.*"

The young man showed no sign of surprise. *Hamlet* is popular in Russia, like many of Shakespeare's plays, which have been brilliantly translated. He said, "Exactly."

"And what did you do with the card?"

"I am afraid I – I threw it away. It just seemed too personal. There had been so much stripped bare, at the inquest."

"I understand," said Maxim, very gently. He added, "What was the name of the psychic?"

Alexey frowned, thinking. Then he shook his head. "I'm sorry. I don't remember. A Russian name. But not Koldun, I'm certain of that. I'd have remembered someone who called himself the Sorcerer!"

"It was a man, then?"

"I'm not sure. There was no first name spelled out, only initials. V. K? L. B? I don't remember, sorry."

Maxim sighed. "Perhaps you remember something about the address, then?"

"There wasn't an address. Just a phone number. And that tag line, about contacting the dead."

"Was the phone number from Moscow? Petersburg? Somewhere else?"

"I don't remember that either. It was a flimsy thing. Badly printed, the type was smudged, it was like it had been run up on one of those old Roneo machines."

"I see. There was nothing else you remember? No picture, or logo?"

"No. Not that I remember. I'm sorry. I wish I could remember more," said Alexey. "Do you really think it might be important?" There was a wistfulness in his voice that Maxim, disappointed though he was at a promising lead going nowhere, found touching. He said, honestly, "I can't be sure. I don't know yet."

"But what do you think it means?"

And so Maxim told him.

Chapter 12

Helen told Volkovsky what she'd seen last night, in the lane. "Are you absolutely sure he's a policeman?" she finished. "He looks more like a thug."

Volkovsky smiled. "I'm sure that doesn't hurt, in his line of work. But I can assure you, Helen, that he truly is who he says he is. He's interviewed me. He's been on the Trinity case since the beginning."

"But why is he here now?"

Volkovsky looked at her. "I fancy he may suspect Alexey of having something to do with his father's death."

Helen gripped the arm of the sofa. "But that's absurd!"

"Of course. And the Australian police found nothing to link Lyosha in any way with his father's death. But that is precisely what worries me now."

Helen swallowed. "You don't mean that you think that man has uncovered something incriminating? Surely – surely you can't believe that."

"Helen, I know poor Lyosha is innocent as a lamb. But it is my duty to try and protect him, and to do so I must try and think like that man out there. He's no fool, that is certain. But I think he could be ruthless. Even – unscrupulous."

Helen breathed, "Do you mean he – he could be trying to frame Alexey to get … a result on the case?"

Volkovsky smiled ironically. "Perhaps. But I rather doubt it's for that reason. Getting a result might be good for a man's morale but it does little for more important considerations."

She stared. "I don't understand."

He sighed. "Helen, my godson is rich. *Very* rich. A tempting target for a man who is not paid very much."

Helen's eyes widened. "Do you mean that policeman might be trying to blackmail Alexey in some way?"

"The thought has crossed my mind. As a Russian I'm ashamed to admit it, but our police don't have a very high reputation. Why come all the way here, on his own, when he could have summoned Alexey for official questioning in Moscow? It has a strong smell of corruption to me."

"Oh my God." Helen looked around, wildly. "What are we going to do?"

"I would call his superior in Moscow but I can't be sure he isn't on it too. These things have happened before. We're going to have to sit tight and wait to hear what Lyosha has to say. If the man has made that kind of approach to him, we can act then."

"And do what? If all the police are corrupt …"

"There are other ways." He gave a faint smile. "I've not been the general manager of a successful investigative agency for nothing. Everyone has a weak spot, Helen. This man will have one too, and we'll find it, and use it against him." His voice was hard, his eyes cold. Thank God he's on Alexey's side, Helen thought. I wouldn't want to be in that policeman's shoes!

At that moment the door opened and Alexey came in. There was an odd expression on his face. "Are you okay?" said Helen.

"Yes. No." He sat on the sofa next to her and took her hand. "At least I …"

Volkovsky interrupted. "Where is he, Lyosha?"

"Gone to the bathroom."

Volkovsky said, softly, in English, "How much?"

Both Helen and Alexey looked at him, startled. Alexey said, "How much what?"

"How much money did he ask for in return for not spreading lies about you?"

"Money? Spreading lies? About what?"

Helen cried, "Did he – did he accuse you of anything?"

He looked at her. "He did at first. But that was just a lead-in to other things."

"To blackmailing you," said Volkovsky.

Alexey shook his head. "No. No. You've got it wrong, Kolya. He wanted to know if I was aware of a project – or a person – code-named Koldun."

Helen saw the astonished expression that passed over Volkovsky's face. "But he asked us about that already. I mean, the staff at the Trinity office," he explained.

Alexey frowned. "You didn't tell me that, Kolya."

"No. I'm sorry. But he asked so many questions, and that was just a tiny part of it."

"Well, it doesn't matter, anyway. I told him the truth – that I had no idea. And then he asked me all sorts of questions about Dad. About whether he had any interest in the occult."

"*What?*" said Helen.

Alexey explained, "Koldun means sorcerer in Russian."

"It was just a code-name, surely," said Volkovsky, slowly.

"He seems to think it means something more. He's looking into the possibility that Dad and his partners may have secretly decided to employ a sorcerer as a consultant."

Astounded, Helen said, "What? I know you said magic is a big thing in Russia. But they were running a *business*!"

Alexey and Volkovsky looked at each other. It was the Trinity manager who said, calmly, "I personally know of several companies that use the services of occult practitioners of various types, either on a retainer or for the occasional consultation."

Helen couldn't believe what she was hearing. "You mean a business would actually get someone to read their stars or cast a spell or ... all that sort of stuff? But that's crazy!"

"No, Helen," said Alexey, gently. "It's just the way it is. You use whatever advantage you can in business. Why not that as well? We Russians discount nothing."

Helen was speechless. It was one thing to learn to accept the mysterious in ordinary life, but quite another to cope with the idea of a sorcerer in the hard-headed world of business. For the first time since meeting Alexey, she felt impossibly foreign. And it wasn't just his calm reaction to the idea that stunned her. It was that the shrewd, down-to-earth Volkovsky hadn't flinched either, and that the theory had actually been put to them by a policeman.

"Don't worry," Alexey said, giving her hand a reassuring squeeze. "We don't necessarily think that's what happened. And Dad wasn't normally the type to have any truck with such things. But then the policeman jogged my memory about something." And he explained about the psychic's card.

"But he might have been just consulting the psychic for a personal matter," said Helen, bemused.

"He might. Of course," put in Volkovsky, smoothly. "I can personally guarantee that there's never been a sorcerer or any other psychic on our books at Trinity. But, of course, there were things we didn't know about. So we can't rule it out." He turned to Alexey. "You really don't recall the name of that *ekstrasens*?"

Alexey shook his head. "I've been racking my brains, but nothing comes up."

"If that policeman's theory is correct, then your father might have been, shall we say, exploring possibilities for Trinity. You're right that he'd never shown interest before, but things can change. And your father was highly intelligent and flexible in his thinking."

Alexey gave a sideways glance at Helen. "He was willing to try anything. I know. But he wasn't alone in Trinity."

Helen was slowly getting used to the idea. "Yes, wouldn't his partners object?" she asked.

Volkovsky shrugged. "Not necessarily. Barsukov was a thorough cynic in these matters, but Galkin had a certain interest. He consulted an astrologer sometimes, I believe. And where Ivan Mikhailovich led, the other two followed. He'd have persuaded them." He paused, and his tone suddenly changed. "But don't you think that policeman's been rather a long time in the bathroom?"

Startled, Alexey and Helen looked at him. She whispered, "Do you think he's snooping?"

"Yes. He's either not convinced you've told him the truth, Alexey. Or he thinks he might find something here which will back up his theory. Something he does not intend to share. Did he explain to you why he came alone?"

Alexey shook his head. "No. Is that important?"

"It could be. I rather suspect that our friend the senior lieutenant had to come alone because he isn't acting in an official capacity."

Somewhat glad to be back on solid, understandable ground, Helen said, "You mean, he might still be looking to blackmail?"

"It's possible." Volkovsky took a cell phone from his pocket. "I stored Serebrov's office number here after the first interview, on his request." He hit the number, and spoke, briefly. "*Spasiba*," he said, finishing the call. His eyes shone. "We've got him, my friends. When I asked to speak to Senior Lieutenant Serebrov, I was told that he was on two weeks leave. Now why would a policeman be wasting his holidays working on a case he should have left at the office? There must be something in it for him. A kickback of some sort.

Not money, perhaps. For his own reasons, he wants to get his hands on Koldun, whatever or whoever it is, and he thinks it might be here. You remember what Lebedev said to us today, Lyosha, don't you?"

"About the rumor of something big that had been brewing in Trinity? Yes, but he's a liar and a fantasist. You know that."

"Yes. But even such people can accidentally hit on a shred of truth. And it's Koldun that's brought this officer to your door, alone. Why, we'll have to ask him that directly," said Volkovsky, cheerfully. "Ah! I think it will be most enjoyable turning the tables on our dear beloved *militsiya*, don't you?"

Chapter 13

Volkovsky jerked his head at Slava, who had come upstairs with them. The bodyguard nodded, and drew out a handgun from his inside jacket pocket. Helen held her breath as Slava quietly turned the handle of the door. Alexey gripped her hand, tightly. Only Volkovsky and Slava seemed perfectly calm.

The policeman was sitting on the bed, his back to the door, carefully examining something. So intent was he that he did not turn until it was too late, and Slava did not give him a chance to make good his mistake. With the gun in his back, there was nothing the policeman could do but turn to face the others. He spat something in Russian. There was no need to know the words to know what they meant. *What do you think you're doing, you bastards?*

Volkovsky smiled, but didn't reply. He walked over to where the policeman had been sitting, and bent down to pick up the thing Serebrov had been examining. He held it up so the others could see. It was a small digital camera. Looking at the detective, he raised an eyebrow. Serebrov shrugged but said nothing.

Volkovsky turned on the camera, and hit the button to replay the stored photos. There were about two dozen of them, and they were all of the house and the grounds. Many were of very poor quality, hazily focused and taken at odd angles. Alexey said, blankly, in English, "What the hell …"

Volkovsky spoke to the policeman, who made a brief answer. Despite his predicament – and the gun in his ribs – Helen thought he did not look at all frightened.

Alexey said something sharp in Russian. The detective gave him a shrewd glance. He nodded. "*Da.*"

"He's lying, Lyosha," said Volkovsky, in English. "It's got to be his camera."

Alexey shook his head. "No. Dad bought a camera exactly like this last year, just before one of his trips back here. But why would he have bothered to take these sorts of photos? It wasn't like him to …"

Volkovsky said, "Wait." He spoke harshly to Serebrov. Helen thought the detective didn't appreciate whatever line of questioning the other man was pursuing, for his hazel eyes gleamed dangerously. But he answered calmly enough, in laconic phrases.

"Kolya, I really don't think he is working for gangsters," said Alexey, in English, so Helen now knew what Volkovsky had said. "If he was, he'd have had back-up of some sort."

"Maybe, but you know he tricked his way in here," said Volkovsky, sharply. "He's not on the case. He's on leave. If he's not working for a Trinity-hungry gangster, then he's up to mischief on his own account."

Alexey didn't reply. Instead, he spoke rapidly in Russian to the policeman, who looked at him for an instant. Then Serebrov said, precisely, quietly, in accented but good English, "Yes. That is so. I was transferred from the case. Indeed it's been transferred from my department altogether."

You could have heard a pin drop. Slava's gun wavered for an instant. But the policeman did not even attempt to free himself.

"You speak English," said Volkovsky, accusingly.

"A little. I studied it at university."

"*University*? But you're a policeman."

Serebrov gave a faint smile. "Yes. That is so." He turned to Alexey. "You are correct in your assessment. I have taken the law into my own hands because I do not believe in whitewashing a failure of justice."

"Well, well, well," said Volkovsky, with an incredulous expression, "an idealistic policeman! Wonders will never cease."

"Oh, not idealistic. Just tired of being lied to."

"If lying offends you so," said Volkovsky, with an ironic lift of the eyebrows, "then you will tell us the whole truth about what you were doing here, and what you thought you'd find in the bedroom of a dead man. The house was already searched by the local police."

"Yes, but not thoroughly," said Serebrov. "There was no reason to – it was known no computer files or documents were kept here, and Makarov had not been back to the house for many months before his death."

"So why do it now?" said Alexey.

"Call off your guard dog, if you want me to answer any more questions."

"You can't give orders around here, Senior Lieutenant," began Volkovsky, angrily, but Alexey cut him off.

Walking closer to Serebrov, he said, "Give me your hand."

The policeman's eyes narrowed. Helen thought he might refuse. Then he shrugged, and held out a hand. They shook, and Helen saw Alexey's wary expression relax, and something like surprise flicker over Serebrov's face. Alexey turned to Slava, gesturing him to step aside.

Volkovsky said, urgently, "Lyosha, wait ..."

Alexey took no notice. He spoke sharply in Russian to Slava. The bodyguard looked at Volkovsky, who shrugged. He lowered the gun and stepped away reluctantly. The policeman looked pointedly at the bodyguard. Alexey understood. He waved Slava out of the room.

The bodyguard left, but hovered just beyond the doorway, uncertainly. He didn't understand Alexey's attitude, Helen thought, and, meeting Volkovsky's eyes, she knew he too had reservations. She thought of how last night, when she'd seen Serebrov from her window, he'd reminded her of a forest predator. How did they know that wasn't what he was, police or no police? What did any of them really know about the man's motives, apart from what he'd chosen to tell them?

The detective picked up the camera, and addressing Alexey alone, but still in English, said, quietly, as if continuing an interrupted conversation, "I was sure that the answer to the riddle of your father's death, and those of his partners, lay somewhere in the secret jobs they'd taken on. I knew there was no paper or computer trail of those. But I was also sure your father, being a cautious man, wouldn't obliterate all traces of important business, even that which had to remain a secret. I came here because I thought he might have told *you*, Alexey Ivanovich, even in a riddle which you may not have understood at the time."

"He didn't," said Alexey.

"I know that now, yes. But after we spoke just now, and you told me of that card in your father's book, another idea struck me." He paused.

He said he spoke *a little* English! Helen thought. That was definitely a lie. She must have been rather obviously staring at him, because he darted a hostile glance at her.

Then Serebrov went on, "Unless you physically obliterate a computer hard drive you can always find files, even if deleted. Paper files are more difficult to discover, as long as they are typed or written by hand, and not printed on computer. I believe the Koldun file was originally a paper file, which was destroyed. But today it struck me that another copy might have been made. That the file might have been photographed in its entirety, and stored in another medium. So that's when I went looking. And I found this." He held up the camera, pressed on its side, and ejected a tiny memory card.

They stared at him. Alexey was the first to speak. "I don't understand. Those photos we saw, they're not of a secret file."

"No. Of course not. They are a decoy," said Maxim Serebrov, calmly. "I was looking for a small digital camera, and I found one. I did not expect to find the files easily. Your father was neither stupid nor careless, Alexey Ivanovich."

"I don't know much about digital cameras," said Volkovsky, impatiently, "but I do know that you can't have hidden photos on a card. Either these mysterious photos of yours are there on this card – or they're not."

"You are correct, Nikolai Pavlovich. They are not," said Serebrov, meeting his eyes.

"Then what?"

"The small internal memory of the camera is filled with the same kinds of photos. I checked. And this card has been placed in it to draw suspicion away, in case some snooper wondered why there wasn't a card in it. I think there must be another memory card. For otherwise, why take such useless pictures? The card I hoped to find, with the secret files, must be concealed elsewhere."

"Here?" said Alexey.

"Perhaps. Or perhaps in Moscow. His apartment. His office."

"We have an office in St Petersburg too," said Alexey, eagerly.

Serebrov shrugged. "It could be in any of these places. I don't know. All I know is that it doesn't require much of a hiding place. Look how tiny such a card is."

Helen spoke for the first time, and all eyes turned on her. "But why do you think the card is in Russia? Because if I understand your theory correctly, the paper files must have been in Australia, and Mr. Makarov shredded them before he died. Why wouldn't he have kept the memory card there too?"

Maxim Serebrov gave her a sharp glance. "Alexey Ivanovich has already told us his father bought the camera before a trip to Russia. I believe he took photos of the original documents before he left. Then he kept the documents in Australia and brought the photos here, on the memory card, to be put in a secure hiding place. At the time, he did not realize he was in danger. He was merely following an instinct that he must keep the copies in different places." He turned to Alexey. "Was this trip of his before Barsukov's death – that is, before last August?"

Alexey said, "Yes. I remember because there was a concert I was in at the Conservatorium. Dad had been invited. But then he had to go to Russia." He paused. "You are saying, then, that you think my father was killed because someone was after the Koldun file?"

Serebrov said, "I'm not sure. It is a theory only."

"A man came to see us today," said Alexey, with a glance at Volkovsky. "A low-life petty criminal with no reliability or credibility whatsoever. He'd told us he had some information on the break-in."

"What break-in?" snapped Serebrov.

"Someone tried to get into our Petersburg office a week or two ago," said Volkovsky.

"Did you inform the police?" asked Serebrov, sharply.

"It didn't seem worth the bother," said Alexey, smoothly, with another glance at Volkovsky. "Nothing was taken. They didn't even manage to get in. Anyway, what I was going to say was that this man Lebedev claimed to have information as to who might be behind it. Turned out he was having us on. Scamming us," he explained, when Serebrov looked a little puzzled. "But he did say something interesting, that might fit in with what you say. He said rumor had it something big had been brewing in Trinity."

"Did he explain?" said Serebrov, leaning forward. His eyes were bright, but his body was very still, and once again Helen had the uncomfortable sense of watching a dangerous, predatory creature.

"No. It just sounded to us like he was trying to ..." He broke off as a cell phone chirped. Not his, but Volkovsky's. "Excuse me," Alexey's godfather said, taking the phone out of his pocket and flipping it open. "I'll just turn it off – no, wait. I think I'd better answer this."

"Who is it, Kolya?" said Alexey, sharply.

For answer, his godfather showed him the number flashing on the screen. "It's the St Petersburg office," Alexey told Helen and Serebrov, as Volkovsky said, "*Da?*" into the phone, then listened. As he did, his eyes widened. He rapped out a question, and Helen saw the expression on both Alexey and Serebrov's faces change. They were listening intently now as the phone conversation went on. Something was wrong, Helen could see that. But what? They could all speak and understand English, but her Russian was practically non-existent. And it was so frustrating not to be able to follow things.

But Alexey had seen her expression, and understood. He whispered, "It's Feodor, our office manager from Petersburg. Some thugs of Repin's just burst into the office, tore it half to shreds, and terrorized the staff."

Helen's eyes widened. But before she could speak, Volkovsky handed the phone to Alexey, who spoke rapidly into it. Clicking it off with a terse, "*Da sveedanya,*" goodbye, he turned to them.

"That mongrel Repin," he spat. "If he thinks he's going to get away with it, he's got another bloody thing coming. I'm going to get the police onto him right now."

Volkovsky said, "I doubt that would do much good. You know what they say about our dear friend Boris Alexandrovich Repin."

He shot a glance at Serebrov, who remarked, calmly, "That he has half the Petersburg force in his pocket. I happen to think that is not true – for nobody can quantify the exact number," he added, drily.

Volkovsky laughed. "Is that just Moscow prejudice speaking?" For the first time, there was warmth in his tone.

"We have more than our share of rogues," said the policeman, stolidly, "but I know Repin's reputation all right. After all, he hardly confines himself to our celebrated city of culture, does he? And if he is after something, he usually gets it." He looked at Alexey. "From what I overheard, those thugs announced they were delivering a message from Boris Alexandrovich to the boy who thinks he can fill a man's shoes. I take it, then, this is directed at you, Alexey Ivanovich, and that you have decided to keep Trinity?"

"Yes. Not only do I have no intention of selling to Repin or anyone like him, I have no intention of selling at all. In fact I have plans to reform the company and change its direction."

"I see. May I ask you a question?"

"Of course."

"Why not simply transfer your company to Australia?"

Alexey said, blankly, "What?"

"I have heard it is a good country. A young, peaceful country. Without such dangers and obstacles as must face you here. And these days you could even help relocate key staff there."

Helen met Volkovsky's glance. He was wondering where this was leading, as she was. Alexey said, quietly, "It is important to do it here."

"Why?"

"I belong *here*. I am Russian. And so is Trinity. Corruption – it's the curse of our country. You know that, officer. I am not interested in politics and never will be. I am not interested in power or fame. But I do believe in doing something within my own circle, something useful, something real, in the small way that I *can*."

Serebrov's expression did not change, but Helen knew something in him had shifted. But all he said was, "I see."

Alexey said, fiercely, "And I will *not* allow thugs to dictate to us. Kolya, we leave for Petersburg as soon as possible."

"No," said Volkovsky. "I mean, *you* must not go, Lyosha." Alexey made a movement of protest, but Volkovsky held up a hand. "Please, listen to me, Lyosha. Can't you see, that is exactly what Repin's hoping for? That you'll rush off in a fit of youthful passion and fall right into his trap – on *his* territory. No – let me go for you, while you stay here. Don't play his game, Lyosha – be cunning. Patient. It won't be what he expects."

"But you could be in danger too ..." began Alexey.

"I'm just an employee. This is aimed at the top. You heard what Feodor told us. The thugs were delivering a message meant for you."

"I agree," said Serebrov, firmly. "It is exactly how these kinds of people think. Though it puzzles me as to why Repin should have his thugs broadcast his name like this. From what I've heard, he doesn't usually operate in this manner. I assume you think that he was also behind the earlier attempt, the break-in?"

"Stands to reason," said Alexey.

"Yes – but once again, it seems most unlike Repin to try and fail. If he'd sent people to break in, they'd have broken in, no question. This sounds more – amateur. And Repin is nothing if not professional. He is brutal and ruthless, but highly intelligent. Besides, I know that right now he's on holiday in Egypt, with his family. We always keep a watching brief on such people, you know."

"I don't see how that prevents our friend Boris from being behind this," said Volkovsky, tartly. "In fact it makes it more likely, as he appears to be in the clear."

"True enough," said the policeman, calmly. "But if you are to get to the bottom of this, you need to keep an open mind and not rush to conclusions."

Volkovsky nodded. "You're right." He turned to Alexey. "I should like to propose something, Lyosha. If the senior lieutenant is agreeable – and if you agree too of course – I should like to ask him to accompany me to Petersburg. His professional insights would be of great value to us in investigating this matter."

Alexey said, warmly, "I quite agree. Senior Lieutenant, would you consider helping us?"

Helen watched Serebrov's face as he said, calmly, "Why not? I'm certainly aware of Repin, but I'm equally sure he's not aware of me, as a minor Moscow policeman. I have a good friend in the force in St Petersburg, he's always very well-informed. And I have two weeks leave, so I do not have to account for my time." His voice was steady and his face calm, but his eyes betrayed a certain satisfaction that Helen found troubling. But she did not know how to say it without looking like she was interfering in Trinity business. So she kept quiet.

"Excellent," said Alexey's godfather. "Then it's decided. We'll catch the Petersburg plane from Yaroslavl first thing in the morning."

"Wait a moment," said Alexey. "It's possible we can catch up with Lebedev before he heads back home. He told us he was going to that cafe in town and not leaving before midday, remember?"

"Yes, but that was because he thought we might change our minds about –" began Volkovsky, when Alexey cut him off.

"So we have …" He looked at the clock. "It's not quite midday. With any luck, we might just catch him."

"We'll send Slava after him," said Volkovsky. And he motioned to the bodyguard to come back in.

*

But it was a wasted journey, as Slava reported on his return. The cafe owner told him the man answering to Lebedev's description had been and gone more than half an hour before. No, he had no idea where he was headed. Lebedev hadn't confided in him. "He's from Petersburg, so that's probably where he's gone," Alexey said, "so tomorrow you can try and run him to earth too." He seemed more relaxed, Helen thought, as the four of them sat over the remains of Katya's fine buffet lunch. She didn't feel relaxed, though. She was jumpy with the sense of something going on that she didn't understand. She would have liked to share Alexey and Volkovsky's confidence about Maxim's presence, but she couldn't. She couldn't help remembering that vision of him yesterday in the night-time wood, and the gleam of satisfaction in his eye as he was brought into the charmed circle. Her veins hummed with unease. But she also saw Alexey was eager to discuss their plan of action in more detail with the other two men, so after coffee, she reluctantly got up and said she must be going home.

Alexey insisted on driving her, though she tried to protest she was perfectly able to walk back by herself. On the way there, he said, "I keep saying this at the moment, I know – but I'm so sorry, Helen. I so much wanted us to spend the day together."

"It's okay," she said, gently. "I understand you have to sort this stuff out."

133

He flashed out, "That's what makes it worse, because I feel like my hands are bloody tied, I have to let others do my dirty work for me and it pisses me off, it really does."

It was the first time she'd heard him sound so angry. She laid a placating hand on his arm. "Of course it's frustrating, Alexey, I get that, but you know Nikolai's probably right about Repin trying to trap you into rushing off to Petersburg."

"If it *is* bloody Repin and not some other puppet-master," he retorted. "Yeah, yeah, I know, he's probably right but that makes me even more pissed off. How can anyone take me seriously as Trinity's new owner if I hide out in the backwoods like a frightened rabbit? This is *my* company now – I want to take responsibility. And that means putting my neck on the line if I have to."

Helen quivered. "Don't say that."

He looked at her. "I'm not afraid, Helen."

"I know you're not. I know you're not scared of anything." Her breath caught in her throat as a tremor prickled under her skin. "But the rest of us ... we're not like you, Alexey."

"That's where you're wrong," he said, his tone changing, becoming gentler. "I'm just like everyone else. There are things that *do* scare me. Most of all, of – of not living a real life. Of hiding from things. Of not having the courage to do what I *know* is right."

She cried, "You have plenty of courage. You don't need to prove it. You don't!" She hesitated, then plunged in, "Alexey, that policeman ... frankly, I don't trust him. How did he just happen to be on the spot when your people rang up from Petersburg, and could then insinuate himself right into the thick of things?"

"He didn't insinuate himself. It was Kolya's idea to ask him. He was here to ask about that Koldun file. And that idea he had about the memory card – it's a great one. I always thought secrets were what got Dad and the others killed. If we can at least start unravelling some of them, then maybe we can get closer to finding out what happened to them."

She swallowed. "Do you think – do you think Repin might be behind that too?"

"I don't think so. Repin might have seen an opportunity when the company was left without anyone to run it, as he thought. But three murders is quite another thing. If there was a hint of that, the police would have got onto it."

"But you heard what they said about Repin having the police in his pocket."

"Yeah, but Dad and his partners were pretty influential and had some very powerful connections. No way even someone like Repin would want to touch them. But I don't have any connections, and I'm young. That's why he probably thinks I can be bullied into giving up. My instinct is that Senior Lieutenant Serebrov is a straight shooter and has no connection to Repin or any other gangster."

"I still think there's something a bit odd about him," she said, stubbornly. "Listen to this." And she told him what she'd seen, the night before.

"I'm sure there's a good explanation for it," Alexey said, after she'd finished. "But I'll ask him about it." He looked at her, and said, quietly, "Helen, he is a sad man. A man who has been disillusioned by life, but who still believes in doing things right. A man who has suffered, and who is to be trusted."

"But how do you know that?"

"I just do," he said, simply. "I – I sense things about people."

"But – how …" She trailed off as she remembered him insisting on shaking Serebrov's hand.

His expression now showed he guessed what she was thinking. "Oh, it doesn't always happen. But I know, when it does – that I *must* trust it. Besides," he added, with a little smile, "Kolya has good judgment, about people. Sums them up pretty well. And I am certain he'd never, ever have asked our friend to join him if he thought there was any problem. In fact, I think he feels it's better to have the persistent copper inside the tent with us, as it were. If you get my meaning."

"So he can keep an eye on him?"

"Precisely," said Alexey, with a faint smile.

"Well, I agree," said Helen.

"Good. Because then, between us, we have the situation sorted."

He pulled in at the side of the road and stopped the car. He reached over to her and took her in his arms. "But that's quite enough of that now," he said, tenderly. "Tomorrow – let's forget about all of this. Let's ditch the guard dogs and go off on our own. How does that sound?"

"Wonderful." For the moment nothing mattered but his nearness, and the promise of the next day.

Chapter 14

The next morning, Helen woke from an uneasy sleep to find that a rain, soft and insistent as muffled footsteps, was padding at the window. Going downstairs, dressed in a light jumper over a denim skirt, she was a little surprised to find Sergey in the kitchen with her mother. They were going to Yaroslavl today, Therese reminded Helen. She'd hardly been listening when her mother had mentioned it last night, her mind too full of all that had happened at Alexey's.

"You sure you and Alexey don't want to come along, darling?" Therese said. "It's not very nice weather for the picnic you're planning, is it?"

"We'll manage. But thanks."

She watched from the window as they left, noticing how the old blue Lada was polished so that it shone, and how smartly turned out Sergey was, in his dark gray trousers, white shirt and black jacket, his salt-and-pepper hair surely newly cut. Noticed too, the bright, animated look on her mother's face as Sergey ushered her into the car. It was clear that Therese was looking forward to a day out with the taxi driver. He wasn't the kind of man her mother usually went out with, but so what? Why shouldn't her mother want to break out of habit too, to be free, to take a risk? I can only give her my blessing, Helen thought, and smiled. Not that her mother would ask her permission!

The rain had quite eased by the time Alexey turned up on the motorbike, and they decided to keep to their original plan. He didn't say much about what had happened yesterday, other than that his godfather and the policeman had left early that morning and would call in the evening, and by common unspoken consent they left it at that. The next few hours belonged to them, and them alone, and were not to be clouded by anything else.

They roared off, spinning down the road at an exhilarating rate, her arms around his waist, the wind whipping at her hair under the helmet he'd insisted she wear, though he himself went bareheaded, shouting with laughter as they took the corner and flew along the next road, startling a passer-by into jumping for the safety of a nearby hedge. Round the next corner came a big lumbering tractor and the driver waved a fist at them as they squeezed past him at the last minute. Racing on, they sped through the main square at such a rate that people and buildings went by in a blur of color. Not quite a troika, but the next best thing, Helen thought, happily.

Out of town now, flying along a road that soon narrowed and turned into a track. And then they were in the forest, with big trees growing overhead on either side of the path. The bike's wheels spun and crunched on the dirt and stones of the forest track, and Alexey had to slacken his speed. But though it was slower going, it did not seem to have rained as much here as in the town, for the track was almost dry. A little further, Alexey stopped in a kind of lay-by. "There's this lovely place I know just in there," he said, pointing into the trees. "You can only go there on foot, there's no track. Coming?"

"Wait a moment, I want to take some photos of you," she said, fumbling in her bag. "I haven't even got any yet, you know."

"Well aren't you lucky," said Alexey, laughing, but he posed willingly enough for two or three, and then insisted he take photos of her, and then selfies of the two of them together, before he said, "That's quite enough of the paparazzi session, I think," and taking her by one hand, and the laden bike-bag in the other, he plunged with her into the forest by the side of the path.

It was cool under the trees, fragrant with pine-scent, and quiet, the silence broken only by their footsteps, the odd bird call, and the skitterings of small animals, somewhere deeper in the forest. Dodging brambles and briars – one nearly sent Helen sprawling – they skittered through the forest themselves. Not for long, for they soon came to a beautiful little clearing, carpeted by lush green grass. Almost hidden from sight in one corner was a simple shelter, built of bark and twigs, which Alexey said was used by berry-pickers and mushroomers in the season, but was quite empty right now. But the loveliest and most unusual thing of all was the half-circle pattern of little creamy flowers, almost in the center of the clearing.

"Well, what do you think?"

She breathed, "It's absolutely magic. And those flowers! It's like a fairy ring. You can just imagine them dancing here."

He smiled, and bowing to her, he said, "Well, my sexy little fairy, may I have the pleasure of this dance?"

"You may," she said, laughing in delight and surprise, and they waltzed around together in a dance that had no real form but that made them both laugh in delight, and then Alexey started singing, an old song Helen recognized because it was on her mother's favorite CD, a jazz number called "I Won't Dance". He had a baritone voice, rich and deep as black velvet or the darkest chocolate, and the sound of it made her tingle from head to toes. Then he asked her to sing with him, her voice and his mingling, their bodies drawing closer and closer, breathing in each other's smell, the touch of each other's warm skin, eyes in each other's eyes.

Breathing hard, Alexey whispered, "Helen ... Helen ... do you want ..."

"Oh yes," she cried, fiercely, nuzzling at his neck, "Yes ... yes – now – right now ..."

He picked her up and carried her to the little shelter. He put his coat on the soft grass and she lay down on it, then reached up and pulled him down to her, unbuttoning his shirt, stroking and kissing his mouth, his shoulders, his chest, the hot salty taste of him on her lips, the feel of his skin under her hands, satiny-smooth with the sharpness of bone beneath. So glorious he was she could barely breathe for desire, and he was shuddering, whispering her name, kissing her face, her ears, her lips, the nape of her neck. He slipped the jumper off her and unhooked her bra and looked at her for a long, shuddering moment and whispered, "You're so beautiful – so beautiful – so beautiful. Oh, *Yelena, ya tibya lyublyu* ..." and she understood the words instinctively and whispered, "Oh Alexey, I love you too."

His lips were on her breasts, the nipples hardening under his touch. She pulled the shirt off his shoulders then his hand moved under her skirt, she couldn't wait anymore, his touch sending pulses of the sweetest fire through every bit of her as, arching her hips up, she guided him into her. He slipped in so sweetly, so powerfully, that she cried out in sheer delight and surprise. And quite soon there were no more words, no more thoughts, only feelings and sensations as she gave herself up completely to him, and he to her.

Back in the past, before Simon had turned her to stone, she'd always enjoyed sex. But for weeks after what had happened she had hated the very thought of it. She'd felt ugly, stupid, repelled and repellent. Later, when she had begun to feel a little better, when the images had begun to fade, or at least to lose their power to wound, some of her friends had said the only way to get over "that bastard" and how he'd made her feel was to go out and get it on with a guy, any guy. They meant well. But she couldn't. The past had been under her skin like a thorn she couldn't remove. Now, though, it was not only as though Simon had never existed; it was as though there never had been anyone other than Alexey.

*

Much later, when they lay quietly wrapped in each other's arms, Helen said, softly, "I've never felt like this before."

"Neither have I, *maya milaya*," he said. "Never, my sweetheart." And he kissed her, tenderly. "But I hoped that one day I might meet someone like you. Someone I'd want to make love with forever, who I'd want to share my life with for always."

Her breath caught in her throat. "Me too, but I thought – I feared maybe it was something that happened only in books. In films. In daydreams and fantasies. Not in real life. But this is better – way, way better than any dream." She smiled mischievously. "Not even my wildest, sexiest dreams."

His arms tightened around her waist. "You're absolutely bloody gorgeous, you know that?" He kissed her, fiercely. "I'll never be able to have enough of you, never." And he proved it again, most satisfyingly, and afterwards she said, feelingly, "Wow, Alexey, that was so freaking good," and he said, teasingly, "You think?" and kissed her on the nape of the neck.

She said, "I feel warm right through to my toes," and he murmured, "Yeah, me too, but do you know what? I'm bloody *starving*. How about you?"

"I could eat a horse," said Helen, cheerfully.

"Oh bugger. Clean forgot to pack one of those." They both laughed helplessly at the ridiculous joke.

Katya had excelled herself with cold herbed chicken, home-made mayonnaise, rye bread and a delicious home-made sparkling blackcurrant drink in which they toasted each other. For afters there were fresh cherries and some tiny jam tarts. It was a true feast, and they did justice to it, while talking as lovers do, of everything and nothing. But they did not speak of the future, for the present was all that mattered to them just then.

Presently, they packed everything up, and walked back through the woods to the track. It was still very quiet. The bike lay where they'd left it, and there was no sign of anyone having passed. They might as well have been the only two people in all the world.

They had just left the forest track and had stopped so that Helen could put the helmet back on, when an old woman appeared up the road, walking very slowly and carrying a pair of overloaded plastic supermarket bags that looked like they might break at any moment. Helen recognized her at once. It was Mrs. Feshina.

Before Helen could speak, Alexey said, "Wait a moment," and setting the bike on its kickstand, he got off and hurried to Mrs. Feshina. Helen followed. Alexey said, "I'll take the bags, you help her, okay?"

Helen nodded. She looked at Mrs. Feshina. Mrs. Feshina looked at her. Helen tried a smile. Rather to her surprise, the old lady smiled back. Alexey formally introduced himself, then Helen. They shook hands, solemnly. Impulsively, Helen offered her arm for Mrs. Feshina to lean on for the walk back to the bike, half-expecting the old lady might refuse. But she didn't. She looked exhausted, pale, her forehead was beaded with sweat. She leaned on Helen's arm and slowly, patiently, the three of them made their way back to the bike. Alexey said something to her, and she answered.

"She says her house is about a kilometer away," he translated. "Bit slow to walk there, at this pace. I'll take her on the bike."

"Okay. I'll wait for you here."

They'd been speaking in an undertone but Helen had the feeling the old lady had heard every word. Not that it would mean anything to her, in English. But her eyes, those strange, milky-blue, half-blind eyes were fixed on the young people's faces as if she were learning them off by heart. Alexey spoke to her, obviously asking her about riding on the bike. The old lady darted a glance at Helen, and said something in reply.

"She says you must come too," Alexey translated.

The back of Helen's neck prickled as her unease of the other day returned. "Why?"

"She wants to give us tea. To thank us, she said."

"Oh." The tension relaxed. "I see."

"We'll put her parcels in the bike bag –" Alexey suited the action to the words " – then I'll get on. You help her up behind me, then you squash up behind her. She's only little, and you're not exactly big either. Hang on."

It was true, the old lady was a mere bag of bones, and light as a feather, and she was very quiet between them, her eyes half-closed, as though she were going to sleep. A herby smell came off her, not unpleasant, but quite strong. They went along very slowly and carefully till they turned off the road to a narrow track that led back into the forest. A short time later they drew up outside a tiny wooden *izba*.

Its timbers were weathered, its iron roof splotched with rust, the delicate carvings around the windows a faded blue and white, while the overgrown garden was full of flowers and herbs. As Mrs. Feshina led them down the path, something swooped from one of the birches by the gate, and landed on her shoulder with a fussing of feathers. Helen gave a startled exclamation.

"Oh my God! It's that magpie!"

"What ..." began Alexey, before going on, "Oh, our lucky mascot friend you mean. Are you sure it's the same one?"

"That silver ring around its leg," she said, pointing. "Unmistakable." Her eyes were shining. She smiled. "Some coincidence, eh?" she said, echoing Alexey's words the other day.

"And then some," he answered, his own eyes shining.

The old lady was looking curiously at them. Alexey said something to her. She replied, animatedly. "It turned up one day in her garden a few years ago," he translated. "She thinks it escaped from a lab. Anyway, it adopted her. She calls it Daria." He added, with a little smile, "If she's a witch, it must be her familiar, eh?"

Helen didn't answer. She looked at Olga Feshina. The old lady looked back steadily, and on her shoulder, the bird Daria also regarded Helen with utter calm. She said, softly, "Tell her I first saw Daria the day I arrived. And then later, in the woods."

Alexey did so. The old woman nodded. She spoke, and he translated, "She said Daria is a very wise bird. She knows many things. I told her also how we'd met and she said Daria did us a good turn, and she was glad of it."

"So am I," said Helen, softly. "Oh, so am I, Mrs. Feshina," and she impulsively kissed the old lady on one soft, faded cheek. Mrs. Feshina beamed, and with a cheerful gesture motioned them both to come into the house, and take their shoes off at the door.

*

The house had only one room, and it was very warm, for the stove – the same type of old-fashioned one as in Irina's house – was going. Glancing at the neat pile of logs by the stove,

Helen wondered how the frail old lady managed. Maybe someone chopped her wood for her. In the corner closest to the stove was a narrow iron-framed bed; in another a small kitchen area with a stone sink, and shelves neatly stacked with preserves, as well as a few old books and magazines and a radio. In the center of the room was a table cluttered with stuff, including a battered samovar. Two wooden chairs with pokerwork cushions, and a rocking chair stood by the stove. There was no electricity – Mrs. Feshina cooked on the wood-stove, and for light there were two kerosene-style lamps. No obvious bathroom, but there was a tin bath under the sink, and an outhouse visible in the back garden. Mrs. Feshina might be poor, but she'd still made her cottage cozy and bright with color and personality. An icon of the Madonna and Child glowed in a niche near the table, there were little carvings on a shelf along with a row of books, a large framed photograph of a family group on one wall, and on another an attractive collage made of colored pictures cut out of magazines. An embroidered red and white spread covered the bed, and vases full of lily of the valley and lilac in purple and white scented the room, along with bunches of herbs hung over the stove.

Olga Feshina waved them to sit down, and fiddled around with the samovar, Daria the magpie still on her shoulder, head under its wing, drowsing. As the old lady carefully poured the hot tea into some surprisingly fine painted cups, Helen suddenly found herself catching her breath. *I am in a world deeply strange and strangely deep*, she thought, *a world both simple and mysterious, as far away from my old life as it's possible to be, and I don't feel spooked or uneasy or even out of place any more. No, it feels completely natural.* She shot a glance at Alexey and he smiled, his socked foot brushing her calf briefly, lightly, under the table, and the thrill of their love-making washed over her again in warm sweet waves.

Olga Feshina handed them the tea, and a pot of jam. Alexey said, to Helen, "You're meant to put it in the tea. That's traditionally how it's drunk."

It was surprisingly good, the thick dark, slightly smoky taste of the tea blending with the berry jam in a sweet rich mixture that went right into her bones. As they drank, Alexey talked to the old lady, drawing her out on her life, discovering she wasn't strictly speaking a local, but had come to Uglich as a bride, following her husband, who worked in the local Chaika watch factory. They'd lived in one of the ugly apartments in the new part of town, she'd brought up her daughter there but always yearned for a cottage in the quiet of the forest. Her husband had died many years ago and her daughter now lived in the city, but she had not forgotten her mother's dream and a few years ago she and her husband had bought Mrs. Feshina this small place. She lived alone but was not lonely because her daughter and her family kept in touch and she also had all the life of the forest to keep her company. And Daria, of course. Helen couldn't understand the words but the rhythms of the old lady's speech were as restful as a soft song to her ear, and she felt herself slip into a dreamy state of contentment.

They finished the tea. Olga Feshina offered them more. Alexey thanked her, but said they should be going. Then Olga Feshina looked at Helen and held out a hand for one of hers. The old lady's fingers deftly traced the lines in Helen's hand. She looked up at the young woman, and said something.

Alexey translated, "She says you are the firebird come from far distant lands."

Helen said, puzzled, "I don't understand."

"Neither do I. She says she can't explain it. Not that she won't – she can't. It's an image that came to her when she took your hand. Like a kind of vision, if you like."

"You remember I told you the other day about that book I used to love when I was a kid?" said Helen slowly.

"Yeah. *The Tale of Prince Ivan, the Firebird, and Gray Wolf.* I loved that story too," he said.

"Anyway, like I told you I hadn't thought of it for years, until Uglich. Do you think that somehow she might – might have picked up on that, if you know what I mean?"

"I do." He turned back to Mrs. Feshina.

"She says she doesn't know about that," he translated. "She knows the story of course but she doesn't think it has to do with that. She says the meaning will reveal itself. When you're ready."

Helen looked at the old woman, who returned her gaze steadily. She said, "Well, then, can you ask her why she gave me that doll?"

Alexey spoke to the old lady. "She just wanted to. That's all. She says it's Vassilissa the Wise, from a fairytale."

"Oh. I never got to thank you properly," said Helen, to the old lady, as Alexey translated. "But now I want to thank you, very much. I really love it."

Mrs. Feshina smiled, and nodded, and patted Helen's hand. Then she looked at Alexey, and spoke again. He nodded, and gave her his hand. She grasped it. A look of surprise came over her face. She looked him straight in the eyes, and spoke softly, making Helen's palms prickle. In the flow of incomprehensible speech, she'd caught one familiar word, spoken more than once. *And that word was Koldun.*

Alexey's expression had darkened as she was speaking, and when she drew to a halt, he asked her a sharp question, to which she calmly answered. They spoke together a little while longer, and Helen longed to know what they were saying. But he didn't translate, and it wasn't until a short time later, when they'd left the cottage, that Helen had a chance to ask him.

"Alexey, you're like her, aren't you?" she said, as they went out of the gate. It wasn't at all the question she'd meant to ask; it had come out of her mouth quite unbidden, and it astonished her almost as much as Alexey, whose eyes widened.

"What do you mean?" he said, slowly.

"I saw the look on her face when she took your hand. I think she recognized something. You said you sense things in people. But it's more than just an instinct. You have ... a ... a gift, don't you? Like she does. Through touch."

"And if I do – doesn't that scare you?" he said, after a moment.

"No." She wasn't quite telling the truth.

"Well – her gift – it's different. Stronger. It's like a kind of ... second sight. Mine's not like that. Like I told you, I just sense things. Not in everyone. Just in some people."

Helen said, quietly, "What did she tell you? Please. I know she spoke about the sorcerer. I heard her say *koldun*."

"Yes. She did. But it's not what you think."

"What is it, then?"

"She said that I was haunted by a sorcerer. Like my father before me. She'd had a dream, she told me, weeks ago. That my father's death, and the others', it was due to a curse. A sorcerer's curse."

Helen stared at him, not quite succeeding in keeping the dismay from her voice as she faltered, "A *curse*?"

"I know it sounds crazy. But she's a long way from crazy. So I've got to take it seriously."

Helen struggled to understand. "You mean – she's warning you – about the sorcerer behind the Koldun file? But how does she know about that?"

"She doesn't. The old lady's not a supernatural detective. And she's not a prophet. She doesn't tell you the future. It's not like she's receiving a news flash. Second sight – it's not like that. She sees ... visions, possibilities – sort of living metaphors, in you. And the real meaning – it's often quite different to what it seems to be at first."

She said, uneasily, "But it's strange that she should speak about the very thing that we –"

"Helen, she doesn't know *anything* about the Koldun file, or Trinity, or employing sorcerers, or about what's been going on. And let me tell you, I gave her the third degree about it."

"Then what *does* it mean?"

"I don't know. But I'm not going to let myself get worried about it. And neither should you, Helen. Really." He spoke tenderly but firmly, closing the subject.

Chapter 15

They had just got back to Alexey's house when the phone rang. It was Nikolai Volkovsky. Alexey put the line on speakerphone so they could both hear. "Hello, Kolya."

"Hello, Lyosha. Is Helen with you?"

Alexey smiled at Helen and replied, "Yes. We've just got back from a day in the forest."

"Ah! That's why your cell phone was not answering, it was out of range. Did you have a good day?"

"Very good, thank you," Alexey said blandly, with a wink at Helen, who squeezed his hand, feeling warm all over. "What's up?" he went on.

"Just wanted to give you a progress report. Not that there is much. We haven't got very far yet I'm afraid. Questioned everyone in the office and looked at the security tapes – but these men knew what they were doing. There were four of them, and they all wore balaclavas, dark clothes and gloves. Impossible to get a conclusive identity. And they came in through the one area where there are no cameras – the emergency exit – so the security guards, who as you know are in that downstairs room, didn't even see them on the screens until it was too late."

"Do you think they were actually Repin's men?"

"They said so, but like Maxim Antonovich says, anyone can say anything. He thinks it's possible some rival gangster could be using Repin's name in vain, maybe even from the Moscow mafia. He has a reliable contact in the Petersburg force with a good network of informers, and we may get something from him tomorrow. We're going to have to stay at least another couple of days, if not more."

Helen listened tensely as Alexey asked, "What about Lebedev? Did you track him down?"

"Zaitsev, Maxim's contact in the Petersburg police, found us his address. According to his neighbors he hasn't returned yet from his trip. Zaitsev's put a watch on the place so as soon as he turns up, he'll let us know."

"Good. Kolya – how is everyone in the office?"

"A little shaken, but coping well. Feodor got a little roughed up when he tried to stop the intruders from smashing one of the computers. He's got cuts and bruises, but nothing major, the hospital's checked him over, no broken bones or anything like that. The other staff were unhurt. And the office – well, it's a mess, but that can easily be cleaned up. Even the computer – it was just a spare one, and all the files it contained were duplicated elsewhere. As to the documents in the filing cabinets, they too are duplicated, so no real harm done there."

Helen mouthed, "Ask him if it seemed if they were looking for anything in particular."

"Good thinking," Alexey said, and asked. Volkovsky answered, "You mean, for Koldun? Maxim doesn't think so. And certainly they took nothing away."

"So that must mean Repin – or whoever it is – has no idea it exists."

"Possibly. We think it most likely that this incident was meant as some kind of warning. We're going to have to do something about improving security, at the very least. Maxim thinks it's not up to scratch."

"Of course. Do whatever you must."

"Now, Lyosha, another thing. Feodor wanted to know about what they should do about those remaining contracts you were doubtful about."

"Tell them we'll look at each one on its merits," said Alexey, with a glance at Helen. "If they are the right sort of jobs for the right sort of clients, then there will be no problem. If not – then we will cancel them."

"But, Lyosha, it might not be so easy as all that. And if we acquire a reputation for unreliability …"

Helen saw Alexey's expression harden as he said, "If we acquire a reputation for unreliability by refusing the money of bad men, then we should be proud of that."

Volkovsky sighed. "Very well. If you say so. But then you must resign yourself to a good deal more trouble."

"Then I do."

"It's not just you, Lyosha. It's our people, too."

Alexey snapped, "Like you said, we will improve security. And you will also issue a statement making it clear I am *solely* responsible for the change in Trinity's direction, so that any quarrel anyone has with that will be only with me."

Helen cried out, "Alexey, no! You can't do that!"

Volkovsky said, "She's absolutely right, Lyosha. You can't. Firstly, because it is not true. We are all in this together. And secondly, because to do such a thing – it would be extremely dangerous. For all of us."

There was a silence. Then Alexey said, quietly, "What do you propose, then?"

"Let me and Maxim Antonovich think it over. Between us we will come up with a plan."

"You are getting on well with him, then?"

"He is a good man to have on our side," said Volkovsky. "Now, Alexey, the memory card. It must be found. That is what you could do. You and Helen could look for it in the house."

"I don't think it's here, Kolya."

"You can't be sure. And I know it's not as exciting as dashing off on a white horse brandishing your fiery sword," said Volkovsky, drily, "but it's important. Maxim Antonovich thinks the card is the key to understanding what happened at Trinity."

"And you, Kolya? What do you think?"

"I don't know. Perhaps."

"Always the cautious one, eh?"

"Someone's got to be cautious," said Volkovsky, and you could hear the smile in his voice even over the phone, "because it sure as hell isn't going to be you, Lyosha!"

*

They looked for a couple of hours. They flipped through books in case the card had been placed there. Pulled out drawers to see if it might have been taped to their underside. Felt in the family photo album in case it might have been hidden behind a photo, or even taped to the inside of the binding. Looked through bags of flour and rice, in bottles and boxes and all sorts of things. While they were doing that, Slava popped his head around the kitchen door to ask if it was okay if he and the other staff walked into town for a drink at the local bar. He looked a little surprised to see them rummaging around on their hands and knees but made no comment, even after Alexey told him brusquely that of course it was okay, and they didn't have to ask permission. After he'd gone, Helen said, "Your godfather probably told him he had to ask us."

"I know," said Alexey, and he sounded annoyed. "Honestly, Kolya can be so old-school sometimes, it drives me mad!"

"He just wants the best for you …"

"Knowing that doesn't make it easier to cope with." He gave her a mischievous glance. "But listen, my dear

Mademoiselle Clement, I do believe the card is nowhere here. I also believe that for the next couple of hours or so we are all alone in the house, and what do you think we should do about that?"

It didn't take much figuring out.

*

Later, Alexey said, dreamily, "I've had an idea. How about we go to Moscow tomorrow?"

She twisted round to look up at him. "What for?"

"The card's not here. It's not in Petersburg. So I reckon it's in Moscow. At the office. Or the apartment. We can make a day of it. We can look for the card – and I can show you Trinity head office and introduce you to our people."

Her eyes lit up. "Oh, Alexey, I'd love that!" A pause. "Only, Nikolai said ..."

He broke in. "He only banned me from Petersburg."

"Slava and Oleg will have to come along and ..."

"To hell with that. We won't tell them we're going. You don't really want those two eavesdropping on us, do you?"

Helen looked at him. "No, but ..."

He took her hand, and kissed it, softly. "Do you really think I'd ask you to come, *milaya maya,* if I thought it was unsafe?"

"No," she said, "I know you wouldn't. But you can't be sure – and besides, how can we possibly drive to Moscow and back without anyone knowing? It's hours away."

"Who said anything about driving? We'll fly. There and back within a day. Direct from here."

Helen stared at him. "There's no airport in this town. You have to go to Yaroslavl for that."

He smiled. "True. But there's a helipad here."

She squeaked, "You're not saying we go by *helicopter*?"

"That's exactly what I'm saying."

"No – don't tell me – you're a helicopter pilot in your spare time, along with everything else!"

He burst out laughing. "Sorry to disappoint, my love, but no. The only aircraft I've ever flown is an ultralight. I'll hire a local pilot. No worries at all. So – are you on, or not? I'll go and organize it now, if so." He gave her a teasing glance. "But if you don't like helicopters or you don't like flying, that's okay, I'll go by myself and ..."

Helen's eyes flashed. "Don't you dare! I'm coming with you, whatever."

He smiled. "You're trembling. Scared, *maya sladkaya?*"

"No, no, no. Not at all. Just so happy. And excited. What did you just call me, by the way?"

"*Sladkaya*—" he said, nuzzling at her neck. "Means sweet one."

"You're going to have to teach me all those words to say to you too," she said, kissing him, "and the right way to say them and everything."

"Only if you'll teach them to me in French," he said. "Deal?"

"Deal," she said, happily, "*mon amour, mon chéri ... je t'aime,*" and she moved slowly down his body, touching him with hands, with lips ...

"Wait a moment." He laughed, "How do you think I can concentrate on learning a foreign language when you're ... oh God, Helen ... Helen, Helen ... what are you doing to me?"

Chapter 16

That night, back in her own bed at Irina's, Helen lay awake for a while, thinking about all that had happened. Thoughts of the future had not troubled her when she was lying in his arms, but they troubled her now. In a month she'd have to leave, when her visa ran out. What would happen then? This was not some fling, not the rebound remedy her friends had urged on her. This was the real thing and the thought that she and Alexey might be separated made her stomach clench, as she remembered what he'd said to Maxim, when the policeman asked him why he hadn't moved the business to Australia. His life was here. He'd chosen Russia. And it had chosen him. But not me, Helen thought. I'm a foreigner. I find it fascinating here, I even like it, but I'd never belong. And I'm not sure I even want to. I'm not Alexey, or even Irina. I don't have that beat of blood in my veins, that instinctive understanding, that links a person to a country. I can never be Russian. So how can my life be here? But how can it be *anywhere*, if it isn't with Alexey?

Then worries about the future evaporated as she recalled his touch on her skin, the expression in his eyes, the smell of him, the beauty of him. Don't be afraid, she told herself, he's not afraid and neither should you be. It will work out, somehow, because it must. *Because we will it.* She fell asleep on that thought, and slept soundly, dreamlessly for the rest of the night. Waking refreshed and eager to start the day, she showered, dressed and went downstairs to find her mother at work on her laptop on the kitchen table.

"Already hard at it, Mam?"

"Sad, I know. But I woke rather too early. Couldn't get back to sleep." She glanced at her daughter's bronze silk shirt, black linen flares, cropped jacket and high-heeled boots. "You look stunning. What's the big occasion?"

"Well, we thought we might have a day out in Yaroslavl. See the sights. Eat in a flash restaurant. And like you told me the other day, best to dress up for that."

She felt a bit guilty about lying to her mother, but it was easier than telling her they were going in a helicopter to Moscow. There'd be questions. Fussing. Anxious requests for a phone call when they arrived. She wanted to be free.

Therese smiled. "Sounds perfect. Have fun."

"Thanks, Mam. We will. You have a good day too. Productive."

"Thanks, *chérie*. And remember, we've been invited to Galina's place tonight."

"Who?"

Her mother looked sharply at her. "Sergey's sister. I told you."

Now Helen dimly remembered her mother mentioning it last night. "Would they mind terribly if maybe I didn't ..."

"Helen! I told them you were coming. And you said last night that was okay. Please be back by seven-thirty."

"Okay," said Helen, vaguely. She'd heard the motorbike engine. "He's here, Mam. I've got to go."

"What's the big hurry? You haven't even had your breakfast, tell him to come in for a minute," protested Therese.

"It's okay, Mam, I can have it at Alexey's. And you don't want to sit around chatting, I know. You need to get on with your work." She kissed the top of her mother's head. "Have a good day. See you tonight."

A day out on the motorbike was what everyone had been told, including Slava and Oleg. "Told them the phone would be out of range too," Alexey said, as she got on the motorbike. "So we're all set." His delighted grin gave Helen a sudden, touching glimpse of the impish little boy he must once have been.

They raced through the town, heading a kilometer or two north to the helipad. There were two or three choppers parked there, and the pilot was waiting for them in a building nearby. A thick-set middle-aged man with a rather military air, he introduced himself laconically as Konstantin and did not seem in the least surprised that two young people should be his passengers, or that one of them didn't speak Russian. Yes, he agreed in answer to Alexey's question, they'd be in Moscow in about an hour and a bit. No, he didn't expect any delays. Weather conditions were fine, and everything had been cleared.

Though Helen had often flown, it had only ever been in planes, and big ones at that. She'd never even sat in a helicopter before, and she couldn't help feeling a little spurt of anxiety in with the excitement as she climbed into the big white machine.

Alexey grasped her hand as they buckled themselves in and put on their headphones. "Don't worry. It's great. You'll see. I've been up in them in Australia a couple of times and I really enjoyed it."

Helen nodded, dumbly, staring out through the windscreen as Konstantin started the engines and the rotors started turning. She couldn't help a small gasp as the helicopter slowly rose vertically in the air for several meters, and then seemed to lean slightly forwards and began to accelerate. Her stomach lurched. She felt as though she were on a Ferris wheel, or a roller-coaster. It wasn't an unpleasant sensation – she quite liked Ferris wheels and roller-coasters – but it was unexpected. Not like a plane at all. Alexey lifted up her headphone flap and whispered, "I'd love to fly one of these things one day."

"It looks … complicated."

"Yes, much more than a plane. Anyone who's driven a car can learn to drive a plane, though there's more to it of course. But a helicopter's different. You have to use both hands and both feet to drive it. See that control there in his hand? That's the cyclic, which controls whether the chopper's going to go forwards or backwards, left or right. The one in his other hand – that's the collective, which controls the up and down motion of the helicopter, and also the engine speed. And those pedals under his feet – they control the tail rotor."

"You know a lot about it," said Helen, smiling at the enthusiasm in his voice.

"Mishka used to have a picture book about planes and helicopters when he was a kid. Wanted to be a pilot before he decided boats were more his thing. It had all these cutaway pictures and things. I used to look at it sometimes." His tone changed. "Hey, look down there, Helen! Can you see it? That's the place where we were yesterday."

She could see a little patch of green in the dark trees below. Her heart beat fast as images from the day before flooded into her mind. But she said, pertly, "It could be anywhere."

"No, it couldn't." He grinned. "You women – you have no sense of direction!"

"And you men are such boasters!" she retorted, cheerfully.

They fell silent, looking out of the window at the unfolding landscape below. Once you got used to the motion of the helicopter, thought Helen, it was really quite exciting to look down from that height, onto the forests and rivers and cities that spread underneath you like a living tapestry. Because they were flying lower and slower than a plane would, you could see so much more too, and more clearly. Time seemed to go so quickly that Helen was surprised when the taciturn Konstantin pointed out the sprawl of Moscow below.

"We're landing at a small airport called Bykovo," said Alexey, pulling off his headphones, "helicopters and private jets go there. It's a little way from the city, but I've organized for a car to pick us up and take us back there this evening, okay?"

"You're the boss," said Helen, teasingly, and then gave a startled, "Ooh!" when her stomach dropped as if she were in an elevator, as Konstantin began to make his descent.

Chapter 17

The Trinity head office was situated in a side street off Okhotny Ryad, the big wide boulevard that runs past the Duma, the Russian parliament building, in central Moscow. Everything about it was unexpected to Helen: the nondescript building in which the office was housed on the first floor; the modest entrance, with a simple wooden door with a discreet plaque on it announcing "Trinity Consultancy", in Russian and English; and the lack of obvious security guards.

In the reception area, furnished with a couple of shabby leather armchairs for visitors and a low table on which reposed several magazines, a big-haired young woman of about Helen's age sat on a swivel chair at a plain desk. Behind her was a wall untidily crowded with framed certificates and testimonials, and a cheap reproduction of the Trinity icon. With its rabbit-warren confusion of cramped little offices and dull furnishings, the whole place might look at first sight like some shabby '60s government department, one of the more boring ones, say administration. But the computers on the desks were brand-new, the telephone system state of the art, there were security cameras discreetly positioned, and the young man in the casual jacket who greeted Alexey at the entrance had a way of carrying himself that hinted he was more than a mere doorman. It seemed the low-key, flying-under-the-radar approach was deliberate, part of the company's mystique, which had enabled it to survive the political and social turmoil of the last twenty years when others had long since fallen by the wayside.

On the way from the airport, Alexey had called the office and asked that everyone gather in the meeting room. And he'd told them Helen was coming along to observe, that she was a business student in London, and wanted to see how it was done. The cover story had been Helen's idea; she'd have felt weird coming in just as his curious new girlfriend.

As they approached the meeting room, followed by Alla the receptionist and Grigori the security man, Helen could hear a buzz of conversation coming from behind the door. All talk ceased when they entered, as the dozen or so people seated around the table in the center of the room turned their eyes toward them.

For the first time, she felt nervous. But it all went fine. Alexey greeted them all in his usual warm, easy manner, briefly introduced Helen, and then sat down. Helen sat next to him, and took rapid stock of the people around her.

Three-quarters of the Trinity staff were male. There was quite a range of ages, with the oldest person looking to be in her fifties, and the youngest being Alla. Several looked in their twenties and early thirties. Appearance-wise, they were also a mixed bunch: from an elegantly besuited middle-aged guy with Central Asian features to a closed-faced young tough with a blond rat's tail and leather jacket; from pretty, plump Alla with her helmet of glossy black hair to a formidable-looking hatchet-faced woman in a severe gray hairstyle who sat with arms folded.

Alexey said, "Helen, I want to introduce everyone, one by one. But perhaps you could say a quick word to them first?

Most of them understand at least some English, some are very good at it, for the rest I can give a quick translation."

Helen nodded, nervously. She felt almost as though she were at a job interview. A really important job interview. Trying hard to sound calm and businesslike, she said, "*Dobry dyen*. I am honored to be here as an observer, and I promise I won't get in your way."

"We are glad to welcome you," said a tall thin man with a shock of wild hair and glasses perched on the end of his nose, who seemed to speak for them all. "Any friend of Alexey Ivanovich's is a friend of ours, and we hope you will find your time with us interesting."

"Thank you. Thank you so much," said Helen, blushing, feeling like a fraud.

Then Alexey introduced each person in turn, and she concentrated, trying to remember them all. Fortunately it was only first names he used, or she'd have become completely lost. As it was, it all passed in a bit of a blur. Alla and Grigori she knew already. The other women were easy to remember, with the formidable woman, who was revealed as surprisingly friendly, being the office manager, Sonya. A flash, mini-skirted blonde was Yulia, head of IT; and a young woman in jeans and red jumper, introduced as a junior researcher, was Natalia. Among the men, she knew she'd remember Zakhar, Mr. Rat's Tail, field investigator; Igor, a short round man with a shock of red hair; and Timur, the gray-suited Central Asian financial manager, as well as Ilya, the chief researcher, the tall thin man who had welcomed her in his excellent English. The rest varied as to proficiency in the English language, Ilya told her, but only three of them – Sonya and two of the men – had practically no English at all.

Then Alexey started talking animatedly in Russian. She couldn't understand everything he was saying, but from one or two words she caught, and an intake of breath from a couple of people, she realized he was informing them about what had happened in Petersburg. There were anxious questions then but, from what Helen was able to judge, Alexey succeeded in reassuring the staff. Then he began speaking about more general things, interrupted by people asking questions, and she quickly got lost. She knew he hadn't said anything about the memory card, or the Koldun file. He'd agreed with Volkovsky that nothing should be said about it till more was known.

It was getting stuffy in the airless room, and she felt a headache coming on. Murmuring an apology, she slipped out to the bathroom.

There was a small plastic glass in a toothbrush holder on the sink, and she filled it with water, and was rummaging in her bag for some paracetamol when a sudden sound made her spin around – just as a black-clad figure climbed in through the window and into the room.

For a heartbeat, she could only stare. Then she made a dash for the door, but too late, as another sinister figure dropped into the room. In an instant, she was on the floor, efficiently gagged and bound, as a third sinister figure appeared. A helpless Helen could only watch as they took the key out of the inside of the door and went out of the room, locking it firmly behind them.

Chapter 18

As soon as they were gone, Helen tried shuffling on her side across the hard tiled floor, trying to reach the door to bash on it with her boots and alert the others. But it was hard going. She winced as every jerking movement made the tightly knotted plastic rope cut deeper into her skin. The gag in her mouth made her feel sick and her head, pressed against the tiles, beat like a drum.

She heard a crash. Another. A shout. Many shouts. A pounding of feet, slamming of doors. Yelling. There's only three of them, she thought, and more than a dozen of us, it'll be over in seconds, they don't have a chance. Then her heart nearly stopped as she heard an unmistakable sharp cracking sound and someone screaming.

Oh my God, they've got guns, they're going to kill everyone! Sobbing, she beetled desperately across the floor. And then – the lock rattled, the door was flung open. Alexey was in the doorway, pale, eyes wild. Behind him crowded several shocked faces, but Helen hardly noticed as he bent down to her and rapidly untied the gag, the ropes. She began, "Oh Alexey, I'm so sorry that I couldn't warn –"

"Don't worry about it," he said, his eyes on her face. "Are you okay?"

"I'm okay," she said, quietly, taking his hand. "Just a bit bruised. It'll heal."

"Those *bastards*," he spat.

"How's – how's everyone else? I heard the gun go off – did anyone ..."

"No. Grigori got a nasty crack on the head but no one was shot. Thank God."

"And thank *you*," said Ilya, gravely, from behind him. "If you had not been there, Alexey Ivanovich, then I think one of us would not be going home tonight. Maybe more than one. You are a real hero, my friend."

Alexey went red. "Oh no. No. No. I was just lucky."

At that, Zakhar, who was standing next to Ilya, burst into a torrent of excitable speech, half-Russian, half-English, recounting how Grigori had been the first to rush out of the meeting room after they heard the crash, but before he could draw his gun, he had been knocked out cold by one of the intruders. The man had snatched the gun and shot into the air, screaming at everyone to get back, then the intruders had backed toward the front door. Two of them turned tail and ran, but the third, the gunman, quite deliberately moved toward the terrified employees and aimed his gun straight at them. And it was then Alexey had moved – "like hot lightning!" exclaimed Zakhar – had knocked the gun out of the man's hand, and the breath out of his body. "It was astonishing, magical, like something in a movie! And then a whole swarm of us came at that scum, and knocked him out cold and locked him the bathroom where Igor and Arkady are standing watch over him. But if it hadn't been for Alexey and his judo move ..."

"Zakhar, please don't go on like that," muttered Alexey.

At that moment, red-headed Igor came in and said something to Alexey. "The guy's come to," Alexey told Helen. "They've moved him to the meeting room. I'm sorry, but I'm going to have to leave you for a moment to ..."

"No," said Helen. "I want to be in on this. I want to hear what he says."

"Are you sure?"

"Yes."

He hugged her. "Okay then. *Davai!* Let's do it!"

*

Stripped of his sinister mask, the man on the floor of the meeting room looked a pitiful sight, not at all like the fearsome creature of Helen's imagination. Thin and small, he sat with his knees up, his arms wrapped around them, shaking, his face hidden, his ribs showing under the black pullover, the very model of a strung-out junkie.

Alexey sent everyone out of the room except himself, Helen, Ilya, Sonya and Igor, saying that a crowd of hostile faces would only spook the intruder, and prevent them from getting anything useful out of him. But as Ilya remarked, whether you could trust anything such a man said was questionable. Still, they had to try.

Alexey squatted on the floor, his face level with the man's knees, and said, quietly, a simple Russian phrase that Helen understood perfectly: "Who are you?"

The man didn't reply. Alexey repeated the question. Still no reply. Beside Helen, Sonya clucked impatiently and was about to say something when Alexey reached out a hand and touched one of the man's hands, clenched tight around his knees. The man's head jerked up. Revealed, his face did not belie earlier impressions. Deep-set blue eyes were set in a ravaged, hollow-cheeked face. In a weird echo of Alexey, he whispered, "*Who are you?*" His voice was hoarse, thin, frightened.

Sonya gave a startled exclamation. Before any of the others knew what was happening, she marched over to the intruder. Grabbing him by his stringy hair, she stared into his face. He squealed, but she took no notice. She dropped him and spoke rapidly, excitedly. Alexey looked astonished at first, but Ilya nodded, thoughtfully.

Alexey turned to Helen and said, "Sonya says this man used to work here as a cleaner a couple of years ago. Nikolai Pavlovich fired him when he caught him going through office drawers one night."

"I'd forgotten him," said Ilya, "but Sonya swears it's him. She did not recognize him at first. He has become very thin. But his voice, yes. She says his name's Grisha. She can't remember his last name. But it will be in staff records."

Alexey said, "Sonya said he told Kolya that he'd get even one day. But nobody's seen anything of him for ages."

"But somebody must have found him," said Helen, "and hired him to do this."

"Exactly," said Alexey, grimly. "And now he's going to tell me who that was." He turned back to the man, and spat something at him in which Helen recognized the name "Repin".

A sly smile flitted across the man's face, and he said, very clearly and simply, so even Helen understood it, "*Nyet. Ivan Mikhailovich Makarov.*"

Alexey recoiled as though he'd been struck. Recovering himself, he said something Helen understood instinctively. "What did you say?"

Grisha had an ugly smile on his face. He mimed a phone conversation. He said, "Ivan Mikhailovich, *da.*"

Sonya and Ilya yelled something at him, but Alexey just stared, stricken. Helen said, quickly, "Is he saying your father called him?"

Alexey nodded, numbly.

"Then either he's taunting you or someone put him up to saying that and he really doesn't know who hired him. Look at him, Alexey. He's a junkie. He can't think straight. Ask him who his mates are. We've got to find them." Alexey nodded. "You're right. I'm an idiot, getting spooked by this little rat." He turned back to Grisha, and growled something which Helen took to be a question about the other two.

Grisha didn't answer. Alexey repeated the question. This time, Grisha made an obscene gesture, and Alexey completely lost his cool, and yelling, lunged at the man. Everything happened very fast then as the intruder, driven by blind panic, jumped up and ran straight at the window, shattering it in a shower of exploding glass, his body disappearing into emptiness.

For an instant, no one could move. Then they all raced to the window at the same time as the others, alerted by the noise, burst into the room.

But there was no broken body lying on the pavement below. Instead, Grisha, bloodied but definitely alive, was staggering to his feet. Zakhar, followed by several of the other men, had already sprinted out of the office after him – but too late. For Grisha, driven by desperation, was not about to hang around, and by the time the men appeared in the street, he had already gone. Even so, the fleet-footed Zakhar might have caught up if by bad luck he hadn't run straight into a feisty group of dawdling *babushkas* who weren't going to give ground to anyone, especially not some rude little punk in a rat's tail and a leather jacket! As he recounted ruefully later, he wasted precious seconds squeezing politely past the scolding old ladies and by the time he turned the corner into the boulevard, he was only just in time to see Grisha sprinting across the busy road, to the wild honking of startled drivers. An instant later, he disappeared down the escalator that led into the big underground shopping mall in the square on the other side, and though Zakhar and the others followed in hot pursuit, they lost Grisha almost immediately in the heaving mall crowds.

Chapter 19

Alexey was berating himself. "If only I hadn't lost my temper, he wouldn't have slipped through our fingers. God, what a *durak* I am. What a bloody fool."

"Don't," said Helen. "At least we know who he is."

"Fat lot of good that is," he said, despondently. "He could be anywhere."

Sonya had looked up the staff records, found Grisha's surname – Chekushkin – and an address and phone number for him. Trouble was, when she'd called the number, the woman at the other end said that Chekushkin had moved out of the apartment nearly two years ago. No, she had no idea where he'd gone.

"I'm sure we can find him," Helen said, comfortingly. "That cop – Serebrov – he probably knows all the Moscow low-lifes. Alexey, I know it's not going to be easy to tell Nikolai, but you've *got* to call him."

"I know," said Alexey, glumly.

"I'll go and help clear up while you call him," said Helen, discreetly.

Alexey nodded, and picked up the phone. As she went out of the room, Helen heard him say, "Kolya?" in a here-we-go sort of voice. She gave him a thumbs-up and, closing the door gently behind her, went off to help the others.

In the short time they'd had, the intruders had made an amazing mess, mostly in the reception area, but also in a couple of the offices. They'd violently swept the framed certificates, testimonials and icon off the shelf, wrenched open filing cabinets, torn files up and strewn them around, and overturned Alla's desk, complete with her computer. Helen set to work with others in the reception area, wading through shredded paper, smashed glass, broken computer components and splinters of wood. Nobody spoke much; the adrenaline of the attack and its immediate aftermath had drained away, leaving everyone feeling flat.

She was sweeping up stray pieces of picture frame and glass when she saw it. She almost missed it at first because it was so small. And even when she did spot it, her brain couldn't take it in properly, as she stared at the tiny sliver of blue plastic, with the label on it reading 'Sandisk, 4GB'. *It was a digital camera's memory card.*

She picked it up. She knew she had to tell Alexey at once, without alerting anyone else. She looked around. No one had noticed. Thrusting it out of sight into her pocket, she went to find him.

He was still on the phone, but when she came in, closed the door and he saw the expression on her face, he said, "Wait a moment," and put the phone down.

"What's up, Helen?"

She handed him the memory card. His eyes widened. "Where ..."

"It must have been hidden behind one of those frames and fell out when it got broken."

"My God." He took the card from her. "It's got to be the one."

She swallowed. "Yes. We need to – to see what's on it."

"Yes. Hang on." He picked up the phone again and spoke, rapidly, in Russian. There was Volkovsky's voice at the other end, exclaiming, and then another voice came on the phone – Serebrov's. After a moment, Alexey spoke, a stream of speech that sounded annoyed. Serebrov spoke again and this time Alexey said, "*Da, da,*" and clicking off the phone, put it down. He looked at Helen. "They wanted us to wait until they got here to look at it. I said there was no way we'd wait that long, because even if they manage to get a plane straight away, which I doubt, they're not going to be here for three or four hours at least. And I can't wait that long to know."

She swallowed. "No. What did they say to that?"

"Maxim said we have to be careful. Look at the images but not make any copy of them. No saving to the computer, no printing out. He thinks we should do it away from the office. No one here knows about the Koldun file and he doesn't think they should learn about it. Not yet."

She shot him a glance. He said, "I know, I don't like the implication either. I can't believe – I don't think anyone here is – is *not* to be trusted. But well – I think I'd like to see it first, anyway. Before anyone else does. Except for you," he added, quickly.

"What are we going to do then?" She spoke in a whisper.

"We'll go to my apartment and look at it there. We'll need something to view it on. Not a camera. Screen's too small, and if there are printed files, we'll never be able to read them. We could use the laptop in the apartment to ..."

"Wait," Helen said. "What about one of those digital photo frames? We can view it all but there's no record, no computer footprint or anything. And if we get a good big one, it'll be easy to read documents too."

He smiled. "Great idea. We can buy one in the mall across the road and then get a cab to the apartment. I'll tell the staff we're going out for a while, they don't need to know why."

*

Alexey's large and elegant family apartment, furnished in his father's preferred coolly modern style, was on the top floor of a building on Tverskaya Street, a large central boulevard that is sometimes known as the city's equivalent to the Champs-Élysées, sweeping down with a thunder of traffic and glitter of lights to Red Square and the Kremlin.

The view from the living-room was stunning, but Helen was too preoccupied to do more than only half-notice her surroundings as Alexey let them quickly into the apartment and locked the door behind them. Taking the phone off the hook, and not opening the blinds – on advice from Maxim – they sat on one of the big pale leather sofas. Alexey looked at Helen. There was a hectic light in his eyes, and his white knuckles told of his tension. She put an arm around him and hugged him. "Are you okay?"

He said, tightly, "Yes. I'm fine. Let's do it." He pulled out the big digital photo frame they'd bought and, with slightly shaking fingers, he set it up on the coffee table and inserted the card in the slot.

At first, it seemed like there was nothing. Picture after picture came up blank. And then, quite suddenly, there it was. A page of flowing Cyrillic script. Alexey focused the image. He stared at it. "It's Dad's writing," he said at last. "It's ... weird. It's not at all what I thought – it's like some kind of memoir." Touching a finger to the screen, he translated the lines, slowly. "*So many years since I thought of my father, and yet he has never really left my mind. He was a great man, but there was that about him which did not let me get close. I loved him but I was afraid of him as a child. Only later I understood him better. He did what he had to do without flinching. He was a solitary man, who had been born late to his parents, my grandparents, when they had almost given up hope of a child, and so growing up he had no brothers or sisters and very little other family. I never met his mother, my grandmother, she died before I was born. I remember my grandfather as a stern old man who rarely spoke. We did not often go to his place when I was a child, and my father went alone to his funeral."*

He scrolled on. Another image appeared on the screen. More script. *"If there were secrets in my father's life, I did not know them. That is, I know there were secrets, but they were secrets of his profession, things he wouldn't have told even under torture. But secrets about himself, I do not know. He never had a mistress, of that I am sure. He was not a man for women. Not for men either, I hasten to add, just a solitary man. He had made his choice with my mother, and he stuck to it. To do otherwise might have jeopardized his work, left him open to manipulation, and that was anathema to him. I know nowadays people like him are painted as cruel monsters, but in his own way he had a pure heart, which sought only the good of the motherland. He could not be corrupted, by money or influence or even mercy. With me, however, he was not unkind."*

He scrolled onto the next image. Not script, this time, but print, a paragraph from a book or journal article which had been heavily underlined before it was photographed. Alexey read it out, blankly: *"Disturbing dreams about the dead usually indicate unfinished business with the dead person. More rarely, they may indicate an actual haunting, with a message from beyond that must be deciphered. Even more rarely, they may point to a form of psychic attack, for example, possession, or a curse. If such dreams persist, professional psychic help should be urgently sought to determine an accurate diagnosis."*

They looked at each other. Alexey said, quietly, "This has nothing to do with Trinity. This can't be the Koldun file. It's totally personal. That psychic's business card I found … Dad must have been having dreams about his father. That stuff he wrote – it must have been something he was trying to work out in his own mind. My God, Helen. I had no idea. He never said anything. I wish – I wish he had. It would have made him more – more human. More approachable. I could have understood, if he'd only trusted me with it."

Helen put an arm around him. "You don't know what he was going to do with this. Maybe he was writing it down for you. Maybe he was going to give you this, if he'd had time."

"But why hide it, Helen? That's what I don't understand. Why hide it at all if ..." He broke off, with a startled exclamation. The next image had appeared. It wasn't handwritten and it wasn't a memoir, but a typewritten cover sheet.

"What is it, Alexey?" she said.

"Helen, I was wrong. Quite wrong. This is it. Listen." He pointed at the screen, and read out, translating, *Koldun Psychic Unit, First Planning Meeting. Present: I. M. Makarov, S. D. Galkin, S. G. Barsukov.* My God, Helen, it wasn't just *one* sorcerer they were planning to employ. They were putting together *an entire psychic unit*!"

"Freaking hell," breathed Helen.

"That date – that was a few months before Galkin died," said Alexey, scrolling to the next page, which was back to handwriting. "Let's see what they – oh *shit*!"

"What's up?"

He pointed at the screen. "They're not proper words. More like a jumbled collection of letters – and see – numbers here too. It looks like some sort of code." He scrolled on to the next image, but it was similar, and so was the next and the next and the next at least ten or fifteen pages after.

"That's all we bloody need," Alexey exclaimed. "Can't make head or tail of this stuff. Never was any good at puzzles and crosswords and things. How about you?"

"Not great either." Helen thought rapidly. "But look – I've got this idea – I saw a film once where spies made a really tough code using a particular book or something as a key. They took bits out of it and jumbled the letters around and the numbers referred to pages, something like that."

"Trouble is," said Alexey, sighing, "if Dad and his partners did use a book code, it's just about unbreakable, unless by some miracle you can find out what book they were using as a key. And if only they knew that, then it's going to be just about bloody impossible. I mean, we'd have to wade through just about every book they might have read or have on their shelves or ..."

"Or there might be a clue somewhere on this card," said Helen, thoughtfully. "For example, what about that extract you read out before, about dreams? Maybe if we can find out what book it came from – like maybe if we put that extract into Google and see what comes up."

"Yeah," said Alexey, "it'd be great if it could be as easy as that. But somehow I doubt it. Let's see if there's anything more on the card first."

He scrolled on. Blank image. Another blank. Another, and another. And then suddenly, there was a photo.

Not a written item, this time, but an actual picture. A bizarre but oddly beautiful photo, of a man's face, rather out of focus, but gazing steadily at them, behind a wash of brilliant colors in a kind of halo effect all around and over his head – pale yellows, reds and purples, with irregular black spots at intervals.

Alexey said, blankly, "That's Dad."

He scrolled on. Another similar photo. The same man's face, still out of focus, behind a veil, a wash of color. The next was similar. Each photo was slightly different, with the colors changing shade a little, but otherwise they were all exactly the same format.

Helen said, "What on earth are they?"

"Kirlian photographs," said Alexey, quietly.

"Kir what?"

"Kirlian photographs. Named after the Russian guy who invented them, Semyon Kirlian. I forget exactly when it was but I think it was in the 1930s or '40s that he discovered a strange photographic process. It doesn't use an ordinary camera but connects electric voltage to an object – living or non-living – on a photographic plate. The image created then shows all those colors."

"Wow, that's amazing," she said. "Very artistic."

"It wasn't about art. Kirlian thought it proved the existence of auras. Everyone's supposed to have one. They're invisible to most people, but it's a rainbow of colors that comes off you. That's supposed to show the inner you. Your health, your emotional state, your spiritual state. It's your – presence, if you like. Your psychic signature. And each color means something – each shade is supposed to be a pointer to something going on inside you. There are psychics who specialize in reading them, either from what they can see of your aura, directly – or from interpreting a Kirlian photo-graph." He shook his head and stared at the image on the screen. "Heaps of people go to aura-readers here. But I never in my wildest dreams would have imagined Dad, of all people ... *Why* would he want a photograph of his aura?"

"Because of those dreams," she said.

"You might be right. But it's just so ... hell, after all this I feel more than ever that I never really knew him at all." He paused. "Well, we'd better have a look at what else is there, I suppose."

The next image was blank, and the next, and the next, and so on for a few more, until suddenly, up came an image with a sign reading "Quick Time Movie". It was one of those short videos you can take with a digital camera. But there was a problem.

"The display thing won't play it," Helen said, "you need a computer for that. Or a camera," she added, excitedly.

"Mine's got a card the same size so it should fit. Hang on, I'll get it out of my bag."

She ejected her card and inserted the Koldun card. Turning on the camera, she clicked rapidly through the images, with Alexey looking over her shoulder. The "Quick Time Movie" logo appeared. Helen said, "Ready?"

He nodded. She pressed "play." And the video started.

There was a bird, in a little cage that was sitting on a table. The camera zoomed in on it; an ordinary bird, a sparrow, actually, sitting on a perch, hopping nervously about. A second or so of that, and then suddenly the sparrow stood stock still, staring. It began to twitch, to jerk – and then it fell off the perch, crumpling into a pitiful little bundle of feathers at the bottom of the cage. And then the video ended.

There was a stunned silence, then Alexey said, blankly, "That was deliberate – the bird, it looked like … like it was poisoned, and just, just … to watch it die, to make a video of it … It's revolting. Oh my God. Why – *why* would he have done that?"

Helen's stomach churned. She faltered, "You – you don't know *who* made that video. You can't see the person behind the camera."

"No," he said, sadly, "but it's on Dad's card. It's got to be him."

She looked at his stricken face, their eyes met and she knew what he wanted her to do. Picking up the camera, she brought up the video, looked at him again and, when he nodded, she clicked the delete button. And the horrible little video was gone. Forever.

Alexey took her in his arms. Kissed her, fiercely, desperately, without a word. And she didn't speak either, but kissed him back, her arms around his neck, his heart pounding against her chest.

Presently, he sat up and said, very quietly, "Thank you."

"What for?" she said, lightly.

He smiled. "For understanding. For being right."

She smiled back. "Careful. I might hold you to that." She paused, and said in a rush, "Alexey – I – I think we shouldn't mention that clip to anyone. Not ever." The vision of that poor little bundle of feathers came into her mind and she shuddered. "I think we should ... try and forget it."

He looked at her, for a heartbeat of time. Then he nodded, and the last of the shadow vanished from his face. "Yes. Of course. We must."

Chapter 20

Maxim hated flying. Nobody knew, because he'd never told anybody, and when he had to fly – which was rare, thank God, because of police budgets – he had learned to hide his anxiety to such an extent that not even Marina had ever realized it, attributing his reluctance to take the package holidays she dreamed of to his miserliness, another of her complaints about him. Now he sat with a stolid face and still hands in the narrow, uncomfortable seat, the very picture of Zen-like calm. Because of their last-minute booking, he and Volkovsky had had to take separate seats rows apart, and so he was wedged in between a preoccupied Italian-suited businessman fiddling with his briefcase, and a long-legged teenage boy plunged in a fat book with a lurid cover of vampires and werewolves. Trying to distract himself from his discomfort and the cold churning of his stomach, he turned over in his mind the events of the last couple of days, and what they might mean.

The Petersburg incident had puzzled him from the start. Yes, it was true that Boris Repin was known to be an aggressive acquirer of shares in other people's businesses, by way of extortion, bribery, blackmail, mysterious fires, assault and intimidation of all sorts, so trashing an office would be right up his street. But he usually limited his attentions to certain types of business – up and coming restaurants, new clubs, small building firms. Easy prey. Trinity was a quite different proposition. Sure, young Makarov might be a less formidable opponent than his father, and sure, he might not have as many connections; but would Repin take the risk? Maxim's feeling that it was out of character for Repin only grew as he talked to the Trinity staff, and viewed the security footage of the incident.

His thought that Repin's thugs wouldn't announce that they were delivering a message from their boss had been backed up by his friend Zaitsev in the Petersburg police. They wouldn't need to, Zaitsev had said. For Repin's heavies did not go about masked and disguised. No, quite the opposite – their faces were well-known, for that was part of Repin's hold on potential targets. If you saw those ugly mugs in your doorway, you'd know what to expect, if you didn't do what the crime boss wanted. But though Zaitsev agreed this could be a sign that this incident wasn't of Repin's doing, he also cautioned against Maxim ruling it out altogether. "They say only the grave cures the hunchback," he said, "but you and I both know, Maxim, that you can never rule out the unexpected. And if young Makarov's right and Repin was behind one of the takeover offers he received, then Repin's ambitions have diversified, so why not change tactics, too? Perhaps he thinks this sort of thing would frighten the eggheads in Trinity more. Sinister black clothes, balaclavas, gloves – the whole silly caboodle that whizz kids like that would be familiar with from movies."

That was true. More than one of the shocked workers had even *said* how it was just like in the movies. Simultaneously alarmed and excited, they weren't the easiest or most reliable of witnesses to interview, and he was glad that Volkovsky had offered to sit in, because his knowledge of the staff might help in clarifying Maxim's own mind, and dispel the nagging suspicion that somebody knew more than they were letting on.

Volkovsky had told him that the Petersburg office had a different focus to that of Moscow, not only more high-tech, but also handling most of the foreign clients. It was a smaller staff than in Moscow, mostly young – the oldest, the manager, Feodor, having only just turned thirty-five. They were fluent in more than one language – English, German, French, Danish – and up to date and sophisticated, except when it came to knowledge of the underworld of their own city, in which they appeared to be innocent babes in arms. Except for Feodor. And the nightwatchman, Andrei.

Maxim had checked all the staff. Nothing jumped out at him. He'd had his suspicions about Andrei at first, until Zaitsev told him that the man's uncle had been one of Repin's victims, and that Andrei would no more do Repin's work than he would cut off his right arm.

But though the feeling of a false note, somewhere, persisted, Maxim had got nowhere in pinning down where the source might be, and Zaitsev's informers hadn't yet come up with any proof of Repin's involvement or lack of it. In the city's underworld, there were whispers about what had happened, but nobody knew the truth of it. Repin ran a tight ship. But even if the Petersburg attack wasn't down to him, Zaitsev said, once Repin heard about it, he'd be weighing up his options – find and punish the cheeky beggar who'd taken his name in vain, or allow people to think it *was* him, for his own reasons. "What's more, even if this isn't down to him, it might well give him ideas," Zaitsev said, "which could be the worst outcome for Trinity. So tell them to beware."

Which was exactly what Maxim had told Volkovsky, as they'd sat comparing notes in a hotel bar the previous evening. "Repin and his like are sharks attracted by the scent of blood – they scent weakness – and it's striking that from what you and the others have told me, in the past you have not had such incidents. But now …"

"This is the first serious incident," said Volkovsky, defensively. "The other things – the calls, the attempted break-in – they were minor. Very minor."

"Yes, but it's escalating, and you know that, Nikolai Pavlovich. In the old days, nobody would have dared. I know you're doing your best to keep a lid on things, but from the outside it must look like Trinity's lost its way with your impulsive young dreamer of a godson who, it might be said, doesn't understand what he's doing and has made the company fair game."

"Oh no, no, no," said Volkovsky, firmly. "People who think that are quite wrong. Alexey may be young, yes, but then so was his father when he started Trinity. And he's a lot like his father." He smiled, thinly. "And people like Repin – or whoever's behind this – will learn that soon enough."

"Then what about the girl?" asked Maxim.

"What about her?"

"How long has he known her?"

"Not long. He met her just a few days ago. Love at first sight, he told me." He smiled. "She is very beautiful. And my godson has a passionate nature. It's all or nothing, for him."

"That doesn't worry you?"

"No. He's been through a difficult time. And he's been thinking too much about Trinity, not enough of himself. A romantic fling won't do him any harm."

"Nikolai Pavlovich, even from the little I observed, it can hardly be called a fling. They seemed exceptionally close."

Volkovsky said, drily, "My friend, they are young. In love. They think it'll last forever. Don't you remember what that's like?"

Maxim ignored this. "He's the owner of Trinity. And in a short space of time, she has become very close to him, so close he lets her in on his business secrets. And when I arrived and she realized I was a policeman, she seemed bothered, to say the least. It all makes me feel unsettled."

Volkovsky burst out laughing. "Maxim Antonovich, you speak as though she were some kind of spy! Some sort of honeytrap."

"It has been known to happen," said the policeman, stiffly.

"Not in this case. She was bothered to see you, as you say, because she'd seen you before, Maxim. Skulking in her lane in the middle of the night."

For an instant Maxim had no idea what Volkovsky was talking about. Then he realized. He said, defensively, "I couldn't sleep. Went for a drive. What the hell was she doing anyway, spying out of her windows that time of night?"

Volkovsky shook his head, smiling. "You are a stubborn man, my friend. But I can assure you that Helen is exactly what she appears to be." He paused. "You see, as soon as Lyosha spoke so glowingly of her to me, I had her checked out discreetly by Pasha – Pavel Dutov, that is, our senior investigator in Moscow. Everything is fine. I also had Pasha check out the *bona fides* of the person at whose place she's staying at – Professor Bayeva Simmons – and that checks out too. She's a respected American academic with expertise in folklore, who's writing a book about bears in Russian history and myth."

"Does your godson know you made these checks?"

"Of course not. He'd be furious if he knew. But I don't leave things to chance. Not with all we have at stake in Trinity. Not after what happened to Ivan Mikhailovich and the others."

"I'm glad to hear it," said Maxim, tightly.

Volkovsky grinned. "Listen, friend, let the young be young! If they want to believe in the beautiful myth of true love – who are we to disillusion them? Life will do it to them soon enough. Now, then – how about another glass of that excellent Georgian wine?"

*

Now, Maxim thought, staring straight ahead of him as the plane dipped and began to make its descent toward Moscow, events this morning in Trinity's head office had proved both that things were escalating, and that Alexey had plenty of courage. Even if he had also made a grave error putting the intruder in the meeting room. But who was to know Grisha would take a header through a glass window? That was the sort of thing that happened in movies. The only time Maxim had seen it happen, the fool who had tried it had ended up smashed to pieces on the pavement, his throat pierced by broken glass. He didn't know Grisha Chekushkin – in a city the size of Moscow, no individual could possibly know the name of every inhabitant of the underworld, especially if he was small fry – but he'd make it his business to find out now.

Volkovsky had told him Chekushkin apparently had a good record when the cleaning firm that had the contract for the Trinity offices had hired him. But six months after he started working shifts at the office, and not long after Galkin's death, Volkovsky had caught the cleaner red-handed, snooping in Barsukov's office, and sacked him on the spot. It was then discovered that he'd falsified several of his references, and had a hidden drinking problem, though he'd never been drunk at work. The embarrassed cleaning firm had not only barred him from any further employment with them, but also put the word out to other firms that he was not to be trusted. "I don't know what happened to him after that," Volkovsky said.

Maxim could imagine what might have. With no qualifications and a black mark against his name, Grisha

185

would have found it impossible to get a legitimate job. That left illegitimate ones, of which there were plenty. And drugs to add to the drinking. All in all, an unsavory character at the end of his tether, an unpredictable quantity on a job like he'd been sent on today. It made it even less likely that Repin was orchestrating these attacks against Trinity, for the gangster might be brutal, but he wasn't stupid. You asked for trouble, the wrong sort of trouble, employing drug-addled types like Chekushkin. And the claim that the ghost of Alexey's father had employed him didn't stack up with Repin's style, either. He didn't play those sorts of games. It might just have been a stupid random idea of Chekushkin's to hide the real identity of the man who'd hired him. But it was more likely that whoever had hired him had given that name deliberately, to rattle Alexey.

The striking thing was, though, that the Moscow thugs, like their counterparts in Petersburg, had shown no sign of knowing about the existence of the Koldun file. They didn't ask for it to be produced. They didn't try to search the office. They'd been sent to trash and terrorize. So that meant whoever had hired them didn't know about it either. Which meant, Maxim thought, either that *my theory about the Koldun file being the key to the murders was wrong, or we are dealing with two unrelated criminal plots, and two criminal masterminds. One the murderer, one the vandal. One aware of the Koldun file, the other one not. One, seeking to scare Alexey into giving up Trinity. The other, killing the three directors for a motive as yet shadowy. Two criminals, with two different motives. All in all a most frustratingly complicated prospect,* thought Maxim ruefully, as the wheels landed smoothly on the runway.

*

But a little later, in the Makarov apartment with Volkovsky, he cast such speculations aside as Alexey scrolled through the astonishing images on the screen. Beside him, Volkovsky kept uttering exclamations; but Maxim said nothing. Inside him, though, excitement was growing. He'd been right. Not only was the secret file a reality, but he felt more sure than ever that somehow it was the key to the murders. The vague rumor of "something big brewing" that the man Lebedev had mentioned – and he hadn't been found yet, either – was not just a rumor. The Koldun psychic unit hadn't been set up within "official" Trinity. But it was possible it had been operating separately, part of the "shadow side" of Trinity that had already been hinted at by the staff. But whatever the outcome, the psychic's visiting card Alexey had remembered was most interesting, more immediately interesting to Maxim than the reams of coded pages which he knew were likely to take a long time to break.

Alexey had told him about their idea of the book on dreams, or whatever it was, being a possible clue, but also that though they'd searched on Google using the extract, so far they had not found a match, either from a book or a journal. Privately, Maxim rather doubted that the key would turn out to be so simple. He had his own idea about where to start, and after a time, he got up and said, "This is all very interesting, but in the meantime we are forgetting about another important lead."

"And what's that?" said Volkovsky, vaguely, still staring at the pages of code as though he'd crack it by sheer willpower.

"Grisha Chekushkin," said Maxim, calmly. "He might still give us some valuable information, if he can be found. I can track him down through the department's records. If you'll excuse me, I will take my leave of you and start on the search right away."

"Excellent," said Volkovsky, absently, his eyes turning back to the screen, as if he couldn't tear his eyes off it. "We will be waiting for you here."

*

Despite what he'd said, Maxim hadn't gone to track down Grisha Chekushkin. First, he called in a favor from a pal in immigration and asked him to run certain checks. Then he called records at CID and got them to run Chekushkin's name through the system and to text him the last known address. The man's name hadn't come up at all during the Trinity case, so the inquiry would set off no alarm bells, even if by some remote chance either Korolev or the Organized Crime Unit types got to hear of it.

And then there was the most important thing. The idea that had almost instantly come to him as he sat looking at the Koldun file. The *ekstrasens* who had come to see him in his office, before Makarov's death, the one who had made the claims about dark forces and Makarov: he'd dismissed her at the time, of course – anyone would have – but only a fool never changed his mind. He had to speak to her.

The *ekstrasens*, Anna Feodorovna Dorskova, who went by the professional name of Skorpia, lived in a shabby block of apartments in a northern suburb at the end of one of the Metro lines. He hadn't expected her to live in a place like this, he thought, as he made his way up the dirty stairs to her third-floor apartment (the elevator being out of order). She had given him to understand business was going well. But then, these sorts of people were born liars, weren't they?

When she opened the door to him, he saw at once that she recognized him. He also saw she didn't want to let him in, but no citizen would dare to shut the door in the face of a policeman – not unless that citizen was wealthy and influential, that is. And poor Skorpia was clearly neither.

"I am sorry to disturb you, Anna Feodorovna, but I need to speak to you," he said, more gently than he'd intended.

She raised an eyebrow. "Really? You couldn't wait to get me out of your office last time."

He was glad she still had some spirit. He said, quietly, "I may have missed something, and I need to check with you. Can I come in?"

She gave a little laugh. "As if I have a choice!" But she led him into her living-room, or rather the niche off her kitchen that functioned as that. Her apartment was small and shabby, and she herself looked thinner, jumpier, the hard gloss worn off her since last year, when she'd sashayed so confidently into his office, all blonde hair and tight skirt and killer heels. A little younger than him – in her late thirties – she was still a nice-looking woman, but nothing like the vamp of last year. The blonde had grown out and faded to an ordinary light brown, the dark eyes were a little bloodshot, her simple skirt and top were workaday rather than glamorous, and she was holding a cigarette in thin fingers, the first of two or three she smoked while he was there. Her kitchen table was covered with a velvet cloth, and on it was a neat stack of Tarot cards, a pendulum, a divining rod, and other bits and pieces, the usual clutter of her trade.

"So, how may I help you today, Senior Lieutenant?" she said, in an ironic tone, motioning him to sit down.

He didn't beat about the bush. "Your story about Ivan Makarov and the sorcerer – you lied, didn't you?"

She went red and jumped up, knocking her half-smoked cigarette off the ashtray. "Is that what you've come to do? To persecute me?"

"Not at all," he said, calmly. "Answer the question. You lied, didn't you? Not about the sorcerer or Ivan

Makarov – but about *how you knew*. You pretended to see it when you put your hand on his photograph. But that was hokum, wasn't it? You just didn't want to say that years ago he had come to you as a client. And that you persuaded him there was some kind of sorcery at work on him."

From red, she went white. She sat down, heavily. She picked up her cigarette and took a long draw on it. She whispered, "How – how do you know?"

"New information has come to light," he said, coldly, watching her face. "Well?"

"I – it wasn't persuasion. It was ... seeing. A vision." She swallowed, looked away. "And it wasn't me."

He stared at her. "What do you mean?"

"It wasn't me. I – I just used the story."

"Whose story?"

"A – a friend of mine."

"Another psychic?"

She nodded.

"Who? And why didn't she –"

"*He*, Senior Lieutenant," she corrected.

"Well, why didn't he come forward himself?"

She gave a thin smile. "Lev was troubled about it, but he wouldn't have talked to the police. It wasn't his style."

"Wait a minute. You say *wasn't*. Past tense. Does that mean ..."

"Yes. He's dead." She swallowed. "Regrettable accident, they *said*. Lost his footing on Metro escalators, broke his neck. At the time, I thought it was true. He was old, you see, and there was no reason to suppose then that anything else had happened. But then *he* came round."

Maxim was getting confused. "Who came round?"

"Ivan Makarov, of course."

"*What?*"

"Yes, Senior Lieutenant, Ivan Makarov came to see me a few days after my ... after the story appeared in the paper. He wanted to know how I knew ... He didn't ask gently."

"He assaulted you?"

"Gave me a slap or two. I'm not brave, Detective. I told him. And then he said –" She paused. Her fingers shaking, she lit another cigarette from the stub of the last one. "Then he asked me who else I'd told about Lev. I said no one. He said I must have done. That he had tried to protect Lev, but someone had still got to him. But I knew he was lying."

"What do you mean?"

"The wolf hires himself out cheaply as a shepherd," she said.

Maxim knew the proverb, and its meaning. "You think he was hinting he'd had your friend murdered?"

"Of course. He was a clever man. He'd never admit it outright. But he was letting me know, so I'd understand. Would keep my mouth shut. And so I did. What else could I do?"

"You could have come to me."

She laughed without humor. "That's a good joke, after how you treated me last time."

"You cannot blame me for your own failure," he said, tightly. His phone beeped at that moment with a text message. It was the office with Grisha's address. He went on, "I understand you were afraid of Makarov. But he's been dead for months now. You could have come forward. He can't touch you anymore."

"Can't he?"

"For God's sake, you're not telling me you believe that a ghost can –"

"You forget my profession," she said, with a rare flash of humor. "I am bound to believe in all kinds of things. But no, I am not talking about a ghost. Or not in the ordinary way. If

Ivan Makarov was a *koldun,* a sorcerer, then you know what they say about sorcery even outlasting death."

Maxim's scalp prickled as his whole understanding shifted. "Makarov was a sorcerer *himself?*"

She looked puzzled. "I thought you said you knew."

"I only know the bare bones," he said, blandly. "Not the full extent. Tell me exactly what you know."

"Lev knew almost at once that Makarov had a latent psychic power. Something that had only just begun to emerge, but that could be powerful if its full energies could be unblocked. You see, though psychic power usually manifests itself when you're young, in rare cases it can manifest later in life, often in very driven people." She saw his raised eyebrow, and misinterpreted it. "If you don't believe what I'm saying, then I don't see why you …"

"It's not my job to believe or not," said Maxim, calmly. "It's my job to investigate. Continue. Please."

"Very well. A sudden letting-go of that focus may then allow the psychic energies to start flowing through. And that can be very dangerous, because if you have grown up with your psychic power, you gradually get used to it. But a sudden discovery like that, later in life – it can knock you right off balance. You must learn to channel the energies into some-thing constructive, or God knows what might happen."

Maxim thought of the Koldun file. Was setting up a psychic spying unit in your own company a constructive way of channeling your new energy? Aloud, he said, "There was no doubt in your friend's mind, then?"

"Oh no. None at all. Lev was very gifted in recognizing these things. He was the real thing, you see." She added, quietly, "Not like me. I mean, I do have some – some slight gift, and I dress it up, I admit. A good deal of our work is psychological. Summing up people quickly. Understanding little signals they're not even aware they give off. But Lev

– he was extraordinary. He really saw into people's hearts. Their souls."

Maxim said, uncomfortably, "If he knew so much, why didn't he foresee his own death?"

"Ah. The age-old skeptics' question. Think of it this way. Even the best of us are only given incomplete knowledge. The gift is not a guarantee. It doesn't give you access to everything. How could it? If we had such power, we'd be gods then – or demons."

He looked at her. She smiled. "You're thinking how surprising it is that a charlatan like me should make so much sense."

He couldn't help starting. She smiled again, and crushed out her cigarette. "I told you, any *ekstrasens* who hopes to make a living must have a little skill in reading people."

He said, harshly, "Tell me *exactly* what Lev told you about Ivan Makarov. And when he told you."

She looked at him. "You must promise not to say you heard this from me."

He shrugged. "I assure you I am not in the habit of divulging informants' names." He saw her mutinous expression. "All right. I give you my word."

She said, "Very well. Lev told me after Galkin's death. There was a picture in the paper of the three directors. Lev recognized Makarov. He said he'd come to see him once. He didn't know who he was – Makarov had given a false name – but he remembered the face. And what happened."

"Why exactly did Makarov come to your friend?" This would prove if she was telling the truth, he thought.

"Because of the bad dreams."

"Bad dreams?" he said, casually. "He was a tough businessman."

"Some dreams are unbearable. Even for tough businessmen. Maybe even for tough policemen," she added, ironically.

"What were the dreams about?"

"I don't know, other than they were about someone who had – passed on. And that I only know because Lev also had a … a reputation for reaching the dead, for understanding their messages."

"I see," he said, coolly. "A man of many talents."

She didn't rise to the bait. "He was. But he saw at once, when he was in trance. The dreams weren't the cause, but the *symptom* of the crisis in the man's nature. He wasn't being *literally* haunted by a ghost. He wasn't under a curse or under a psychic attack from someone else. No. The true cause was the power, blocked. The power of the sorcerer. That had passed to him through the blood."

Maxim looked at her. He thought of the pages of things he'd seen, and Ivan Makarov's halting, awkward words about his father. He thought of KGB Major Mikhail Petrovich Makarov's fearsome reputation. Could they have been more than natural, those cruel talents of his? A coldness swept over his body briefly as he said, "How did Makarov react?"

"He took to the idea with remarkable calm, apparently. As if – something had clicked inside him. Lev said he'd never seen anything like it."

"And then?"

"Makarov asked whether Lev could tell him more. How should he use this power? How great was it? Things like that. Lev told him that wasn't his province. Makarov would have to go to other people for more information. And to work on things himself, in his own time. But Lev warned him to be careful. Not to make sudden changes in his life, but to allow himself to discover the energy slowly, to release it constructively. Eventually, he'd come to understand what he needed to do."

"And?"

"And that was it. Lev never saw him again."

"Are you sure? Makarov didn't come back and offer him a job?"

She stared at him. "A job? No."

"You are quite sure?"

"Of course I'm sure."

"When did your friend Lev die?"

She answered, promptly, "June last year. The fifteenth of June."

"Two months before Barsukov's death, then."

"Yes. But like I told you, at the time I never thought that there was any connection. He was old. The escalators are long, steep. He slipped. It happens. Or so I thought. Until Makarov came calling."

Suddenly, he felt very sorry for her. He said, gently, "I can look into the case. Into your friend's death."

She looked quickly at him. "Thank you. But there's no point. The man who had him killed is dead."

"We don't know for sure it was Makarov. It might still be worth checking out. What was Lev's full name and date of birth?"

"His surname was Kirov. Lev Grigorevich Kirov. I don't know his exact date of birth, but he was nearly eighty when he died. A grand old age. Not many of us live to that age."

"Mmm," said Maxim. "And his old address and phone number?"

She gave it to him, and he wrote it down, though now the man was dead, it wouldn't be of much use. "Did he have a visiting card? A business card, I mean?"

"Yes," she said. "But it wasn't much good. Done on the cheap, you know. On one of those old-fashioned Roneo machines. I kept at him to change it, but he wouldn't. He was unworldly, poor Lev. Didn't realize these days you needed something showier."

Flimsy paper, smudged type, Roneo style, he thought, remembering Alexey's description. Yes. There could be no lingering doubt it was Lev Kirov whom Alexey's father had gone to see. Getting up, he said, "Anna Feodorovna, I must go. But I'd like to thank you. You have been very helpful indeed, and I had no right to expect that."

She shot him a surprised look. But all she said was, "You're welcome."

"One more thing – your kind of people. You must know a great many."

"*My* kind of people?" she said, with a raised eyebrow.

Maxim said, quickly, "Sorry. I mean, psychics. Witches. Wizards. Aura-readers. Healers. And ..."

"Et cetera," she finished, deftly. "Yes, Senior Lieutenant, I do."

"I'd like a list of the people in Moscow that you consider best in each ... special field."

Her eyes were sharp. "Yes. A wealthy businessman like Makarov would only have gone to the best to follow up on his discovery. And what about the tendency?" He looked confused, so she added, "White magic, or black magic?"

He swallowed. What *was* he getting himself into? If anyone in the department found out about this, he'd be a laughing-stock. "Er – both."

"Very well."

He took his notebook out of his pocket, scribbled down his name and cell phone number. "Call me when it's ready. And please ..."

"I know. Don't tell anyone," she finished for him, with a smile. "You can count on me for that, Senior Lieutenant Serebrov."

*

On his way to Chekushkin's place, Maxim's phone rang. It was his pal in immigration, with the information he'd asked for.

"The girl Helen Anna Clement came into the country with her mother direct from Britain about two weeks ago," said the man. "Their visa expires in four weeks. The girl has never been to Russia before. Her mother, however, has been before, there is a record of a visa for her about two years ago."

Maxim's ears pricked up. "Did the mother fly direct from Britain back then? Or France, perhaps?"

"I thought you'd ask that, so I checked. She didn't come straight from Britain. Or France. And she didn't fly. She came in by train."

"Did she come in to Petersburg from Finland by any chance?" said Maxim, eagerly. Finland was where Galkin had been killed, and the time frame was right.

"No. Into Moscow, overland from Belarus and Poland."

Maxim thanked him and rang off. So that was it, then. Well, it had only been a possibility, he thought, as he turned into the street where Chekushkin lived.

If Skorpia's apartment block had been shabby, this one was positively grim. With its facade riddled with concrete cancer, entrance awash with a tide of trash, including used syringes, dirty stairwell walls graffitied with obscene messages, it was the kind of place Maxim knew only too well, though he hadn't been to this particular block before. Climbing wearily up the filthy stairs to the second floor – of course the elevator was not working here either, probably vandalized beyond repair years ago – he was thinking this would be a wild goose chase for Grisha would have made himself scarce, if he knew what was good for him. But when he got there and saw the splintered door, he knew, even before he saw the body sprawled on the ragged armchair like a grotesque rag doll, its throat cut from ear to ear, that Grisha Chekushkin hadn't even had the most elementary notion of what was good for him.

Chapter 21

"He'd been dead for some time. At least three, maybe four hours before I found him. Even if I'd gone straight there, he'd have been dead."

Helen watched the detective's face as he spoke. He was speaking in English, clipped, unhurried, apparently calmly. Not a flicker of emotion, not a hint as to his thoughts could be read in his expression. Or rather, lack of it. It made her feel even more uneasy.

Volkovsky said, sharply, "But *why* didn't you go straight there?"

Serebrov was unruffled. "I thought he'd keep. And there were other things I wanted to check. The psychic your father consulted," he went on, turning to Alexey. "I found out who he was."

"How ..." began Volkovsky, but Alexey cut him off, impatiently. "Who was it? Did you go to see him? What did he say to you?"

There was a pause. Then Serebrov said, slowly, "He was an old man named Lev Kirov. But he didn't say anything to me." Another pause. "Because he was dead."

They all stared at him. Alexey said, blankly, "I don't understand. Did you find him too?"

"No. He died at least eighteen months ago. Before Barsukov's death. Accident apparently. But I suspect otherwise. He was murdered."

"By the same person who killed my father and his partners?"

"Perhaps. But there are – other possibilities." His steady gaze met Alexey's, who went pale.

"You don't mean … that my father – had him kill –"

Volkovsky broke in, angrily, "This is mere unfounded speculation. I demand you withdraw this outrageous accusation."

Serebrov smiled, faintly. "I did not accuse anyone of anything. I merely stated that there were other possibilities."

But Helen knew he'd meant to stir things up. Deliberately, to see what happened. A sense of dread crept over her. What was he up to?

Alexey said, quietly, "But why? Why for God's sake would he – why would *anyone* want to kill a psychic they'd gone to see about a dream?"

"Because of what the dream revealed," said the policeman, grimly. "Because of what Kirov told him. Your father became convinced he had a latent psychic power. Something that came down to him from the blood. That had been blocked most of his life because of his single-mined focus on his company. But that was now emerging."

There was a stunned silence as three pairs of eyes stared at Maxim. Then Volkovsky said, disbelievingly, "You surely cannot mean that Koldun refers to – to *Ivan Mikhailovich*? That he thought he was – a – a *sorcerer*?"

"Yes," said the policeman, simply.

"Good God, man, that's ridiculous," began Volkovsky, but Alexey interrupted him. He was very pale, but his voice was steady as he said, "How do you know that?"

"I have my information," said the policeman, watching him, Helen thought, like a cat watches a mouse.

"And – is there … is there any doubt in your mind as to the – accuracy of this information?"

"Not the slightest."

Alexey sighed. Then he said, quietly, sadly, "I see."

Helen hated to see him so cast down, and it made her say sharply, "Aren't you jumping to conclusions, Senior Lieutenant? Alexey's father might well have believed he was a sorcerer, but that doesn't make him a murderer! I'd have thought if he'd really wanted to – to hide his secret – he'd surely have got rid of this Kirov person at the beginning, when he was told about it. The fact that he didn't suggests, doesn't it, that this man and his knowledge was no danger to him."

Serebrov's attention turned to her. His hazel eyes had a strange gleam to them. He said, softly, "Well thought-out, Miss Clement. But I'm afraid that my information suggests otherwise."

"Your information, your information!" she said, fiercely. "You keep repeating that, but you won't tell us where you got it from. Who was it exactly who tried to pin Kirov's death on Alexey's father?"

His eyes weren't friendly. "None of your business."

Her fists clenched. She burst out, "But it's *Alexey's*! Why should we trust your informant – or you, come to that? If you really wanted to get at the truth, you would have gone to find that creep Grisha at once. You say he would've been dead anyway, but we've only got your word for that!"

The policeman's face was no longer impassive, his hostility clearly showing. But he said quietly enough, "That is not so. After I found him, I called the ambulance, and the uniformed police. It will be in their report."

"You don't get out of it so –" Helen began, angrily, but Alexey put a hand tenderly on her shoulder, interrupting her.

"It's all right, darling, we've got to hear it all." He turned to Serebrov, and said, firmly, "What did your informant actually say?"

"That your father issued certain threats."

"To Kirov?" said Alexey.

"No. To my informant. But he did mention Kirov's death." Another pause. "To be fair, it was, however, rather ambiguous. Whatever you might think, I do not keep a closed mind on this –"

"Like hell," Helen muttered, under her breath.

"And so I think Miss Clement is most likely right and your father had nothing to do with Kirov's death," went on Serebrov, his glance flickering over her. "The timing of his death, between Galkin's and Barsukov's, suggests that whoever killed Kirov suspected he might know something about Galkin's death. Now that could have been Barsukov – and it could have been your father – but I don't think it was either." He turned to Volkovsky. "I think that's where Grisha and Kirov are connected."

"What do you mean?" said Volkovsky, sounding startled.

"In the matter of timing – because you caught Grisha snooping in Barsukov's office not long after Galkin's death, didn't you?"

"Yes."

"Well, perhaps Grisha found something in Barsukov's office that identified Kirov, and tipped off whoever was responsible for Galkin's death. Or maybe he was even contracted to kill him. Grisha Chekushkin had no visible means of support but he had plenty of money for drugs. Hard drugs. And he was moving in criminal circles, that's certain. To me, the murder of Lev Kirov provides a link between the partners' deaths and the attacks on the Trinity offices both here and in Petersburg. It was a link that, to be frank, I couldn't see before I knew about Kirov. I had almost become convinced we had two separate criminal plots here – the murders, and the vandalism. But now I'm sure it's not the case. It's all connected. We are dealing here with one criminal, and a very dangerous, flexible and devious one, with a good many resources at his disposal. Somebody who's not afraid to change his method, who plans carefully, is patient and impulsive by turns, whenever it suits. Something else has been made clear to me now – I had an instinct the Koldun file would prove crucial, but now I think it is absolutely central. It is at the dark heart of this case, I am convinced of it."

Helen shivered, remembering what she'd felt, holding that memory card in her hand, the feeling that it was evil.

Alexey said, "But how? I mean, yes, if my father – if he really was – or thought he was – a … a sorcerer, that's one thing. For him to plan setting up a psychic unit based on that discovery, okay. I get that. But to *kill* him for it? Are we talking about some witch-hater here? Some religious fanatic who thinks all such things are the works of the devil? And what about the others? There's no indication that either of them thought they had – powers, is there?"

"Not that I know of. But I can't be sure. Anything's possible, at this stage. But it does seem increasingly likely to me that that it was their plans for Koldun which got them killed. But I think a religious motive is most unlikely. It was something much more cold-blooded. A rival, maybe – someone trying to stop them. Perhaps there is something in their plans that threatened somebody. We don't know, yet. Not until we can read what's in those other pages."

"We've got to crack that code," said Alexey.

"Yes," said Maxim. "But listen, and listen well. You are the heir and now the sole director of Trinity. You are already under attack because of your decision to keep the company on. But now – if even a breath of a whisper gets back to whoever's behind this that you've actually found the Koldun file – documents which the murderer may have believed were destroyed – then you will be in the gravest danger." He turned to Helen. "Did you tell anyone else about your find?"

She faltered, "No. Nobody except Alexey. And he told you, and Nikolai."

"Did anyone see you find it?"

"There were other people in the room with me when I found it – but I don't think anyone was taking any notice of …"

He looked thoughtfully at her. "Who were they, Miss Clement? I mean, who was in the room with you?"

Helen said, "Ah – Alla was there, and Sonya I think – and – um – maybe Ilya. Not sure, though, can't really remember."

"I see." His voice was hard, and Helen had the impression that he didn't really believe what she was saying.

"What do you suggest, then?" Alexey said.

"We neutralize the danger of the card, to you, and to Trinity. And to do that it should not stay here in this apartment, or go back with you to Uglich. For if anything leaks out, whether innocently or not, you'll be in great danger. So here's what I propose: first, allow people in the office to know something important was found, but that it has been put for safekeeping in your bank vault."

"But I don't see how –" began Alexey.

"Wait. Let me finish. The card must be put in a bank safe-deposit box, but not in your usual one, rather in a branch a fair distance away, or even in a completely different bank. This must be done this very day. Till you have cracked the code, that is where it must stay."

"An excellent idea," said Volkovsky, warmly.

"But if we don't have the pages, then how can we crack the code?" said Alexey. "We need to at least have a copy of the pages."

"Of course we do," said Volkovsky, eyes alight. "But I think we only need the first coded page to do that. If we print out one single copy of it – I have a photo printer which we can use for the purpose – then that's all we need to find the key. We're going to need the services of a really good cryptographer."

"What about Foma?" Alexey said. "Yulia's right-hand man," he explained to Helen and Maxim. "Brilliant at cracking."

Helen tried to remember Foma. He'd been one of the quiet ones, she thought.

"Can he be trusted?" Serebrov said.

"Pretty sure he can," said Alexey. "Don't you, Kolya?"

"Never seen anything to suggest otherwise," said Volkovsky. "He's been working for us for years. But as a safeguard we should tell him as little as possible, aside from the code-name, and that the code may be text-based. It's an off-the-books job for a client, we'll say. It's not the first time he's been asked to do one of those." He smiled. "And if we tell him we think it's an impossible task, he will take it as an absolute point of honor to crack it."

"Excellent," said Alexey. "We'll do that, then. Print the copy first then take the card to the bank."

"You should disguise it," said Maxim. "Not just put it in the safe-deposit box as is, I mean. Nobody except us should know what is in it. I suggest something simple, though – perhaps an envelope inside a padded bag."

*

An hour or so later, it was all done, and the bag with its strange cargo was locked away in the safe-deposit box of a far-flung suburban bank branch Alexey had chosen, and put in the vault personally by him, with only the bank manager in attendance. Now no one but Alexey could access it, unless it were a proxy appointed personally by him and bearing a signed document from him. As to the print-out, Volkovsky took that to Foma's apartment after work, so as not to alert anyone else in the office.

It was after six when Helen and Alexey finally got back to the apartment. They would not be going back to Uglich tonight. Volkovsky wanted them to go back the next morning, but Alexey had said firmly that he would see. He would not accept another bodyguard; he said there was quite enough in-house security at the apartment. But he agreed that he would be in regular touch with Maxim and his godfather and that he would take no chances.

Helen called her mother, not without some trepidation. But after the first astounded, "*Where* did you say you were?" Therese Clement listened in silence to her daughter's garbled half-truthful explanations, "Sorry, Mam, but it was a spur of the moment thing. Alexey thought it would be fun to hit Moscow for a bit – we went in a helicopter, we had this really good pilot, ex-airforce, Alexey thinks – anyway we meant to get back tonight but things got a bit hectic and we decided to make a weekend of it. We'll be back Sunday or Monday – I'll call you when I know."

Her mother said, blankly, "Okay. But why did you tell me this morning you were going to Yaroslavl?"

"I'm sorry, Mom. I thought you'd freak out if I told you we were going in a helicopter."

"Damn right I'd have had something to say about it," snapped her mother, "but so what? If you want to go off for a romantic weekend, that's up to you. Just don't lie to me about it, okay?"

"Okay. Sorry."

There was a pause, then her mother said, in a different tone, "I'm sorry too, Helen. Didn't mean to jump down your throat like that. It's just – it was a bit of a shock, that's all. Are you having a good time?"

"Yes. We are." She didn't mention what had happened at the office.

"Then that's good. Oh well, I suppose I'll just have to make apologies for you tonight. At Galina's place. Sergey's sister. You know."

"Oh *shit*. I totally forgot about that."

"Why does that not surprise me?" said her mother, wryly. "Ah well, you take care, have fun, and see you soon."

"You too. Mam?"

"Yes?"

"I love you."

"I love you too, *chérie*," said her mother, and Helen could hear the smile in her voice. "See you when I see you, then." And she rang off.

Helen went to find Alexey, who'd kept a discreet distance while she called her mother. He was munching on some olives and nuts in the kitchen, a bottle of vodka and two glasses at his elbow.

She smiled at him. "Hey, that looks good."

He poured them each a shot. "To us!" he said, and they drank.

She took a handful of olives and nuts. "Well, that's it. Mam freaked out a bit at first but she was okay in the end."

"Good," he said, coming to her and sliding an arm around her waist. "Now then, *ma petite mademoiselle*, we have the night to ourselves."

"Yep," she said, joyously, resting her head against his shoulder. "We do."

"And you know what? I don't want to talk about sorcerers or secrets or Trinity or anything like that. In fact, right now I'd really prefer something other than talk altogether. Or even drinking vodka. How about you?"

"Suits me just fine," she murmured, heart pounding as she reached hungrily for him.

Chapter 22

If their love-making the day before had been glorious, this evening's took it to a new level of intensity as they explored each other, bodies silk-slipping, hotly fusing, breathing in sights, sounds, smells, touch, taste. And now it was wildly passionate, now glowingly tender, now slow and languid, now hot and urgent. For the lovers, time had stopped, the bed was their kingdom, the bedroom their universe and nobody and nothing existed outside of it. And at the end of it, as they lay sweaty, exhausted and exhilarated in each other's arms, Alexey said, softly, "I could die happy right now."

"Oh, don't say morbid things like that," she cried, a little coldness tracking up her spine. He nuzzled at her neck and whispered, "We're going to live forever, you and I, right?"

""Right," she said, "and we're going to make love every day of it. Like, many times a day."

"Wow," he said, laughing, "what are you going to do to me, girl?"

"Just wait and see," she said, teasingly, and just when it seemed it *couldn't* happen again, it did. Alexey fell asleep then but Helen couldn't, and she lay there staring into space, her arm slowly growing numb under Alexey's shoulder.

Extracting it gently, she got up and, flinging on one of Alexey's shirts from the wardrobe, she padded into the kitchen and made herself a cup of tea. Taking it into the living-room, she stood at the window and looked out at the glittering night city, sparkling fairy lights strung out along the roads as if there was about to be a party, colored streams of car headlights, floodlit buildings against the black sky. From this distance, framed in the big double-glazed window, it was a strangely serene scene, like a living painting.

"How do you fancy going out in that?" said Alexey, behind her.

"Oh, I do," she said, hugging him. "But do you think it's okay? I mean, safe?"

"Christ, I'm not going to be a prisoner, no matter what anyone says. Besides, the card's in the bank, and Kolya spread the word about it being locked up, just like Maxim said, so we've done everything we can." He gestured at the city. "Out there, it's buzzing. Heaving with people. Safest place to be, out in public. And I want to show you Moscow by night. What's the matter, you too tired to go out, babe?" He gave her a teasing sidelong glance.

She smiled. "No. Why, are you?"

"Never felt better. Let's hit the town then." He grinned. "Maybe better change though, yeah? Very fetching what you're wearing, but ..."

"Pot calling the kettle black," she said, pinging the elastic of his silk cartoon-covered boxers, "don't you think?"

In the mall, where they'd bought the photo display, Helen had also bought a pack of knickers and a T-shirt, for her beautiful silk shirt had had to be washed, but it was so light that it was already dry. She put it back on, and the flares and jacket and boots, and twisted her hair up with a bronze band she'd also bought in the store. Alexey had extra clothes in the wardrobe so that was easy for him and in his deep green linen shirt, cream pants and jacket he looked so stunning she couldn't stop looking at him.

*

Outside, the Friday night air was balmy, and the streets buzzing. It was as if the whole city was out and about. Nightclubs, bars and restaurants were crammed full, cars streamed by on the roads, from flash Italian and German sports cars and hulking SUVs to nippy Japanese hatchbacks and battered Russian workhorses. And crowds of roaring motorbikes headed for the Sparrow Hills where, Alexey said in his Aussie idiom, the bikers did "wheelies", showing off shamelessly. Red Square heaved with people: teenagers out on the town, scrubbed-up families promenading with blasé children, wide-eyed foreign tourist groups shepherded by brisk guides, people having their photographs taken with buskers in fancy dress. Behind the baroque crimson bulk of the historical museum with its costumed guards were food and drink and souvenir stalls, still doing brisk business, while a loud rock band with a mini-skirted singer in high-heeled boots and a fur hat played on a stage in a corner and a wispy man parading two little performing monkeys in red jackets and a dejected eagle on a perch called meekly for coins from the watching crowd.

For quite a while, Alexey and Helen wandered around happily, hand in hand, loving the bustle, loving too being a young couple like any other, for here no one recognized Alexey and no one dogged his footsteps. They didn't go to a restaurant for dinner but just bought sausage and onion sandwiches from a stall and a cold glass of strong-smelling *kvass* from a cart, and had it on a bench while the crowds swirled around them. Tiring of bustle, they walked to the river and stopped on a bridge for a moment, arms around each other, gazing out over the black rippling silk of the Moskva river, shot through with broad and thin brushstrokes of moonlight and electric light, together. Helen said, "You know, last time I was in Moscow it freaked me out. I couldn't cope with it. It was just so different to what I was used to. But now …"

"Yeah, now?" he said, when she broke off.

"Now, it's like the most exciting place in the world," she said simply, "it's like everything around us is mirroring how I feel – do you know what I mean?"

"I do," he said, and drew her to him. They kissed passionately, emerging to a gleeful chorus of klaxons and whoops as a band of bare-headed young bikers and their girls swept past. Alexey and Helen laughed and waved back, and then they walked hand in hand back to the Kremlin, and the Alexandrovsky gardens behind it.

Against the back wall of the Kremlin, a smartly uniformed guard watching over the Eternal Flame and the Tomb of the Unknown Soldier stood stiffly in his gilt-framed glass niche, like a giant toy or a colored statue. Frozen in mid-movement, the bronze bears and wolves and horses and peasants which decorated fountains and canals in the gardens could have kept him quiet company had it not been for the cheerfully noisy crowds surging through.

Alexey and Helen found a secluded spot to sit, under a tree near the water, her head against his chest, his arms around her. She took a photo of them holding each other, and because it was night and on flash, the photo was soft-focused, almost magical, the lights of the city smudged behind them like one of those aura haloes. Alexey began to sing, softly, a song she didn't know but whose melody was nevertheless hauntingly familiar, his rich dark voice inhabiting it fully, enveloping her in a cloak of beauty like the moonlit night.

"What was that you were singing?" she breathed, when he'd finished and the song died away on the warm scented air.

"It's so lovely. I think I've heard it before but I don't know what it's called."

He smiled. "It's one of the Russian classics. Almost a cliché. It's called *'Moscow Nights'*."

"Clichés like that," she said, lightly, "I can live with very happily."

"That's what I reckon. The words are beautiful too." He translated some of them, softly, "*Nothing can be heard in the garden, oh how dear they are, these Moscow nights – the river is flowing and standing still, made of moon's silver, a song is heard and not heard on those quiet nights – Now the dawn breaks, please my darling don't forget these Moscow nights.*"

"Oh, that's gorgeous. Magical."

"Songs like that create a special kind of magic."

She looked up at him, at his dear face illumined in the moonlight. She whispered, "Oh Alexey, don't you ever regret not … not going on with music?"

"I don't know," he said, looking into her eyes. "If I can get Trinity on an even keel – if things turn out how I hope – who knows? Perhaps in the future I might go back to thoughts of singing in public. But for now, I do not miss it. Anyway," he said, brushing her hair with his lips, "singing to you in the night garden means much more to me right now than the applause of any crowd. I am completely content."

Her heart was full. "Oh Alexey. So am I."

There was a little silence, and then he said, "Helen, how would you feel about living here?"

Startled, she looked up at him. "What do you mean? Live here, in Moscow?"

"Yes. Or Uglich, if you prefer. Or Petersburg. In Russia, is what I mean."

She was silent a moment, remembering what she'd thought last night. Then she said, slowly, "I – I don't know. I really like it here, in lots of ways. But it also ... I mean ... I feel so foreign, sometimes. Things are so different. I guess I need time to think about it."

"Of course you do," he said, smiling. "You take all the time you need. I'm sorry for putting you on the spot like that. Patience, Kolya's always telling me. Don't really follow his advice well, do I?"

"No, you don't," said Helen, a ripple of laughter in her throat, "in just about every way, you give poor old Nikolai a real run for his money."

Alexey shook his head. "Poor old Nikolai, my foot! Don't let his mild manners fool you, Helen. My godfather is tough as boots, with an iron will." He stood up and held out a hand to her. "Shall we go and find something more to eat? I'm starving."

"Aren't you always?" she said, happily. "I think you're just greedy."

"Guilty as charged," he said, cheerfully, sweeping her into his arms. There was no doubt, she thought. No doubt at all. He saw them sharing the future, as well as the present. How it would work, she might not know yet. But she would, when the time was right.

*

Leaving the gardens, they had a drink in an intimate little bar, and afterwards wandered slowly hand in hand back to Tverskaya Street. Falling into bed, they made love for the final time that day – tenderly, gently – and fell asleep still entwined in each other's arms. In the morning, Helen awoke to find Alexey gone. But he'd left a note on the bedside table. *Out to get us some breakfast. Back soon. Kolya called. Meeting with him and Maxim this evening. Rest of day's ours. Love you. A xxxx.*

Helen looked at the time. It was ten o'clock. Stretching luxuriously, she got up and went to have a long hot shower. They'd gone to bed very late and not gone to sleep at once either of course, but she didn't feel tired. Indeed, she felt an immense sense of well-being. Wrapped in Alexey's dressing-gown, she stood at the big window, looking down at the morning city spread under her, and happiness flooded through her. She went to the CD rack, took out a recording of traditional Russian music, and put it on. The melancholy, lively, haunting melodies filled the air and she danced to them in front of the window, arms stretched out to embrace the city below her, feet gliding soundlessly on the thick carpet. And as she danced, her eyes prickled with ecstatic tears and a glorious shiver rippled down her spine.

She started as the front door banged. Alexey was back. She ran to greet him, hugging him so hard as he stepped into the hall that he protested, laughing, "Hang on, let me put these bags down. Now, there, that's better." He held her tight, looking into her face, "What was that about – did you think I'd run away or something?"

"No, I just love you," she said, simply.

"And I love you too," he replied, kissing her. He cocked an ear. "You've been playing Dad's records."

"Yes," she said, lightly. "I'm getting more acquainted with Russian culture. As it seems that might be a pretty good idea."

Their eyes met. He understood her meaning at once. His face lit up. "Helen, are you sure?"

"No," she said, quietly, "but what does that matter? It's an adventure. You *can't* be sure with adventure, can you? That's the point. You just have to get on with it."

"Oh yes," he said, and his whole face lit up with an enormous smile. "Oh yes. Yes!" And he kissed her on the lips, hard. "I've brought back something for you," he went on, rummaging in the plastic bags and pulling out a little gift-wrapped parcel.

She unwrapped it carefully and found, nestled in a box in tissue paper, a beautiful little round brooch. Made of black lacquered wood, it was edged with delicate gilt scrolling, and in the center was an exquisite painting of a bird, rather like a bird of paradise or a peacock, with a crest and outstretched wings and a long, sweeping tail, its plumage glowing in shades of red and gold.

Helen stared at it. Alexey said, a little uncertainly, "It's the firebird, you see. Do you like it?"

"Oh yes. Oh Alexey – it's so – so … it's just so – perfect."

"Whew," he said, with a grin of relief. "I'm glad you think so. The lady in the shop – she thought it was a funny sort of choice, kept trying to point me in the direction of heart lockets and … Hey, what's up? Don't cry … don't cry …"

"Sorry, I just can't help it," bawled Helen, on his shoulder, "I'm just so happy and I can't believe my luck, that's all."

"You are the funniest, sweetest thing," he said, half-laughing, half-serious, sweeping her up to him, "the loveliest girl in the world – there – let me pin it to your shirt." He turned her around so that she'd face the hall mirror. "What do you think?"

"It's gorgeous," she whispered, stroking the painted bird, gently, a warmth in her fingertips tingling all through her.

"Listen to this," Alexey said. He picked up the box the brooch had come in and gently pulled out a little slip of paper. He read, "*One of the legendary traditions of the firebird is that when one of her long golden tail feathers drops to earth, light and inspiration follows, and a new story begins.* I think that's the meaning of old Mrs. Feshina's vision, when she said you were the firebird, come from far distant lands. That is the gift you've brought me, Helen – new inspiration and new meaning."

She murmured, "Oh Alexey, no – it's *you* who has brought that to *me*. And the courage to know it."

His smile was very tender as he said, "You had that courage in you already, or you'd never have been able to find it in the first place. I'm sorry, my beautiful firebird, but I think you're just going to have to accept that you are the light of my life."

"Oh, Alexey," she murmured, overcome, leaning against him.

"Helen, I want to ask you something."

"Ask away," she said, happily.

"You know that day we first spoke to each other?"

She nodded.

"Well, I'd *never* before been to that little wood near your friend's house. I didn't even know it existed. Normally, if I went for a ride, it was in the forest. And I hadn't even done that in ages. But that day I changed my route. I went in a direction I'd never gone before." Another pause. "I had no idea why – until ..."

"Until the moment you asked me if I wanted a lift back."

His eyes widened. "Yes. Oh yes. It was *precisely* at that moment. Up till then – I was so flustered; so deafened, blinded, by my own stupidity. I had seen you once already. I had wanted so much to speak to you and couldn't. Now, the second time, there we were, I'd touched you, had felt that connection, so deeply – and yet it was all wrong. I'd frightened you, hurt you. I felt like fate was determined to thwart me. I cursed my bad luck, but I was just going to apologize profusely and – and go – but then, somehow, the only way I can explain it is ... it was as if – as if scales fell from my eyes. And I could see."

She looked at him and said, softly, "What did you see?"

"I saw a picture, clear as a bell. A crossroads. We could take one path, together. Or go on opposite ones, alone."

A shiver of awe goose-fleshed her skin. She said, "Alexey, I had – *the same vision*. A right-hand path, business as usual; a

215

left-hand path, you and I. Oh, Alexey ... What does it mean, if we both saw ..."

He said, quietly, "It means that – how can I explain it? That our souls are keyed to the same music. To variations of the same melody." He took her hand and, bringing it to his lips, kissed it, softly. "Tell me, my darling firebird," he whispered, "do you think you'll ever regret taking that left-hand path?"

"Never," she cried, a wild thrill coursing through her. "Not for one instant."

Chapter 23

They had a late breakfast, or rather brunch, consisting of an array of delicious little freshly baked pies, or *piroshki*, with various savory fillings, as well as fresh fruit and thick creamy yoghurt, and just as they finished, Volkovsky phoned. Maxim had heard from Zaitsev in Petersburg, he said. Lebedev, the supposed informant, had turned up back in his home town. But he was in no fit state to talk. In fact he was in no fit state to do anything anymore, for his drowned body had just been fished from the Neva. He'd been brutally bashed and dumped in the river. Nobody had seen anything. Zaitsev had searched his apartment. Nothing useful had been found there either. That lead was now literally at a dead end.

Maxim had not had much more luck with Grisha's associates. "He managed to get some possible names," Volkovsky said, "but the men in question were nowhere to be found. They've gone to earth."

"Or into the river," said Alexey, drily.

"As you say. Anyway, that's the situation right now, Lyosha. We should have more for you this evening. Everything all right at your end?"

"Absolutely," said Alexey, smiling at Helen.

"And you're taking care, Lyosha?"

"Of course."

"I wish you'd think of going back to Uglich till we get this sorted out."

"We'll see, Kolya," he said, firmly, and rang off.

"Frustrated every way we turn," he said to Helen. "Repin – or whoever it is – seems to be one step ahead of us all the time."

Helen shuddered, and he was instantly contrite. "Don't worry, Lenochka. He won't come near us. I promise."

"How can you promise that?" she cried, "when you don't even know for sure who it is?"

"Trust me," he said.

"Oh, I do. But …" She saw his expression, and swallowed the rest of her words.

"Maxim and Kolya are on it. They'll figure it out. You'll see."

"Okay," she said, trying to sound convinced.

"Now – let's think of something better. What do you want to do for the rest of the day? Aside from the obvious," he said, grinning.

Blushing a little, she said, "I don't know. Do you want to go back to the office and see how the staff are getting on?"

"It's Saturday, Lenochka." He'd told her yesterday that was one of the pet-forms of Yelena. She loved the tender sound of it on his lips. "Nobody's working. But I might call round there this afternoon anyway, see how the clean-up's going. Sonya's supervising, she called this morning, as did Ilya."

"How are they?"

"Fine. Angry, actually. But not scared. They're real fighters, those two. Same can't be said for some of the others." He sighed. "But you can hardly blame people if they're reconsidering their options right now." He spoke reasonably but she knew by the sadness in his eyes that even if he didn't blame the nervous ones, he had hoped for more. And maybe that was exactly the enemy's aim. Not to frighten Alexey into giving up a thriving company, because as Kolya said, perhaps they already had the measure of him and knew he couldn't be chased off; but more a war of attrition targeted at the weak spots, at those who could be intimidated into running away. So in the end Alexey would be faced with the ruin of his hopes, for what good was a reform plan if there was nothing left to reform? And then the sharks could move in with ease.

The insidious malice of it made her so angry that it chased the fear away. She burst out, "Alexey, I hope you know that if there's anything I can do to make things better, anything I can help you do to stop those sodding bastards, anything to help you keep Trinity going, anything at all, I'll do it!"

"I know," he said, "thank you," and he kissed her, very tenderly. They were quiet a moment, just holding each other close; then he said, in a lighter tone, "How about we go out for a bit? What do you fancy? A museum, an art gallery, a walk?"

"Actually, if it's not too boring for you, I'd really like to go shopping," she said. "I could do with a change of clothes."

"Not boring at all," he said, "but you've got to let it be my treat. No protests accepted," he added, laughingly putting a finger to her lips, "so don't even try."

"Yes, sir," she said, demurely, looking at him under her lashes.

He caught his breath. "If you look at me like that, you wicked girl," he said, "we'll never end up going out."

"And that would never do," said Helen, flashing him a pert look, "because I really do need to get those clothes."

"Come on, then." He took her hand pulled her to the door. "Forget taxis, we'll walk. I need to calm down."

*

Moscow is a city of parks: some formal and elegant, like the Alexandrovsky gardens; some big and rambling, like Gorky Park where holidaymakers ride troikas in winter; and some modest and sunlit-green as tiny patches of woodland with surprises to happen on – a bandstand, a cart selling cornets of nuts, a merry-go-round, a group of statues. Such a one was the little park they walked through, stopping at a place where, against a background of greenery, stood an unusual grouping of sculptures depicting two children in the center of a ring of grotesque, even monstrous, figures.

The boy and girl glowed brightly bronze; the grotesque figures had been left to weather green. Alexey read out the plaque underneath: "Childhood is threatened by adult vices," he said. "There's indifference; and violence; and drunkenness, and greed – and so on."

"It's amazing," said Helen. And she shivered. "But kind of horrible too. Scary." She'd never seen anything like it.

"Yes," he said. "It's pretty controversial. Some people say it's enough to give kids nightmares. But I think it actually does that to adults, not children. I'd have thought it was so cool, when I was a kid. I loved everything gruesome. Not that it was up then. It's not all that old."

Yet somehow it looked like it had been there forever, this extraordinary bronze allegory like a dark fairytale made manifest. She said, "It would have scared me stiff. I'd have imagined those monsters coming to life. By a night of full moon or something. I'd have imagined them slowly uncreaking their metal limbs and lumbering toward the kids, who'd try in vain to escape."

"So different, eh! I wonder if we'd have liked each other, when we were kids?"

"Probably not," she said, pertly. "I'd have thought you were a rough noisy brat, and kept well away."

"And I'd have thought you were little Miss Prim and Proper, and pulled your plait," he said, and did just that.

She squealed, and hit him on the hand. He growled and said, "Right, Miss Prim, I'll get you for that," and made a grab at her, but she twisted out of his grasp and ran away, laughing. He ran after her, catching up with her just beyond the sculptures, said, gleefully, "Now you'll never escape," and swept her into his arms, much to the approval of two old ladies sunning themselves on a bench nearby.

Walking hand in hand through the park a little later, he said, "You know, I think we'd have done exactly the same thing as kids, we'd have ended up playing catch and kiss," and she gave him a sidelong glance and said, "Oh yes, I bet you were *very* good at catch and kiss," and he gave her a mischievous look. "You have the wrong idea about me, I was a quiet, good little boy, not a noisy brat at all."

She snorted. "Yeah, whatever. I hardly think that someone who immediately thinks of yanking a girl's plait is all that much of a goody-two-shoes."

"If that had been the only way to get you to notice me, I'd have done it in a flash," he said, smiling.

"Well, then, I rest my case," she said, firmly, her pulse quickening.

*

He would have taken her to an expensive shop, but she'd have none of it, and in the end they found a Zara store and, after parading in and out of the fitting rooms under Alexey's appreciative glance, she finally selected an emerald green top, a pair of skinny cream trousers, a short fitted lavender-blue dress, and a pair of slingback shoes in the same soft color. The last two items were at Alexey's insistence; she needed a new outfit for dinner tonight, he said, and Helen easily let herself be persuaded. At another place, he bought her a beautiful pure white evening shawl in a knit so fine and lacy it was like the most delicate cobwebs, and a silver silk nightie that slipped like water through her fingers and made her blush as she looked up to see the look on his face.

It was well past lunchtime by the time they finally left the shops, but they stopped for potato pancakes and tea in a little cafe before heading to the Trinity office, where the cleaners were hard at work under Sonya's beady eye. The window had already been replaced, there was new office furniture and fittings arriving to replace the items that had been broken, and the mess was slowly disappearing. Alexey rolled up his sleeves and set to, carrying up boxes from delivery vans as they arrived, while Helen and Sonya unpacked glasses and crockery, phones and computers. Then Zakhar and Natalia turned up to lend a hand, and a little later, Ilya. Soon what could have been a grim task turned into an unexpectedly cheerful gathering, crowned by Zakhar producing a bottle of vodka and a jar of gherkins from somewhere and everyone toasting a job well done.

So Helen and Alexey were cheerful as they got in the taxi which would get them back to the apartment in time for the meeting with Serebrov and Volkovsky, and not in the least bit ready for what awaited them when the concierge intercepted them in the lobby and handed Alexey a letter that had been brought in by a messenger that afternoon, when they were out. It looked ordinary, the name and address printed on the envelope, but Alexey frowned.

"What is it?" said Helen, as they went up in the elevator.

"There's nothing to say who this is from," he said, turning it over.

Helen's throat clenched. "Don't open it. It could be a – a bomb."

"No," he said, "it's much too thin for that."

She stammered, "Or what if it's poisoned – anthrax like that guy in the States? Or I remember reading once about this

Saudi terrorist in Chechnya who was killed by the Russian Federal Security Service with a poisoned letter – there was a contact poison on it that went through his skin."

He looked astonished. "Anthrax! Secret service poisons! Helen, what the hell are you imagining here?"

"Okay, so maybe I'm paranoid, but I still don't think you should open it," she said, defiantly, as they went into the apartment. "Call Nikolai and the policeman. Please, Alexey."

He sighed. "Okay. If it makes you feel better." He made the call, the letter lying unopened on the hall table. Helen watched it as though at any moment it might rise up against them. But it did nothing of the sort, only lay there looking ordinary, and when Maxim and Volkovsky arrived a short time later, it was still lying there, quietly. To Helen's relief, both men took her fears very seriously, and Maxim ordered them all to stand back while, wearing thin rubber gloves and a face mask, he carefully slit the envelope open over the bathroom sink and extracted what was within with a pair of tweezers.

It wasn't a letter, but a thin piece of card. On the front were a few computer-printed words. Maxim passed the card over to Alexey, still in the tweezers. He read what was written there, his face darkening, but said nothing. Then he turned the card over and, looking over his shoulder, Helen saw what was printed, and her scalp tightened with fear.

It was a computer-generated graphic, very basic – a long black shape with the top edges cut off, and a cross at the top. Crude it might be but she knew at once what it was. *A coffin.* Helen cried, "What does it say on the other side? Oh, what does it say?"

It was Nikolai Volkovsky who answered, quietly, "*There's more than one way to change your mind.* That's what it says, Helen." He looked as though he might say more, but Serebrov, taking the card back from Alexey, spoke first.

"Alexey Ivanovich, did the concierge describe the messenger who brought this?"

"No," said Alexey. His lips were tight, his expression grim.

"Did you notice anyone loitering outside when you got back?"

The young man shook his head. Serebrov looked at Helen, who also shook her head, mutely, her eyes on Alexey's thunderous face.

"Might you have been followed today?" the policeman persisted.

"No," snapped Alexey.

"Are you sure about that?"

"Absolutely bloody certain. Oleg taught me what to watch out for, one day."

Volkovsky raised an eyebrow. "*Oleg* did that? Then he's smarter than he looks."

Alexey ignored this and rounded on the policeman. "If I'd really thought we were being followed, do you think I'd have exposed Helen to it?" He glanced at her and she could tell all his heart was in his eyes. "I'm not such a reckless fool as all that, Senior Lieutenant."

"I never said you were, Alexey Ivanovich," said Serebrov, calmly. "I would have expected nothing less of you. But I had to know."

"What *I* know," said Alexey, his color high, his eyes flashing, "is that whoever sent this must be a complete and utter moron, because if he thinks this *pathetic* stunt is going to make the blindest bit of difference, then he must have his head so far up his ass that –"

"Yes, yes," said Volkovsky, cutting in hastily, "of course, Lyosha, I quite agree, but we must still take it seriously. After what happened yesterday, you must see that."

"I see, that someone made a stupid blunder," Alexey said, biting off the words. "And it sure as hell wasn't me." He looked at Serebrov. "We have a piece of evidence now that we didn't have before. Isn't that so, Maxim Antonovich?"

"It is," said the policeman, gravely. He took a plastic bag from his pocket and dropped the card and the envelope in it. "It's possible that we may find DNA traces on the card or the envelope, or information on the type of computer and printer used. And the concierge might remember more, if pressed."

"Mights and maybes and possiblys," said Volkovsky, tersely, "and if beans grew in the mouth, then it would be a kitchen garden! What if you don't get anything out of all that? What then? We can't just wait while you find out. Lyosha, you must go back to Uglich."

"That would be wise," agreed Serebrov, with a meaningful glance at Helen. She said, "Alexey – please. You've got to listen to them."

She could see the volcanic struggle inside him, the defiant pride and anger, warring with tenderness and concern for her. He said, his eyes never leaving her face, "Okay. We'll leave tomorrow morning then." He put an arm protectively around her, and she knew he'd agreed for her sake, and her sake only. It didn't matter. He would be safe, and that's what counted for her.

Volkovsky said, "Good. Now as for tonight, you will stay here and ..."

Alexey's eyes flashed dangerously. "We were planning to go out to dinner."

"Out of the question," snapped Volkovsky. He looked to Serebrov for support, but the policeman discreetly said nothing.

Alexey hissed, "I will not be dictated to, even by you, Kolya. In the name of God, we were out last night, and all day today, and nothing happened, nothing! Aren't you forgetting something? The card came here, Kolya. *To this building*. So why would you imagine it's safer here than out in the streets? You can see for yourself it's not so!"

Volkovsky had paled, his lips set. He snapped, "I can see no such thing, and neither would you, if you had any damn sense!" They glared at each other, fists clenched, like two antagonists, and Helen suddenly couldn't bear it anymore. She cried, "Stop it! Don't you see that's what they want? What they're after? They're trying to set you all against one another, and it's working, because listen to you, just listen to you!" And she burst into tears.

She hadn't meant to, but it was the best thing she could have done. In the face of her tears the tension between the two men dissolved as they sheepishly apologized to each other and to her. Serebrov slipped out discreetly during this time and soon returned with the news that, though the concierge could only give a fairly sketchy description of the messenger, he'd also said he believed that the man's van had borne the logo of a particular courier company. That could be checked quite easily. They had a good deal to go on, he said comfortingly. Besides, just as a barking dog rarely bites, a killer rarely signaled their intention so blatantly. In his opinion Miss Clement was quite right, the intention behind the card was not to issue a death threat so much as to cause instability, like the attacks on the Trinity offices. And then, he observed blandly that in restaurants, as far as he knew, a table for four might be reserved just as easily as a table for two. As he spoke, he glanced at the other two men, and Helen saw by his expression that he understood Alexey's attitude, and even admired it; but that he also knew Volkovsky was right to be wary. She knew that because she felt exactly the same way; and so she was immensely relieved when both Alexey and his godfather smiled wryly and nodded. She knew he had found precisely the right compromise, and her estimation of the big policeman grew a little.

Chapter 24

So the evening ended not in tension or recriminations, but in a cozy little backstreet restaurant, and if it wasn't the romantic night out Helen and Alexey had planned for, it was perfectly safe and uneventful, the sinister little card not forgotten, but not discussed by mutual consent. Helen even enjoyed herself in a way. Nikolai, she knew already, was a good conversationalist; but drawn out by Alexey's warmth, or perhaps loosened by liquor, Serebrov showed a talent for mimicry and anecdote which she'd never have imagined could lie in such a hard, impassive man.

Later, they adjourned to the apartment, and over more glasses of liqueur, Alexey started singing, and Volkovsky and Serebrov joined in with him. For all his bulk, Serebrov had a surprisingly light tenor voice, and Volkovsky a rather subdued baritone, not as deep or rich as Alexey's but perfectly capable of holding a tune, and as the three voices threaded together in perfect harmony, Helen found the tears springing to her eyes. She would happily have just sat and listened, but after a while Alexey insisted she sing too, and she began a little hesitantly on one of her favorite French songs, "À la claire fontaine", a sweet sad song which they all seemed to know, at least the melody if not the words. She soon forgot to be shy in the simple pleasure of fellowship, and music, and Alexey's tender eyes on her.

Volkovsky and Serebrov stayed over with them in the apartment that night, Alexey's godfather in a spare bedroom, and the big policeman claiming one of the living-room sofas. On her way to bed, very late, Helen glimpsed him sitting there, a blanket wrapped around him, methodically checking his revolver, and she felt glad of his presence.

*

Even though they missed the noisy freedom of being alone, there was another sort of pleasure for Helen and Alexey in loving each other quietly that night, feeling like secret teenage lovers, in suppressed giggles lest the bed creak too much while Volkovsky snored like an old walrus next door and Serebrov was watchful as a big cat in the living-room.

They fell asleep at last, and she woke to bright sunlight to find Alexey leaning on his elbow, looking at her with a strange expression in his eyes. She said, on a catch of breath, suddenly remembering the coffin card, the fear, "What's wrong?"

"Nothing, nothing at all." He picked up her hand and kissed her fingers, one by one. "It's such a glorious day, we'll have a beautiful ride home, my Lenochka," and she knew that it wasn't just for her sake he was going back now, but for his too, for *their* sake, their fates entwined, together.

She snuggled into him and whispered, "I don't want to be apart from you, not even for a few hours," and he smiled and said, "I was hoping you'd say that, so will you come and stay with me?"

"Try and stop me," she said, fiercely, making him laugh in delight.

*

Konstantin the helicopter pilot was as unsurprised and laconic as ever when they turned up flanked by Serebrov and Volkovsky, and he didn't even bat an eyelid when the big policeman asked him for his license, and the helicopter papers. Producing them with an inscrutable face, he waited patiently while Serebrov ran his eye over them, and though he said nothing when he got them back, only nodded, Helen saw there was a sardonic twist to his lips that told a different story. At last, they were cleared to go, and as the big machine rose up and wheeled away to the north-east, Helen looked back and saw the tiny figures of last night's guardian angels fast disappearing and a tiny ripple of unease went over her, quickly swept away in a flood of relief. Maybe it was because he hadn't slept well enough, maybe because the worries were getting on top of him, but Volkovsky had been uptight that morning over breakfast, and more than once Helen had feared that his anxious fussing would make Alexey lose his cool again. But the young man must have made an overnight resolution, for he endured it all patiently and with good humor, agreeing that he wouldn't give Slava and Oleg the slip, that he'd take care, that he'd not go off to investigate on his own, and that, yes, he promised he'd call Nikolai or Maxim immediately if there was any sort of problem. How long this new patience would have lasted if Alexey had been too much longer exposed to Nikolai's anxiety, Helen did not know.

As to Serebrov, he'd been busy trying to hunt up someone at the courier company the concierge had mentioned, and by dint of ignoring the outraged grumbling of "But it's Sunday," and stubbornly refusing to take no for an answer, he'd finally obtained a meeting with the reluctant manager at the courier office for later that day, so he could have a look through the records of jobs for the day before.

"Don't worry, he's a smart guy, our Maxim, and he'll figure it out," said Alexey, beside her.

She started. "You're incredible, how did you know what I was thinking?"

He took her hand and said, teasingly, "I read your mind, Lenochka. No," he added, hurriedly, as her eyes widened, "that isn't true. It was just a lucky guess. Besides, I've been thinking about that too." A pause. "I'm not quite as blasé about that card as I made out last night," he went on. "It was just – well – it puts my back up, when Kolya acts like I'm too young and stupid to know any better."

"Oh, I don't think he was doing that," she said. "He's just worried, Alexey."

"Sometimes it's as if he thinks nobody else knows how to worry like he does. Like he won the world gold medal in the anxiety stakes."

She gave a hoot of laughter. "You can hardly blame poor Nikolai! You give a pretty good impression at times of not having any idea what anxiety means."

"It's not true," he said, quietly. "It's just that – what is the point of it? Worrying doesn't stop anything from happening. All it does is make you miserable for no good reason. And it stops you thinking straight about finding a solution. That's all."

He was right, she thought, squeezing his hand. When had worrying ever made anyone stronger? If you allowed it to, it ate at your resolve and your courage, but also at your clarity of mind. It was as insidious as the malice that lay behind the attacks on Trinity. But it was a self-inflicted wound, a weapon you turned against yourself.

Presently, they touched down in Uglich. And there, waiting for them, was the big black Mercedes, and Slava and Oleg. No Yuri. His daughter in Ekaterinburg had been taken gravely ill and the chauffeur had had to leave, Slava told them. In his absence either Oleg or he would drive them, should they wish to go anywhere. Yes, he'd picked up the motorbike as instructed, he answered Alexey's next question. It was back at the house. All was in order. And Katya had prepared a fine lunch.

Alexey and Helen shook hands with Konstantin and Alexey handed the pilot an envelope stuffed full of notes, which he counted at once. He looked at Alexey, sharply, said, "This is more than we agreed." Alexey held his gaze, and nodded, and for the first time, a smile broke over Konstantin's face. But true to form, he didn't waste much time on speech, just nodded, shook Alexey's hand, said "*Poka,*", which Helen knew meant "see you later", and stalked off.

Back at Irina's house, Therese was in a bustle of preparation for what she called a "traditional Sunday". Irina hadn't returned yet – she was expected back within a day or two – but Sergey's sister Galina was picking Helen's mother up to take her to the Sunday liturgy at the Transfiguration Cathedral in town, and then there would be a barbecue at Galina's house afterwards. "It's not that I'm a very regular churchgoer," Therese Clement told Alexey, when he asked, "I'm more of an Easter and Christmas Catholic, if you know what I mean. But the other night at dinner, I happened to mention that I wanted to go to an Orthodox service last time I was in Russia, but had been too shy to do so, in case I caused offense by crossing myself in the wrong way or standing when I should be kneeling and so on. And then Galina offered to take me, which was very kind of her."

"Isn't Sergey going too?" said Helen with a little smile.

Her mother said, calmly, "Well, he would have done, only he had a fare to take to Yaroslavl this morning, he couldn't refuse it, the money was too good. He'll be at the barbecue though. Galina says that he and Sasha, her husband, will be doing all the cooking, in fact." She gave them a sideways glance. "Well, that's enough of my plans. What about yours? You look like you came to tell me something important."

"Actually, yes, Mam," said Helen. "Alexey and I – that is, I'm going to stay at his house."

"I see." Her mother's tone was a little sharp, her expression unreadable.

Alexey and Helen looked at each other. It was the young man who said, gently, "Madame Clement – Therese – I hope you do not think I am trying to come between you and your daughter – but Helen and I, we need to be together."

There was a little silence. Then Therese said, on a soft sigh, "I know. Oh, I know, Alexey. I understand. It is just that I ..." She broke off, then went on, more strongly, "It's not that I didn't expect it. From the first day she's met you, Helen has been ... different. No, not bad different," she went on, holding up a hand to forestall her daughter's movement of protest, "not at all, but still – you see, a mother is always a mother, no matter how old she or her child are. She wants to keep her child from hurt. She wants her to be cherished by others, as she cherishes her. Do you see?"

In her emotion, her mother had reverted to a French way of doing things, Helen thought, talking about me in the third person though I'm right here. Years of living in England had modified that kind of response, though back in France with Grandpère, she sometimes slipped into it again. But if Alexey thought it strange, he didn't show it. Instead, he said, gently, "I do see, Madame Clement – Therese – I do see very well. And I promise you that you have nothing to fear." His eyes in Helen's eyes, he took her hand and said, "For I will always love and cherish you."

Helen's heart swelled with so much love and pride and gladness that she felt almost choked by it. She whispered, "And I, you, Alexey, always." She saw the color flame into her mother's pale cheeks, saw the sudden shine of her eyes.

She knew it wasn't embarrassment at hearing this public promise, made between lovers. It was a tidal wave of emotion that made Therese whisper, "Then I can only be glad to step aside."

"Oh, Mam." Helen impulsively hugged her. "You don't need to do that, I love you just as much as ever, don't look so sad!"

"I'm not sad," said Therese, wiping her eyes, "I'm just – okay, so I am a little sad," she agreed, laughing a little now, "but it wouldn't be natural if I wasn't, for a time that passes, for a time when my child does not need me in the same way as she did, and you are not to concern yourselves with that. All I want, all I've ever wanted, my darling Helen, is for you to be happy and I can see you are and for that I have to thank you, Alexey. And I am thankful, oh so much, and you won't ever forget that, will you?"

"No, Therese, I will not," he said, gravely, and then he took her hand and kissed it in a beautiful old-fashioned way, and said, "Thank you for understanding."

"Understanding is not hard," she said, softly. "It is trust that is not so easy."

"Of course," he said, "and I do not expect it to be." His voice was as steady and honest as his expression. Somehow, then, everything was different, Helen thought, as though something watchful, almost fearful, in her mother had relaxed. And as she went upstairs to pack her bag shortly after, she left her mother and her lover nattering cheerfully over a glass of tea, and it warmed her all over.

A little time later, Galina arrived. Two years older than Sergey, she was a good deal like him, with the same kind of friendly light blue eyes, and the same kind of headlong speech as her brother, only she was plumper, her hair had not been allowed to go gray but been dyed a soft, flattering fair shade, and she only spoke a few words of English.

She was also much less circumspect in front of Alexey than Sergey had been, chatting away to him apparently quite unselfconsciously in Russian but also, as Alexey said later, not asking him any direct questions. She didn't seem in the least put out that they had missed dinner at her place the other day; and segued quite naturally into inviting them round for lunch too, a proposition they could hardly refuse.

As they finally managed to extract themselves from Galina's chatter and make their way back to the car, Alexey said, shaking his head, "Amazing! I'm sure she managed to find out a great deal about me without even appearing to."

"You should offer her a job at Trinity," said Helen, smiling.

"Maybe I should," he said, laughing, "she'd make a great investigator. Talk about determined!"

Chapter 25

At least this place had an elevator that worked. That made for a nice change, thought Maxim, as the elevator groaned up to the ninth floor, even if said elevator also carried a distinct whiff of overcooked cabbage. But there were much worse smells, he thought, as the elevator doors clanged open and he stepped out.

It had been a frustrating day, so far. The courier company's records showed a call had come from a man who said an envelope had been left with him. This proved to be the bar-man in a seedy little bar; but he wasn't the sender, nor did he know the person who had dropped it off, with money and instructions, as he hadn't been curious. It was that kind of place. When pressed, the barman said the man who'd left the envelope might have had a German accent, but that was all. And even that was doubtful.

So Maxim had decided to follow another trail, and it had led him here, to this place. The sort of place where a retired civil servant who'd never gone above a certain rung might live. Someone with a bit of money set aside, but not much. Someone who'd never been quite ambitious enough, or far-sighted enough, or ruthless enough …

The man who answered Maxim's knock was small and frail-looking, with wispy white hair and hazel eyes behind wire-rimmed glasses. He was wearing tracksuit pants, a zipped-up fleecy jacket and slippers, and looked like he'd just got up, though it was nearly midday.

"Luka Viktorovich Nevsky?"

"Yes," said the old man, in a surprisingly steady voice. "And you are?"

Maxim knew he was expected. His informant had arranged it. But he still took out his ID and showed Nevsky. "Senior Lieutenant Maxim Serebrov of the Criminal Investigative Department," he said. "I believe our mutual acquaintance has told you to expect me."

"You better come in," said the man, and shot a glance down the corridor before ushering Maxim in. The policeman hid an inward smile. It didn't matter how low down the ladder, how unimportant a KGB employee had been, like Nevsky, old habits die hard.

The apartment was small, almost as small as Maxim's own, but unlike Maxim's, it was very tidy. Almost obsessively so. Every flat surface was clear, and showed not a speck of dust. The few photographs on top of the bookshelf were arranged in a neat row; the books themselves were ranked in order of size and spine color. The single armchair was neatly positioned to face the small TV, which had itself been put on a high table in a corner, while in another corner an open door revealed a tiny bedroom, equally as tidy. Nevsky motioned Maxim to one of the two chairs at the small dining table, went to close the bedroom door, and coming back, said, "May I offer you something to drink, Senior Lieutenant?"

"Thank you. But no. I believe our mutual friend has told you why I have come?"

"Yes. You are interested in my time in the archives. Specifically a particular time. The 1970s."

"That is so."

Nevsky frowned. "You understand, I was not at any time in possession of any secrets. I was just a humble clerk. Otherwise I would not be speaking to you now. For I still believe in the honor of the sword and the shield, Senior Lieutenant." He was referring to the KGB's coat of arms.

"Most laudable," said Maxim, blandly. "But I am not after any secrets, I assure you. Merely a possible memory. Did a Major Mikhail Makarov ever visit the KGB archives when you were employed there?"

Nevsky shot him a sharp look. "Comrade Major Mikhail Petrovich Makarov of the Second Chief Directorate?"

"The very same."

"Yes. Several times."

"Do you know why?"

"In his work, he had sometimes to check the – the background information we might hold on a suspect. All officers did this sometimes. Or had files sent up to them. But the comrade major preferred to come down himself."

"I see. So you knew him."

"I wouldn't say I knew him. I never had the personal contact with him, my superiors did that. But I knew him by sight and by reputation, if you understand me."

"I do. What did you think of him?"

"It wasn't my place to think."

No, I don't suppose it was, thought Maxim. Aloud, he said, "What I meant was – what had you heard about him?"

"That he was an excellent officer," said Nevsky, promptly.

"Anything else?"

"That he was much feared by our enemies and much respected by his colleagues."

"He was never promoted beyond major, though, was he?"

"So? Perhaps he didn't want to be promoted beyond that rank. He was a man who liked what he did. Who wanted to work on the frontline, not be kicked upstairs to paperwork and politics."

That at least I understand, Maxim thought. "He was a skilled interrogator, wasn't he? I have heard he could break a man in under an hour."

"Yes. He was extraordinary, I believe. There were many, many convictions of spies and subversives to his credit. And he hardly ever used the classic interrogation techniques. He had his own. I heard it said that it was as though he saw direct into people's souls. If such a thing as a soul exists," he hastened to add.

Maxim smiled to himself. Poor old Nevsky obviously hadn't caught up yet with the idea that atheism wasn't fashionable anymore. He said, "Was there ever any talk that this … talent of his wasn't natural?"

"Whatever do you mean?"

"I think you know, Luka Viktorovich."

"There was some talk," said the man, reluctantly, "but it was silly tattle peddled by gullible people. Typists. Empty-headed girls. What can you expect?"

"What did they say?"

"Oh, it's too stupid."

"Please. What did they say?"

"That he was – uncanny. An absurd idea."

Maxim didn't comment. "Did he have particular friends in the service?"

"I don't know for sure. But I believe he kept to himself."

"I see. What do you know about his private life?"

That threw Nevsky. He said, "What?"

"Was there any gossip about his private life? Any secret life?"

"No. At least not that I heard. Major Makarov was an exemplary character. No vices whatsoever. He hardly drank. He didn't smoke. He had a clean family life, and utter dedication to his work. I heard that in his office there was not a single personal memento."

Maxim could see he wasn't going to get any more from the man. "Well, then, I will leave you to your Sunday, and I thank you very much for your help, but if there is anything you might remember later, perhaps you might care to call me on this number?"

"Very well, Senior Lieutenant," said the old man, taking the scrap of notepaper. "But I doubt I have very much more to tell you. Oh, do say hello to our mutual friend, won't you? And tell him he owes me a drink."

Chapter 26

In her dream, she was in a room. A very small, very dark room. She was paralyzed, facing a corner where *something* crouched. She couldn't move. Couldn't look away. Couldn't turn her head. She could only stare at the thing in the corner. Not that she could see it – for it was made of dense darkness, like the blackest night. But she could *smell* it. There was no escaping the smell. It was rank, like the stench in the den of a wild animal. But worse than that. Much worse. In the dream, she thought it was the smell of evil. Of hatred. Of black despair ...

It was very quiet in that dream-room. Her ears were full of silence. A heavy silence that seemed to clutch around her heart, squeezing, slowly, slowly, while the stench grew worse and worse.

And then – then the thing moved. She heard it. Her terrified mind broke the spell, speeding her up through layers of consciousness like a desperate sailor escaping a stricken submarine, and with a gasp she woke.

She was in bed. In Alexey's bed. He was lying beside her, deeply asleep. The room was quiet. Not dark. Pale light was filtering through a crack in the curtains. As her breathing slowly returned to normal, she thought, *Don't be afraid of your dreams*. Easier said than done, at least while you were in the middle of them. She could rationalize it now. It's only a dream: subconscious fears you hardly understand, mingled with fears you are aware of. Like the memory of the black coffin graphic on the threatening card. Was that what it had been about? A formless enemy, waiting in the dark.

Alexey's godfather Volkovsky had called Alexey last night about Serebrov's lack of progress so far in tracking down the identity of the sender of the card. And last night, relaxed after a surprisingly enjoyable, rather boozy barbecue lunch at Galina's which went on till early evening, Helen had persuaded herself that it was okay, and that she'd vanquished the demon worry. But she must still have been troubled, deep down. And it had come out in that awful nightmare. Though now she was fully awake, the power of the dream, the special quality of its hideousness, was slowly fading. Thank God.

She slipped quietly out of bed and went to the bathroom. On the way back, she happened to glance out of the window and saw Oleg's dogs in the garden, prowling around restlessly, their coats shining blackly under the moon. With a little tremor, she went back to bed, trying not to think of the other day, of being bailed up by them under the tree, lest the image was the last thing in her mind before she fell asleep and it triggered another nightmare.

But it didn't. Quite the opposite, she sailed into a sweet dream of flying, not alone this time, but with Alexey, and nothing and no one troubled them; there was just the blue sky around them, and then, quietly, everything faded into a long dreamless sleep. And when she awoke, it was to the sound of her name, spoken by Alexey, already dressed and fresh from the shower, bringing her breakfast in bed.

"I thought we might have a day on the river today," he said, brightly. "Hire a rowboat. Go fishing. What do you think?"

"It sounds lovely," said Helen, buttering her warm, sweet yeast bread, "only I can't fish and I'm not all that good at rowing either."

"Then I'll teach you, you'll see, there's nothing to it."

"Says you," she retorted, but smiling.

He said, "You know what, Lenochka? I thought, when I woke this morning – this place – it's ours now, yours and mine, and for the first time I feel at home in it."

She kissed him, tenderly. She thought how in the past she had been afraid of the future ambushing her. She'd tried to control it, set goals. She'd had her life in hand. So she thought. Till the fates whacked her hard and then future and present both disappeared and there were only fragments of the past endlessly replaying, like a stuck music loop. Now – she wasn't brooding about the past; but she also didn't fret about the future. Not any more. She'd never felt more alive, never felt more present in the moment, more at home, in the world, in life, in her skin, with him. So what did bad dreams matter, when she felt like this?

*

Under the trees by the Volga, the mosquitoes swarmed; but on the river, there were none at all, and it was perfectly delightful, a tiny breeze ruffling the calm blue waters, the boat bobbing peacefully along as Alexey rested at the oars. They fished most of the morning and caught only one fish in the end, but it was a lovely day, they were together, with their whole lives in front of them like the flowing waters of the Volga. After a lunch of the excellent sandwiches and home-made juices Katya had prepared for them, they simply allowed themselves to drift, talking softly at first then falling into a companionable silence, watching the river, and all that was going on beside and on it. For there were several other people out on the water too, and they exchanged greetings with them, in the quiet, laconic way of any river fraternity. There was something curiously pleasing about it, thought Helen, something oddly satisfying in being part of the ordinary intimacy of people in the vastness of nature. The river put things into perspective, like watching the stars at night. It gave you a sense of the grandeur of the eternal. But the little boats on the water reminded you both of the fragility and the simple warmth of human life. Yet they weren't alien to each other, the bigness and the smallness; they were part of the same thing.

She said, "Do you believe in God, Alexey?"

If he was startled, he didn't show it. He smiled and said, "Yes. Do you?"

"I don't know. Sometimes I think I do. Sometimes not. Don't you feel like that?"

"No," he said, simply.

"You just believe, is that it?"

"No," he said. "Not really." He took her hand, put it on his wrist. He said, "Can you feel that?"

Puzzled, she said, "Your pulse?"

"Yes."

"I don't understand."

"That's what I feel about God," he said. "It's not a belief. It's something that is like my pulse. There all the time. Do you see?"

She looked at him, catching her breath. "I do. But I'm not sure I'd call it God."

"Whatever you choose to call it," he said, gently, "it's there."

"Yes," she said. "It is."

He looked at her. "What brought that on, Lenochka?"

"Just being here, with you," she said, simply.

He smiled. "You know what? I've sometimes wondered what heaven might be like, and now I think I know. What we share. Our love. No matter what happens – we will always be together in these moments. I think that's what it will be for us, in the next life. Those moments, over and over, always fresh, always beautiful."

She shot him a glance, uneasy again. It was the tone in his voice, the look that had briefly flickered in his eyes, like a dark shadow briefly seen moving in the depths of the sea. She said, "What's wrong?"

"Nothing. I'm just idly speculating. Being a village theologian." His voice was warm, his smile impish. Had she just imagined what she'd seen in his face before? She said, tartly, "Well, I prefer our heaven in this life, thank you all the same. Besides, I never fancied all that stuff about pure spirits and sitting around on clouds strumming harps and all that sort of thing."

He laughed, and kissed her. "Neither do I."

*

It was an hour or so after they got back to the house that Helen's cell phone rang. It was her mother.

"How's your day, darling?"

"Lovely, Mam. We've been fishing."

"Fishing?" said her mother, in an incredulous tone, as well she might. Her daughter had never been renowned for an interest in fishing before.

Helen laughed. "We just caught one fish but it's a reasonable size."

"Good," said her mother vaguely. "But listen, Helen – Irina's back. And she'd like you both to come for dinner. Tonight, if that suits."

"Hang on, Mam." She put a hand over the phone and asked Alexey.

"Okay, why not?" he said. "I'd like to meet the famous professor."

Just before they left for Irina's, Volkovsky called. He was back in St Petersburg, he said, following up a lead from Zaitsev on Lebedev's associates. "There's nothing further from Maxim in Moscow yet," he went on, "but I know he's continuing his investigations. He keeps his cards close to his chest, does our policeman friend. And he's slow. Methodical. But he'll get there. Oh, and by the way, there proved to be no fingerprints on that message. Whoever sent it used gloves. The only fingerprints were on the envelope, and they were the courier company messenger's, and the barman's. It's faintly possible DNA testing may uncover more, though unlikely. But it's slower in any case and we'll have to wait for results."

"What about Foma and the code?" asked Alexey. "Has he made any headway on that?"

"I'm afraid not. But he's keeping at it. He's another one who doesn't give up. And this is a real challenge to his pride so I'm confident he'll do it sooner rather than later. Now, is everything all right at your end?"

"Quite all right," said Alexey, smiling at Helen.

"I will call again tomorrow if I have news," Volkovsky said. "In the meantime, don't worry."

"Of course not," said Alexey, ironically, and when the call ended, he immediately tried to call Maxim, but the number was engaged, so instead he called Ilya, and spoke to him for a few minutes, in Russian.

At last he rang off and Helen said, "So? What was that about?"

"I just wanted to know if Ilya had anything new to report."

"And did he?"

"No. He's been going through the CCTV footage of what happened the other day, trying to zoom in on the faces of those other two guys."

"And?"

"Without success. They were much cleverer than Grisha. They never faced the camera and besides they had those balaclavas. He's trying to see if he can blow up other details, like shoes and so on, but doesn't hold up much hope he can identify them from that. Okay, then, we'd better go, we're already late for our dinner date."

Chapter 27

Irina's eyes were bright with frank interest as Helen introduced her to Alexey. "Pleased to meet you, Mr. Makarov."

"Alexey, please, Professor. And I am sorry we are late. My fault. I had to take a call."

"*Nichevo*," said Irina, cheerfully. "No worries. Dinner's not spoiled, and Therese and I just had ourselves another glass of wine, so we're happy. And none of this professor business, either, Alexey. My name's Irina. Now what do you have there? Wow, did you guys catch this yourselves?" she exclaimed, her words tumbling over each other, as Alexey presented her with the fish wrapped in clear cellophane.

"We did," said Alexey, grinning, "And I know it won't feed four of us, let alone the five thousand, but maybe you can have it tomorrow. And here's something else that I hope you might like." He presented her with a bottle of French champagne, cold from being in his father's cellar.

"Hey, any apology gracefully accepted if it comes with a fresh fish and most especially with real champagne," said Irina, laughing. She poured four glasses and they toasted each other and then sat down to a meal of delicious roast lamb and vegetables. And if Helen had feared the conversation might flag, she was soon reassured, for Alexey asked about Irina's favorite subject, the book she was writing, and that kept everything flowing nicely.

Irina told them she was working hard on one of the most important chapters in the book, about cases of feral children brought up by bears. "There's not as many documented cases of that as children brought up by wolves," she said, "but they're just as interesting. And some of them are very recent. For instance, in 2001, a sixteen-month old baby girl was found in a bear's den in Iran. She was being fed by the mother bear!"

"That's really weird. You'd think a bear's natural instinct would be to kill a human, or at least to avoid them," said Helen.

"You're right, honey – and nine times out of ten that's exactly what happens. But occasionally, a female bear will accept a young baby or toddler as part of her family. Usually it's when they have cubs of their own. I guess a protective instinct kicks in."

"But how the hell does a kid end up in a bear's den in the first place?" asked Alexey.

"They get lost – the parents are hunting or foraging and the kid wanders off – or they're abandoned because the parents can't feed them or sometimes because the child's mentally disabled. What mostly seems to happen is that the child crawls into the den, when the mother bear's absent – and falls asleep with the cubs. When the mother returns, well, she just lets it stay there. Anyway, it's pretty rare, but it's been documented all through time, and all over the world – from Lithuania to Turkey, Hungary to India to the States. Anywhere you find bears, really."

"What about in Russia?" asked Therese.

"Here too. The case I'm concentrating on is one I unearthed in my research, of a baby who was found in a Karelian bear-den in late 1934 and who subsequently became part of a most unusual scientific project around feral children. The *Homo Ferens* project. That's 'wild man' in Latin. It was conceived by a Russian scientist called Antonov. His *Homo Ferens* was a top-secret project commissioned by Stalin. So secret there was practically nothing archived at all. It forms the heart of my book. The theme, in a way. And it's taken me years and years to piece together the story, and track down the details."

"So what was the project, exactly?" said Helen.

"Ah..." Irina smiled and wagged a finger. "Maybe you should wait and read my book!"

"Oh come on, Irina, you can't just leave it like that," said Therese, smiling. "We're all bursting with curiosity."

Irina smiled. "Okay. I suppose it started first because of the superhuman soldier experiment Stalin ordered in the late 1920s. A scientist called Ilya Ivanov, an animal geneticist by profession, reckoned he could cross-breed humans and apes to produce a being who would have human-type intelligence but no human morality, who would have animal strength, endurance, cunning and obedience. The perfect soldier, as far as Stalin was concerned. Anyway, that experiment was a complete failure, not one embryo resulted from it."

"Yuck," said Helen, revolted, "what a disgusting thing to even try."

"Stalin didn't care about that, honey, he only cared about success. And when it didn't work, well, he punished Ivanov for it, sent him into exile, where he soon died. The whole project was dismantled completely and never tried again. But a few years later, in the 1930s, the guy I've been looking at, Antonov, came up with a completely different superhuman project. Not nature, but nurture. Not genetics, but upbringing. Now, there's a famous fairytale about Ivashko, the bear's son, who's brought up by a bear and has superhuman strength and agility but little concept of morality. Despite all that, Ivashko gets on really well in life. Antonov thought that this story contained a kernel of truth. But he also knew that though most *real* feral children have certain senses sharpened enormously and do have superhuman strength or agility or whatever, they are mostly unable to adapt to human life after they are found, especially the older they are. Mostly, they don't learn to speak, they seem unable to learn human ways, they pine for the wild, and they die young. But Antonov thought he could modify these patterns, and that a way could be found that would grow a superhuman and useful child, like in the fairytale. The child would be brought up by the bear – but the whole thing would be controlled, so it wasn't just left up to the animal. The child would be in constant interaction with the bear, but carefully monitored."

Helen said, "You mean, he would watch it all happening?"

"Yes. But from a distance. From an observation hide. He wouldn't interact with the children himself though."

"The *children*?" said Alexey. "There was more than one?"

"Oh yes. It all started after Antonov discovered the existence of the Karelian child – who I've called Baby K, nobody knows his real name. So Baby K was the first subject. But not the only one. There were by my reckoning about eight to ten children involved."

"There were that many children found in bear-dens back then?" said Helen, surprised.

"Oh no. Only Baby K. The others – Antonov obtained through other means." She paused. "There were many orphans in those days. Abandoned children." She saw their expressions. "Look, Antonov thought of himself as a rational scientist. The old concept of the soul, morality, all those things had been rejected. To Antonov, it was all about new frontiers. The continuation of evolution but not by random means. He really thought he was helping to bring into being a whole new species. He did not intend cruelty to the children. In fact, I think he meant well."

"Meant well?" said Alexey, incredulously. "He sounds like a complete maniac."

Irina looked at him. She sighed. "He was single-minded, yes. Obsessive, yes. A maniac? Well, you have to remember the times. Against the Stalinist background of mass murder, Antonov's experiment really was small beer. But I find it, and him, interesting, because of that mixture of science and fairytale. It is not my job to pass judgment, Alexey."

"Of course not. I didn't mean that," said Alexey, hastily, "and I'm sorry if it sounded like that. It's certainly a fascinating subject."

"It sure is," said Irina, smiling. "Endlessly fascinating. But that's quite enough about my stuff, I'm tired of holding the floor and I'm sure you're all sick of hearing about it." She looked at Alexey. "It's your turn to spill. I hear you've taken the helm of your father's company. And yet I also heard you'd planned a career in music. What gives, then?"

Alexey smiled and said, "Well, it's like this ..." And he began to tell them about how he had decided to take on Trinity. He didn't tell them everything; and he certainly did not mention the recent troubles. But Therese and Irina seemed very interested, and made the right sorts of responses at the right sorts of moments, and Helen could see by the expression in her mother's eyes that her already good impression of Alexey was only growing by the minute, and it made her very glad.

*

But a short while later, Irina ambushed Helen when both Therese and Alexey were out of earshot in the garden. "Listen, honey. Don't take this the wrong way. Think of it as an old woman's paranoia, if you like – but are you sure you're being wise?"

Helen bristled. "What do you mean?"

"His kind – they're trouble. Dashing, rich young men, used to having their own way. After what happened with Simon, aren't you the least bit worried?"

Helen stiffened. "He's nothing like Simon! And he's not a *kind*. He's just himself."

"In any case, you hardly know him. You only met him, what, a week ago? Less? No wonder your mother's worried."

"She is *not* worried," retorted Helen. "We've spoken about it, and she's fine."

"That's what she might tell you, and I know you might think I'm an interfering old bitch, but I care about you. And about Therese. And I *know* when she's worried."

"Mam likes him," said Helen, stubbornly.

"Sure she likes him. Hell, I like him. He's likeable all right."

"Well, then ..."

"But look at you, Helen. You hang on his every word. You practically live in his pocket. Nobody else seems to matter."

"That's not true! And Mam understands. I know she does."

"Sure she does. It's what happened to her, with your father. God, you should have seen them together. Couldn't keep their eyes and hands off each other. It was – intense. And she was so happy at the time. Everything that separated them – their culture, their experiences, their personalities – didn't matter a damn, back then. But it ended up mattering very much, Helen. Too much."

"Alexey is not my father," said Helen, fiercely. "And I'm not my mother."

"You are from different worlds," said Irina. "He's Russian. And you're a Westerner. You speak a different language. And I don't just mean words. It's what's in your head. The mind-set, it's just not the same."

"I can't believe you're saying this, after all you've said about Russia, and how much you love it!"

"Sure I do, at least most of the time, but I don't kid myself I understand it completely. And I'm not trying to have a relationship with a guy, either. Things are complicated enough as it is. Hell's bells, honey, I'm part Russian and I've lived here on and off for years and I still don't get it sometimes."

"Why do we always have to *get it*?" snapped Helen. "Why can't we just accept it's different, and take it from there?"

"All very woo-woo and mystical," retorted Irina, "but you have to weigh up the risks."

"Risk is the price we pay for living! If someone told you, Irina, that this book you're writing – the work you love so much – if someone said that it is dangerous trash and that you should give it up – what would you do?"

Irina gave her a sharp glance. She shrugged. "Touché. I'd tell them to go to hell."

"I don't want to tell you that, because I know you care about me and Mam – I know you are saying these things because of that – but please, understand. This is the most important thing that has ever happened to me and I will never turn my back on it. No matter what. Never. Ever."

Their eyes met, for a long moment. Irina sighed. "Hell, I can respect that. Completely. You have made your choice and you are sticking to it, come what may." Her tone changed, became softer, apologetic. "And look, honey, I'm sorry if I spoke out of turn. Damn bad habit of mine, blurting out what I shouldn't." She stuck a hand out. "No hard feelings?"

Helen took the proffered hand. "It's okay." And oddly enough, it was. Irina had been challenging, but that was a good thing. Unlike Mam, she thought, Irina never saw me when I was feeling bad, so she isn't wary, she doesn't spare me at all and that's kind of stimulating. It was all out in the open now, with Mam, with Irina, I stood up for myself and for Alexey, I found exactly the right way to defeat her arguments, and she respects that. I know she does. It feels like the air's been cleared between us, for good.

Chapter 28

This apartment was almost comically the polar opposite of Nevsky's, Maxim thought: cheerful, colorful and cluttered with pictures – including a wall covered in icons – and memorabilia of all sorts. Behind a closed door, he heard a woman's voice, crooning to a fretful child. It made a sudden pang go through him. How much have I lost, he thought, sadly, through my own stubbornness? I could have been happy with Marina, if I'd tried. If she'd mattered more to me than my own pride. This man might have a job I consider strange, irrelevant, fake, even. But he has a family. Something real. Something warm. Someone to care if he was hurt, or lonely. Someone to mourn him when he was gone.

"So," said the man he'd come to see. Josef Oberlian was a big, vigorous-looking man in his late thirties, with an Armenian accent and a steady dark gaze. "You were quite mysterious on the phone, Senior Lieutenant. To what do I owe the honor of this visit?"

Maxim pushed aside the regretful thoughts and became brisk. "I'm sorry to call so late," he said, "but I wondered if this man had ever come to you as a client." From his wallet, he took a newspaper photograph of Ivan Makarov and showed it to him. The Armenian glanced at the picture, then back at the policeman. He said, "This is the man from that Trinity case, yes? You are investigating his death?"

Maxim saw no reason to deny it. "That is so."

"Why show me this? Why come to me?"

"A friend of mine told me you are regarded as the best aura-reader in Moscow," Maxim said, discreetly. Skorpia had texted him Oberlian's details. "I know Ivan Makarov had his aura read. I also know that he only ever sought out the best, in any field of life. Therefore if he did go to an aura-reader, he would have come to you." The Armenian inclined his head in recognition of the compliment, but said nothing. Maxim went on. "It would have been at least two, maybe even three years ago."

"That was a fair time ago, Senior Lieutenant! And you understand, I have had many clients before and since. Some of them are regulars. Others come only once or twice. It is not always easy to remember those."

Maxim looked hard at him. "But I think this man *did* visit you, didn't he? You displayed no surprise when I showed you his picture."

"Yes. You are quite right. But I had forgotten him until I saw news of his death on TV."

"And yet you did not contact the police."

The steady gaze did not waver. "Why should I? There was nothing linking a client's visit some years ago to that client's suspicious death in a business scandal. He did not consult me about his work, Senior Lieutenant."

Maxim had to admit that was fair enough. "So, he came to visit you. What happened?"

Instead of answering directly, the Armenian said, "Do you know how we aura-readers work, Senior Lieutenant?"

"Not really. Please enlighten me."

"People come to us for various reasons – usually because they have problems of one kind or another, health problems, for example, that doctors can't work out. Or maybe they fear they are under psychic attack of some sort, such as by energy vampires. But as well as physical or psychic problems, people can also come to an aura-reader for curiosity's sake. Because they want to know if what they perceive of themselves is the truth. Or they want to get to know themselves better. For their spiritual advancement – or for other reasons."

"Mmm," said Maxim, non-committally. "And what category did Ivan Mikhailovich Makarov fall under?"

"The man whose picture you showed me?"

"Yes."

"He was definitely in the second category. Now, let me explain – a very small percentage of us can see people's auras clearly, with the naked eye. Most of us see them only dimly, however, and need to take photographs to focus our perception."

"Kirlian photographs?"

"Exactly. Anyway – I was originally of the second breed of aura-reader, with only a slight natural talent, but over the years I have greatly sharpened my … perception." His dark eyes flicked over Maxim's face, thoughtfully, and the policeman had the uncomfortable feeling that his aura was getting a thorough look-over. "However, I always work with photographs initially, as that puts clients at their ease. But there is another reason why I do it."

"And that is?"

"It is less dangerous, Senior Lieutenant," said Oberlian, quietly. "You see, an aura is the visible emanation of a person's innermost being. Intensely personal, yes? But the photograph is made by an impersonal machine. It is then like an X-ray. Ultrasounds. Scans. The client does not link you, the professional aura-reader, directly with the photograph. You are merely the interpreter of it, like a doctor is of scans and X-rays and the rest. No one can blame you for what is there or not there. The machine does not have an agenda. It cannot threaten you. It cannot be a danger to you. It merely – *records*. With some people – it is *absolutely* essential they know that. That they think that without the machine, you can see – nothing. Or very little." His eyes met Maxim's. "Do you understand?"

Maxim nodded.

"This man Makarov – who by the way did not give his real name – was one of those sorts. I would have wanted him to think that I saw very little without the photograph. Do you see?"

Maxim said, "Yes I do."

"In fact, his aura was very bright. And dominated by the kinds of colors that give off a certain – danger signal."

"Red, black, indigo, yellows," said Maxim, promptly.

"Ah. You must have seen a copy of his Kirlian photo."

"It's come up in the investigation. What does it mean?"

"Without the actual photograph, I can't give a complete picture, you understand. It all depends on the shades of color and where they're distributed. But if I may make gross generalizations: red is associated with a strong ego, passion, conviction, certainty; indigos and yellows with varying degrees of psychic abilities; and blacks with – shall we say – negative qualities. All in all, an image showing a person of a certain – formidable sort. Not one you'd want to interfere with. If you get my meaning."

"Yes. I'd like to see your file on Makarov's Kirlian photos, please."

"No. I'm sorry – what I mean is, if a client is not a regular, I do not keep any such files, Senior Lieutenant. I destroy my notes and give all copies of the photos to the clients, including the negatives as well. Another form of insurance, you might say."

Maxim said, "I see. But Makarov didn't come just once, did he?"

For the first time, the man's calm gaze wavered. "What?"

"He returned a few weeks or months after he'd originally come, and asked you to be part of a new venture he was starting. Offered you a job, in short."

Oberlian stared. "What? He did no such thing."

"Are you sure? Please tell me the truth, because if you do not –"

"I *am* telling the truth, Senior Lieutenant. Yes, he came back. But no, he did not come back to ask me to join any venture. If he had …"

"Yes?"

"I'd have said no."

"When did he come back?"

"About three months after the first session."

"What did he want?"

"Simply another session with the camera, Senior Lieutenant. He wanted to know if certain areas of his aura had become enhanced."

"The yellows and indigos, I presume? The psychic area?"

"Yes. You are quite correct."

"Had they? Become enhanced, I mean?"

"Yes. They had been paler in the first session. The shades had deepened."

"Can you explain that?"

"He had been working on them."

"How does one do that?"

"Mental exercises. Visualization. Meditation. Experimentation. Those are the tried and true methods. Slow, yes. But tried and true. You can even buy machines to do it, if you are impatient. And foolish."

"How so?"

"I have heard many inflated claims about such machines. But none stand up to proof."

"What sort of machines are we talking about?"

Oberlian shrugged. "Hand-held devices which use microwaves, electromagnetic radiation, laser or acoustic waves, or even simple electrical charges, to artificially interfere with the brain. It's believed some such devices have been used as weaponry. But it's claimed by those who sell them over the Internet that they can also enhance and stimulate the mind's abilities. Psychotronic devices, they are sometimes called. The kind the Parliament banned a few years ago but which our Defence Minister not long ago mentioned as having some interest for our military. And there's a flourishing black-market trade in them. Why, I could order one today over the Internet if I so chose."

"But you say none stand up to proof."

"That is so. These devices have been on sale for years. No doubt many people have bought them. But I have observed no corresponding rise in psychic power among the general public, and my clients present with the same mixture of abilities, or lack of them, as way back when I first started. No, Senior Lieutenant, they're fool's gold, sold by shysters."

"So you don't think Makarov would have been using such a thing?"

"Certainly not. Whatever else he might or might not have been, the man was clearly no fool. Besides, he told me himself he'd been using mental exercises and experimentation. There really is no substitute for good old-fashioned work and practice. Of course, if someone were one day to discover a process which did away for the need for the hard slog in the psychic realm, that would change the face of the world. Myself, though, I think such a thing will remain firmly in the domain of fiction." He smiled. "I certainly hope so, or all of us professional psychics would be out of a job."

"I see. Very interesting. Did Makarov come back a third time?"

"No. He did not. He thanked me, paid, and left with his photographs. I never saw him again. Until – I saw a report about his death on TV."

Maxim took out two other newspaper photos from his wallet. Galkin. Barsukov. He said, "What about these two? Did they come to see you?"

Oberlian looked at them. "These are the other two men in the case, am I correct?"

"You are. Well?"

"No, Senior Lieutenant. I am certain they never came to me. But if you have found their Kirlian photos, then I will remind you that I am not the only aura-reader in Moscow."

"No, of course," said Maxim. Then he added, "Is it possible to read the aura of a dead person?" He was thinking of Major Mikhail Makarov.

Oberlian looked startled. "What?"

"I mean – if you are given a portrait, or a photograph of them?"

"I see. Well – it's possible – but it is likely to be inaccurate, because it will be at second-hand."

"Ivan Makarov didn't ask you the same question?"

"No, Senior Lieutenant. He did not."

"I see. Well, thank you, Mr. Oberlian, you have been most helpful."

"May I make an observation, Senior Lieutenant?"

"You may."

"Sometimes things are not what they seem to be. A man may think he knows what he's doing – his aura may be bright, clear, powerful – but that doesn't mean he really *does* know. Contrary to what many people think, an aura is *not* your destiny. It is not fixed, and cannot, *must* not, be used to foretell the future. It should not be used as an infallible guide. It is merely a reflection of your innermost self. But even that can change." He gestured at the wall of icons. "Only God knows everything. We humans – we are rather more limited. We see through a glass darkly. Some of us better than others, that's all."

"What are you telling me?"

"I am telling you that what may seem to us to be our greatest strength may instead be our fatal weakness. You may be lured to your death by the very thing which, in your blindness, you may consider to be your chief strength."

*

As he went back down in the elevator, Maxim could not get those words out of his head. *The very thing which, in your blindness, you may consider to be your chief strength.* What was Ivan Makarov's strength? His passion for Trinity, of course. And that newly discovered "psychic" talent of his, which he had decided to put in Trinity's service. Trinity, which indissolubly linked the three directors: that, and their loyalty to each other.

But Makarov had been the company's heart. The driving force of the triumvirate. And whatever the truth about his "psychic power", Makarov had *certainly* been a powerful man. A man not to easily cross. And yet a charismatic man. A man who still, even after his death, inspired the loyalty of his subordinates. Family strengths, those. The KGB major, that fearsome old heart-devourer, had had them in spades, too. And now, it seemed, Alexey ...

He looked at the time. It was well past eleven by now. Still, he might as well try. He took out his phone, dialed Alexey's number. It was picked up after a few rings. Alexey said, "Hello?"

Maxim could hear voices in the background. It sounded like the TV was on. He said, in Russian, "I'm sorry to disturb you, Alexey Ivanovich."

"It's okay. Film's just about over, anyway. Helen and I have been sitting up watching my favorite childhood film. Lev Atamanov's *The Snow Queen*. What's up?"

"Nothing's up. But I just need to ask you a question. Is that okay?"

"Fire away."

"Since you've been in Russia, has anyone approached you about writing a book about Trinity? Its history, famous cases, et cetera? Someone claiming to be a writer of some sort – a journalist, even maybe?"

Alexey sounded startled when he answered, "Well, I've had calls from journalists wanting to know what I was going to do with Trinity – but Kolya fielded all those. You can ask him if you like. But a book on Trinity – no way."

"Did anyone ever approach your father about such an undertaking? Either a book – or a series of in-depth articles?"

"Not as far as I know. And he'd never have agreed, even if such an approach had been made."

"It would have been couched in highly flattering terms."

"Dad didn't care about flattery. If you think that's how the killer might have wheedled his way in, I really can't see it. Dad would have smelled a rat at once. He'd have suspected espionage of some sort."

"What about the others? Galkin and Barsukov?"

"Well – I can't say. But I doubt Dad would have let them. He was pretty much on top of things, you know."

"Even though he didn't live in Russia anymore?"

"Well, they might have done something behind his back – but why would they? If they were working on their unit plans – and they wanted to keep that really secret – they'd hardly want to go blabbing to the press, would they? But Maxim – why on earth do you ask? What's happened? Who have you been talking to?"

Chapter 29

Alexey clicked the phone off. "That was Maxim," he told Helen. "He went to see these two guys …" And quickly, he recounted what Maxim had told him of his visits to Nevsky and Oberlian. "But he started with this strange question – about whether anybody had contacted me about writing a book on Trinity. Or had contacted Dad and the others. He has some idea that this could have been a way to get into the inner circle."

"But you don't think so?"

"No, I don't. It's an ingenious theory, but I don't think it stands up. They'd never talk to a writer about Trinity. But it's made me think. What if it had been about something else? About a hobby, say? Dad had no hobbies, and anyway he'd have just said no on principle, he hated talking about himself, his instinct was always to be secretive – but the others – I'm not so sure. Galkin, for instance, he fancied himself as a big-game hunter. So if somebody claiming to be, say, from a hunting magazine had suggested doing an article about him – he'd probably have agreed. Say then that they suggested doing it in the field – actually following him on a hunt – then they might have had an opportunity to …"

"Yes, but wouldn't he have talked about it? And wouldn't someone have seen him going off with this person?"

"Yes. You're right. It doesn't really work." He paused. "The aura-reader told Maxim he thought Dad had been somehow … working on his psychic powers. That he'd been practicing. I – I – I thought at once of that – that video we saw."

Helen saw the shadows in his eyes. She said, "Did you tell Maxim about it?"

"No. I can't. Stupid of me, but …"

"No," she said, putting an arm around him, "it's not." Tenderly, she added, "But it's late, and it's been a tiring day, and we shouldn't think about any of this right now, but just go to bed."

"What, are you sleepy, Lenochka?" he said, kissing her hair.

"Who said anything about sleep?" she murmured, taking his hand and leading him up the stairs to their room.

*

In the early morning, Helen was having a dream about crossing an iced-up river on a troika, when there came a sharp cracking sound. The ice was breaking up, and she'd be drowned, she thought, terrified, and jerked herself awake, only to realize that the sharp sound hadn't just been in the dream. She heard it again. Her half-asleep mind tried to understand it. A car backfiring, a firecracker going off, a gunshot. *A gunshot!* She sat up like a jack in the box.

"Alexey! What's that?"

But his side of the bed was empty. She jumped out of bed, flung a cardigan over her nightie and ran barefoot down the stairs. As she did, the clock in the hall struck seven.

There was no one in the living-room or the hall or the kitchen or any of the other rooms. But the back door was open. She ran out into the overgrown garden, and saw Slava, gun in hand, bending over something lying on the ground. Shock made her yell, and he turned. His impassive gaze swept over her body in the thin clothes and she felt herself shrinking from him. But all he said, pocketing the gun, was, "Better you go in, Miss."

But now she could see what was on the ground. A body, yes. But not human. A dog. One of Oleg's dogs. A little further, another body. The other dog. She stared at Slava. Whispered, "What ... what have you done?"

"He had to do it. They attacked Oleg," said Alexey, from behind her, and she jumped. He was pale, grim, his lips set.

Beyond Alexey, Oleg was sitting, propped up in Katya's arms under a tree a short distance away. His eyes were closed, his skin was gray, there were bloodstained towels wrapped around his legs, and one arm. Katya's face was blotched with tears, her eyes glassy. Helen whispered, "What ... what happened?"

"Oleg went to feed them as usual and for some reason they just went berserk. I'd got up early, heard him scream and ran out, and with Slava and Katya we managed to drive the dogs off, and then Slava shot them." Alexey swallowed. "He's bled a fair bit, that makes the wounds look worse than they are. I've had a look, I think they're not deep – the doctor's coming, anyway, so we'll know soon. But I – I think he'll be okay. As long as the dogs didn't have rabies."

"Rabies?" Helen said, aghast. She remembered a story her grandfather had told her once, about when he was young and one of his village friends had been bitten by a mad dog and nearly died. He'd foamed at the mouth. Needed three people to hold him down. Was brain-sick for ages, and never the same again. *La rage*, rabies was called, in French. The same as rage, as wild anger. She'd thought it never happened anymore.

Alexey saw her expression. "It's very unlikely indeed, but better to be safe than sorry. He'd had those dogs years, Katya said, they'd never gone for him before."

"Well, maybe not him, but other people, yes," said Helen, shivering a little as she pulled the shawl closer. And she told a startled Alexey then what had happened the other day. As he listened to her story, his expression darkened.

"Then they were already out of control, and Oleg must have known that," he said, tightly. "I wish you'd told me."

"I know. I'm sorry. But I didn't want to get Oleg into trouble. Him and Katya – I got the impression they really needed their jobs."

He flashed out, "For God's sake, I wouldn't have sacked him for that!"

She swallowed. "I wasn't hurt, so I thought it was best."

He looked quickly at her. "Forgive me, Lenochka. I didn't mean to jump down your throat. Of course you did the right thing at the time. It's just that I'm a bit – shaken – and thinking of what might have happened."

"I know," she said, gently, "but it didn't happen to me, but to poor Oleg, and at least you got to him in time." At that moment the doctor came into the garden, a thin little woman with a harassed expression. She went briskly to Oleg, bent over him and examined him, spoke to Katya, and to Alexey, who had approached them. He beckoned Slava over, and together he and the bodyguard carried a now conscious but groaning Oleg gently out of the garden, and the doctor, Katya and Helen followed.

They laid him in the doctor's car on the backseat and Katya went with him to the hospital. After Helen had dressed, she and Alexey followed in the Mercedes – stony-faced Slava had stayed behind to bag up the dogs' corpses and bring them in for pathology testing. At the hospital, Oleg was given painkillers and a sedative, and his wounds were dressed, the doctor confirming Alexey's judgment that they weren't nearly as bad as they looked. And after he had been thoroughly examined, they were also told that neither he nor his wounds were showing any sign of rabies infection, that it was pretty much certain he didn't have it, which was a relief, but not a surprise to Oleg himself, who, weak though he was, had recovered a spark of indignant energy when he heard that's what they'd suspected. "As if my dogs would have such a thing! As if I wouldn't have known!" he'd protested to anyone who would listen. But if there was no rabies there might be other dangers, said the doctor, firmly, and she ordered that a tetanus shot be given to him. As they hovered in the corridor waiting to be allowed to go back in, Alexey said to Katya, "You must tell me if there is anything I can do for you."

"Thank you," said Katya, and then she hesitated and went on, in a rush, "You do enough already. You pay for extra care. You are very kind. But ..."

"What is it, Katya?"

"I regret, Alexey Ivanovich," she said, formally, "but we cannot stay in Uglich. We go back to Moscow as soon as Oleg is well."

"I see," said Alexey, tightly.

"It is not you. You are good boss. But the dogs, you see ... they were Oleg's – friends. He works with them years. And Slava – he just shoot them."

"They were dangerous! He had to do it. Surely you understand that. Not only did they attack Oleg, but I hear now they also went for Helen."

Katya flushed and shot Helen a sideways glance. "Yes," she whispered. "But never they are like this before. And – and Slava – you did not ask him to shoot, he just does it. Ask no questions. Give no mercy. We cannot work with him anymore."

"I see," repeated Alexey. His tone was icy. His eyes flashed.

"I am sorry, Alexey Ivanovich," she said, helplessly.

His voice was hard as he said. "Very well. I'll make sure you are paid all you're owed. You can collect your things when you want." And he turned his back on her and stalked off, away up the corridor toward the exit.

Helen turned as if to follow him, but checked herself. Something bothered her. Something which scratched at her instinct like a splinter under the skin. Impulsively, she burst out, "There's something else, isn't there, Katya? Something you didn't tell Alexey. Something about Slava." She remembered the way the man's eyes had crawled over her. "Katya, did he try to ..."

Katya met her eyes. She shook her head.

"Then what is it?"

"Dogs never do this before," Katya said. "Slava, too. He know Oleg long time, but he does this. I think there is badness in that house." She paused. "People say, a curse ..."

She broke off, but Helen had heard enough. She said, sharply, "That's rubbish. The newspapers dreamed all that up. Look, Katya, I'm sorry Oleg got hurt, but it was his dogs did it, no one else and you shouldn't try and blame it on –"

Katya cut her off. "If you please," she said, coldly. "I go back to my man now. Goodbye." And she left Helen planted there.

Alexey was just outside, by the car. He opened the door for her to get in, and got into the driver's seat. He looked at Helen. Took her hand. "I'm sorry, Lenochka."

"About what?"

"Walking off like that."

"It's okay," she said, squeezing his hand. "I – I just stayed to try and get some sense out of Katya. I had the impression she was hiding something."

"And was she?"

"Well ..." She hesitated, but didn't want to lie. "She said your place was cursed. That it made the dogs go mad. I think that's what she meant, anyway."

Alexey looked at her. He said, very quietly, "I thought it must be something like that."

"What? You knew?"

"I guessed. The way she kept harping on about this being out of character for the dogs."

Helen said, "You know, Katya said that Slava had behaved oddly too."

"Hell, she's just trying to pin the blame everywhere but where it belongs," he snapped. "Any old story will do." His lips were set again in that thin line, his face hard as stone. Helen thought, shakily, I can almost imagine being frightened of him, when he looks like that.

But he must have sensed what she was feeling, for he stopped the car. Turning toward her, he held out his arms. He murmured, against her hair, "Forgive my bad temper, Lenochka, this has all shaken me up more than I like to admit, but I'm not making it easy for you, and I'm sorry."

"Don't be," she said. "It's all right. I understand ..." She hesitated. "Did Slava have a theory, about why the dogs had gone for Oleg?"

"No. Slava doesn't do theories." He gave a crooked smile. "He just acts."

At that moment, his phone rang. It was Volkovsky. "Slava's just called," he said, without preamble. "Told me what happened. Are you and Helen all right?"

"Fine," was the laconic answer.

"I never thought much of that young man. Oleg, I mean. No judgment. But how is he?"

"He'll live. In fact it's not nearly as bad as it might have been." A pause. "But he and Katya have resigned."

"Really?" said Volkovsky, sharply. "Then that saves us the trouble of sacking them. Now then, I'm going to arrange straight away for someone to take Oleg's place, and –"

"No," said Alexey.

"What do you mean, no?"

"Exactly that."

"Look, Lyosha, I know Slava's reliable but he can't be everywhere at once. It's a lot of work for him on his own. Let me arrange for ..."

Helen held her breath as she saw the pinch of Alexey's nostrils and feared an explosion. But all he said was, "Slava will be enough. Thank you, Kolya."

"If you're sure ..."

"I am," he said, firmly. "Now, Kolya, any news at your end?"

"Well, I'm at the Peters office right now, going through the CCTV tapes for the hundredth time, I've got Feodor with me, he's much better by the way, sends his greetings."

"And mine to him," said Alexey.

"Good. Yes. Oh, and you remember that advertisement we placed in that English-language magazine some years ago? Well, Zaitsev tells me that one of his contacts told him the woman who wrote it had an affair with Repin later and they'd talked about Trinity. It doesn't prove anything but it is interestingly suggestive. I'm following it up, going to see the woman tomorrow, she's not with Repin anymore, and he's still away on holiday in Egypt, so she's willing to talk, off the record."

"She's brave then."

"No, in need of money," said Volkovsky, drily, "if I have your permission to spend some funds that way, Lyosha."

"Of course. If you think it'll help."

"Every lead is worth following at this stage," said Volkovsky, and rang off.

Chapter 30

They had just finished a simple lunch of sandwiches and salad when Slava came in to tell them that someone was at the gate, asking for them. An old lady. No, she didn't want to come in, he said, in Russian. She was in a hurry.

So they went out, and there was Olga Feshina. Looking more frail and birdlike than ever, she was in the passenger seat of an old gray car, with the driver, a disinterested middle-aged man, sitting reading a newspaper. She introduced him as her son-in-law, Vanya, he was taking her to her daughter's, she said, it was her granddaughter's birthday and she'd be staying there a couple of days. Then she drew Alexey aside and talked to him for a short while; and though Helen couldn't hear the words or wouldn't have understood if she had, she could see their effect on Alexey; his expression was grim again. What could the old woman be telling him?

Olga Feshina's speech came to a halt. She looked at him, and put a hand on his shoulder, briefly. He looked at her without a word, his expression blank. She sighed, and raising a hand in farewell to Helen, the old woman turned and got back into the car. Her son-in-law barely looked up from his paper. Whatever Mrs. Feshina had come to do was of little interest to him, clearly. Not so for Helen, who burned with anxious impatience to know. But Alexey's expression was hardly inviting, and it wasn't until the car had turned the corner of the street and disappeared that she managed to say, "What was that all about?"

His face was still closed. "Nothing important."

"Come on. This is *me* you're talking to!"

"You don't want to know," he said, harshly.

Her heart raced. "Please, Alexey. Please don't shut me out."

Something flickered in his eyes. "It will only upset you more, after what happened this morning. And I don't want –"

"No. *This* is upsetting me. That you don't want to tell me. Because you don't trust me." She was on the verge of tears, where hurt mixed with anger.

He grasped her hand. His eyes were full of pain. "No. Never think that. Never. I trust you absolutely. More than anything. More than anyone."

"Then tell me. Alexey, please."

He looked away for a moment. Then turning back to her, he said, heavily, "She told me she'd had one of her dreams. But this time, it was different. Because it was, she said, not a dream that came from her. It was an actual message from beyond the grave."

The very roots of Helen's hair seemed to grow cold. She stared at him. She couldn't speak.

He went on, in a strange, hollow voice, "She saw Dad. He was kneeling in a snowy field, full of crosses. A kind of graveyard, out in the wilds. He carried a gun, as if he'd been hunting. He wore a fur hat, and an old, shabby fur coat over his clothes. And all of it was sticky with blood. There was blood on his face, his hands, and staining the snow at his feet."

Helen's throat tightened.

Alexey said, tonelessly, "My father was kneeling in the blood, among the crosses, and she saw he was weeping, the tears mingling with the blood. Then he put his head down and when he raised it again, she saw that –" He broke off.

"She saw *what?* Alexey!"

"She saw that it wasn't him, any longer. It was no longer his features, his face." His eyes were full of a nameless horror. "Helen – the face – it was – *it was mine.*"

This was a crossroads for them. Just as in the forest. She could try and comfort him with lying words. She could stay silent and hold him, and hope her love would be enough. But that would be wrong. She knew that. So she said, "Did ... did Mrs. Feshina explain what it meant?"

"She only said he was – restless, unquiet. She said that she ... that she could not tell me precisely what the dream meant. Not because she didn't want to but because she couldn't. Its message was meant for me and it was up to me to understand what he was saying."

"But I think it's a warning, Alexey." The words burst from her, as if a flash of lightning had suddenly lit up the truth.

He looked at her, startled. Then he whispered, "Yes. You see it too, don't you? It's a warning. That I will – become like him. That I cannot escape it. That one day I will turn into my father – with blood on my hands, and destroyed lives on my conscience."

"No," she said, desperately. "No. That is not what I mean. I – I think you are looking at things the wrong way. The face she saw – you say it was yours."

"Mrs. Feshina said it."

"But she might be wrong, Alexey. Because she doesn't know. She doesn't know about your grandfather."

He stared at her. She went on, hurriedly, "I saw a photo of him the other day, remember. I know *you look just like him.*"

He faltered, "Oh Helen ... What – What are you saying?"

"Your father – if it was him she saw –" She gulped, as she realized the true import of what she was saying. She, a girl brought up in the clarity and logic of a secular society where such things as ghostly visitations were dismissed as superstition, was giving her allegiance to quite another world. Her head felt tight, her skull booming with the weird knowledge flooding her like the icy water of truth, which must be told, no matter what the cost. So she went on, "I think your father is trying to warn you – to tell you – that what happened ... it goes back – it goes back to your grandfather. Remember what Mrs. Feshina said, the other day, about you being haunted by a sorcerer – like your father before him? It's him, Alexey – him. *Your grandfather.* Remember Maxim telling us that the psychic your father first went to see – Lev Kirov – he told your father the power of the sorcerer had come to him from the blood. Which means, from his family. And his father – well – you told me yourself what Maxim said he'd heard from that old KGB guy Nevsky. *Your grandfather saw into people. Into their souls.* If he gave off that kind of power, people would think that, wouldn't they? Feel it, instinctively. And even his – colleagues, they'd fear that. Give him a wide berth. Even in those times, when you weren't supposed to believe in anything like that. He *was* a sorcerer, Alexey. A real one."

There was a long silence. Then Alexey said, in a hard voice. "Yes. Yes. And that power of his – it – it *wasn't* good. He was ... the darkest of dark sorcerers. Using his gift, his power, to see into people's souls – not to heal them, not to help them, not even to seek the truth – but to hunt them down, to devour their hearts, dismantle their minds. To destroy them utterly."

She said, gently, "Perhaps he didn't see it that way. Perhaps he thought he was doing the right thing. That he was really seeking the truth. That he was destroying evil."

"He might have told himself that, but it wasn't true. It wasn't true, Helen. He was a monster. It wasn't only his victims who suffered, but their families. Their friends. Suffering and pain, rippling out from him for decades. God, how he must have been hated and feared. And yet he died in his bed ..." He broke off, and then went on in a rush, "That catchy media phrase – the Rusalka Curse – that's alluding to death by drowning, and the fact Rusalka week is before Trinity, but you know, the *rusalki* – they want to avenge things that were done to them, when they were alive, when they were human. They are avengers of dark crimes, never admitted and never acknowledged. But they don't necessarily go for the one who did it, anyone will do, if they can't get him."

She stared at him. "You mean ..."

"Yes. Maybe it was my *grandfather* who did the bad things, but he was dead, beyond hurting now, and Dad ... maybe it was in the very excitement of his own discovery – in the exploration of his newly revealed psychic power – the power that had come through his accursed father – that Dad woke up those ghosts."

Helen said, heavily, "It might even have been the Koldun project that triggered it. Someone – someone they interviewed for the unit – must have discovered your father's ... origins. Someone who was – one of your grandfather's victims. Or at least a member of their family." She shuddered. "It's awful to think that such evil could come of such suffering. That victims would turn into killers, visiting the sins of the father on the innocent, on your father – and on his friends. Because what had *they* done? They weren't associated with your grandfather in any way, were they?"

"No. They'd never met him. Their families weren't acquainted at all. But they were from KGB families too. That might have been enough. And besides they were – they were the weak link. They were the way to my father. Killing them off one by one ... This person – I think they wanted my father to suffer. Not just to kill him straight away, that would have been too easy. They wanted him to be afraid. To look over his shoulder. To lose his friends. To wonder who ... how ... why ... And all the time they were hunting him they made him look in the wrong direction – he'd think gangsters, rivals, were after them, or someone wanting to steal his ideas – his Koldun project – which is why he destroyed those papers and hid that card. Even then, he must not have suspected who – why ... He must not have known until the very last moment. When it was too late. But he would have been made to see then. Because the killer would want him to know. They'd want him to die, knowing. To go into the afterlife with that awful knowledge, with that stain on his soul." His voice broke. He was trembling all over.

She took him in her arms and held him tight, hard, without speaking, hugging into him her warmth, her love, the deepest urges of her soul, every ounce of her being; wrapping him with a steady, glowing strength she hadn't even known she had until that moment. She'd been so in awe of him before, as if he'd been an invulnerable hero in a fairytale. But now she knew better. He needed *her*, too. He wasn't a hero in a fairytale. He was a real, vulnerable human being, and her own true love. This was no one-way street. In the darkness of this terrible revelation – in the painful, horrified understanding of what his father must have gone through – he really needed her. She held him, wordlessly sending him every bit of her strength, her total love and trust and understanding, and after a moment, he stopped trembling, put his head on her shoulder and wept. And as he did, she felt the dreadful tension slowly easing from him, the horror ebbing, the bitterness of his old feelings for his father transforming, not into sweetness – that would have been too much, too soon, and perhaps could never be – but into a real sorrow that was the beginning of healing.

Presently, he grew calm. They hugged in silence; then, arms around each other, walked slowly back to the house. It wasn't until they went in through the gate and had walked up the path to the front door, that he stopped and said, "Helen – I know where we must look now."

For a moment, she didn't know what he was talking about. "What?"

"Lev Kirov," he said. "He was the right age. That is why he must have been killed."

"I don't understand."

"I mean, Kirov was about the right age to have known someone who was a victim of my grandfather's. Or a relative. According to Maxim's informant Kirov was troubled after seeing a picture of my father and his two partners in the paper, after the death of Semyon Galkin, and learning what Dad's real name was. Perhaps it clicked then. The connection with Dad's father – to someone whose history he knew."

Helen breathed, "Yes – and maybe he tried to confront them about it."

"That's why they killed him. Because they thought he'd denounce them. Or maybe he didn't confront them but they suspected anyway that he was on to them – and got rid of him, just to be safe. Either way, I think, Kirov must have been the only person who knew the truth about their background. They must have hidden it."

"But *why* would you hide the fact you or your family had been a victim?"

Alexey sighed. "I know, it doesn't seem right, does it? But lots of people do it. It's wanting to forget, it's shame, it's fear. Even now, when the Russian state talks openly about remembering victims, not forgetting their suffering – when we have a national remembrance day for Stalin's victims, for instance – there's lingering unease. But in the past, it was much, much worse, in my grandfather's generation of course, but also in my father's. It doesn't surprise me at all that someone would want to hide such a history. Especially as – as there never really was any justice meted out – and those who profited by the system ... well, they survived and prospered, and so did their children, and their children's children." A spasm crossed his face, and she knew what he was thinking, and she cried out, "Yes, and that's unjust – unfair – that people who did bad things wouldn't be punished. But their children and their children's children aren't responsible. To kill them just because you can't get at the real perpetrators anymore – that's worse than unjust. That's *evil*. And there is no excuse for it."

"No, of course there isn't," he said, softly. "No excuse, and no forgiveness. But understanding, yes. I don't mean to say that my father deserved to die, and neither did his friends. But I need to understand what I am up against if I have any chance of knowing the truth. I feel as though I've been just glimpsing things in a fog, and now I can see ahead clearly." He paused, and his voice changed as he went on, grimly, "I don't intend to rest until we find this person, Helen. To hunt them down, as they hunted down my father. But not to kill them. To bring them to justice. So that my father – so his spirit can go to rest. Do you see?"

"Yes," she said. "I do. But, oh – Alexey – I'm scared. This person – they must be insane. But they must also be so – so cunning. So clever. And they must also have underworld connections, to set up those attacks on the Trinity offices. You remember how Grisha said that your father had hired him?"

"Yes. I do. And that stupid card they sent. They're playing mind-games. Trying to spook me. But also trying to make me look in the wrong direction – just like they did for Dad and his friends. To make me think it's Trinity they want. To hound me until I crack and then ..."

"Don't," she said, sharply, "don't. Oh Alexey – you know what it means – they had Grisha killed so he couldn't tell you anything. And now they could send a hitman to –"

"No," said Alexey, firmly. "I don't think that's their style at all. If they'd wanted to kill me like that, they'd have done it in Moscow. They knew I was there – they'd have heard that from Grisha's mates. You're right, I think they must have underworld connections. But I am certain they did not use them to kill my father and his friends. There was no third party, no hitman involved. However they did it – it was up close and personal. This person knew how to approach each of their victims, without suspicion. Each time, it would have had to be different. Tailored to each individual. For me, once they think I've been nicely softened up – I think I'd get an approach about the attacks on Trinity. An offer of information. Or maybe even an offer to help crack the Koldun code. Something like that."

He spoke quite calmly and steadily. But Helen shuddered. She said, "Oh God – what are we going to do now?"

"We'll call Nikolai. And Maxim. Tell them what we're thinking. And take it from there."

Chapter 31

When his phone rang, Maxim had not long left the Trinity cryptographer Foma's apartment. The cryptographer hadn't cracked the Koldun code so far, but he had some useful ideas. He was working on the notion of "Koldun" itself, he explained. Looking to see if the code might be based on, say, stories of famous sorcerers. Like the one from Russian folklore, Koschei, who had kept his soul deeply hidden in different objects, so that he could not be killed. That had struck him at once, Foma said, because it was such a perfect metaphor for cryptology itself. But no, he went on, it was not as simple as that. Churn the data as he might, number-crunch as diligently he could, try as he might to find as many editions of the story as he could, he'd come to the conclusion that the Koschei story did not fit the template of the code.

Still, he didn't look at all dejected by that, and indeed Maxim suspected he'd have been disappointed if it had been so easy. He was going through many other possibilities, he told Maxim: stories of sorcerers from Voldemort to Sauron, Dr. Faustus to Merlin, Rasputin to Simon the Magus and lots more. And even if that failed, there were all sorts of associated possibilities. Hundreds, thousands of them. A lesser man might have blanched at the prospect. Not Foma; he was thrilled by the challenge, determined in his bloodless blood-hound way to track down his elusive quarry without fail.

Just as Maxim reached the Metro station, his phone rang. "Ah, it's you, Alexey Ivanovich," he answered. "I am glad to have you on the line. I have just come from Foma's, and though he hadn't made a breakthrough yet with Koldun, there's something I …"

"Wait, Maxim Antonovich," Alexey said, in Russian. "There's something *I* must tell you first." The young man spoke gravely, quietly for a little while, and when he'd finished, it was the older man who found himself quite without words.

Recovering after a moment, Maxim said, "You are quite right. This is a most promising line of inquiry. And I should have seen it myself."

"But it was you who put us partly on this track," said Alexey, "going to see that old KGB man. So you must have had an instinct about it."

"Perhaps, but I didn't follow it to its logical conclusion. Truth is, I had decided it was a dead end and I've been con-centrating on the coded document today."

"But that's important too," said Alexey, "especially if it proves to be records of interviews and lists of names for the psychic unit. Maxim Antonovich, you were going to tell me something about it. What is it?"

"Nothing definite," said Maxim, "just a possibility."

"Something Foma discovered?"

"No. Something that I thought afterwards. It was because of that Koschei story – Foma's been trying to fit it to the code, without result – but it got me thinking about a secret hidden in several layers. And I wondered if perhaps we persuaded ourselves too easily that the Koldun project *was* in fact a plan for a secret psychic unit."

"What do you mean?"

"If you think about it, the level of secrecy seems excessive – it's not as though such units have never existed. But more cogently, I have not found any evidence yet to suggest candidates being interviewed. For instance, I was told that neither Lev Kirov nor Josef Oberlian, the aura-reader I interviewed today, were approached about such a job. And yet they were supposed to be among Moscow's finest, and Trinity's first port of call, you'd think."

"Perhaps they're lying."

"Perhaps, and in view of what you've told me just now, I will certainly make further inquiries. But I wonder if the project could have been about something else. Something connected with psychic phenomena, yes; but in a different way."

"Whatever do you mean?"

"We've been assuming that the heading on that cover sheet – *Koldun psychic unit* – refers to a group of psychics Trinity were setting up as a work unit. But what if it they were developing *some kind of device or process that would actually enhance psychic power*? Oberlian told me that's the Holy Grail of psychic research. And worthy of complete secrecy until whatever it was could be released."

"Could such a thing exist?"

"Oberlian seemed quite skeptical, but not altogether dismissive. And it is only an idea. A vague one at present. In any case for the moment we should leave the Koldun file to one side – nothing can be done there, and nothing known for sure till the code's broken – and concentrate on this much more urgent matter you have raised."

"I've spoken to Kolya too," said Alexey, "and he thinks we should put together a list of people whose careers overlap both the psychic and criminal worlds. You might need to go and see your original informant again."

"You mean the person who told me about Kirov?"

"Yes. And Maxim – I'm sorry – but I need to know who this person is."

Maxim hesitated. Then he made a snap decision, and said, "Of course you are right. She's an *ekstrasens* by the name of Anna Feodorovna Dorskova, she practices under the name of Skorpia." He explained how he had first come to meet her. "And that is why I think that we can cross her off any list of suspects," he finished. "And it's not because she says she was a good friend of Kirov's, but because she was so determined to profit by Kirov's story as to come and see us and then, rebuffed, sell her story to the media. The killer would not have done that; not drawn attention to himself in such a way. It does not fit the psychological pattern at all. An attention-seeking killer would have made damn sure there would have been some sensational clue left at each crime scene – might even have left some kind of calling card. The fact they didn't, even after the media started dubbing it the 'Rusalka case', after Barsukov's death – suggests a very different sort of mind. Vengeful, discreet, secretive, ruthless. Certainly not a boaster or a seeker after glory. Not like poor Dorskova."

"But wouldn't the killer have thought she knew something about their identity, after her story appeared in the paper?"

"Not necessarily. I've read the piece. She didn't mention Kirov's name at all in the interview, and everything was all vague mystical talk about sorcery and your father, and veiled hints he might be linked to his partners' deaths. And so it was he who took offense. Although there is another possibility and that is that the killer never saw the piece at all."

"Yes," said Alexey. "Do you think you can trust what this woman might tell you about Kirov's circle, or will she simply try again – to profit by things? To make herself more important by pretending to know more than she really does?"

"It's a possible risk, yes. But I think she's learned her lesson the hard way. She's not a bad woman, just a flawed one. But of course I won't accept what she tells me without double-checking. And I will also check on Oberlian's antecedents as well. In case."

"I intend also to do my own investigating," said Alexey.

Maxim said, sharply, "I must advise you, Alexey Ivanovich, that it really would not be wise for you to come to –"

Alexey interrupted him, firmly. "Before you go on, Maxim – like I just told Kolya, who made the exact same point as you, I have no intention of leaving Uglich and coming to Moscow or St Petersburg. Not right now, anyway. But there are other means open to me, even staying right here. I could investigate what there is on KGB archives on the Internet, for instance. I don't know if I can find anything of any use, but it's worth trying."

"Hmmm," said Maxim, in such a doubtful tone that Alexey laughed.

"You are not a fan of the cyber-world, I take it, Maxim Antonovich," he said.

"No. That I am not."

"Then we must agree to differ and each take our own path. Agreed?"

"Agreed," said Maxim. "But, Alexey Ivanovich ..."

"Yes?"

"Take care. And when you are hunting through the shadow forest of the Internet, please don't forget about the real wolves. Trust in God – but keep your eyes open."

Alexey said, gravely, "I will. You can be sure of that, Maxim Antonovich." And he ended the call.

*

Maxim had an urgent call to make now. But nobody answered the phone. His sense of dread grew as his calls went repeatedly unanswered. By the time he reached the street, he was in a lather of anxiety, and took the stairs two at a time, arriving panting and breathless at the door, fully expecting it to be smashed, and the apartment broken into. But everything looked normal. So he knocked. Once, twice, three times. Louder and louder. No answer. Something was wrong. Something was very wrong ...

He was just about to run at it and try to burst in the door, when all at once it opened and Anna Dorskova herself stood there, looking tousled and cross. "What the hell is this damn racket ..." she began, then saw who it was. Her eyes widened.

Maxim was so taken aback by this sudden deflation of his dark imaginings that at first he could only goggle at her. Then he said, lamely, "Sorry to disturb you, Anna Feodorovna. I thought you were ... I thought there was something wrong. I tried to call. More than once."

"I turned my phone off because I was asleep," she said, sharply. "Is that a crime?"

"No, of course not. I'm sorry. I just wanted – to ask you something. Urgently."

She gave a faint smile. "Well, I suppose you'd better come in," she said, stepping aside. "Would you like a cold glass of kvass, perhaps?"

"Oh – thank you. That is, if it's no trouble."

"No trouble at all. I need one myself." She went out to her little kitchen to pour the drinks, and he sat there waiting. It was strange, being here again, he thought. He hadn't really expected to come back here. Or at least not so soon. But as she came through from the kitchen with a foaming jug of the mild black-bread beer known as kvass, and pickles and olives on a tray, he was suddenly glad he'd come, and not just because she might be a useful source of information. Despite the tousled look – or perhaps because of it – she looked much more appealing than she had the other day, her face less wary, her eyes clearer, her mouth softer.

She set down the tray in front of him, and sat down opposite. She poured out the glasses, and handed him one. She gave him a smile, lit up a cigarette and said, "Help yourself to the snacks. Now, Senior Lieutenant, what is it that's so urgent?"

He took a gulp of the cold drink and said, on an impulse, "I had to tell Ivan Makarov's son who you were." She made a startled movement, and he went on, "I know I promised not to tell anyone – but he is a fine young man, brave and honorable and I think true-hearted – and he's in grave danger from the homicidal maniac who has already killed several times, including your own dear friend Lev Kirov. He could not be left in the dark. Do you understand?"

She had gone pale. Her lip trembled. She said, "Are you sure that the same person ..."

"Yes. I am. And I also think you may perhaps be able to help us identify this madman. Before he strikes again."

She stared at him. "How ... can I ... possibly ..."

"By giving us a picture of the circles your friend moved in. His colleagues. Friends. Professional contacts."

"You think someone Lev *knew* killed him?"

"I'm afraid so, yes."

"But, Senior Lieutenant ... Lev – he knew so many people. He was old. Greatly respected and loved. He – it would take years to enumerate everyone he knew."

Leaning forward, Maxim said, earnestly, "We are looking for three characteristics in particular which may help you to narrow down possible suspects. We believe this person is probably connected in some way with the psychic community and that they may also have some kind of link to the underworld. But the most important thing is a connection to someone with a background as – as a so-called enemy of the State. As a subversive."

She looked at him, a weary contempt in her eyes. Then she said, biting off the words, "I should have known."

"Should have known what?"

"That no policeman could be a decent man. But I must say I'm surprised that you should resort to those old tricks."

Maxim was completely bewildered. "What old tricks?"

"Subversives, enemies of the State, criminals, social parasites, anti-social elements – why, it has quite a ring to it, doesn't it? A ring straight back to our dear undead past. No, Senior Lieutenant. I will not help you to frame some poor wretch who ..."

Maxim glared at her and hissed, "I'm not trying to frame anyone. Don't you understand? This person betrayed your friend – killed him in cold blood. And killed three other people who, whatever their failings as businessmen, were innocent of whatever happened to the killer or his family. Do you believe in the sins of the father being visited on the son, Anna Feodorovna? Because if you do – then you must accept that it is not only the Trinity people who suffer. People like your friend are necessary collateral too. You must think then that it is okay that they are betrayed and killed just because of who they are. What they know."

She swallowed. "How dare you! How dare you – I never said ..."

He leaned forward. "Listen to me. I believe this person knew your friend Lev Kirov *intimately* – and had confided only in him the secret of his past – that is, that he, or a close family member, had been a victim of the cruel power of the State."

She shook her head. Stared at him. Said wonderingly, "Could it – be – that you really don't know?"

"Don't know what?"

"That Lev Kirov was himself a victim of the cruel power of the State, as you so eloquently put it. As a young man, he spent ten years in a northern Gulag, after being convicted of possessing banned literature." She paused, and gave him an ironic smile. "To wit, underground copies of the mystical texts of Gurdjieff, Blavatsky, Andreev, Steiner and Rerik."

"I'm – I'm sorry," said Maxim, with an effort, feeling stupid and wrong-footed. "I'm afraid I – I had no idea." Why didn't you think to check the old man's background before now, you damn fool, he cursed himself, no wonder she's looking at you like that.

She looked sharply at him, as if summing him up. Then her face cleared. "Look, it was like this. Lev knew several other people who similarly had been recipients of the State's attentions like himself. And some most certainly had links to the underworld, as they had been imprisoned as what used to be called 'anti-social elements'." That was the Soviet euphemism for common criminals. She added, "But none of them concealed their past, as far as I'm aware. And certainly not these days. I know some people are ashamed of what happened to them, but not those in Lev's circle, I can guarantee you that. They were survivors, and tough with it. But the one you seek – you say they did conceal it – and that only Lev knew their secret. If that's the case, then I'm afraid I have no idea who it could be."

"What about his clients?"

"You mean – that it could be a client who had concealed their past?"

"Yes."

"It's possible, yes. If a client told Lev in confidence – or if Lev found out – then he would keep the secret, if he knew that's what the client wanted. And then you might also have a link to – to the underworld. All sorts of people came to ask for Lev's advice and help. He made no distinction between people. But I don't understand why he'd be killed for –"

"You told me your friend was troubled, after Semyon Galkin's death. Perhaps, you see, it wasn't just because he recognized Ivan Makarov, but because it sparked off an idea in him – that something he'd heard recently; something he'd been told in confidence by a client – could provide a link to Semyon Galkin's death. Maybe it was only a hint – but if he was still seeing this client, then he may have shown what he was thinking. Even if unconsciously. And the person realized their danger, and acted."

She stared at him, swallowed and said, in a small voice, "Then – then when I went to you – and to the paper..."

"You could have been in very great danger too. If the killer had perceived it to be so. But for whatever reason, they didn't. We must be grateful for that."

Their eyes met. She said, quietly, "What do you want me to do?"

"If there is any way you could help me to get to Lev Kirov's records, I'd be grateful. Perhaps you might know for example where his personal papers might have gone. If he had a diary, for instance."

She nodded. "He did have something like that – but I don't think it's what you're after. It's not a standard diary – not a record – more like a kind of compendium of his thoughts over the years. Way before he died, he lent it to a mutual friend who is writing a book on great modern Russian psychics. I can give you his name and details" – and she did – "I'm sure he will be happy to show the manuscript to you. But I can tell you here and now – there are no names, no addresses, nothing to identify clients or indeed anyone else in it. Lev was a very discreet man. He kept his client records in his head, not liking to entrust those kinds of things to paper. Understandably so, given his experience. And he worked alone. No one else had access to his clients. So any records – I'm afraid they died with him. I could try and rack my memory for anything he might have said – but I'm not sure it will be of much help. Apart from Makarov, I never heard him say anything directly about a client. I'm so sorry."

That was that, then. Maxim suddenly felt very tired. Every time that it looked like there was a promising break-through in this damned case, it hit a brick wall. He said, sadly, "Well, thank you, anyway. You have been most helpful once again, and under most trying circumstances. I am sorry to have caused you distress today. And if ever you need my help – if you feel threatened or concerned in any way – contact me at once. I give you my word I will do anything I can to keep you safe."

She looked at him, her face softening. Gently, she put out a hand to touch his knee, very briefly. "You are a good man, Senior Lieutenant. I am – sorry – that I jumped to conclusions and abused you before. You did not deserve it."

"You have nothing whatever to apologize for, Anna Feodorovna," said Maxim. "I should have explained myself better."

"Please. I – if it is agreeable to you – please just call me Anna, if you wish," she said, quietly, reddening a little.

He looked at her, surprised and glad. And said, "Thank you. I will. And please, my name is Maxim. Maxim Antonovich."

A lovely smile lit up her brown eyes, and she held out a hand. "I am very pleased to meet you, Maxim. And I hope to see you again soon."

"And I you, Anna."

And they shook hands, warmly, smiling at each other as delightedly as schoolchildren unexpectedly promised a treat. How wonderfully strange life's ambushes could be, Maxim thought, as he took the stairs down two at a time again but from sheer, thankful cheerfulness this time.

Chapter 32

Helen had seen that photo in the album, the one where Major Makarov had been looking away, and even then the resemblance had been striking, but this was altogether different. This photo was full-face, and it was uncanny. She'd looked at it a few times now and still she couldn't get over it. The young man who looked out from the small black and white photograph could have been Alexey's double. Different haircut, of course, and different clothes and setting – the photograph had been taken in the mid-1950s, in a forest, he'd clearly been hiking, judging from his backpack – but the features of the face were the same, the eyes, nose, mouth, even the set of the shoulders under the sheepskin coat. That was disturbing enough; but what made it more so was that, despite the striking resemblance to Alexey, there was something fundamentally different about the man in the picture. And that was to do with the expression in Mikhail Petrovich Makarov's eyes. Or rather, the lack of it.

Helen didn't know how to explain it. It wasn't to do with the fact that Mikhail Makarov was unsmiling, or that his face was perfectly still. It wasn't a deliberate withholding. Not a masking of emotion. Not even a challenge. It was the gaze of someone truly unreadable.

And it wasn't just in that photo. In a crumpled older photo, he was with his parents at a riverside beach. They held him, a beautiful blond child of about four or five, protectively close between them – both of them in their forties or so, his mother Lara plump and dark-haired and smiling, his father Pyotr tall and fair-haired and unsmiling. Helen remembered how Ivan Makarov had written that his father Mikhail had been born late, when his parents had almost given up hope of a child; and it was clear both doted on him, even though Pyotr Makarov wasn't smiling. But even then he did not have the same expression as his son. Pyotr's was hard, the gaze of a man used to command. He didn't look like he'd have been a pleasant sort of guy. But he was readable. Whereas the child gazed out from that photo with the same unblinking stare as he did as a young hiker; as he did in the couple of other framed photos from Ivan Makarov's study: one of Mikhail walking with a young Ivan in the park, and one of him in KGB dress uniform standing stolidly beside Ivan who was in army uniform.

Alexey said, pointing at the last one, "He died only a few weeks after this one was taken, when Dad was away." He paused. "You can see, can't you, why it should give me the creeps to look at my grandfather?"

She nodded.

"When I was a kid these pictures used to scare me. I always tried to avoid seeing them. Looking at him – it felt like – like looking in the mirror, but in a twisted way. And I felt like – if I looked at him too long, I'd get sucked in and never come out again. It was like … like the eyes were hungry. Do you see?"

"Yes," she said. "I do."

"That's why I stuck them all in Dad's desk drawer, but I couldn't bring myself to throw them away, because – well, because he'd loved his father, no matter what he'd been, and it didn't feel right to … But now, I just look at them and I think, you were a lost soul. And you have no power over me. Not anymore."

Helen squeezed his hand. "That's good."

He smiled. "Yes. It is." He put the photos down, and hauled her to her feet. "Come on, babe, let's call it a day. I've had more than enough."

They'd been in the study for a few tiring hours, fruitlessly trawling the Internet. They'd first googled "KGB Major Mikhail Petrovich Makarov" in Russian and English, but not surprisingly there wasn't a single mention of him in a document or an image. Thinking of the different people who might have had a grudge against him for family reasons, they first tried Boris Repin, the Petersburg gangster suspected of the attack on the Trinity offices. There were several images of *him* on Google, the man certainly didn't hide away. He'd been pictured at the opening of nightclubs, at a mayoral function, at the ballet, in a hunting party. Big, blond and hard-eyed, even in the photos he exuded the confidence of the alpha predator. Described as a "well-known Petersburg business-man" and a "generous benefactor to charity" (he had given money to help rebuild a ruined church, among other things), he had a checkered past, as might be imagined, but though he had done prison time in his youth as an "anti-social", there was no record of any past family connection with the kinds of things a KGB major might have investigated. Repin's parents had divorced when he was young, both had been factory workers. There was no indication at all they, or their parents before them, had ever been in trouble.

More to eliminate possibilities than a real hunch, they then put in Grisha Chekushkin's name, and Lebedev's, but there was nothing about them at all, they were too small fry. They widened the search to KGB archives and ended up with millions of hits. They'd refined the search to dates and places but even then it was clear it was going to take a long time.

*

That night, Helen had a strange dream about Major Mikhail Makarov. In the dream, he looked just like he had in the hiking photo, only he didn't have a pack, and he wasn't posing, he was just wandering in a dark forest, a small, lonely figure under towering dark firs growing thickly together. His blond hair shone faintly on his collar and behind him was a trail of gleaming white pebbles – or was it crumbs? They were the only points of light in that dark place. As he walked the trail of pebbles – or crumbs – faded but still he walked, and now only his hair shone, and then it too faded and he got smaller and smaller till he disappeared like a shadow into dark. That was all; the dream ended as suddenly as it had begun, but she found herself awake with tears on her face, and she had no idea why.

Beside her, Alexey lay fast asleep on his side, one arm flung out of the covers. The room was very quiet, very still, and the moonlight came in at the window. For an instant, in the strange stillness, Helen couldn't shake off the feeling that her dream was like Olga Feshina's vision – that it was saying something vital, which she must understand.

But it was only for an instant, for she wasn't quite awake; and before she even knew it, she was asleep again, and when she next woke, it was bright morning and Alexey was bringing her a cup of tea. She hadn't forgotten the dream. But in the light of day everything had taken its proper place again, and she knew that it *was* just a dream, a vivid and symbolic one, sure, most likely brought on by a memory of Alexey saying his grandfather was a lost soul. But nothing like Olga Feshina's vision at all.

So she didn't tell Alexey about it, because it didn't seem important, and as the day wore on and they scrolled their way carefully through pages and pages of information about

Gulag prisoners on the Internet, she completely forgot about it. After the frustrating experience yesterday, they'd decided to narrow the search down only to persons accused of the kind of "crime" Lev Kirov had gone down for – not so much politicals or even "anti-socials", but those accused of "mysticism and occultism". It seemed a more fruitful line of inquiry in view of the fact the killer was most likely a member of the psychic community in one way or the other, and possibly had inherited the ability from a family member. But it was pointless. There was practically no information available on those kinds of prisoners. On Google books they found reference to a book called *The Occult in Russian and Soviet Culture*, and were able to consult some of its pages, but though there were a few references to people being imprisoned for "mysticism and occultism" and possessing banned texts of that nature, there were no actual names named.

They took a welcome break for sandwiches and coffee, fed up of the endless, tedious trawling. The unexpected thing about doing this research though, Helen thought, was that, tiring as it was, the sheer volume of it was enough to muffle the horror of what they were looking for, and enough, almost, to stifle the nagging feeling of unease that they were missing something important, something that was in plain sight and yet invisible. And then Alexey had his idea.

"We need to go at it from a different direction," he said. "It's hard for us to really dig properly into the past, just on the Internet, because most of that stuff must be still secret, or no one's transcribed it – but what about the present?"

"What do you mean? To look at prisoners now?"

"No, no. Instead of the identity of the criminal, maybe we need to focus on their method. See, Lev Kirov was killed by pushing him down the Metro escalator – so that must have been spur of the moment – but the deaths of my father and the others were carefully planned. Nobody knows how it was done. There are such things as untraceable poison – like an injection of potassium chloride which in solution can bring on a heart attack – but I'm sure that was thought of already. But if we're right about the killer – about them having some kind of psychic talent, I mean – then – maybe that's how they did it."

Helen felt the frightening implication drop coldly into her veins. "You mean – they devised some kind of psychic murder method?"

"Yes. It might also ..." He paused, as though the words were difficult to bring out. "It might explain how – why – they got close to my father and his partners."

She stared at him, trying to understand.

He went on, "Let's say Maxim's right and Koldun was not a work unit but the development of some kind of device to enhance psychic power. What if, in fact, the device they were developing was a ... a weapon, based on an enhancement of the most dangerous kind of psychic power – killing from a distance?"

Helen shivered, as much from the haunted look in his eyes as the vile prospect that his words opened. At such moments, it felt as though he was retreating from her into a nightmare world she couldn't reach, and it chilled her to the bone. She faltered, "But is that even possible? I've heard of people pointing the bone. And curses. But you have to believe in that sort of thing for it to have any effect, don't you?"

"Yes. And my father wouldn't have been interested in something as traditional and erratic as that." His fingers raced across the keyboard, putting in the search term "murder by psychic means". Up came a whole lot of stuff, most of it about psychics helping police in murder cases, but there were a few pages canvassing the possibility of psychic murder itself. And then they found a website which had a section on what was called "psychic self-defense", which mentioned three possible methods of psychic murder: a sorcerer's curse; a desperate energy vampire's hunger (though that was described as manslaughter rather than deliberate murder); and the skills of a psychic skilled in psychokinesis, or telekinesis as some people called it. The writer went on to say, "*in psychokinesis, which literally means 'mind-motion', the psychic uses his or her mind to move objects or physically interfere with them in some way. Repressed emotion is often at the base of psychokinetic power: these psychics usually have powerful emotions, rigidly controlled, building into a vast energy that can literally bend reality. Such a person might be able to interfere with the electrical workings of the heart. A famous case in the '50s and '60s was that of the Russian psychic Nina Kulagina. In a famous experiment, she showed she could stop and restart a frog's heart, by the power of her mind. So why not people's? In fact, Kulagina herself had given a hostile psychiatrist who did not believe in her powers a real fright one day by doing just such a thing, proving that it was possible. But what if the psychic had no intention of restarting the heart? Then it would be murder, plain and simple – and completely undetectable by ordinary means.*"

There was no more about heart-stopping experiments on that site, but plenty of Google hits for Nina Kulagina. And a YouTube clip of that "famous experiment" with the frog.

They clicked through to watch it, and as the clip rolled on, Helen's skin goose-fleshed, nausea roiled in her belly, her throat seemed to close up. For the grainy black and white video of the dumpy woman in her dowdy clothes and bun staring at the hapless frog, and it struggling then falling over, reminded her horribly of something else she'd seen recently.

Alexey was pale. She knew he was thinking, feeling, the same thing. She took his hand. He held on to it so hard that later she could still feel the pressure of his fingers against hers. When the clip ended, he said, very quietly, "You said ... that video on the card – the one you deleted – it might not be something Dad had … done. What if – what if it was the record of a testing session they made? A test of a psychic who later …" He broke off.

She swallowed. "Do you think this person is related to Nina Kulagina?"

"No," he said, more strongly. "Her profile doesn't fit. You saw what it said in those pieces. Not only wasn't she harassed or persecuted, she was accepted. Rewarded, even, by the government. No. I don't think it's anything to do with Nina Kulagina. It's just someone like her. Who has the same abilities."

But now Helen started seeing the flaws in the theory. "If your father and his friends had tested this – this person – and they knew that they could kill a sparrow like that – could stop its heart like that Kulagina woman stopped that frog's," she said, "then surely they'd have been really careful! And when his partners started dying, your father would have suspected who'd done it. He wouldn't have been fooled. He'd have gone to the police, surely, told Serebrov. Or at least tried to track them down."

"Yes, but he might not have been able to find them."

"Still, he wouldn't just wait till they got to him, would he? He'd have done something. And remember what it said about Kulagina. She was utterly drained by the effort of the frog thing. And the frog was tiny. If you tried to kill a person that way – imagine the vast amount of psychic energy you'd need. You'd probably put so much strain on yourself you'd run the risk of triggering off your own heart attack first …"

He looked at her, the color returning to his face. "That's true. Oh, you're right, it's not possible. It doesn't fit with Dad's character at all. Unless he was – hypnotized or something. And I can't see that happening. Not for a minute. Besides, he drowned, and so did the others."

Paradoxically, she now felt uneasy. Were they being too hasty in discounting the idea? "We should check it out anyway, Alexey. I mean, the video. See if – if there's any record of anything like it."

He didn't say anything so she just entered in the search "sparrow death psychokinesis" first on YouTube – bringing up nothing – then on Google, going more general with "bird heart psychokinesis" and trying out different search terms but not coming up with anything that resembled what they'd seen. So she tried broader terms, such as "Russian psychic experiments" and "Russian animal psychic experiments". Various things came up, mostly to do with measuring the psychic abilities of animals, or using animals in weird experiments. There were even a few about Ivanov's experiments with apes and humans in Stalinist times, which Irina had mentioned, and one passing reference to Antonov's bear project. But that was all. The sparrow video had certainly left no traces on the Internet – but then, why should it? If it was part of Trinity's ultra-secret project, then it would hardly be in the public domain in any shape or form. And though they'd googled the Koldun project more than once, in several permutations, unsurprisingly there wasn't a single reference to it on the Internet at all. The Trinity partners would hardly have gone to the trouble of encoding files and then allowed their project to be splashed into cyberspace by some Wikileaks clone.

I shouldn't have deleted the video, Helen thought. Yes, it seemed like the right thing to do at the time, and yes, there was no person pictured in the video, but perhaps there might have been some other clue. We might have been able to enlarge the pictures, see if anything in the room could be identified, for instance. But now we have nothing and we're stuck – and someone out there might have the ability to stop people's hearts.

Because even though she'd tried to persuade herself and Alexey that it was a nightmare story to keep them awake at night, deep down she wasn't so sure. And all at once she'd had more than enough. "I need to get out, get some fresh air," she said, getting up.

"Yes," he said, slamming the lid of the computer down. "That stuff makes you feel sick. Dirty. Let's go out on the bike."

He'd never gone as fast as he did that afternoon, taking corners at breakneck speed, sending stones skittering every which way, and it frightened Helen, in a way, but it was a healthy fear, not the ugly thing that had shadowed their day till then. It felt as though they could outrun the shadow of the past, the fear, the horror of it. And she found herself wishing they could just keep going, leave everything behind, everything and everyone, vanish over the horizon, losing themselves in this vast land, and never come back. Never have to look back. Never.

Chapter 33

Maxim had spent most of the day cross-checking the list of psychics Anna Feodorovna had given him, with a list of criminal records. So far he'd drawn a blank. Josef Oberlian, for instance, had nothing in any police record apart from visa matters – which were all in order. And he had no family connection to any Gulag prisoner.

He'd looked up Kirov's prison record. Just as Anna had said, the man had spent ten years in a Northern Russian prison, but since that time had stayed out of trouble. Then, feeling a little ashamed, Maxim had done a quick check on Anna herself – but apart from a couple of traffic fines, she was pure as the driven snow. Married at the age of twenty-one, divorced five years later, she had no children but two married sisters and a widowed mother living in a small town in the Urals. Her father had died years before. She held a license as a registered psychic, but had also worked in cafes, shops and as a cleaner in a school. Earlier, she had also earned a degree in literature, which appeared to have stood her in no good stead whatsoever. Really, thought Maxim, she and I are peas in a pod, a disappointment, a promise not fulfilled, disregarded flotsam and jetsam in the impatient current of the new Russia, drifting toward our forgotten end.

It made him feel sad, but also tender. He remembered the feeling he'd had in Oberlian's apartment the other day. The feeling that he'd lost too much, in his stubborn pride. He didn't want to make that same mistake again. And so he picked up the phone and invited Anna to dinner that night. She did not sound surprised, only glad, and on the phone her voice was bright as a girl's.

Heart light, he had then gone looking for Kirov's papers, that Anna had told him were with a man named Igor Rimsky, the "mutual friend who was writing a book on great modern Russian psychics". Rimsky proved to be a thin, earnest, ponytailed young man in his late twenties, and he seemed happy enough to show Maxim the papers. Anna had already briefed him, he said. There was a thin bundle of papers, flimsy typescript in a cardboard folder. Maxim flipped through the first couple of pages. He looked at Rimsky and said, "When exactly did Kirov give you these?"

"About a year before he died."

"I see." Before Galkin's death, then – so they probably wouldn't be of much use. Still, he had to be sure. "I'm afraid I'll have to take these away for a while."

"Fine. I'm not up to my chapter on Lev yet. I'm a very slow writer, I'm afraid. Please look after these notes, this is the only copy in existence."

"Of course. Thank you."

"It is my pleasure. Anya said you were investigating Lev's death. That means a lot to her. To me. To all of us who knew him. We had thought no one was interested."

"Did you have any suspicion at the time that your friend's death was not accidental?"

"No."

"Nobody for instance searched Kirov's apartment after his death?"

"I don't think so. But Lev wasn't very tidy, Senior Lieutenant. So if someone had made a mess of things ..."

"You wouldn't have been able to tell."

"Quite so. But nothing was missing. As far as we could see. Lev had very little worth stealing, of course."

"And you're sure he kept no other records of his work than this manuscript?"

"Positive. And only Anya and I knew about the manuscript. Lev was a modest man. I had the devil's own job even persuading him to let me see it."

At the door, Rimsky said, "Anya said you had a suspicion a client may have ... been responsible for Lev's death."

"It's possible, yes," said Maxim, cautiously.

"There are no actual records of clients in the papers, Anya told you that, right?"

"She did."

"He didn't write about cases. At least not in their actual details. If you get my meaning. But there are some which I would call disguised stories. It's possible that among those might be something useful."

"I see. Thank you."

"Don't mention it. Good luck."

Back at his apartment, Maxim started going through Kirov's manuscript. It was just as he'd suspected, not a memoir or autobiography, but rather a kind of philosophical work, though there were bits and pieces of life history in there to be reconstructed if you cared to, bits of memoir, about his childhood, the prison camp, and other things, especially spiritual experiences, for it was soon clear Kirov had been a devoutly religious man who believed his psychic gift came directly from God. He also believed it should be used only to help other human souls in trouble, but he was not blind to the fact that not every person with psychic gifts felt that way. Though it wasn't at all the kind of thing Maxim normally liked to read, there was something engaging about it, not a trace of self-pity or self-importance, and he soon began to develop a real respect and liking for the man whose presence seemed so strong in these pages. But as to trying to get hard evidence, to identify anyone from the "disguised stories" or semi-parables that Kirov used to illustrate his work, that was quite another question. And then he came upon one that made the back of his neck prickle.

Two people who share nothing but a similar secret come separately to my door. They are plagued by disturbing dreams about the dead. They do not know each other, they are as different as could be, in surface and in the depths, in body and in soul, in word and deed, tongue and heart.

One serves power and lives in action; the other is a seeker and lives in thought. One walks in the shadows; the other in the light. Yet in each of them I see another shared secret: I see the gift that has only dawned on them late in life. A soul-power that could be very great indeed. And in each of them I sense it could go either way. And so I warn them that to make such a discovery so late can cause a revolution, but whether of velvet or blood only they can choose.

On the face of it, a person who has walked all of life in the shadows may plunge further into the night, while a person who walks in light goes deeper toward the sun. It seems immutable truth. But the truth of the soul is a deep mystery. For while the night may hide the malefactor, it may also be the time of healing sleep; but one can be burned coming too close to the sun.

He re-read the story a couple of times. A psychic gift, discovered late ... Could it be that one of the men was Makarov? He could have been described as one who "serves power and lives in action", who "walks in the shadows". That could fit with his secretiveness, and with Trinity's work. But it was possible to see it the other way. He *could* be the "seeker, the thinker" who "walks in the light" – because bringing things to light was also Trinity's business, and Makarov had been an investigator – a seeker of truth – and a highly intelligent man, a "thinker", as much as a man of action.

Could this be how Makarov had met his murderer? As a fellow client of Kirov's? It was possible.

Anna had said Lev Kirov had begun to suspect someone after Galkin's death. But he'd suspected the wrong person. He'd suspected Makarov ... and that was why he'd spoken to Anna about him. Oh if only he'd come to us, Maxim thought, despairingly. If only he'd said something. But there was no way he would. Not with his history. Certainly not to people like me ...

Now he was speaking, from beyond the grave. But oh, Lev Grigorevich, Maxim thought, why couldn't you have been more specific? How can I possibly get to your murderer if you won't give me more than this?

*

Now, as he looked at Anna in the soft light of the little restaurant, he thought how lovely she was. Her freshly washed hair shone with subtle honey lights that, to Maxim's eyes at least, were far more attractive than the bright blonde she'd once affected. She wore smoky eye shadow that accentuated her dark-lashed brown eyes; her lips were touched with coral pink, and she wore an evocative floral perfume. Her soft short-sleeved dress was of the same color as her lipstick, and she wore it with a lacy jacket and high-heeled black sandals. She looked fresh and lovely, and he felt as clumsy as a dressed-up bear beside her. He'd dragged out his best suit from its mothballs at the back of the closet, and teamed it with a new brand-new shirt and a tie; he hated wearing ties, they made him feel like his neck was too big. He'd shaved carefully, trimmed his moustache, and wetted down his unruly dark hair. It felt odd to be walking out of his apartment dressed to go out for dinner – he couldn't remember the last time he'd done that, for since Marina there had only been a few one-night stands with women picked up in bars. But somehow, despite the discomfort of the suit and tie, it didn't seem odd at all to be sitting across the table from Anna, talking not like a policeman and his informant, but a man and woman enjoying each other's company over some particularly succulent lamb *shashlik* and full-bodied Georgian wine.

They kept away from business talk, concentrating instead on personal things; and though they both avoided the dangerous topic of ex-spouses, she spoke about her family, and he of his. He was not close to them and, since his mother's death, never bothered to see his siblings, who shunned him anyway because he was a cop, as did his increasingly cantankerous old father, whose only topic of conversation these days was how great things had been in Soviet times, ignoring the fact he'd moaned about it at the time. And then the conversation moved to Anna's first meeting with Lev Kirov.

They'd met in a park, she said, not long after she'd first arrived in Moscow. He'd rescued her from a would-be bag snatcher and they'd become good friends. He'd seen so much and suffered so much and yet he was the least bitter person she had ever met in her whole life; there were tears in her eyes as she spoke. Maxim took her hand without speaking and she didn't snatch it away but looked at him and went on, "He spoke very occasionally of his time in the prison camp and told me that it was there that his gift was honed and perfected and that he really began to understand things about the human soul. I remember him saying once that was what Communism had intended to do – to engineer human souls, and create a new man – but that it had ultimately failed, as all such things must fail, because there is no humble acknowledgment of mystery, only diseased pride pushed to madness. And Lev lived by the truth of mystery, if you understand me."

Maxim nodded. "I do understand, but it makes my work all the harder," he said. "There was a story I read in his manuscript today ..." And he told her what it was. "Did he ever talk to you about those people?" he asked her, at the end.

"No," said Anna. "He didn't. He wouldn't, you see, because he kept other people's secrets as well as his own. He allowed people their mystery, he did not try to unpeel it." Her expression changed. "But do you think it was one of them who ..."

"I don't know," said Maxim. "I don't even know if one of them was Makarov. It is just a feeling. I have no evidence."

"Feelings *are* evidence," said Anna, simply, "that's what Lev would have said." And her eyes met his, and he knew she wasn't just referring to the case.

By the time they left, it was nearly eleven. Maxim accompanied Anna on the Metro back to her apartment. She invited him in for a brandy and they sat around for a while longer, drinking and talking against a soft background of old pop songs on her tape recorder. Then he got up to leave, saying he had to catch the last Metro home. He'd half-hoped she might protest, tell him to stay; but she didn't, though she kissed him goodnight in a way that promised him much, all in its own good time, if he was prepared to be patient. Going back out from her warm apartment into the cool night, he smiled as he imagined what that would mean, and his imaginings filled the rest of the journey home.

Chapter 34

Katya came to collect her and Oleg's things the next day. She spoke to Alexey, and not at all to Helen. Or to Slava, though from where she stood talking to Alexey, the guard was only a short distance away, washing and polishing the Mercedes till it gleamed. Not that it hadn't before. Helen, watching from the living-room window, saw that Slava, too, was pointedly ignoring the girl. Katya had said there was nothing between her and Slava. Maybe there hadn't been. But maybe, just maybe, what she'd hinted at, of his strange behavior, of implying that he had the same kind of "curse" on him as the dogs – was that a clue to something else? Something she was ashamed to voice to anyone? Slava wasn't the seducer type; but given any encouragement at all, he'd take what he thought was being offered, even if it wasn't really. Oh, I'm being unfair, Helen thought, completely unfair. And if he had done anything like that, anyway, Katya would have told Oleg, and … and what if Oleg had confronted Slava, and he'd set the dogs on him? But the dogs wouldn't have obeyed Slava, he wasn't their master, she told herself, and besides Oleg was conscious yesterday, he'd most certainly have told us if Slava had done anything like that. But what if he was frightened of Slava, if the other guard had some kind of hold over him, so he couldn't tell the truth? No, I really must stop this, she thought, I am imagining things just because I don't like Slava, because it makes me uncomfortable when he's around.

The taxi drew away. Alexey came back inside and said to Helen, "Well, that's it. I'm glad we parted on better terms this time. It's a weight off my mind. I really didn't feel I'd handled it at all well the other day."

"It wasn't your fault," said Helen. "You don't have to take everything on yourself, you know. They're adults and they're responsible for their own lives and their own reactions." As she said it, an unexpected insight came to her, about her own experience at Changeling. Maybe she'd been blind to the realities there and had misunderstood the situation because she was not long out of school and she'd seen the company as some kind of protective surrogate parent, not as the pragmatic, even ruthless, business it actually was. A few weeks ago, it would have been a disconcerting thought that would have sapped her confidence. Today, it seemed illuminating, a useful step on the way to understanding herself and the world.

"Thanks for that, Lenochka," he said, grinning, and she realized what she'd said might have sounded a bit patronizing, though she most certainly hadn't meant it that way.

She said, hastily, "What did Katya say, about Oleg?"

"He's okay. They had the results of his blood tests, there's nothing wrong with him, he definitely doesn't have rabies. Just as well they could find out that way."

"How do you mean?"

"Well, turns out the pathology people at the hospital mislaid the dog corpses Slava delivered, because some idiot there put them in the pile for incineration, so they never were able to test them. The doctor was pretty cranky about it, but things aren't always exactly efficient in these smaller hospitals. Anyway, at least Oleg's okay. And Katya's calmed down too ... Now, listen, Lenochka, I've got to go and run a few boring errands, the bank and all that sort of thing to pay up Oleg and Katya, Slava's going to drive me, do you want to come?"

"No, I might just stay and relax, and maybe make us something for lunch." She didn't feel like being in the same car with Slava, but she didn't want to tell Alexey that.

*

On such passing whims, such apparently unimportant decisions, can everything change. Later that day, she was to think, if I'd gone with Alexey, I wouldn't have seen it. And who knows what would have happened, then?

She was gathering together ingredients for a quiche in the pantry, twenty minutes or so after Alexey and Slava had left, when she noticed it. A slip of shiny paper, fallen under the shelf where the cheese bell sat. She picked it up, turned it over.

It was a photo, trimmed up, showing a man, dressed in camouflage gear and sporting sunglasses, planted in front of the body of a huge elk. Just behind him, another man, with a steady, impassive gaze. It was Slava. A souvenir of hunting, she thought. It was of a size to keep in a wallet and must have dropped out when he was getting the cheese for his eternal pasta last night. Well, she'd give it back to him when he ...

She looked again, puzzled. Something about the other man's face struck her as familiar, though he was a total stranger. She couldn't see his eyes, but there was something about the shape of the face ... the jut of the jaw. And then, in an electric flash, it came to her, and she gasped.

"Miss?"

She whirled around. Slava was standing in the kitchen. Calm, girl, calm. Don't let him know what you've found. If he's here, Alexey must be back, too. So play it cool. Closing one hand over the photo, she backed away from the pantry and gabbled, "Oh hi, you're back, I'm just making a quiche for lunch, do you like quiche?"

He didn't say anything. He didn't move, just stared at her. His eyes were completely devoid of expression. He said, "He not back."

"What?"

His voice was flat, without inflection. "Alexey Ivanovich. I get him later."

"Oh. I see." Her palms felt sticky, her skin prickling with nerves. More than anything, she wanted to get out of the kitchen. Away from him. But she didn't want to run past him. Didn't want to alert him that anything was wrong. She gave him a nervous smile.

It was a mistake. In two strides he was on her, grabbing her wrist, dragging her toward him. There was no mistaking the expression on his face now, and in a start of horror, Helen understood why he'd told her Alexey was still in town. He'd been signaling to her that "the coast was clear", and her smile had proved to him that she shared his ugly thought. She threw herself back and yelled, "No! No!"

But in her agitation the hand hiding the photo unclenched and the picture dropped to the floor. Slava saw it at once. Shock flooded into his face, and loosened his grip. Helen grabbed her chance, and ran.

Out the back door. Not into the garden where she'd be trapped but up the side of the house. She could hear him behind her. Any moment he'd catch her. She couldn't think. Could only feel. Ran like she'd never run before. The front. The Mercedes. Parked in the driveway. The door was open. The key in the ignition. She made a dive for it, but Slava was too quick. He shoved her roughly aside, sending her sprawling onto the gravel. Before she could recover, he'd jumped into the car, slammed the door, and roared off in a shower of dust, tires squealing as he went.

She stumbled into the house, to the hall phone – her cell phone was upstairs – and feverishly dialed Alexey's number. When he answered, she gabbled, "Alexey, something terrible … come back, come back quickly – Slava – he's one of Repin's men –"

"What?"

"I found a photo – he's taken the car – he's gone – he …" But she couldn't finish, she was trembling with delayed shock now, her throat felt thick, her ears buzzing, her gravel-rashed knees and elbows stung. The phone dropped from her nerveless hand as she slumped to the floor, hugging herself, knees drawn up to her chest, trying to stop her teeth from chattering. After a moment she began to feel better, her mind clearer, working properly again. Getting to her feet, she went back to the kitchen to retrieve the photo. But it was gone.

When Alexey jumped out of a taxi a few short minutes later, she was at the staff quarters, trying to pick the lock of Slava's room with a bent pin. He hurried toward her. He was very pale. He took her in his arms. "Lenochka – my darling Lenochka – are you all right?"

"Yes, yes, yes, I'm fine," she said, impatiently, but then without warning she burst into tears, and he held her tight and it was just what she needed, the loving warmth of him, the knowledge he was safe, nothing really bad had happened, she had unmasked a traitor in their midst before it was too late. Presently she was able to tell him her story, without faltering, and as he listened the expression in his eyes darkened. "If I catch him I'll kill him, I swear to God," he growled. "Not for me, but for you. That bastard. And I wasn't there when you needed me …"

"You weren't to know, love," she said, tenderly. "And I'm okay, I really am," and it was true, she was steady now, steady with the knowledge that fate had been kind to them and disaster had been averted. "It was lucky, really, what happened."

"*Lucky?*"

"Yes, because, whatever he was up to, whatever he was planning, he can't do it now." Her voice quivered. "Can't you see? He can't do it, Alexey."

"No," he said, soberly, "he can't," and his eyes met hers, and she knew he understood what she was saying. With Yuri gone, and Oleg and Katya – and was it possible Slava had engineered all that – then Alexey had been exposed, with Slava as his only guard. How long would it have been before something happened? Not straight away, no. Slava would have waited. Waited till they were lulled into a sense of false security before …

She shuddered. It didn't bear thinking about. And the important thing was – it hadn't happened. Slava had made a mistake. It was pure chance she'd found the photo. He hadn't known he'd mislaid it. But the shock in his face when he saw it had given him away. He knew he was blown. That's why he'd run.

"We need to get into his room," she said. "In case there's anything else. And then we need to call Nikolai, and Maxim."

"There's a master key somewhere. I'll go get it. I've called the local police already. Told them Slava had stolen my car. Gave them the number. They might be able to stop him."

*

But Slava was long gone and the police didn't catch up with him. Helen and Alexey got into his room and found it obsessively tidy, everything arranged in military precision. A search of every inch of it produced very little. No more photos. No clues. And apart from a luridly jacketed paperback book on the bedside table, very little of any personal nature either. They flipped through the paperback anyway, but not surprisingly there was nothing hidden in it. But in the small bathroom Alexey found a small brown pill-bottle in the wastebasket, and though there were no pills left in it, there was still a fine residue of powder coating the bottom. "It's a long shot, but we might as well get it analyzed," he said, "just in case it's connected to what happened with the dogs …"

He rang Nikolai then, and even from across the room Helen could hear the Trinity manager's startled yelp.

"It can't be true, it can't! We checked out Slava – you remember, Alexey, Pasha did it?"

"I do. I saw the file. It was pretty thorough."

"There was absolutely nothing to connect him with Repin. Is Helen absolutely sure it *was* Repin in that picture?"

"I'm sure," said Helen, taking the phone. "I've seen his picture on the Internet. There's no doubt, Nikolai."

"Oh well, at least thank God for fools! I can't imagine Repin will be best pleased with him, blowing his cover like that. Hell, to think … If you hadn't found that photo, Helen …"

"I know," she said, swallowing. "I keep thinking of that."

"But you did find it," said Volkovsky, his voice firming, "and we are all greatly in your debt because now a clear and present danger has been neutralized."

Helen's voice trembled a little as she said, "Do you think there's any chance that he – he'll come back?"

"No. I think he'll stay well away," said Volkovsky, reassuringly. "And I have a hunch that Slava wasn't there to hurt Lyosha, anyway."

Alexey took the phone back. "But what about the dogs?"

"That might be a simple coincidence. After all, the dogs tried to attack Helen too."

"Yes, but …"

"We must not make the mistake of assuming that everything is linked, Lyosha. Or we will get confused and go up the wrong track. I think myself that Slava was there as Repin's eyes and ears. There's no doubt in my mind now that Repin has his eye on Trinity. I went to see that ex-mistress of his this morning. And she told me that just over three years ago, he'd had a secret meeting with Galkin."

"But why would Galkin meet with Repin?"

"She didn't know. But it's possible that Galkin was exploring options, shall we say, on his own. Or it may be unconnected. Galkin was a hunting enthusiast, like Repin. Anyway, it's a connection we didn't have before. And now we know Slava was Repin's mole."

"Have you spoken to Maxim about it?"

"No, but I will. Have you spoken to him?"

"Not yet. Will you?"

"Sure," said Volkovsky. "He might as well have all the information in one go." His tone changed. "Now, don't take this the wrong way – I don't think you're in any physical danger from Slava, but your security has been compromised. I've got a few things to finish up here, but I'll catch the plane back tomorrow morning, and arrange for the house to be thoroughly searched, in case Slava installed surveillance equipment of some sort. Until we can get the house swept clean for bugs, you should stay somewhere else. A hotel, perhaps."

"What about Irina's place?" whispered Helen to Alexey. "I'm sure she wouldn't mind and it might – might be better than a hotel." She didn't want to say, *I'd feel safer for us to be there, surrounded by people I know and trust, rather than a place full of strangers*. But Alexey understood. He squeezed her hand, and spoke to Volkovsky.

"We'll try and arrange to stay at Professor Bayeva's tonight."

"Is that wise? They will want to know why you want to stay there. In a hotel, no one asks questions. And I'm not sure it would be good if they knew the truth of what happened. They will be frightened. This will be of no help to you."

"We'll think of something," said Alexey. "Maybe that the house has to be fumigated against vermin, something like that."

"And so it does, in a way. Very well. If you think that is the best thing. I will be there in the morning as soon as I can get a car from the airport in Yaroslavl."

Chapter 35

Helen felt a little guilty about how easily her mother and Irina had accepted her explanation about why they needed to stay overnight. Only a little guilty, though, because in fact they were so transparently pleased to see the young couple, so delighted to have their company, that in the end it had all felt quite natural, and quite right.

The cozy little *izba* felt much more secure than Alexey's big, echoey house. And the ordinary chatter they engaged in over dinner, and later, over cups of tea, was soothing and cheerful after the emotions of the day. Therese talked about the places she'd recently visited, Helen talked about fishing in the Volga, Alexey and Irina had a spirited discussion about whether it was Lev Atamanov or Walt Disney who had made the best classic animated films of fairytales (surprisingly, or perhaps not, Irina turned out to be a staunch defender of Disney). By the time they went to bed, Helen was feeling mellow. She and Alexey made love quietly under the bedcovers and she fell asleep in his arms, with the soft night pressing in at the window.

But she woke much later to a terrible feeling of oppression, a terror so great she could hardly breathe. The room was dark, very dark. But there was something there. A thing whose being seemed made of the night. A presence that stood upright on its hind legs and watched her with stony, unblinking eyes.

A *bear*. A huge bear, watching her with that alien gaze. The more she looked at it, the more she was paralyzed by it. There was a suffocating tightness in her chest, something like a claw gripping at her heart, squeezing ... With a huge effort, she managed to moan, "*Help – help –*"

"Helen, Helen ... what's wrong? What's wrong?"

Alexey's voice. Alexey, holding her. What was happening? Her face was wet with tears. Her heart was pounding. She was shivering. But she was not alone, facing a bear, she was in bed with Alexey, the door was closed, there was nothing in the doorway, the room was warm, and silvery moonlight came in through the window. She realized she'd been asleep, and now she was awake.

"I –" She swallowed. "I – I'm sorry I woke you. I just had a horrible nightmare. But I thought – I really thought I was awake."

"They're the worst sort," he said, gently. "Lucid dreams. Do you want to tell me about it, Lenochka?"

Usually, she wouldn't have wanted to, because recounting a nightmare to someone else seemed to fix it in her mind, to give it a daylight shape that should not be. But this one was different. This was a terrifying visitation and she knew it must be spoken out loud to dissipate its power. So she nodded and said, "I was in this room, and the door was open, and there was a bear, a huge bear – and it's hard to explain, but I couldn't look away – and I felt like it was trying to ... get into my head – to hypnotize me or something so it could get me – and – that's all that happened, but it was horrible ... horrible. I suppose it was because of the things we looked at on the Internet – but oh, Alexey, it felt so real."

He did not tell her it was "just a dream". He held her close against him and murmured, "I know. I know, love. I know."

"You weren't there. In my dream. I – I was alone."

"Oh my poor Lenochka, my poor love. I'm here now," he said, kissing her, softly.

"Oh, Alexey, don't ever leave me," she cried, and he answered, fiercely, "Never ever, and that's a promise," and then they were moving together, making love again, passionately, desperately, but silently.

Presently, they fell asleep again. She didn't have any more dreams, bad or good. When she awoke, it was to find Alexey still fast asleep, one arm outflung from the quilt. She looked at him for a moment, so beautiful, so vital, so warm, so much himself, so much hers, and, her heart turning over with love and thankfulness, she kissed him on the bare shoulder. He stirred but didn't wake – and getting up quietly, she put on dressing-gown and slippers and went downstairs.

It was 8.30 and her mother was alone in the kitchen. Irina had already gone off to her study to work and Therese told Helen she was waiting for Sergey to come and pick her up. They were driving to Kostroma today. Did Helen and Alexey want to join them?

Helen smiled affectionately at her mother. "Thanks very much – we'd have loved to – but he's still asleep, Mam, and I don't want to wake him. And you don't want to be late setting off either I suppose."

"No. It's quite a distance. I might even overnight there."

"With Sergey?"

"Well, he's got the car," her mother said, blandly.

"Mam – how's it going with him?"

"What do you mean?"

"Come on. You know."

"Good. He's a very nice man."

Helen laughed. "Mam! I think you've been living too long in England! *Very nice*! Is that all?"

"That's plenty to be getting on with," said her mother, adding quietly, "at my age."

"Oh, Mam! You're hardly old."

"Well, thank you for that, but you know what I mean. At your age, one can afford to fall head over heels. At mine – one has to be more careful."

"But is it – do you think it might get serious?"

"I don't know. And I'm not sure I want to know. Let's just say we enjoy each other's company very much. And leave it at that." She looked at her daughter. "But it's different for you, *chérie*."

"Yes," said Helen, simply. "Alexey is the love of my life."

Therese Clement smiled. "He's a wonderful young man. In every way."

Helen kissed her. "I'm so glad you think that, Mam."

"Even that cynic Irina agrees he's special, and that's saying something."

Helen laughed. "Yes."

"Not that she believes in true love, mind you," went on her mother. "Poor Irina! I only wish she'd found a man who could match that passion of hers. But she never has, and that's a tragedy."

Just then, Sergey arrived. He greeted Helen and Therese cheerfully, without a trace of self-consciousness. He said, "You stay here this night, Helen?"

"Yes." She knew he must have seen Alexey's motorbike outside, so she said, "And Alexey did too."

"Ah." He shot Therese a look. She smiled. He said, "Tell him hello from me. He is good man."

"Yes," said Helen, happily. "He is."

Soon after, they left. It was only after the Lada had turned the corner and disappeared that Helen noticed her mother had forgotten her phone, left behind in the clutter on the dresser. Sergey had a cell phone too but she had no idea of the number, so she couldn't call and tell them. Oh well! It didn't matter. She thought about what her mother had said, about her and Sergey, and whether it was true that at her mother's age it was enough that they just enjoy each other's company. But Alexey and her ...

"Yes, we're pretty hot together, aren't we," he said, behind her.

She jumped. "I can't believe it! You read my mind again!"

"Lucky guess again," he said, teasingly. He was already dressed, his hair bright, his eyes full of enticing mischief, and she felt her knees buckling, though she spoke sternly to him.

"I forbid you to read my mind, Alexey Makarov, unless I give you permission!"

He laughed and gave her a mock salute, his eyes sparkling with mischief. "Yes, ma'am, at your service, ma'am!"

"You're crazy," she said, mock-pityingly, and he said, "Yes, I admit it, I'm crazy for you, don't you know, mademoiselle, and what are you going to do about it?" and with that he was whirling her around the kitchen.

"Well, well," said Irina, coming in just then, "and good morning to you too! Must have been a good sleep, you guys are sure energetic dancing at this time in the morning!"

"Ah, hi, Irina," said Helen. "We were just mucking about. Sorry."

"Why be sorry? Looked like fun. Actually, though, I came to ask you a favor, Alexey. It's really annoying – but I just this minute got a call from a guy in Rostov about some really important documents I've been hanging out for, which are finally available. I really need to get there today, and Sergey of course has gone off with Therese. I know there should be a bus soon from the town center. Could I trouble you for a quick lift to the station?"

"Sure," he said. "No problem at all. If you don't mind riding on the bike, that is."

"Course I don't mind. I used to have a biker boyfriend when I was young. Loved the bike, if not him."

"Irina! I never knew that!" said Helen, delighted.

"Hell, honey, you wouldn't believe all the dark secrets of my misspent youth," said Irina cheerfully. "Okay, Alexey, you ready to roll?"

"Sure," said Alexey, and giving Helen a kiss and a "*Poka, milaya.* See you later, sweetheart," he was off outside with Irina, and an instant later they were roaring up the street.

Chapter 36

Helen had a shower and got dressed. Just as she finished, she heard her cell phone buzzing. It was a text from Alexey. *Bus gone, running Irina to Rostov. Back couple hours. Love you. A xxxxx*

Love you too, heaps, she wrote. *Drive safe. See you soon. H xxxxx*

She looked around her, a little uneasily. So she was alone till he got back. Well, so what? What was there to fear here? Only bad dreams, her memory told her. Only bad dreams that felt totally real. Stop it, girl. Don't think about it. Keep your mind busy. She washed up the breakfast things and sat down with a book, a collection of Russian short stories, but fell almost immediately on a spooky story by Nikolai Gogol, about a cursed painting that haunted everyone who owned it. Maybe it was the story, maybe it was the remnants of the dream, but soon Helen decided she really didn't want to be inside.

Laying down the book, she went out into the garden, closing the back door firmly behind her. Oh, it was much better out there, in the sunlit green. The birds sang, the lilac filled the air with scent, things felt normal, and she began to feel ashamed of her fears. Dreams, what were they, really, even the powerful lucid ones? Just ragtag and bobtail leftover bits of thoughts and feelings and memories. They were the last thing she should be afraid of. Real life was more dangerous, but right now it was less dangerous than it had been yesterday, before she'd unmasked Slava. Now he was gone. He wouldn't be returning. Now they knew Repin was behind the attacks on Trinity too and had solid leads to go on. He'd be stopped. And Nikolai would be here soon, his presence, experience and knowledge a reassuring bulwark against the malice of their enemy.

She came to the study. The door wasn't locked. So she went in. Irina's laptop and printer sat on the desk, with a thick stack of printed manuscript paper next to them. By each side of the desk was a filing cabinet, repainted a soft pale blue, and on the floor was a rug of the same color, while a framed photograph of a Russian forest scene hung on one wall.

Helen sat in the chair and picked up the first page of the manuscript, the title page: *Gods, Protectors and Enemies: The Bear in Russian Thought and Culture, by Irina Bayeva Simmons.* She flicked through the manuscript, till she came to a chapter called "The Homo Ferens project". Settling down in the chair, she began to read, and was soon completely absorbed in the extraordinary story it had to tell.

The Homo Ferens project
    Prologue: Northern Russia, winter 1935

The old hunter was just as he'd been described to them by the villagers: small, tough and wiry, with a large, recent, livid scar that ran across one cheek to thin lips, and a pair of very pale eyes in a weathered face under a shock of long silver hair. Unlike the villagers, those eyes showed no fear in front of the two strangers. In his expression was no eagerness, either. No interest. Nothing at all. And yet their gaze was fixed on the two strangers, and there was something about the old man's very lack of expression that made the two strangers feel, just for an instant, a tremor of an ancient, outlawed terror.

To believe in such things – to think that a man could really turn into a beast and curse people with evil magic – was a sin in the new Russia, a thought-crime you kept to yourself if you didn't want to end up before the commissar, accused of superstition and obscurantism. But old terrors are not so easily eradicated by new ones, especially in the villages, and even the most enthusiastic Party informer might hesitate to denounce a man such as the one who stood before them, a benighted relic of a bygone age.

But the two strangers were not villagers, or informers. They were new men, with no belief in any kind of superstition, be it God or miraculous icons or witchcraft or shape-changing beasts or anything that broke the iron laws of materialism. Or so they'd always thought. Until now.

"Where is it?" growled the fairer of the two strangers, who despite being older than the dark one, had a harder, fitter air. He advanced menacingly on the old man, who did not flinch in the slightest, but looked at both of them with the ghost of a smile as the darker man signaled hastily to his companion to keep quiet.

"You are in a hurry, my lords," said the old man, using the forbidden honorific, blithely ignoring the fact that "comrade" was now the accepted term.

He knew, the old devil, thought the dark-haired stranger, with an inward smile. Knew that he was a walking insult to the State and yet somehow he must imagine that he was protected, because of his reputation, and because we have come to his door as petitioners. The dark stranger could feel the hostility of his companion; knew that to him it was incomprehensible that they were kow-towing to this hideous old relic. But it didn't matter what he thought or felt; for despite the fact the fair-haired man was older, it was the young, dark stranger who was in charge. It was he who had the only blessing that counted, before which all others, real or imagined, meant nothing at all. And he knew that the old man couldn't be hurried.

So ignoring a puzzled glare from his companion, he said, very politely using an address he knew the old man would expect, "Dedushka – grandfather – forgive our haste, but we have come a long way and must be back in town before nightfall. Please tell us in your own words how it happened. You were hunting bear, is that correct?"

"Yes, as you see," said the old man, simply, pointing to his scar. Rolling up a sleeve, he showed them deep scratches on his arms, and on his chest. "She was very nearly the death of me, for that creature had a powerful soul."

The stranger nodded, taking care not to let his true feelings show on his face. Soul, indeed! What was soul? A thing that did not exist, could not exist. Why did the old fool persist in such nonsense when he must know full well that he simply had great instincts, honed over years into perfection? After all, to survive in the forest, any hunter worth his salt needs to develop skills that to the untrained eye may look magical, like a sixth sense. A silent footfall. An unerring sense of direction. An understanding so complete of the ways and customs of his chosen prey that it is almost as though he is reading their minds. All the villagers had spoken of the hunter's skill in that. The fact they'd also implied there was something supernatural about it did not mean it was true. The old devil had created his own legend. And the superstitious peasants believed it.

The old man leaned toward him. "Remember this – of all the animals in the forest, the bear is the closest to man. If you do not forget, then you will not go far wrong. If you do, then *doom will come on you –" he turned to the other man "– and on you."*

"How dare you threaten us, old –" began the fair-haired man, furiously, but the dark-haired man raised a hand to hush him. He said, quietly, "We will not forget, dedushka."

An old Russian legend speaks of how the first bear was once a man who, refused hospitality by his fellows, plunged into the forest, vowing revenge on mankind. The stranger knew the legend, and the many stories of men turning into bears and bears into men and of children taken in by she-bears and raised as their own. It was what had brought him here after all, to this stinking cottage deep in the heart of the forest. It was what kept him patient now in the face of the old man's insolence. Simply killing him and taking his prize, as his companion had wanted to do, would be of no use, if they did not know the story behind it.

"I'd been tracking her for three days," the old man said, abruptly launching into his hunting narrative. "That isn't unusual. Only a fool expects to kill quickly, and fools don't last long as bear-hunters. But this bear, when I got closer, and saw the shape of her soul, I realized she was wary but not for herself. Cubs, I thought at once. And I remembered that last summer a bear-trainer came to the village and let it be known he'd pay good money for a new cub to train, his beast being sickly and weak and likely to die. This was the first she-bear I'd come across in months that had cubs. I didn't intend to kill her. Just take her cub when she was away from the den."

"But that is not what happened?"

The old man frowned, as if annoyed by the interruption. "No. I came across the den on the afternoon of the third day. I had just seen what was in there when she returned." He paused. "I had not expected her to. She was a long way away. But then—" He gestured into the dim recesses of the cottage, and now, their eyes used to the dim light, they could just about make out what looked like the shape of a cage, covered with a blanket – "it must have called her back, soul to soul."

The fair-haired man could not restrain himself any longer. "What you say is impossible," he burst out. "There is no way on this earth that—"

"And what do you really know of this earth, eh?" The old man rounded on him. "You cannot know anything of the truth of things for you are blinkered like the horse of a carter who does not wish his beast to know he is alive in case he should take it into his head to escape."

They glared at each other. The other stranger said, quickly, "Dedushka, forgive my friend, he does not mean to—"

"If he is your friend," snapped the old man, "then you are the fool I did not take you for, for there is no friendship in such as him. But as you are not a fool, I presume you are trying to butter me up. But I do not care for butter and never have." A malicious glitter had come into his eyes. "You come here with no respect, only lies and soft words. Do you not think I do not know what is in your hearts? Enough. Our business here is done. I have changed my mind, and I ..."

He never got the chance to finish what he was going to say, for with a roar of rage, the fair-haired stranger pulled out a gun and shot him dead.

What I have written above is a fiction; a recreation of what might have been, deep in a cottage in a Northern Russian forest, in the darkest days of Stalinism. I do not really know if it happened like that. It is a leap of the imagination. But it is based on truth, a truth so extraordinary that it dwarfs any fiction. For what if fairytales are not fantastical imaginings, but the truth of the world, written down in a metaphorical way to encode knowledge for the wise? What if myths can be made to come true? This is not my imagination's leap, but that of another: it is the challenge of Anton Antonov, the gauntlet he throws down to our conventional views of human nature and history.

Anton Ilyich Antonov was born in 1899 in Danilov, near Yaroslavl. His mother was of a Karelian family reputed as white witches; his father, who originated from the mid-Volga region, was a minor civil servant with revolutionary ideas. Brought up by his mother on tales of shapeshifters and spells, and with a certain psychic talent himself, he turned against traditional beliefs as a teenager, embracing instead his father's revolutionary philosophy and developing his own strong interest in the new science of eugenics. After the Bolshevik Revolution, and a stint in the Red Army during the civil war, he completed a degree at Leningrad University and began work as a scientist in a state laboratory.

It was during this period that he first conceived the extraordinary idea that was to flower years later as the Homo Ferens project. At its root, the idea was a rethinking both of what fairytale meant, and also a bold statement of the possibilities of science and the nature of mankind, which to him, as to many in that revolutionary time, seemed boundless. For a few years he kept quiet about it, working on it only in his spare time. He knew he had to proceed very carefully and in utter secrecy at first. His reborn but now scientific interest in fairytales and myth might be misinterpreted as mystical obscurantism and lead him into difficulties with the authorities; but most of all, his ideas could be stolen by other, jealous but less able scientists, like Ilya Ivanov, the creator of the famous "superhuman soldier" experiment under the direct commission of Josef Stalin, feared dictator of the Soviet Union.

In old Russia, tales were told of such creatures as Ivashko Medveko, little Ivan the bear's son, who, brought up by a bear, acquires superhuman strength and cunning and killed without a thought. Stories were also told of shapeshifters:

sorcerers who turned into bears, wolves, birds, hares and all kinds of other animals. Antonov thought that all these fantastical stories contained at their root a kernel of truth – it wasn't actual shapeshifting that was going on, because that was biologically impossible – but radically transformed behavior, which to Antonov was the true underlying principle of the so-called "soul". These people at times behaved like animals and actually developed animal characteristics of strength, speed, agility and improved senses; but they also had human intelligence, and together this created a superhuman hybrid which could literally manipulate others and create an illusion of "sorcery". So, the hybrids did exist, but they were not the product of breeding between animals and people. Rather, they were the result of prolonged and very early identification with the animal world. But in the old days, this was all scattergun, disordered, and far too individualistic to be of use in modern times, when the exigencies of a new kind of State demanded a new way of doing things.

Researching stories of feral children, Antonov became convinced this was the way. If such a child could be found who could be kept within the animal world but in a way directed by humans, then the problems of complete animal identification – the lack of adaptation to the human world – would be eliminated whilst at the same time, no direct human contact would be encouraged or even allowed, to eliminate the possibility of undue influence until a certain age. He envisaged the result not as the obedient dumb brute of Ivanov's imagination; but like Ivashko the bear's son. It would be an extraordinary creature which would truly be beyond human and be of immense service to the Soviet state.

Eventually, in late 1934, he managed to get the ear of a man who was close to someone who was close to Stalin; and by dint of this, obtained permission to begin, as well as being given a small group of troops to help him.

When, in the winter of 1935, he heard that a baby boy of about fourteen months old had been found by an old hunter in a bear's den in a forest not far from the little town of Kirilov in Karelia, he was overjoyed, and went to get the child at once. Baby K, as we will call him, had been a long time in the bear's care, judging from the physical signs, such as overgrown hair, the ingrained dirt on his body, his calloused hands and knees, and extraordinary speed and agility for a child of his age, as well as a complete absence of speech. He was apparently "scarcely human" and had been kept by the hunter in a cage after he'd discovered it. The child's origins were a complete mystery. Though there were superstitious rumors in the nearby village that he had the "Devil's mark" and was most likely the child of a witch, lost or abandoned in the forest, no real clues were discovered as to his antecedents, and no one came forward to claim him. Which suited Antonov's purposes very well.

The nurturing bear, a massive female, had been killed by the hunter, but Antonov lost no time in introducing the child to another she-bear he'd acquired, who'd recently lost a cub. She took to the child easily, and him to her. Antonov returned to his laboratory, and to the task of raising his Homo Ferens.

But he'd known from the start that one child was not enough for an experiment. Moreover, he could not wait for another feral child to be discovered, for that search could take years, and Stalin's patience was not famous. Children would have to be found, of the right age and from suitably remote locations, to introduce to the bear. If a child did not survive the contact, another would be quickly found. Orphanages were full of abandoned children who would suit, and thus he'd build up suitable subjects. And so that spring of 1935, he began on the work which could have changed the history of humanity – if Stalin hadn't once again changed his mind.

That was as far as Irina had got, printed out at least. Helen was disappointed. It was an extraordinarily powerful story, and Irina had told it very well. She'd no idea her mother's friend could write like that. But then she had said she wanted to write a popular book, a book that would be read by more than just specialists and academics. A book to set the imagination on fire. And it certainly would do, if it was all like that.

And then she gasped as it struck her. *Anton Antonov.* And Maxim *Antonovich* Serebrov. She distinctly remembered Alexey calling him that yesterday. *Maxim Antonovich.* Irina had said that a Russian always had three names, and that the second name, your patronymic, was based on the Christian name of your father. The "vich" part meant "son of". *And the scientist Antonov's Christian name was Anton, just as Maxim's father must have been called Anton.* What if – what if it was a family name? The surname wasn't the same – but Antonov could have been on the female side of Maxim's family – or the family had changed their name – to avoid the disgrace.

Her mind ran wildly on. Irina had written that Antonov had some "psychic talent" himself. There was no indication yet of his eventual fate, but it was safe to assume that if Stalin had "changed his mind again", that meant the scientist must have come to a bad end. The policeman's only in his thirties, she thought, so Antonov could not be his father, not if he'd died in Stalin's time – but he *could* be his grandfather – or great-uncle ... Bu then – how could that be connected to *Alexey's* grandfather, Mikhail Makarov? No way would he have been around at the same time as Antonov. He might not even have been born then. Or at least he could have been no more than a baby. So he couldn't *possibly* have been the one to interrogate or arrest Antonov, if that's what had happened. Wait – wait – wait – what about Mikhail's *father,* Pyotr

Makarov? Alexey had even said he'd been in Stalin's secret police. Could it be that?

Her throat fluttered. No. The links were too tenuous. She was spinning a sinister fairytale out of disjointed scraps, just because of the amazing power of Irina's story. She tried to call Alexey, but the phone immediately went to voicemail. She left a message. She tried Irina's phone but it was the same. They must be out of range. She could ring Volkovsky and …

Without warning, her throat clenched. The back of her neck prickled. Something was there. Something was watching her. Last night's terrifying vision of the bear was in her mind as she turned around – and saw, to her utter shock, *Alexey, standing in the doorway.*

He was swaying as though about to faint. His white T-shirt was stained with what looked horribly like a mixture of blood and dirt, one knee of his jeans was torn. He was pale – pale – so pale – almost as white as the T-shirt had once been – except for a long red mark on one cheek, like a gravel rash. He didn't speak. But worst of all was the look in his eyes, an expression of such horror and despair that it froze her to the spot.

Her mind was in spasms, trying to understand. An accident – he'd had an accident on the bike – he was hurt, injured. The paralysis left her. She ran toward him, calling his name, reached out a hand to him – but the moment her fingers touched his, she felt a jolt as violent as an electric shock. Her body jerked back involuntarily, and in that instant, he vanished.

Chapter 37

It wasn't possible. It wasn't. Sobbing, she pulled open the door and ran out into the garden, calling his name. But he wasn't there. The garden, empty of anything but birdsong and vegetation, mocked her with its sunny normalcy. She ran into the house, looking in every room, out the front door into the street. There was no sign of him; no sign of his bike, either. But still her mind refused to accept that he wasn't there. He must be hiding somewhere. Something terrible had happened, so terrible he was hiding like a child. She ran down the road, calling his name, screaming it. Every muscle in her body ached, every nerve jangled with fire, but inside her, at the heart of her, a terror made of ice and shadow was gaining, freezing her heart, her thoughts, her soul.

She turned the corner – and nearly ran headlong into a car coming the other way. The driver stood on the brakes and skidded to a stop; and as he jumped out, she saw it was Volkovsky. He said, "Helen! What on earth—"

"It's Alexey," she cried. "He's hurt – he's had an accident ... he's in shock – we must go after him –"

Volkovsky looked completely bewildered. "After him? Where? What accident?"

"Please – please – let's find him – let's drive and find him."

He looked at her. "Okay. Get in. But I don't understand where."

"The Rostov road," she said, scrambling into the passenger seat. "Please, Nikolai – quickly, quickly!"

"Okay," he said, getting back in, and reversing the car back up the road, "but really you have to explain what's going on."

She told him about Alexey giving Irina a lift to Rostov, and then about how he'd appeared in the doorway, dirt-stained and bloody, and as she spoke, a feeling grew in her that was also a terrible, uncanny knowledge she'd tried to hide from. Though it had looked so solid, she knew it wasn't Alexey in flesh and blood she'd seen – but a vision – a *double* – of her lover, who was even now lying somewhere on the road, in his own blood. Not dead, though. She clung to that. Not dead. They were so closely connected, he and she, so tightly wound together, that, injured, badly in need of her help, he'd used every bit of his energy to reach out to her through space and time, pushing himself into her consciousness, pleading with her to come and help him.

Volkovsky didn't say, "You must be mistaken." He didn't say, "You must have been seeing things." He didn't say, "This is crazy." He simply patted Helen's shoulder, briefly, and said, "We'll find him, never fear. But we must be calm."

He took out his phone and dialed Alexey's number. No answer. Helen had Irina's number in her phone, so he tried that next. Still no answer. He clicked off the phone and said, "And you're sure they were going to Rostov?"

For answer, she showed him the text.

"Right. Then the next thing is to find out if they made it to Rostov. Do you have any idea where the professor was going to pick up these documents? A local authority office? A museum? A library?"

She shook her head, bleakly. "I don't know."

"Well, we'll try them all."

No one at either the first or the second number he tried knew anything about it. But his call to the Rostov library produced a different result. "They were indeed expecting Professor Bayeva to pick up some photocopied clippings," he said. "But she hasn't turned up yet."

She cried, "Oh my God – oh my God –"

"I'll call the police, in Rostov and Uglich, and see if there have been any reports of accidents." He made the calls, and hanging up, said, "There's been nothing – but I persuaded them to put out a call on their radios and also to truck drivers, and they're going to start a search up and down the road in case the bike veered off into the ditch somewhere ..."

A light rain was falling now but Volkovsky didn't go fast as they reached the Rostov road, so that they could look properly, see if there were skid marks, signs of wreckage, anything. On and on they went, every sense alert.

Helen said, wildly, "We haven't seen a single police car yet. Why aren't they out searching?"

"I'll check on that." He pulled over and made the calls. His expression changed as he listened, and he spoke sharply, briefly.

"What is it? What is it?"

"News has only just come in that a truck driver thinks he passed the bike on the Rostov road only a few kilometers out of Uglich. After that, nothing." He looked at Helen. "It's only a chance – but the Uglich police are going out straight away to search in that area."

"Then we've got to go back too. We've got to help search. We've got to ..."

But she never finished what she was going to say, because at that moment Volkovsky's phone rang again. Snatching it up, he said, sharply, "*Da?*" And then. "*Ah. Maxim Antonovich.*"

The bitterness of the disappointment was so sharp that it felt like a punch in the stomach. She concentrated on the image of Alexey, trying to reach him. But there was no answer. She prayed then like she'd never prayed before in her life, offering up everything – anything – if only she could find him.

Chapter 38

Maxim had woken at three o'clock that morning sweating from a nightmare he put down to too much red wine the night before. In the nightmare, he'd been sure of being onto something that would crack the case. But then it had slipped away from him again. He'd tried to think what it was, but it was gone. Instead, his ears were full of voices. Voices he knew, voices of the unknown. Voices of the dead, voices from life. A babel of disjointed, discordant, unbearable noise. He woke with a headache, knowing that he'd lost it, the clue, the thing that would crack this case wide open. But it was there, somewhere, if only he could concentrate long enough to find it again.

Volkovsky's phone call the day before had shaken him, not because he'd believed in Slava's bona fides, though he'd had no reason to question it one way or the other. What bothered him was that he'd been so sure Repin wasn't behind this, and yet now it looked like he'd been badly wrong. But that wasn't the only thing that troubled Maxim. He also disliked the fact it was Helen, once more, who'd found the important piece of evidence against the bodyguard, and that now that important piece of evidence was gone. He'd said as much to Volkovsky.

"In God's name, Maxim," the Trinity manager had sighed. "The girl is an innocent, and it was pure chance she happened on that photo."

"That's what she told you," Maxim said, stubbornly. "She had no witnesses apart from Slava, and he's gone."

"Yes, and why would he have run if he'd been framed?"

"They might be in it together," Maxim said. "To make it look like –"

"Stop complicating things," Volkovsky snapped. "I told you what Repin's ex-mistress said. There is a history there we didn't know about."

"Perhaps, but it doesn't mean that –"

"Repin's still away, but Zaitsev's trying to find a way to contact him," Volkovsky cut in. "Till then, or till we can catch Slava, we must assume the logical thing: that Repin is behind all this, and his absence proves it; he wouldn't want to be in the country when it all occurs." His tone changed. "Have you made any progress on the other leads?"

"Not yet," said Maxim, stiffly, stung by the manager's tone. Volkovsky sensed it and said, "I'm sorry, Maxim Antonovich, I am tense and apt to snap. I know you've been doing the best you can, as have we all. Now, can I ask you a favor?"

The favor was to call on Foma the next morning, to check in person on the progress of the decoding of the Koldun file. Well, now it was the next morning, but after his bad night Maxim had slept in rather later than he normally would, and so it wasn't till nearly 9.30 that he presented himself at the cryptographer's door. He knocked once. Twice. No answer. He was about to knock a third time when an elderly woman came out of the next-door apartment and said, "You're wasting your time. He's gone away with friends. I saw him leave this morning, very early. I'm awake much too early these days," she said, a little defensively.

Maxim was instantly on alert. "What did the friends look like?" When she hesitated, he pulled out his ID and showed her, hoping she wouldn't clam up. But instead she said, promptly, "One was middle-aged, average looks, thin face, balding. The other was young, blond crew cut, big muscles, sunglasses, you know the type."

Yes, he did. Slava, thought Maxim, grimly. The other one didn't ring any bells, though. He said, "What did Foma do?"

She stared at him. "Do? He just went along with them." Then she caught his meaning. "Oh you think he was being forced – no, no, he was quite willing. They seemed on the best of terms."

"Was he carrying anything?"

"A suitcase. And that computer bag of his," she said, instantly.

Maxim sighed. "Did you happen to see their vehicle?"

"I'm not very good on cars. The makes I mean. But it was one of those foreign jobs. Black. New."

The Mercedes. Hurriedly, he thanked her and left. He needed to know the identity of the third man, so he called Ilya Orlov from Trinity and asked if the description given by Foma's neighbor might tally with that of one of the intruders who had attacked the Trinity's offices. But Orlov told him he'd not seen the men's faces, he'd only be able to remember their voices and general build. And then he added, hesitantly, "It's stupid of me – but actually the person that description most makes me think of is Pasha – that is, Pavel Dutov, our senior investigator. But, of course, it can't be him."

There was no *of course* about that, thought Maxim, hurriedly hanging up after getting Pasha's number and address. The investigator didn't answer his phone so Maxim went round to his place – only to find that the bird had flown. He called police headquarters to have an alert put out for the Mercedes and the three men, and discovered that the car, which had already been reported as stolen from Uglich, had been found abandoned at a Metro station on the outskirts of Moscow. It was a Metro line that went to one of the airports, and he called through there at once. There was no record of the men having taken a plane, at least not in their own names, but Maxim gave a description of them anyway, in case. He wasn't confident they'd be found – they could easily have slipped out of the country on false passports – or taken a train instead, or bought a car – but he had to do something.

Next he called the bank manager to find out if any attempt had been made to check the memory card out from the vault. None had, but he warned the manager about the men anyway. Maybe they didn't know yet about the card or where it was; but he could not be sure they wouldn't find out, somehow. A Repin spy had been caught red-handed at Alexey's, the house might well be bugged, and the young man's cell phone was possibly compromised as well. It wasn't impossible that these traitors would find out that the printout – whose code Foma must have cracked, it was the only explanation for his sudden departure – was linked to a mysterious memory card found in the Trinity office. After all, everyone knew *something* important had been found. And the printout itself might have yielded clues that it was printed from a memory card file.

If all this doesn't stop soon, thought Maxim, grimly, Alexey Makarov will have no company left to helm. Between deceitful betrayers and scared deserters, it will have self-destructed, and his beautiful dream will be at an end.

Not long ago, Maxim would have shrugged his shoulders and thought that was how the world worked. He'd have thought that the likes of Trinity wasn't worth fighting for. He'd have thought that a wealthy young man like Alexey was a mere dilettante who would soon move on to something new; that he was cushioned by his privilege from the fallout of shattered dreams. And that in fact he had invited his troubles by his recklessness and impulsiveness. Yet now Maxim was filled with rage at the cold manipulation and deceit that was so carefully and relentlessly white-anting the company poor Alexey had put so much passion and trust in. For the first time, he felt a real sense of fellow-feeling for the young man. It wasn't all that long ago that he himself had been Alexey's age; not so very long ago that he'd had stars in his eyes and fire in his belly. The stars had faded now, and the fire was mere embers. But they hadn't gone out. And he was damned if he was going to let it happen.

He called Alexey's number. No reply. So he called Volkovsky, and told him very quickly what he'd learned. Volkovsky said, bleakly, "No. Oh *no*. It can't be true. Foma's neighbor must have made a mistake."

"I'm afraid she didn't. Put me on to Alexey, please, I need to speak to him directly."

Volkovsky cried, "But I can't. Alexey's missing."

The shock of it punched through Maxim's veins. "He's *what*?"

Volkovsky explained. Maxim said, sharply, all his suspicions returning, "Where's the girl?"

"With me. She's in a dreadful state."

"Of course."

"Don't take that tone. There's no doubt it's true. I saw the text he sent her. And they were definitely due to pick up something in Rostov. But they never made it. I'm beginning to be afraid he's had an accident and –"

"There is another possibility than an accident," broke in Maxim, grimly. "If her story is true ..."

"It is, I'd wager my life on it."

"Very well then. Let's say they set off for Rostov – but on the road were ambushed and abducted."

Volkovsky gasped. Then he said, "My God. You could be right. But it can't be Slava, we know he was in Moscow at

Foma's apartment this morning. Repin may have had other men in place though."

Maxim interrupted him. "Is the girl's mother with you?"

"No. Why?"

"Where is she?"

"Maxim ..."

"Ask the girl where her mother is."

"Speak to her yourself, then."

Helen's voice sounded very small, broken, infinitely sad, and for a moment Maxim felt a qualm. But it had to be done. He said, sharply, "Where is your mother, Miss Clement?"

"My – my mother? Why?"

"Where is she?" he repeated.

"She – she went to Kostroma. With Sergey. But I don't under—"

"Who's Sergey?"

"The taxi driver. Sergey Filippov. He's a friend, and ..."

"Her number, Miss Clement. I'd like her cell phone number."

"What for?"

"I want to call her."

"Well, you can't. She forgot her phone at Irina's house."

"I see. Does Filippov have a cellphone?"

"Yes. But I don't know the number."

"What is the registration of his car?"

"I have no idea. It's a blue Lada. That's all I know. Please, I don't understand. Why are you asking all these questions?"

Words from Lev Kirov's manuscript flashed in Maxim's mind. Different in body and soul, word and deed, *tongue and heart*. Why hadn't he seen that straight away? It wasn't just a nice phrase, it was a clue. Tongue as in *language*. Makarov spoke Russian. The other, not. So, a foreigner.

He said, "Why did your mother come to Uglich? And why did she bring you with her?"

Her voice trembled as she replied, "What has that to do with –"

"Answer me!"

"She's writing travel articles. On the Golden Ring." Her voice dropped even lower. "And I – because I needed – a holiday."

"And you had never heard of the Makarovs before."

"Of course not. What is this?"

"You didn't get ... encouraged to take up with Alexey? Encouraged to get close to him?"

"What? Are you crazy?" Then her voice rose. Sharpened. "No. You're worse than that. Much worse. You're clever. Very clever, Maxim *Antonovich*."

It was his turn to falter, "*What?*"

"You're trying to confuse Nikolai, aren't you? To make him think – for God's sake – that we – that Mam ... that she could be involved in – in abducting Alexey. Because that's what you're driving at, isn't it?"

"It is the only thing that makes sense to me."

She yelled down the phone at him, "It makes no bloody sense at all! Why should Mam want to – to do such a thing? Why should she have anything against the Makarovs? She's French, not Russian! And what about Sergey? What about Irina? Are you saying they're in it too? Or that Mam would be prepared to sacrifice her old friend to get to Alexey? You bastard. I know what you're doing. You're just trying to divert suspicion from yourself. But I know what you've been trying to hide. I know about your real family, I know about Antonov!"

Chapter 39

Now Helen's words tumbled over one another, as she told them what she'd learned about Antonov from Irina's book. She was driven by fury and fear, and a hatred so scalding and profound that it felt as though it was burning away her insides. Nobody else spoke. They were more than halfway back to Uglich by now but Volkovsky had pulled up the car on the side of the road and was staring at her as though he'd never seen her before, while on the other end of the phone Maxim was completely silent, though she could hear him breathing.

And then, when she'd come to a shuddering, desolate stop, he whispered, "Dear God ..."

She looked at Nikolai Volkovsky. He was very pale. He said, "You found this information in *Professor Bayeva's study*?"

She nodded. "I'll show you, if you don't believe me. You can read it for yourself."

Before he could speak again, Maxim said, in a very different tone, "Miss Clement – I – please forgive me."

It was the last thing she'd expected.

"I have shamefully traduced you and your mother, and for that I am profoundly sorry," he went on, quietly. "But you must believe me when I say that I am guilty of nothing more than bad manners, stupid prejudice and jumping to conclusions. This man Antonov – I swear I knew nothing about him. He is not only not even vaguely related to me. I had no idea he even existed. If I had – everything might have been different."

"How can I believe you?" she cried.

"Please – if you care about Alexey as much as I believe you do – please listen to what I am about to tell you," he said, without answering her question, and then he briefly told her and Volkovsky what he'd seen in Kirov's papers. "I will take the first plane to Yaroslavl and get back to Uglich as soon as I can. But you can't afford to wait for me. You must return at once to Professor Bayeva's study and search it thoroughly. It's possible there may be a lead to where he's been taken."

"But I don't understand ..." Helen began, and suddenly gasped as it all clicked – and in a flash she saw something so terrible – a monstrous picture so blindingly clear – that it was like the moment when she touched the double's hand. The phone dropped from her nerveless hand as she moaned, "No – no – oh no ... no ...no ..."

*

Afterwards, she didn't remember the journey back or how Volkovsky had broken the speed limit. How he'd stopped off briefly at Alexey's house to collect Mikhail Makarov's service pistol and ammunition. Didn't remember getting back to Irina's study, or Volkovsky clicking through the files on Irina's computer without success. She remembered nothing except the blizzard of papers and documents strewn over the floor after Volkovsky had prized open the filing cabinets ...

For a while, they found nothing. No hit lists, no coded plans, no revealing diaries, nothing like that. Just masses of material on bear folklore, none of which appeared to have any relevance to what they were seeking, and she was beginning to think that they'd made a terrible mistake when all at once she found the pictures. Not the ones she'd been half-expecting – no "trophy" photos of bodies, not even any of the Trinity partners. But first, an old black and white photo, a small head-and-shoulders shot, probably from an ID document of some sort, showing a thin-faced man with deep-set dark eyes and springing dark hair. On the back was written, in Cyrillic script, *A. И. A, 1934.* A.I.A. She knew who it must be. Anton Ilyich Antonov. Nothing showed on that face, no clue as to the true nature of the man. No clue as to why ... *why* ...

But the other photos – the small handful of colored, modern ones – she'd seen them before. And not as stills, but as part of a moving clip. And she knew then there was no mistake. For the photos showed a sparrow, in a cage. A sparrow caught in a spasm. A pitiful little bundle of feathers at the bottom of a cage. She knew now *who* had done it – whose eyes had held the bird so still – whose terrifying psychic energy had reached into the poor creature's body and stopped its heart – but she couldn't think about that right now, only set it to one side.

Because Alexey's heart *hadn't* stopped – he *wasn't* dead – she could feel it – deep within her, faint on the air, she could hear a whisper now – the faint, faint trace of his voice – the lingering note of his presence – which told her that somewhere, somewhere, he was still alive. Weakened, yes, but not dead, and not far away – and she clung to the hope that somewhere in Irina's things there was something which might lead them to where he was being held.

Volkovsky shot her a glance. Looking to see if she wasn't going to pass out or go to pieces again, she thought, blankly.

The horror of knowing how ruthlessly Alexey had been ambushed and deceived – and how she herself had innocently contributed – had left her utterly numb. Hatred, fury, even fear, it had all gone. All she clung to was that faint whisper of his living presence...

Silently, Volkovsky passed a piece of paper to her. She scanned it almost without understanding. It was an English translation of a short Russian document, dated 17 March 1936, with the heading of "Report, termination HF".

As ordered, immediate steps were taken to terminate the experiment. Operation successful. Animal destroyed along with surviving subjects. All traces eliminated. The criminal in charge was arrested and under interrogation confessed to false science and deliberately conspiring to bring the State into disrepute.

In its bald way it told a terrible story. But it wasn't that which drew Helen's eye. It was the signature at the bottom. *Lt. P.A. Makarov.*

So Pyotr Makarov had been there on that awful day when Antonov's fantasy world had come crashing down. Pyotr Makarov, secret policeman, had led the operation to "terminate" the *Homo Ferens* experiment. It was Pyotr Makarov's signature on the document. And that was why, in the twisted logic of an insane mind, a Makarov had to pay for the destruction of Antonov. Any Makarov. All Makarovs. Because the murderous, long-dead Pyotr Makarov was unreachable, but his family had continued. Had even flourished. And that was unbearable, to the killer. This was personal. Antonov was no random stranger. No long-gone mad scientist. He was related to the killer. Closely related. Not a father, but maybe a grandfather. And his death, and the destruction of all his hopes, had to be avenged.

I was warned to keep away from Alexey, thought Helen, desolate. Why? Not because I was in danger from him. *But because the killer didn't want to hurt me.*

And that sudden thought gave her hope. A tiny hope ... because now she thought she knew where they might be.

She blurted out, "The stream in the woods. Oh God, it's her favorite place. I think that's where she's got him. I think that's where we must go."

*

You and I, he'd said, we are keyed to the same music.

It was still faint, the whisper, but the sense of his presence was getting nearer. Helen could feel the other thing, too, could sense its massive power the deeper they went into the wood, but she desperately struggled to block it out. She must not be afraid. Must not despair. She must think only of him. Must concentrate only on holding on to him. To that faint thread of his life. Clinging to the fact he was still alive, that there was yet still time ...

Then Volkovsky halted. He pointed to something by the side of the path. It was the motorbike, half-hidden in the under-growth. "I think they must have gone in that way," he said. Before he even finished speaking, Helen had already plunged off the path into the heart of the woods, and he followed, through the thickly growing tall trees and deep leaf-litter, and over rocks and the occasional fallen log that blocked the way.

It was very quiet. It was as if the wood held its breath. Or was under a spell. There were things watching them, Helen knew. Animals, yes – but other things too. She could feel them in the prickling of her skin, the running of her blood: things old as time, as the earth, the rocks, the sky, and the water. Spirit-things that lived in every pore of the wood's skin, that inhabited its ancient flesh, its timeless bones. And they were uneasy. For there was something else within the wood, something that should not be there – the stench of dark magic, a menacing energy that disturbed the timeless spirit-patterns of the woods.

And then suddenly – she could hear it. The only sound in that silent place, besides their own footfalls. The *ssh-ssh-sshh* song of a little stream flowing.

A low, grassy bank, studded with flowers. Birch trees like enchanted sentinels in silver armor. The green scent of firs and pines. And the water, flowing peacefully. And somehow the beauty of it made it all so much worse.

They were on the other side of the stream, sitting against a birch. Alexey was very pale, his eyes were closed, his T-shirt was stained with blood and dirt, there were bruises on his face, his jeans were torn. He was unconscious. But not dead. Propped up, he was held like a shield against the other's chest. And there was something pressed against his throat. The glint of a wickedly sharp knife ...

"Not a step further. Or he's dead." The voice was without inflection of any kind. Familiar yet a stranger's, it rang in Helen's ears like something from a terrible nightmare. She knew it spoke the absolute truth. If they made the wrong move that knife would cut Alexey's throat.

She gathered all her courage and said, as calmly as she could, "It's okay. I just want to speak to you."

A silence, then: "Throw away your phone. That's it. Him, too. And tell him to back off."

Volkovsky looked at Helen. She nodded. "Please. Do it."

"Now, Helen. You can move forward a bit. Okay. That's it. Stop. You wanted to speak to me. So speak."

Helen looked at the woman across the stream, in whose house she had stayed, whose meals she had shared, who had been a dear family friend. The woman who last night had been so cheerfully arguing the relative merits of Atamanov and Disney. Who this very morning had joked about an ex-biker boyfriend. *The woman who'd written that extraordinary book.* And Helen knew now why Irina had aged so much. Why she'd looked so gaunt and drained: the terrifying power she had in her was sapping everything that had once made her human. How much ghastly effort it must have been to maintain the facade of what she had once been!

Helen whispered, "Please – please – Irina … let Alexey go. He's innocent – he's done nothing –"

"Is that all you have to say? Then you might as well leave." The eyes went blank. The vicious dark energy was sucking in all the air around them, making Helen feel breathless. "There is no such thing as an innocent Makarov. His great-grandfather was a murderer. His grandfather a torturer. His father a ruthless bastard. His brother a drug-dealer."

"But he's not like them, Irina. He's not."

When Irina didn't answer, Helen faltered, the words coming choppily, "At least – let me near him. Please."

"Why should I?"

She took the plunge. "Because I think – you – you feel nothing for him – but you still care what happens to me. That's why – why you tried to warn me against him. And it's why you haven't been able to bring yourself to kill him yet. Why you hesitate. Because you know I – I love him."

Irina said, harshly, "He's much stronger than I thought he was, that's all. He has a real core of power. Much stronger than his father. He's resisted me."

"But he's weak now and you have a knife. It would be so easy to kill him but you haven't. And that means –"

"It means only that I want you to understand who he really is," Irina spat out. "You say he's not like the others – but ask yourself, why is he so hell-bent on keeping Trinity? He should have closed it down. Trinity's rotten to the core, riddled with corruption, just like the men who created it. Nothing can make it good. Ha, you believe that shit about reform, don't you? But that's not what it's about. Trinity is about *power*. It is the very source of his father's darkest secrets. The secrets, the power he craves for himself. Nothing will get in the way of that. Certainly not you. Between you and Trinity, what do you think he would choose?"

"I would not – I would never try to make him choose." Helen whispered. "That is not what true love is."

"Sentimental blindness. He's already made his choice. If he is still alive, if he has resisted me so fiercely till now, *it is for Trinity*. Yes, Helen. Don't shake your head. That is his *deepest* truth. At first, yes, I thought otherwise. He came here of his own will, because I told him I'd had you abducted. That you were being held here. So I thought that was the core of him. Love. Not a bit of it! For soon I realized it was Trinity he would fight to the death for. Never for you. That is what I wanted to show you. So the scales can drop from your eyes and you can see what he really is. A Makarov above all else, for whom power will always count far, far more than love."

Instinctively, Helen knew she must not respond. She must not get into direct confrontation. She must not hurl accusations, must not show how deeply she was repulsed by an evil that twisted everything. Because one false move, one word out of place, and Alexey would die. She knew that for certain. She must be one step ahead. She forced herself to say, meekly, sadly, "What you say may be true, but despite it, I can't stop myself. I can't stop loving him."

Irina cried, and for a distressing moment the old, familiar, kindly spirit flashed out, "Hell, I wish you would, Helen. I wish you'd never met him. You *shouldn't* have done. And if I'd imagined for one minute that your paths would cross, I'd never have invited you to my place. You must believe that."

"I do." A pause. She swallowed, and said, in a small voice, "But I *did* meet him. And I *do* love him. And so now ..." She took a deep breath. "Please. Just let me come a little closer. I promise I – won't try anything. If you – if you care for me at all, just let me do this one small thing."

Irina stared at her. Then she said, "Very well. But only as far as I say."

Helen took a step forward. Another. Another. She was at the stream. And Irina said, sharply, "That will do."

So close now, so close, if Helen had stretched as far as she possibly could, she might almost have touched him. She could see the shadow of stubble on his chin, the sweet hollow of his collarbone, the fine golden hairs on his arms, the faint slow flutter of his heart in his chest – it was weak – and weakening by the minute – Oh Alexey. Alexey ...

Part of her wanted to cry, to beg for mercy, to plead for his life. But she knew it would do no good. Irina's insane hatred of the Makarovs was much stronger than her affection for Helen. Much stronger. She would not give in to pleas for mercy. Not for a Makarov. Especially not for the last of the Makarovs. She saw herself as an avenging angel, as a righteous smiter of evil-doers. So Helen had to try another way. She said, softly, "It must have been terrible, finding out what had been done to your grandfather, to poor Professor Antonov."

She'd struck the right note. Irina's eyes lit up. "Oh, he wasn't my grandfather but my great-uncle. My grandmother's twin brother. A very great man. I never even knew he existed, until my mother told me on her deathbed. He was the reason we had to flee, she said. He was a scientist but he committed some crime, she didn't know what, her parents never told her. All she knew was that he was arrested and they'd have been too if they hadn't escaped. That was the way it was in those days. You suffered and you didn't even know why." She paused, then went on, "She'd never tried to find out. But I had to. So I came to Russia. I discovered he'd died in prison. I found out what he'd been accused of. And how his experiment had been *terminated* by Pyotr Makarov, who had worked side by side with him for months, who had accompanied him when he'd found Baby K and took him from the hunter, who with his men had guarded the site, but who when the order came, carried it out *without a shred of mercy or remorse or doubt.*" Her face was twisted with bitterness. "At least six or seven children died that day, Helen, including Baby K. The bear was destroyed. The place was burned to the ground. And Anton was arrested, tortured, sent to that Siberian hellhole. He didn't last six months." She paused. "I felt so close to poor Anton. So close. I felt like – like he and I were kindred souls, calling to each other across time and death. The horror of his fate, of the fate of those children, turned me inside out. Obsessed me. I knew I must do something. But I still thought in the old way. The old timid way. I planned to write a book exposing the whole thing. Make the Makarov descendants suffer shame and exposure insofar as such people can feel it. And celebrate Anton's life and achievements. But then one day, quite without warning, I was set on the right path." There was a strange smile on her face. "Do you remember me telling you about seeing the bear in the Karelian forest?"

Just over a week ago, that was – and yet it seemed so far away. If only, Helen thought, if only I could have seen then what lay behind the familiar face – what hideous stranger had taken possession of my mother's old friend ... But she hadn't. So she nodded now, helplessly, without speaking.

"In that moment, when the bear looked at me," said Irina, "I felt as though something had shifted – like time and space had cracked open. Oh God, I'd spent my entire career writing about magic, about myth, about the other world – and suddenly *there it was, in front of me, real as the bear*! It was a thrilling moment that completely changed the course of my life. That night, I had the first of the dreams. I saw Anton beaten – tortured – covered in blood. I had the same dream the following night, and the next and next. It was intensely disturbing. I couldn't sleep. I couldn't eat. So I went to see a psychic in Moscow."

Helen was shaken, badly, by what Irina had said, for it struck disturbing echoes. The dreams – the sense of the world revealing itself – that was familiar. She fought to keep a grip on herself. She said, "The psychic was Lev Kirov."

"Ah. You know about him. Yes. Lev Kirov. I never told him who Anton was, only about the dreams. And that was when he told me that the dreams were a symptom, not a cause. That I had a great power within me, a great psychic energy, but that it was blocked. He went on and on then about being careful – not rushing into things – as if I was some kind of naive child, the silly old fool! Because I'd known at once what I must use my power for. I knew Fate had at last let me grasp the sword of justice, and I must not let Anton down. I couldn't reveal myself till the time was right – but it all worked so well, because no one ever suspected the fussy professor with her endless research on myths."

Helen said quietly, "You're like Nina Kulagina, aren't you? You've got a power like hers."

Irina snorted. "Mine's much more effective. Her power was crude. Psychic brawn, not brain. Think of throwing a spanner in electric works. Of pulling on a rope till it breaks. That's what hers was like. And it required immense physical effort. Yes, she could stop a frog's heart – but a person's? Never. Certainly not a healthy person, without heart problems. The effort would have killed her as well."

"Then what – how do you …"

Irina's face twisted sardonically. "You think I'm stupid enough to tell you so you can use it against me? Don't push your luck."

But Helen had stopped listening. For at that moment, Alexey's eyes opened, and he looked straight at her.

Chapter 40

It was as though time had stopped. Alexey was looking at her – *but not seeing her*. Staring straight at her, his eyes locked on hers, but there was not the slightest recognition in his expression. Not only was it as though he was looking at her as if she was a stranger, it was worse. Much worse – it was as if *there was a stranger looking out from his eyes*. A stranger with an alien, empty changeling's gaze. The gaze of a lost soul, fixed on her.

It was only for a blink of an instant, for now Helen looked at Alexey's face and saw his eyes were closed. Was she going mad or had she just dreamed what happened? There was a roaring in her ears. A griping pain at her heart, like a hand squeezing, squeezing, harder, harder, an iron band across her chest. She could hardly breathe. Her mind was filled with black mist. For a moment that felt like forever but was actually less than a second, she grasped the full fearsome meaning of Irina's power – how it was *her target's own psychic energy* she used against them, magnified by her own – seeing the deepest dread in their mind and ricocheting it against them, so the shock of it squeezed their heart till the pressure was unbearable, and then –

And then, Helen felt the iron band relaxing, the hand losing its grip, the black mist disappearing. And just like the other day, it was as though a livid flash of lightning had lit up the truth in her mind. She knew whose unquiet, sorcerous spirit reached out to her so fiercely, so desperately through time and space and death to show her the truth. She knew who the terrifying visitation was last night. A lost soul ... A lost soul ...

It was the wild card no one could possibly have expected, and instinctively she knew it changed everything. She said, very clearly, "You have made a terrible mistake. *Alexey doesn't have a drop of Pyotr Makarov's blood.*"

But Irina laughed. It wasn't a pleasant sound. "You really think something as feeble as this is going to change my –"

"Listen to me. He doesn't have a drop of Pyotr's blood because he is not related to him. And not to Pyotr's wife, either. *Because he is the grandson of Mikhail Makarov.*"

"What is this nonsense? Mikhail was Pyotr's son."

"Not by birth. *By adoption.*"

"Lies. There's no record of any such thing."

"Of course there wouldn't be. Pyotr would keep it very quiet, wouldn't he? Or it might come out that he'd not done his duty, after all. That he'd *not* killed all those children. That he'd saved one of them, the most beautiful one, for *the sake of his childless wife who so longed for a baby of her very own.*"

"No – no ..."

"*Mikhail was the bear's son.*" She thought of the lonely figure in the dream-woods, of the bear in the night, of Olga Feshina's vision. She said, "He was the Karelian child. *He was Baby K.*"

Irina had whitened. "No – it's not possible."

"It's ironic, isn't it?" Helen's heart was thumping wildly. Not because of what she was saying, the words were flowing from her like she'd always known them. But because Alexey's eyes were open – really open this time – and he was looking at her – and seeing her, really *seeing* her – and in his eyes there was such a depth of love that she knew at once everything Irina claimed about his "deepest truth" was a lie. It was as if new strength was rising in her, she knew the tide was turning at last, they were winning.

"It's ironic," she repeated, "because you could say Mikhail grew up to make Anton's dreams come true. He became the creature of his vision. How proud Anton would have been of him! Other people would have seen a monster – but Anton would have seen that Mikhail was a true shapeshifter, who could put himself in anyone's skin and look out from any-one's eyes, and know what drove them, and how to break them. *A man truly beyond human, of immense service to the Soviet state.*"

Irina whispered, "You can't know this ... you *can't* ..." Her eyes were bleak holes in a death's head of a face, the knife had dropped from Alexey's throat, she was trembling. She didn't even know he was awake, she didn't see anything beyond the disordered visions in her own mind – everything she thought she knew turned upside-down, everything shattered in the beginnings of a terrible understanding, of a coming, catastrophic defeat.

"Are you willing to take the risk I don't?" Helen was moving closer. "To become what you most hate, the final destroyer of Anton's vision?" Another step. One, two more and she'd be there. "It's over. You must see that."

But suddenly Irina's eyes widened and she gave a howl of anguish and reared up, the knife gripped desperately in her hand. She pushed Alexey aside and came at Helen, and she was too close to duck or dodge, she could only throw up one arm in an attempt to protect herself and then it was as if she'd been punched in the forearm, only there was blood there and she knew she'd been stabbed. Irina raised the knife again ...

But Alexey had staggered to his feet and thrown himself at Irina, she swayed but turned snarling on him, the knife in her fist, striking up with great force under his ribs. In the next instant the world exploded with noise – yells, screams Helen didn't even recognize as her own, gunshots. And Irina jerked back and fell without a sound, the back of her head shattered by the bullet, the knife no longer in her hand.

Helen took no notice of the woman's crumpled body. She crawled to Alexey who was lying on his back with both hands clasped over his left side. His eyes were open but they were shadowed by pain and she saw what he was trying to shield from her – she saw where the knife was – she saw how deep it had gone in – but she couldn't take in the true meaning of it, not really.

She said, "We have to pull it out we have to –" but she didn't even know she was speaking, she was on her knees beside him, her head felt light as though it was filled with air. Dimly behind her she heard Volkovsky's voice. "No, Helen. If you try to pull it out, he will lose too much blood. I have called the ambulance, we must wait till they arrive ..."

She lay by Alexey and took him in her arms so that his head was cradled against her chest but her body was not pressing in any way against his wound. She ignored the pain in her arm, a dull ache though the blood was slowly seeping from it. He was very pale, trembling as though from cold, and she held him tighter, trying to impart as much of her warmth as she could to him.

He whispered, "Helen – I was afraid – that if she knew the real truth – that you are the most important thing in the world to me – she would kill you –"

"I know," she said, and kissed him. "I know. Don't speak. Rest, my love."

"I let her see too much at first – I tried to reach you, to warn you – but it took too much out of me –" His breath was coming hard, he only gasped the words. "All I could do then – make her think she'd got it wrong – that it wasn't you – oh God, it was so hard, she was so strong – but I did it. But oh how I hated denying you, my love ..."

She cried, "Oh Alexey – you never did that – oh I love you so much!"

"And I love you so much, and always while you need me I will be there. Never forget that." He smiled at her, and though his smile was sweet his voice was very faint and there was a swiftly gathering shadow in his eyes that filled her with stark terror. She wrapped herself closer, her body englobing him protectively. "Hold on – they'll be here – very soon. Alexey – no – please don't leave me – don't go – I can't live without you. I can't!"

"Then live *for* me, Helen. Live for me." Without any warning, the light in his eyes went out and his head fell on his chest. Panic-stricken she screamed for Volkovsky who hurried over, took one look at Alexey, took his pulse, and without a word motioned her to move.

He worked on Alexey, worked like a madman, trying to breathe air into his lungs, pressing on his chest. It seemed like an eternity. It felt like no time when he turned to her and cried, bleakly, "It's no good. He's gone. Our Lyosha is gone."

He was panting from his efforts, his hands were shaking, there were tears rushing down his cheeks, but Helen took no notice of his grief, she couldn't feel anything at all, she was completely numb, her mind had seized up.

Blankly, she said, "But Nikolai, he'll get cold if you just leave him lying there like that," and she dropped to the ground beside Alexey and took him in her arms and said, "I'll keep you warm till the ambulance men come. I promise I will. Hold on, my love – hold on – they'll be here soon."

Chapter 41

Nothing existed for Helen except keeping Alexey warm and safe till the paramedics arrived. When they did she told them to be careful because he was in deep shock. They gently put Alexey on the stretcher and picked it up, but not as carefully as she thought they should, and she shouted that if they jolted it like that they would hurt him. Didn't they know anything? They didn't understand her words but they understood the meaning and looked at her with a pity she didn't understand.

Another team was picking up Irina's body but Helen barely noticed that, she didn't even remember her or what she'd done. When a couple of minutes later the police turned up to ask questions, Volkovsky persuaded them to wait to ask her, but she didn't notice that either. All she could think was that she had to go to the hospital with Alexey, she had to be by his bedside when he woke up, her face had to be the first thing he saw.

In the ambulance she sat by him and sung softly to him, or rather hummed, because whatever he said, she didn't think her voice was much good, it would never be like his. She hummed the tune of "Moscow Nights" because she knew that would reach him, remind him of the Alexandrovsky gardens and how he said he and she were tuned to the same melody and so how could he leave her? She didn't see the sad expression on the paramedic's face, or the road flashing past them. But as soon as they arrived at the hospital, she was ready to jump out and follow them, she wouldn't let them just wheel him off without telling her what was happening.

The paramedic was whispering to a doctor, who came up to her and said gently to her, in English, "Miss, we take care of your friend now."

"You're going to operate on him, right? You'll have to be really careful when you do the surgery, if you pull the knife out too quickly he will bleed to death, you know."

"Yes," the doctor said, quietly, "you may be assured we will take very good care." He gave a signal to the paramedics to start wheeling Alexey away, but Helen ran after them and took his hand. She held it all the way till they got to the operating theatre, and then she kissed it before she was barred from the room. She thought she'd just wait outside until they were finished – but the doctor – who's not the surgeon, the surgeon's inside – said, firmly, "You cannot stay here, Miss. The operation will take time. And you have a wound on your arm that must be looked after."

"Oh, that's nothing," said Helen, vaguely. "It doesn't hurt at all, it's just a scratch."

"Nevertheless. It may get infected. Please come with me."

He took her to a small room off one of the wards where there was a narrow daybed. He took Helen's blood pressure and pulse and looked at the wound on her arm, frowned and said, "I must examine more closely but this will hurt. So I will give you anesthetic, yes?"

"Just a local one, then," said Helen, "because I want to be fully awake when Alexey comes out of surgery."

"Yes," said the doctor, smiling reassuringly. He prepared a needle and the last thing Helen remembered was the sting as it went into the vein.

Unconscious, she wandered in a dreamless, pathless darkness, deep as a cave's, as still and as total, where she was hardly even aware of her own being. Then she saw a light and she went toward it. It was still dark around her but the darkness was thinning, fading the more she went toward the light, and now she was beginning to see shapes and then the beginning of colors, and then to her surprise she realized she was standing on a grassy strip rather like the kind you might see dividing a big road. Which in fact was exactly what this one was. In front of her was a road, behind was another. Except the surface of these roads wasn't dirt or asphalt, but a kind of glossy, shifting substance that sometimes looked like water, sometimes like silk and sometimes like the back of some huge creature wallowing in the depths. It made her feel a little dizzy to look at it.

On the other side of the road in front of her was what looked like the beginning of a wood. She was peering at it, trying to work out what sort of wood it might be, when from behind someone spoke her name, and she turned at once, for it was Alexey.

He was standing there on the grassy strip only meters away, smiling at her. He was still a little pale but his eyes were very bright and so was his shining hair. He was dressed in the white T-shirt and jeans but there was no blood or dirt on them or on him. She was filled with joy that he was alive and ran toward him. He held out his arms to her and folded her within them. His flesh was real, she could feel it under her fingers, the softness of his skin, the scent of his hair, the warmth of his arms.

"You're warm," she said, astonished, "you're warm again," and he looked at her and said, "Yes, I am, my lovely little firebird, I am," and kissed her. When their lips touched she felt a melting sweetness that filled every part of her.

But then he untangled himself gently from her and murmured, "You can't stay here, my love. But I must."

"No," she cried. "No. I'm not going. I'm staying here. With you. Don't send me away. Don't leave me. I don't care where we are as long as we are together."

"I won't leave you," he said, "not as long as you need me. But you cannot stay here, you must go, for if you do not, we will be separate forever. You must live, Helen, for only then can our dreams be realized and our love never die."

"No," she screamed, as his solid form began to blur, to dissolve, fading like a ripple in water, like an image on the air, "don't go, stay, Alexey, stay, please, stay!"

But he was gone. And though she called his name he did not answer. She was standing alone on the grassy strip and the shadows were gathering, the clouds coming over the sun, the watery road in front of her was billowing uneasily and then the ground opened under her and she was sucked down into dreamless, dark cave-limbo again.

She woke. She didn't know how many hours after, to find herself lying in a hospital bed. Her arm was bandaged and her head was heavy. There were curtains drawn around her bed and the sounds of a busy ward outside it. Her mother was sitting by the side of her bed. She was pale and her eyes were swollen and bloodshot from crying. She jumped up when she saw Helen had opened her eyes. She clutched her hand and said, in French, "Oh darling Helen – you're awake."

"Yes," said Helen. She looked at her mother and said, very precisely and clearly, "Alexey's dead, Mam. He's dead."

Tears sprang into Therese Clement's eyes. She wept and wept, hugging her daughter. Helen felt the touch but it meant little to her. Dry-eyed, she said, "I want to see him."

Therese opened her mouth to protest – then changed her mind. Wiping her eyes, she said, "Let me get the doctor. He will take us."

She was back quickly with the doctor, who looked at Helen, took her pulse and said, "Perhaps it is too soon. You could still be in shock and it might be dangerous to ..."

"No," said Helen. "It won't be." She added, looking straight at the doctor, "I don't need another sedative or another kind lie. I just need to see him. Please."

"Very well." The doctor sighed.

Volkovsky, Sergey and Maxim were sitting together, waiting outside the ward. Sergey stammered something that Helen didn't quite catch, his normally cheerful face looked utterly miserable. Maxim said gravely how sorry he was. Nikolai Volkovsky's eyes were red-rimmed, but his voice was steady as he told Helen that he had arranged with her mother that they both come and stay at the Makarov house until "things are sorted out", and that if there was anything she wanted or needed, she could count on him. She nodded and thanked them all politely but without any warmth, there was no warmth left in her at all.

*

When they reached the room where he was, the doctor stopped and said, "You are sure? Quite sure?"

Helen nodded. Her mother took her arm. "I will go in with her," she said, to the doctor. Maxim and Volkovsky waited outside, and Helen was glad of her mother's arm for all at once, as they entered the cold white room, a sick dizziness rushed over her, and it was all she could do not to stagger. But her mother steadied her and she managed to keep going, toward the trolley where the shrouded figure lay so still.

The doctor gently pulled back a corner of the sheet and Helen looked into Alexey's face. His eyes were closed and he was pale but he still didn't look dead. He looked like he was sleeping. His hair was bright and his lips were slightly parted. But when she reached out a hand to touch him, she felt the waxy cold of his skin go through her and she knew, *truly* knew, in every part of her, that the most essential part of him, the mysterious spring of his life, the lovely alchemy that made him who he was – was not there. His beautiful body was there, lying indifferent on that cold metal trolley; but his soul had left.

Left this place; but not left her. *I won't leave you, while you need me.* She clung to that. She had to believe in that truth with every bit of her strength, or she would not be able to do what he wanted her to do. She would not be able to live. She bent down to his body one last time and passionately kissed the cold lips, the limp hands. Then she turned to the doctor and said, formally, "Thank you. I am very grateful for your ..." but as she spoke the cold dizziness surged up without warning and she fell to the floor in a faint.

Chapter 42

Maxim long ago learned that when tragedy struck it was no use trying to find the right words, they would never be right no matter what they were, and that was not what was important. Maundering over other people's grief when you were a mere acquaintance and not family or a close friend could only be an irrelevant intrusion. But if it was of any use you also had to be ready to help, in whatever practical and appropriate way you could.

For himself, all he could do was his job. To piece together as much of the story as quickly as he could, so that when Helen was ready for the knowledge, it would be there for her. It was the only way he could think of to try and atone for failing to see the truth before it was too late. Rationally, he knew his nagging sense of guilt was pointless, even self-indulgent. Neither he nor anyone else had any possible reason for suspecting an unworldly and perfectly respectable foreign academic obsessed with bear folklore of having underworld connections, let alone being responsible for the Trinity murders. But reason is not what governs the human heart, and deep in his heart Maxim felt that somehow he should have seen, he should have been able to save Alexey. It didn't help knowing that he wasn't the only one who felt that way. That Nikolai Volkovsky was haunted by his own failures of judgment, and poor Therese Clement was haunted by the notion that as Bayeva's old friend she should somehow have guessed what lay behind the facade.

Only Helen herself did not appear to feel it. But Maxim knew that was because right now there was no space in the girl's being for any thoughts about the killer. When – or even if – she would be ready for what he was putting together he did not know. She was merely going through the motions of life at present. Nothing seemed to really touch her. She ate and drank obediently, if sparsely, she went to bed early, she answered questions politely. She did not weep, even when those around her broke down. Though she insisted on sleeping in the room that had been Alexey's, huddled in the bed that had been his, that still smelled of him, she did not speak of him. But Nikolai reported that she spent hours clicking through the photos in her digital camera, photos she'd taken in the last week of Alexey's life. And Therese said that she heard her daughter crying out in dreams and, on one occasion, had found her sleepwalking in the early hours of the morning. Desperately worried about her daughter's eerie calm, and the fact she refused any kind of sedative or psychological help, she longed to take her home. But she couldn't, not till Alexey's funeral, which would be the day after tomorrow, in St Petersburg. Only then would they fly back to London.

Maxim had no idea how long it would take Helen to get over what had happened. If she ever did, that is. He knew now that he couldn't have been more wrong about the girl. She had been exactly what she appeared to be, a true innocent who'd fallen deeply in love with a very special young man. There had been no plan to get under Alexey's defenses through her. Bayeva had never intended for her to meet him. It had been just an awful coincidence, an accident of fate.

Arriving too late in Uglich to do anything other than take in the news of Alexey's death, Maxim had called Korolev at police headquarters and baldly laid the facts before him, so that he would understand the case must immediately be transferred back to homicide from organized crime. For the first time ever, Korolev had been speechless as Maxim described happenings which clearly demonstrated his own flagrant disobedience. Maxim knew that Korolev could have him sacked or at the very least suspended for his actions. But he needed to be part of the official investigation again and he gambled that Korolev's wrath over his disobedience would soon give way to relief that the mysterious killer of the three businessmen had turned out to be an insane foreigner, and what was more, an unimportant and unknown one, without any difficult political, social or business connections. The fact Bayeva was now dead could only be cream on the cake. It meant no long trial. No hassle with foreign authorities wanting consular access to the prisoner. A quick investigation, a nice tying-up report, and then case closed. Perfect.

He was quite right. After bawling him out, Korolev quickly agreed that, as he was on the spot, it made sense for him to work with the local police. He could start interviewing the witnesses immediately. Korolev said he would square that at once with the local authorities. He also assured Maxim that Nikolai Volkovsky would not land in any kind of trouble over using that pistol. After all, it had been Major Makarov's old service weapon, not Volkovsky's, and so technically he hadn't fallen foul of gun-license laws.

*

Three days after Alexey's death, and already the picture had become much clearer. Bayeva's underworld links hadn't clearly been established yet, but on early analysis it looked like these had been routed through Slava, while inside information on Trinity had been provided by Pasha and, to a lesser extent, Foma. There was no evidence so far that the three men had been involved in the actual murders of the three businessmen and Lev Kirov. Their involvement had been in the final stages of Bayeva's plot, in the attacks on the offices of Trinity and the destabilization of Alexey's plans. It was as though she'd run that part of it as an almost separate strand, and untangling all the elements of it would take some considerable time.

Oleg and Katya had been innocent parties in it all, and tests on the powder found in the bottle in Slava's bathroom showed traces of a nerve agent which had been used to make the dogs more aggressive. A bribe had been paid for the "mistake" of incinerating the dogs' corpses; but the whole thing had been intended not so much to isolate Alexey, but to throw suspicion on Slava once the photo was discovered. For Slava's connection with Repin had been a false trail. The picture had been photoshopped by either Pasha or Foma, from an image available on the Internet, cut and pasted to include Slava and deliberately dropped for either Helen or Alexey to find. The guard's reaction had been calculated to reinforce the impression. It had been a risk, because if Repin had had a scent of what was going on, he would have been very angry indeed. But he was safely away, in Egypt, and unlikely to find out. As far as Maxim could see, neither Slava, Foma or Pasha had had any personal animus against Alexey, and their aim was not specifically to destroy Trinity but rather to enrich themselves. For it turned out to be money, plain and simple, that provided the best motive for their taking part in the plot.

Their bank accounts were immediately frozen, but too late – they had already been cleared. Bank records revealed that for some time Pasha had been running two accounts, one perfectly innocent, with his normal incomings and outgoings, the other a trust account in his young nephew's name, into which he paid large cash sums. Foma, meanwhile, had only recently started depositing unexplained cash into his account, showing that he hadn't been in on the plot for long. But Slava's kickbacks would not be quite as easily documented; as Volkovsky drily observed, "the security man wasn't a great believer in the security of banks."

It was a sentiment with which Maxim could only sympathize. For the memory card so carefully placed in the bank vault had vanished, signed out apparently quite legally the day after Alexey's death, by someone cheekily calling himself Nikolai Volkovsky, who was by default the acting administrator of Trinity till the legal situation was clarified – which could take some considerable time. The real Nikolai Volkovsky was in Uglich and the idiot who had let the impostor sign out the package was an assistant manager in the bank who unforgivably had not been briefed by his superior about the card. Maxim had suspected corruption at first, and both manager and assistant had been hauled in for questioning; but soon it was clear it was blatant incompetence rather than anything more sinister. A full description of the man calling himself "Volkovsky" had yielded a fair match for Pasha Dutov. The assistant manager would have suspected nothing; he'd never clapped eyes on Volkovsky before.

The three villains had clearly decided to go into business on their own account. Their pay-mistress might be dead, but the secrets of the Koldun file could be theirs now. Maxim was more and more certain that his instinct was right and that the file contained some revelation about a new kind of "psychic enhancer" as Oberlian had called it, which the Trinity partners had started to develop. But the Koldun file was gone for good now, and so he'd never know. There wasn't even the printout of the first page, as Foma had taken it with him. As to the rest of the material on the card – the bits Ivan

Makarov had written about his father, the passage from the dream-book, his Kirlian photos – they had a poignancy now in Maxim's memory, but they'd be of no use to the crooks.

Helen had told him about the video she had deleted, the stills of which she'd found in Bayeva's filing cabinet. He didn't say it was a pity she and Alexey had not said anything to anyone else about it. She didn't need to be told. He knew that both she and Volkovsky believed that the clip must have been an early demonstration of Bayeva's psychokinetic power, which had come into Ivan Makarov's possession through the Koldun project. Possibly even that she had sent the clip to the Trinity partners herself, as a kind of lure.

But Maxim wasn't so sure. A thorough search of Bayeva's house had revealed no confessional material of any kind. Secretive to the last, she had left no real clue to her plot or the nature of her power – except for the sparrow stills. And that material about Antonov. But surely she would not have wanted any of the Trinity directors to suspect she had that sort of power anyway, or why on earth would Ivan Makarov, after the death of his partners, not be on his guard against her? No, Maxim thought Ivan Makarov had come across the clip in some other way. How, it was likely they'd never know now. Even if they still had the card, the sparrow clip – which must be a copy of the original – had been deleted. There were the stills of course but he doubted they'd get much from them.

In any case, it didn't much matter. There were other ways of piecing together what had happened and how Bayeva had carried out her murderous plans. Early contact with the FBI had already yielded the information that Bayeva had definitely traveled from her home state of California to Finland, France and Australia around the dates of the deaths of the three Trinity partners. That Finnish trip hadn't been the only one she'd made to that country; over the last three and a half years she had traveled at least twice more from LA to

Helsinki, and when he checked with Finnish immigration authorities, he discovered that she'd also made the trip across from St Petersburg to Helsinki several times, under the cover of her cross-border bear folklore research. Nothing at all to attract the attention of even the most alert person at the time; but now it provided a pattern that could be linked to one of the Trinity partners – Semyon Galkin, who frequently went to Finland on hunting expeditions.

Maxim had the dates of Galkin's Finnish trips checked, and there was no doubt – four or five of them had coincided with Bayeva's, and what was more, most of them had been within the same area. Mostly they had been in different hotels, but once they had even been in the same one. US records provided another small but suggestive snippet – four years ago, Galkin had visited the US on what appeared to be his first and last trip to that country. He had stayed ten days, holidaying in California. Specifically, in LA. At a time when Bayeva was definitely residing in her home town.

In Maxim's mind it went like this: Bayeva and Galkin had first met in LA. Sometime later a relationship had started, instigated most likely by Bayeva. She'd looked old and gaunt in recent times, but Maxim had seen earlier photographs of her which showed a lively, *gamine* sporty charm. And Galkin, who'd not had much luck with women in the past, who was lonely and sought the services of astrologers to find out if he'd ever be lucky in love – for that too they now knew – would have been an easy target. Of the three Trinity men, he was the weakest link.

She must have persuaded him to keep it a secret. Perhaps it had been exciting for him to do so. They'd meet in Finland every now and then – perhaps in Russia too. Cold-bloodedly, all along she must have been meditating her revenge, taking her time, spinning poor lonely Galkin into her web. He wasn't even her real target, just collateral damage in her war against the Makarovs, just like Barsukov, and poor Kirov and drug-addled Grisha. But he was also her entry to the world of Trinity; and unwittingly he must have provided her with useful information. That must have been how she had drawn out Barsukov too. Remembering the email he had found, Barsukov's brief message to Ivan Makarov about "a possible Koldun leak", Maxim wondered if it had been something to do with that. It had been sent only a few weeks before Barsukov's death. Had she anonymously tipped him off there was a leak? Was that why he'd been in France – he'd been steered there by the tip-off? It was a supposition that fitted with what he'd been able to determine of Barsukov's personality, which was a mix of the reckless and the loyal. He'd be determined to get to the bottom of it. But he might not have told Makarov he was going to. And even if he had, neither of them would suspect that the "leak" was in any way linked to Galkin's death. Why would they? There'd been no real reason at the time to suppose Galkin's death was murder. He'd had a weak heart, after all.

Maxim didn't know yet for sure, but he thought that was how it had gone with Barsukov. But in his case it must have been harder. Not so much because Barsukov was a more cynical and suspicious type than Galkin, but because he did not have a weak heart. Maxim had come to the reluctant conclusion that somehow Bayeva's dreadful power had triggered heart attacks in her victims, though in his official report he was going to be careful to present alternative, more palatable theories, such as an injection of potassium chloride or other untraceable poison which could equally stimulate a heart attack. But unofficially he had decided that the feature of the case which had so titillated the media and caused them to dub it the "Rusalka Curse" – the fact all three men had apparently drowned – had not been some kind of flamboyant serial-killer "signature" but a practical way of ensuring that, weak heart or not, the victims would die. Galkin would not have survived a heart attack anyway, water or no water. Bayeva's power would have been enough on its own to kill him. But the others' hearts were stronger. They might just have been rendered unconscious, like Alexey had been. But if they fell unconscious into water and were not found in time, then they'd never recover consciousness. To all intents and purposes, they would have drowned.

Maxim had no real proof yet how Bayeva had got to Ivan Makarov. But as with Barsukov he had a theory. And it wasn't the Koldun file, though Makarov's destruction of the papers the night before his death suggested he thought that was what the killer was after. The Koldun project appeared to be the thing he cared most about; that lay at his deepest, most secret core.

But what if the killer had seen otherwise? What if she had understood that despite his hard, uncompromising exterior, Makarov had been haunted? Haunted by the deaths of his wife and his estranged older son, by dreams of his dead father and the deaths of his two closest friends. Even Kirov's death had meant something to him. Perhaps deep down he feared he was a death-bringer to every person he'd ever been close to. And if he'd been made to think that Alexey was also going to die, then ...

It was horrible, to think of it. For it had been exactly how she'd got to poor Alexey as well. Love. The terror not for oneself but for loved ones.

In Bayeva's diseased mind, the Makarovs were the fount of all evil. She saw no difference between the Stalinist murderer and the young musician. No difference between a cold KGB interrogator and his haunted businessman son or true-hearted grandson. To her they were not individual people. They were one and the same, an undying, monstrous vampire that must be staked through the heart. But the macabre irony of it was that it was *she* who had become the monster. And at the very end, when she realized what a dreadful mistake she'd made – when she knew that it had all been for nothing and her vengeance had turned to ashes – she must have seen that. And it had finally sent her over the edge.

Though part of him would have liked Bayeva alive to answer questions, in his heart he was fiercely glad she was dead. Because of Alexey and his life so cruelly cut short. Because of the deep love those poor young people had shared, and the dreams that would never be. But also because such a monstrous power must not be allowed to flourish on the earth.

Chapter 43

A gray Petersburg day. The streets were slick with the rain that had started as soon as the service was over. "It is a blessing from God," the priest told them, gently, and added, "for Heaven itself is crying."

Heaven might be crying but Helen was not. In church, she stood dry-eyed, holding the mourning candle, while beside her others wept. She stood dry-eyed while the priest chanted the prayers for the dead and swung the incense censor over the open casket where Alexey's body lay like a beautiful wax-work. Tearless, she bent down to kiss the lifeless forehead as they filed past at the end, before the coffin left the church.

There was no eulogy. There is none at an Orthodox funeral, only prayers. It is not a commemoration of this life, but a journey to the afterlife. It is a journey in stages. Forty days, the priest told her afterwards, at the cemetery. That's how long the soul remains on earth before it takes its final leave and departs for the afterlife. Forty days ...

That was what she was thinking of as, dry-eyed still, she looked unseeingly out through the window at the wet streets and boats going by on the canal. The funeral reception was being held in an apartment belonging to the family of Feodor, the manager of Trinity's Petersburg office. It was a lovely apartment, in a large nineteenth-century house. There were a lot of people there, for Alexey's death had touched many. There was a buzz of talk, hushed as befit the occasion, but still talk. Life must go on, after all. People must be people. It was not a bitter thought. There was no feeling in it at all.

Her mother was looking over at her anxiously. Therese was not dry-eyed. Her eyes were red. Swollen. She'd cried at the funeral. She'd cried at the family graveside, where Alexey was laid beside his mother. Tears had welled up in her eyes just before when Helen asked her if she thought the priest was right and the soul stays forty days on earth.

"I don't know, darling," she'd whispered. "But if it helps to think it ..."

"Forty days is not long enough. You have to stay longer," Helen had said, softly. Her mother looked at her and, not realizing it wasn't she Helen was addressing, said, "Darling, you look exhausted, do you want to go and lie down?"

"No. Thank you."

It was the nights she lived for. In the days, he didn't come to her. She didn't know why. She'd tried so hard to see him then too, but she couldn't. Only in photographs that cannot give him back, no matter how much she stared into them. They were frozen moments that would never return. So the days were just time to be endured. At night, though, he was there. But not just in her dreams. She woke up and saw him standing smiling at her. He held out his arms to her and she got up and ran into them. He was himself just as he was, there was nothing ghostly about him. Only he could not speak. But even that didn't matter. Together, they walked through the quiet house hand in hand, and she was happy, truly happy, for she knew he had not left. He was still there, with her.

Forty days. What would the priest know? What would anyone know? *I will always be with you while you need me,* he'd said. She'd always need him. So he would always be there. She could not tell anyone any of this. They had all been so kind but they wouldn't understand. But sometimes she wished it would always be night. That the day would never come.

Outside, a taxi drew up outside the house, and a man got out. He was in a hurry. Helen did not see him. She didn't hear the buzzer sounding, or the man being let in. Her mother had to call her name twice before she turned around. "This gentleman says he wants to see you, Helen."

He was a small man, balding, with gray eyes behind horn-rimmed glasses, and wearing an old suit. He carried a battered briefcase. He blinked owlishly at her and stammered, in English, "I'm so sorry," he said. "I'm so sorry, Miss Clement."

Another mourner she didn't know. Condolences she wouldn't take in.

"I was at the *dacha,* you see. Family holiday." He looked earnestly at Helen, at her mother, at Nikolai who had just approached, at the curious crowd beginning to gather. "There's no phone. No cell phone reception. No TV or radio. And we never get the papers. It's a rule. Leave the city behind. Leave everything behind ..."

She stared at him. What was he prattling about?

"So you see I only found out this morning, on my return. Took the first plane to here." He seemed to catch her expression for the first time. "Excuse, please, I should say straight away. I am V.P. Isakov, advocate in Moscow."

"Advocate?" she faltered.

"Lawyer. Yes? And last week, Alexey Ivanovich Makarov came to see me."

Volkovsky said, sharply, "What the hell are you playing at? You're not the Makarovs' lawyer." His expression was hard, suspicious.

"No, that is so. I am not," said Isakov, calmly. "My practice, it is small. Modest. Nevertheless, Alexey Ivanovich came to see me. I do not presume to know why he chose me but ..."

Helen interrupted him. "When?"

"When he came? Last Saturday morning, around 9 am. Day before I went away." He undid the clasps of his briefcase. "He wanted me to draw up this." He pulled out a folded sheet of paper and handed it to her. "I think you find everything is in order."

She unfolded it. Stared at it. She couldn't understand a word of the body of the text, for it was in Russian. But though it was in Cyrillic script too, she knew the signature down the bottom, written in a firm hand. *Alexey Ivanovich Makarov.* A strange ache started to beat in her head, a pain in her heart. Her beloved wrote those words. It was his hand, on that paper. She thought of that Saturday morning, 9 am. She was still in bed, asleep, in the Moscow apartment. But he'd gone out. Now, she whispered, "I don't understand."

"It is his will. He left everything to you, Miss Clement. I will read it to you in full but that is in short what it says. He writes that he does this because only you can he trust. Only with you can his dream be realized. And so – all of it – it's yours. His property. His company. All his assets. Oh – and this ..." He pulled something else out. A small transparent envelope. And in it, just visible, a tiny blue object. *A digital camera's memory card.*

For an instant, the sight of it was more shocking to her than anything else. She couldn't understand. She remembered Alexey putting the card, in its sealed package, in the vault. She also knew it was stolen the other day. So how could it be here, in the lawyer's hand? And then – quite clearly, as if she had been there, watching, she *saw.* The card was never in the package that went into the vault. Because at the last minute, for some reason – premonition? A double precaution? A wish not to put anyone other than himself in danger? – Alexey had changed his mind. And so, without telling anyone, he'd extracted the card. He'd taken an empty package to the bank. And the next morning, he'd gone round to see the lawyer.

At that very moment, she happened to glance at Nikolai Volkovsky. In that split, unguarded second, the mask dropped, and she saw his true feelings in his eyes. Saw the real man revealed, the cold, ruthless heart behind the mask of the faithful manager, the anxious godfather, the kindly man out of his depth but trying so hard. But it was only a split second; and even as the numbness that had been swaddling her for days suddenly left her and she cried out in shock and warning, he had already pushed his way through the crowd and disappeared.

*

Maxim had been to the service but not the reception. Such events made him uneasy and, besides, he had an important appointment. With someone he'd never expected to be speaking to. Boris Repin, back from his Egyptian holiday and ready to talk.

It was Zaitsev, Maxim's Petersburg colleague, who'd got the approach. Word was, he told Maxim, Repin had not taken at all kindly to his name being taken in vain, and had launched his own investigation, with his own very direct methods of persuasion, apparently without success. But here's the weird thing, Zaitsev said. When news had broken that Bayeva was the killer, Repin had gone completely quiet. And then the word had come through that he wanted to meet.

Now the man sat opposite Maxim and Zaitsev at the cafe table, watchful heavies to one side. Repin was everything you'd expect in an underworld lord who'd come up the hardscrabble way from a Soviet "anti-social". Big and imposing, weight-lifter's shoulders straining under the Italian suit that hid his prison tattoos. He looked at Maxim with a flat blue gaze and, shaking his head, said, "So. What a shocking thing, these Rusalka killings. That foreign bitch must have been completely insane. Well, they do say revenge is a dish best eaten cold – but as to me, I've always preferred hot and spicy. How about you?"

Maxim said, harshly, "Spare me the crap. Tell me what you know. I thought that was why we were here."

A faint smile flitted across the gangster's hard features. "You thought I was here like a vulgar informer, to do your job for you? Then you're not the man I thought you were, Senior Lieutenant Maxim Antonovich Serebrov. Oh yes, I know all about you now; I have my own friends in our glorious capital's *militsiya*."

Maxim glanced at Zaitsev, who shrugged. Maxim said, "I'm not here to bandy words or cross swords with you, Repin. Just say what you came to say."

"I'm a businessman, Senior Lieutenant. Live and let live is my motto. Long as you don't interfere with me, I won't interfere with you."

Maxim got angrily to his feet. "If you think that threatening me is going to –"

"Please sit down. I'm just making a general business observation," said Repin, unflustered. "Nothing to do with the police. As I say, live and let live is my motto. But there are limits even to my patience and when someone tries to pin something on me – well, let's say I don't appreciate it."

"Get to the point."

The flat blue gaze devoured Maxim's face. "I was interested in Trinity, once," he said. "Then I looked into it and decided it wasn't for me. But someone decided to use that knowledge, and build a whole web of lies out of it."

"We know. Bayeva."

An airy gesture of dismissal. "Not the foreigner. *Think*. Trinity offices attacked. Trinity men sought by the police. The rot is on the *inside*, Senior Lieutenant."

Maxim shrugged. "Old news, Repin. We have already ..." And then he broke off, for he realized that Repin had used the present tense, not the past. Repin saw the change in his expression, knew he'd hit home. He said, silkily. "No, I cannot tell you *who* for I do not know. That is your job. But it is the only thing that makes sense. And that is what I came to say."

It was then Maxim knew that his original instinct, right at the beginning – that in the Trinity case they were facing not one criminal, but two – had been right. He knew now why it had been so difficult for him to reconcile the two strands – the Rusalka murders, *and* the disruption of Trinity under Alexey Makarov. Because they were two *separate* strands, run by two different people. For very different reasons.

He was already on his feet and hurrying away, dialing Therese Clement's number as he went.

Chapter 44

They didn't catch up with him. St Petersburg is close to the border with Finland, and even if an alert is put out at once, why should a border guard match the shaven-headed Estonian hunter whose passport appeared completely in order with a certain Nikolai Pavlovich Volkovsky, wanted in Russia for fraud, conspiracy, gangsterism, murder and accessory to murder? A man such as he, who had fooled the world for so long, would always have an escape plan up his sleeve.

But his secret life was rapidly being uncovered. A few days after his flight, after an intensive manhunt, the Petersburg police finally laid hands on one of the Trinity office raiders. Under questioning, the man revealed he'd been hired by Slava Lomakin, acting for someone higher up. He didn't know who the boss was. But it wasn't the first time he'd worked for them. Closer questioning began to provide the first elements of an astonishing truth.

There *had* been a shadow side of Trinity, carrying out occasional but lucrative "black ops" for a range of secretive and unsavory clients. Over the last five years or so, a nucleus of hand-picked operatives – in Moscow, Pasha, Slava and Foma; in Petersburg, Feodor, plus a junior operative named

Ludmila – had been cancering Trinity from the inside, with the help of hired underworld foot-soldiers: thugs, thieves and fixers who never knew what the chain of command was. But the chain did not lead to Makarov, or Galkin, or Barsukov. How could it, when none of them knew anything about it? Obsessed by their own secret – by the Koldun project – they'd lost their grip on what was going on in the company. Trusting to the reliable, unambitious but utterly loyal manager who had never let them down, they had missed the signs and fatally dropped their guard.

Maxim and the rest of his colleagues could have dug for months or years without uncovering the full ramifications of just what it all meant, if, a fortnight after Volkovsky's flight, Helen hadn't received a call in the middle of the night.

She and her mother were still in Russia, staying in the Moscow apartment; they had got an extension of their visa and put off their return to London. Indeed, even when they did go back to London, for Helen it would only be temporary. Everything had changed for her since that moment in the apartment overlooking the Petersburg canal. Everything, that is, except the deep ache of missing Alexey. Except loving him more with every day that passed. Except longing for the moments when her beloved would be there with her.

She saw him during the day now too. She'd glimpse him walking by the river; sprawled laughing in the Alexandrovsky gardens; waiting for her outside a shop, smiling at her from the other side of the room. His voice was in her head and the knowledge of his loving presence everywhere she went. *We are keyed to the same music.* Even when what separated them was death itself.

She knew now why she had to live for him. She knew that she must not let his dream die. She must not let Volkovsky's cold, calculating treachery and Irina's crazy, vengeful hatred win, for that would obliterate who Alexey had been. Who he still was, walking by her side and shining in her heart and soul.

Yes, she had to live *for* him, because he was worth fighting for. Because the dreams he'd fought so hard for must survive. And she would not let him down, come hell or high water or well-meaning advice that it was too much of a burden for someone of her age and inexperience to try to continue with his plans for Trinity. She knew it wasn't so. Her will was strong. Very strong, because Alexey was with her. There was no fog, no uncertainty. The hesitant, questioning girl of the past was gone forever, and would never return.

Her mother, desperately anxious for her daughter, had gently tried to dissuade her. But Maxim understood. He had not argued. He had not canvassed ifs and buts. He had simply said, calmly, "He chose you. And that's good enough for me. Whatever it takes, whatever you need, I will help you to the very best of my abilities."

It hadn't been mere words. Over the last couple of weeks Maxim had gone with her to meetings with lawyers, immigration officials, police, bankers and all kinds of other hard-nosed people whose role in life is to put roadblocks in the way of dreams. He was like the father she'd never really had, keeping her from losing her temper, patiently explaining the finer points of yet another obstacle, informing himself on all kinds of facets of company law so he could help guide her. With the little lawyer Isakov, who had also proved to be something of a rock, he refused to allow authority or slippery shysters to bully, browbeat or bamboozle her. He spoke to the rest of the Trinity staff – shattered by what had happened, several had handed in their resignations – and with Ilya and Sonya's steady support managed to persuade them to hold off for a while, at least till things were sorted out. Both offices were closed till things were on a proper legal footing again, but everyone was still being paid a retainer.

Helen had insisted. She knew it was what Alexey would have wanted.

The night of the phone call, she'd fallen early into a dreamless sleep, absolutely exhausted by another day battling with officials and then with the Russian conversation lessons Maxim's friend Anna Dorskova had been giving her. Early days yet, but Anna was most encouraging as to her progress. Helen had a real ear, she told Therese Clement, with whom she'd struck up an unexpected friendship. She felt sure that before too long the young woman would speak Russian fluently.

"Yelena." The ringing cell phone had brutally jerked Helen out of deep sleep, and she was groggy when she picked it up and clicked the button. But the sound of the voice on the other end instantly woke her up, like a freezing shower.

"Don't hang up," Nikolai Volkovsky said. "Or you'll never know." A pause. "And you want to. I know you do."

She'd been about to hit the end call button. Now she halted. But she didn't speak.

He said, "You might not believe me, but I never intended what happened. Not to Alexey. No – listen. Let me speak. I liked Alexey. I regret his death. And, whatever you may think, I had no part in Bayeva's plot. I had no idea Galkin's death was anything but an accident. I'd been running my operation undetected by then for two years. But when I caught Grisha in Galkin's office, and saw what he'd found, things changed. He had no idea what he'd found. He'd been after cash, trinkets. The photo in the desk meant nothing to him. Not to me, either, at first. Then I wondered – why would Galkin hide a photo of what looked like a shabby American motel? It was that question that eventually led me to Irina Bayeva Simmons and her crazy plot. Not before Barsukov had died too, though."

Helen felt like she was suffocating. "But you knew *then*. And yet you didn't stop it. Even though Ivan Makarov was your friend. Even though he'd made you godfather to his son. You are worse than her. She was mad. You're not. She didn't really know them, not as people. You did. And yet you kept quiet. Worse still, you spun a web of lies, to deceive him. You set false trails, like Repin's. For your own foul ends. So you could have control of Trinity."

His voice was tight. "That company was as much mine as theirs. Just as much! I'd given my life to it. And yet not once did it ever enter their heads to offer me a partnership. Not once. All those years of slaving my guts out and I was still just a salaried employee to them. Never part of their charmed circle. Their most important initiative in years – the Koldun project – they kept from me completely. Didn't breathe a word of it to me. Not a word! I only found out when the policeman did. How do you think that made me feel?"

She said, very quietly, "But Alexey had no part in it. And he *would* have sold the company, if you hadn't persuaded him not to. If you wanted Trinity so much, why do that? Why not wait till it was up for sale?"

"Because I couldn't afford to buy it. Not outright. It was as stark as that. And I was damned if I was going to have to go cap in hand to Repin or anyone like him. Never. No – my operation would function better under Trinity cover. I could run both sides of the business – if we only had an absentee director. A rich young man who hated his father and all he'd stood for. Who'd been years out of Russia. Whose passion was music. Who'd never intended to keep on the business. But who could be persuaded to keep it on, for idealistic reasons. Yet who would follow my advice. Leave it to me. Give me a free hand. It was the perfect solution. It *should* have been the perfect solution. Look, I had nothing against Alexey. I even liked him, like I told you. And then – well, he started to show that he really was Ivan Mikhailovich's son. Showed that under the charming exterior, there was still the iron Makarov will. I tried to persuade him he didn't need to be personally involved, but it was no good. He refused to listen to reason. Refused to listen to warnings."

"You *knew* Irina was in Uglich," she said, breaking in. "Yet you deliberately made sure Alexey would be there – like – like bait for a hungry wolf."

"No! I didn't expect what happened! I didn't plan for it to end that way."

"I don't believe you. You had the gun," she said. "You could have shot her straight away. But you waited. Because you wanted it to happen. You wanted Alexey to die."

"It was *your* fault he was there," he said, angrily. "Yours! If you hadn't persuaded him to stay at her place, and if he hadn't been with you, she wouldn't have got to him that day. Have you thought of that?"

"Yes," she said, very sadly. "I have. But – if it hadn't been that day, it would have been another. She was never going to give up. But *you* could have stopped her. She would have been locked up. He would have been safe. But you never even tried. Because you saw a perfect chance to get your hands on Trinity." She outlined the chilling scenario Isakov had suggested to them, the other day. "If Trinity was seen as irredeemably corrupt – white-anted by gangsters like Repin – if key staff like Pasha started defecting, major fraud was uncovered and its reputation was fatally undermined – then the company would rapidly lose value. And if Alexey died without a will, then you'd have a chance to get hold of it at a bargain basement price. Even for nothing. You could step in as its savior. As its white knight."

He laughed, harshly. "Well, well, someone's been doing their research! Think what you want, Helen, but know this for certain: if Alexey had not been such a headstrong young fool, if he'd not ignored every bit of advice that was given to him – then he'd still be alive today. I'd have protected him from that mad witch. I'd have denounced her long since! Dear God, why did he have to turn out to be so overbearingly like his damned father?"

She said, very calmly, "Listen well to me, you bastard – because these are the last words I will ever speak to you. Whatever it takes – however long it takes – you will pay for what you've done. For I will never rest till you are destroyed. And you will never, ever get your hands on Trinity or the Koldun file or anything that you ever wanted. Never! You have lost, you vile, disgusting traitor. You have failed – because you never understood Alexey and you never will."

He shouted down the phone, "Little fool, you think you hold all the cards but you're wrong! Trinity will be mine one day, no matter what. I have powerful friends. Very powerful friends. And you don't even have a particle of Alexey's will. You'll never be able to keep it. And you might have the file but we've cracked the code, we know what Koldun is, and –"

She disconnected. Switched the phone off. Sat there on the bed staring into space for a moment, then picked up the phone again, and dialed Maxim's number.

Acknowledgments

Writing this book was an exciting and challenging journey and along the way I was greatly encouraged by the practical help and wise advice of other people. I'd particularly like to thank my husband David Leach and my friends and fellow writers Jon Appleton and Wendy James for their close reading of the early drafts, and their many helpful suggestions. Thanks also to Anna for helping me get the intricacies of Russian names right! In Russia, thanks go to the two Sashas, and to Yulia, Elena, Yuri and Valery, whose conversation and anecdotes opened my eyes and my ears to many extraordinary aspects of Russian contemporary life, history and myth during my two visits there in 2010 and 2012.

And a big thank you to the wonderful team at Momentum for their enthusiasm and care for this story, and for delivering it to readers in such a beautiful package.

Note: Alexey's translation for Helen is my own paraphrase of part of the original Russian words of *"Подмосковные вечера"* or "Moscow Nights", by Mikhail Lvovich Matusovsky and Vasily Solovyov-Sedoi (1955).

Also by Sophie Masson

Trinity: The False Prince (Book 2)

Truth is the first casualty of war.

A year and a half have passed since the events that changed Helen's life forever. With Maxim and her other friends, she is fighting to uphold the legacy entrusted to her, but struggles with the weight of memory, the stress of trying to keep Trinity afloat, and the continuing manipulations of the company's enemies.

Meanwhile, in a remote coastal settlement in southern Mexico, a young fisherman is made an offer he can't refuse, triggering a chain of events which will completely transform the struggle for the ownership of Trinity and the secrets of the Koldun code.

For more information, please visit
http://www.momentumbooks.com.au/books/the-false-prince/

www.ingramcontent.com/pod-product-compliance
Lightning Source LLC
Chambersburg PA
CBHW030803260626
47169CB00001B/178